The new Zebra Regency Romance logo that you see on the cover is a photograph of an actual regency "tuzzy-muzzy." The fashionable regency lady often wore a tuzzy-muzzy tied with a satin or velvet riband around her wrist to carry a fragrant nosegay. Usually made of gold or silver, tuzzy-muzzies varied in design from the elegantly simple to the exquisitely ornate. The Zebra Regency Romance tuzzy-muzzy is made of alabaster with a silver filigree ed

D1359498

A STOLEN KISS

"You overstepped your bounds, sir," she interrupted, the shakiness of her voice belying her raised little chin. "You had no—"

"Ah, but Miss Ru—Diana, you enjoyed that kiss as much as I did," he murmured, his eyes twinkling.

Her eyes flashed. "You, sir, are no gentleman!"

"Did you not enjoy it, then? Am I so far off the mark?" He did his best to look chagrined.

She bit her lip, and he watched the play of emotions march across her face.

She sighed deeply. "You are monstrous unfair, Marchmaine."

"Adam."

She sighed again. "Very well. Adam. You are most unfair. I cannot possibly answer such a question." She twisted her hands at her waist.

"And why, pray tell, is that?"

"Because if I answer 'yes,' I should be shockingly brazen. And if I answer 'no' . . . I . . . ah—" She looked away from him.

Adam put his fingers beneath her chin and turned her head back. "And if you answer 'no,' Diana?" he prompted softly.

"I—I should be a liar," she whispered. . . .

THE ROMANCES OF LORDS AND LADIES
IN JANIS LADEN'S REGENCIES

BEWITCHING MINX   (2532, $3.95)

From her first encounter with the Marquis of Penderleigh when he had mistaken her for a common trollop, Penelope had been incensed with the darkly handsome lord. Miss Penelope Larchmont was undoubtedly the most outspoken young lady Penderleigh had ever known, and the most tempting.

A NOBLE MISTRESS   (2169, $3.95)

Moriah Landon had always been a singularly practical young lady. So when her father lost the family estate over a game of picquet, she paid the winner, the notorious Viscount Roane, a visit. And when he suggested the means of payment—that she become Roane's mistress—she agreed without a blink of her eyes.

SAPPHIRE TEMPTATION   (3054, $3.95)

Lady Serena was commonly held to be an unusual young girl—outspoken when she should have been reticent, lively when she should have been demure. But there was one tradition she had not been allowed to break: a Wexley must marry a Gower. Richard Gower intended to teach his wife her duties—in every way.

SCOTTISH ROSE   (2750, $3.95)

The Duke of Milburne returned to Milburne Hall trusting that the new governess, Miss Rose Beacham, had instilled the fear of God into his harum-scarum brood of siblings. But she romped with the children, refused to be cowed by his stern admonitions, and was so pretty that he had the devil of a time keeping his hands off her.

Available wherever paperbacks are sold, or order direct from the Publisher. Send cover price plus 50¢ per copy for mailing and handling to Zebra Books, Dept. 3809, 475 Park Avenue South, New York, N.Y. 10016. Residents of New York and Tennessee must include sales tax. DO NOT SEND CASH. For a free Zebra/ Pinnacle catalog please write to the above address.

Fires in the Snow
Janis Laden

ZEBRA BOOKS
KENSINGTON PUBLISHING CORP.

ZEBRA BOOKS

are published by

Kensington Publishing Corp.
475 Park Avenue South
New York, NY 10016

Copyright © 1992 by Janis Laden

All rights reserved. No part of this book may be reproduced
in any form or by any means without the prior written
consent of the Publisher, excepting brief quotes used in
reviews.

If you purchased this book without a cover you should be
aware that this book is stolen property. It was reported as
"unsold and destroyed" to the Publisher and neither the
Author nor the Publisher has received any payment for this
"stripped book."

First printing: July, 1992

Printed in the United States of America

For Gideon,
my only son
in a bevy of girls,
with love

"And the spirit of the Lord clothed Gideon . . ."

Judges 6:34

Oh, 'twas many and many a year long ago,
On the banks of the stream where the willow trees grow,
On a day when the chill didst the bright morn pervade,
That a lad set about for to woo his fair maid.

He didst stand, cap in hand, on that snow-covered ground,
Knowing well that, at last, his dear heart he had found.
'Twas the spring of his life on that cold winter's day,
But the maid tossed her curls, pursed her lips, said him nay.

And said he to the maid, "How thou dost me confuse
With thy words that insist that thou must me refuse;
For 'tis true, dearest heart, that your lips speak with ice,
But the fire in your eyes somehow doth me entice."

And his lips brushed with hers and he offered his hand.
"Pray, ask not," cried the maid, "wilt thou please understand?
Thou art noble, resplendent in silver and gold;
Who am I, but a maid from a village of old?"

Said the lad, "Feel my heart; it is thine, thine alone;
Come to me, oh my love, I give thee all I own.
Thou art light on dark days, thou art fire in the snow,
Thou art calm in the storm, thou art joy—all I know."

And the maid through her tears pledged her heart, pledged her troth.
"All I ask is thy love, neither gems nor gold cloth."
Now the lad wiped her tears and he took her to wife;
Thus they danced through the spring and the summer of life.

There came children to add to the joy that they knew,
And their woes, shared together, seemed paltry and few.
Oh, the autumn was golden; they walked hand in hand,
And the fire of their love burned the cold from the land.

But the winter of life is upon us at last;
Pray tell how, my dear heart, didst it come, oh so fast?
Though my body be weak and thy hair turned to snow,
Still thy touch flames the fire that it did long ago.

And when cometh the day that this earth we depart,
'Tis my soul that will yearn for the fire of thy heart;
Till some faraway time when a maid loves a swain,
Yea, I know, love of mine, I shall find thee again.

—Sir Isaac Mariner

Chapter 1

"No! Oh, God, no!"

The woman's scream pierced the silence of the night. Adam Damerest, Duke of Marchmaine, stopped abruptly in his pacing of the library and ran a jagged hand through his dark hair. Damnation! Georgie was at least a month before her time! It should be her husband pacing the floor, not he. And where in blazes was the doctor?

As if in answer, the gong sounded from below. Quite forgetting himself and his station, the duke dashed through the open door of the library and down the great stairwell to the entry lobby. He was an indecorous three paces behind the butler as Stebbins swung open the massive iron door of Rossmore Manor.

But it was not, as he'd expected, the masculine frame of the Rossmore doctor that came in out of the cold, shaking snowflakes from his cloak. It was a rather small figure with curling black locks peeping out of the hood of a fur-lined cloak. And a second glance told him the figure was possessed of curves such as he was certain Dr. James Rustin had never had!

Two delicate, gloved hands rose up from the folds of the cloak to push the hood back. "Oh, my goodness, me! It *is* cold out there!" exclaimed a soft husky voice, as its owner shook out a full, luxurious head of ebony black curls. If those curls had at one time been confined in a ribbon, there was no evidence of it now.

Who the deuce *was* she? And what was she doing at Rossmore Manor at eleven o'clock of a frigid, snowy night?

Certainly not paying a morning call!

"Ah, good evening, miss," Stebbins said hesitantly, and the duke stepped forward.

"Thank you, Stebbins. I'll handle this," he muttered, and the butler bowed himself away.

The young woman inside the claret-colored cloak smiled at him, quite as if he had ought to be pleased at her arrival! And perhaps, he mused, under other circumstances he might well have been. If she was not precisely a classic beauty, she was certainly very lovely to look upon with big, round, dark blue eyes set in an oval-shaped face, a delicate nose, and a gracious, curling smile that bespoke frequent bemusement.

None of which, he reminded himself, mattered a whit! He drew himself up to his full six feet, two inches and clasped his hands behind his back. "May I help you?" he inquired imperiously.

She cocked her head, appearing to consider the matter, and a decided glint entered her eye. "Only if you wish to convey hot water and clean linens abovestairs, but I daresay that is best left to the maids, is it not, Your Grace? You *are* His Grace, brother of the Baroness Rossmore, are you not? Forgive me for presuming, but you are not the baron, and I had heard the duke was to visit."

"I am he," he began.

"Yes, well, you must know husbands are useless enough at times like this," she went blithely on, peeling off her gloves. He blinked incredulously. Just what did she think—"And I am persuaded brothers are even worse. No, Your Grace, you'd best betake yourself to the baron's library or some such and pour yourself a snifter of brandy. I shall take care of everything!"

With that amazing pronouncement she began unfastening the top buttons of her cloak.

Adam felt his hands clench. "What the deuce are you talking about? Who *are* you?"

Her eyes grew rounder. "I? Why, I'm Diana Rustin. The doctor's daughter. Did you not know?"

"No, I did not know!" he retorted mockingly. "Where is Rustin?"

"Oh, you must forgive Papa, but he's been over near Midvale ever since this morning attending to Mrs. Caldwell.

We think 'tis twins, you must know," she said with a decided twinkle in her blue eyes. "I've sent word to Papa about Lady Rossmore; but it is quite a distance, and I do not know how long it will take him, especially in this weather. The snow has been falling quite steadily, I'm afraid. You do realize, of course, that Papa can have had no inkling—that is, Lady Rossmore is well before her time."

The duke ran his fingers through his chestnut hair. "I am aware of that," he said tautly, then began pacing the marble floor. "Well, this is a fine thing! My sister is abovestairs shrieking in pain, her husband is on a diplomatic mission in Vienna, and the doctor is delivering Mrs. Caldwell of twins! Forgive me, Miss Rustin, if I am less than sociable. Thank you for bringing me your news, but I really cannot see—"

He stopped abruptly and frowned prodigiously as, without so much as a by-your-leave, she moved toward the cheerful fire burning in the huge fireplace and swung her cloak from her shoulders. She looked about her expectantly. Almost instantly, Stebbins reappeared to relieve her of her garments. Adam glowered at him, but Miss Rustin rewarded him with her gracious smile, then turned to the fire to warm her hands. Stebbins beat a diplomatic retreat, and the duke strode to the hearth to confront his visitor.

He could not help noticing, as he stood just three feet to her side, that her royal blue merino round dress fit her very shapely form admirably. Nor could he ignore the fact that her ebony hair, which she proceeded to pin up and tie back in a matching blue ribbon, was thick and lustrous and curled tantalizingly about her face and shoulders. She twisted it up too fast for him to see just how long it was. He told himself he was not curious. There were more important matters at hand.

"Miss Rustin, exactly what *are* you doing?" he demanded.

She turned to him, her expression immediately contrite. "Oh, I *am* sorry, Your Grace. I did not mean to tarry. I shall go abovestairs straightaway."

"Go above—what the devil are you talking about?"

"Why, I have come to deliver your sister of a child!" she proclaimed.

If she had jabbed him in the stomach with a fierce left hook, he could not have been more stunned. "You? You've—Miss

9

Rustin! What fustian is this? You cannot be serious!"

"But—"

"You will do no such thing! How can you even suggest—why, you are a gently bred girl, not some . . . some midwife!" he fairly spluttered.

"Come now, Your Grace, I am hardly a girl. You may be sure I left the schoolroom many years past. And I *am* the doctor's daughter. I have assisted him at any number of births, not to mention having delivered, on my own, some eight babes—to farmers' wives, you must know—when Papa was otherwise occupied."

He raised a brow. "But you have never, on your own, attended a lady of quality, have you?"

Her lips—beautifully curved lips, he noted irrelevantly—twitched. "No, Your Grace. Are they fashioned so very differently from the lower orders, do you suppose?" she asked ingenuously.

He wanted to throttle her. "Miss Rustin! This conversation is not at all the thing, and nonsensical besides! How could your father permit such a thing? The mere notion is scandalous! Why, you—you are not even wed!"

A gleam lit her velvety, dark blue eyes. "Now, Your Grace," she said placatingly, "I am not *having* the babe, you must know, merely helping to bring it into the world."

At this the duke felt close to the apoplexy. He clenched his fists as he advanced on her, trying to keep from putting his hands to her delicate swanlike neck and wringing it. She backed up as he came closer.

"But," she went on, "if your sense of propriety is so very offended, I shall, of course, take my leave. Perhaps you *do* know of a midwife in the neighborhood who would be more suitable." She had backed herself into a stone pillar and neatly rounded it. Adam followed, scowling at her, his long thin hands itching for her neck. She sought the safety of a wooden settle, grasping its back as she inquired, those big eyes so wide and innocent, "You did not mean to deliver the child yourself, did you? No, I am persuaded not. Oh! I know! You might send for Dr. Willoughby over near Giggleswick. I apprehend that it *is* a bit far, and they say he is bosky these days more often than not; but you might sober him up with black coffee sprinkled

10

with calamint and then—"

He rounded the settle in two long strides and abruptly found his large hands gripping her slender shoulders. "That is quite enough, Miss Rustin!" he shouted.

She gasped softly, and he felt a tremor go through her. And then her body stiffened perceptibly. Even in the candlelight he could see that she had paled. Gone was the gleam in her eye; gone was the bemused smile. She did not say a word. She did not have to; the message was clear. Adam dropped his hands, and she stepped back, clasping her hands at her waist.

"I'll go now," she said with quiet dignity. "If you would be so good as to summon Stebbins with my things . . ."

He stared at her for a long moment, trying not to let his perplexity show. How was it possible that the saucy, self-possessed Miss Rustin had become the stiff, serious, unapproachable woman who stood before him now? She was equally as comely, but there was a certain . . . sadness, a weary resignation in her blue eyes now. Had the mere touch of his hands done that? How? Surely he hadn't hurt her! Had he frightened her? Shocked her? But the serious Miss Rustin did not look frightened, and the saucy Miss Rustin had not looked as if she shocked easily.

He did not understand, but he knew that he preferred the saucy miss. And he also knew that he liked the feel of her soft shoulders beneath his hands, very well, indeed.

But that, of course, was neither here nor there! She began walking toward the shadows through which Stebbins had disappeared. "Ah, Miss Rustin," he called. She pivoted and arched a delicate black brow in question. "You will attend my sister, if you please," he commanded.

The other brow rose, this time in surprise. Her lips twitched, and he could see her relaxing. The saucy miss was returning. "Very well, Your Grace. It is my privilege."

She was mocking him, he thought incredulously, and glowered at her as he indicated with the sweep of his hand that she should precede him to the staircase. He was careful not to take her arm.

Another scream pierced the silence of the manor house as Diana ascended the wide staircase at the side of His Grace, the Duke of Marchmaine. And she reminded herself that she was here to perform a very important task—to help the baroness's child into the world. She must not dwell on the sudden warmth that had flooded her when the duke had put his hands to her shoulders, nor on all the reasons why she could not allow herself to react to that warmth. She would think only of the overweening arrogance of the man. Or better still, she would not think of him at all!

Indeed, as soon as the door to the baroness's suite had closed behind her, leaving the duke in the corridor, Diana took a deep breath and walked through the shadowed sitting room to the bedchamber beyond. She could hear muffled voices—undoubtedly Lady Rossmore was attended by her maid and perhaps the housekeeper. They would all be awaiting the doctor. And if the duke's reception had been less than enthusiastic, Diana was not at all certain of Georgina Rossmore's reaction. A cordial relationship existed between them, no more. For though Lady Rossmore's instincts might have been, when she first wed and came to live here, to befriend the doctor's daughter, she had bowed to pressure from her mother and others and kept her distance.

And then, of course, there was that unfortunate business with Edward, Baron Rossmore. Diana doubted that Lady Rossmore knew of it—certainly, she had given no indication—but she might suspect that her husband's precipitous departure for the Continent entailed more than a sudden desire to serve his country. No matter. Diana knew there was nothing untoward between the baron and herself. She had a clear conscience, and now she must keep her head clear for the task at hand. Surely Georgina Rossmore would not refuse her help now, though when it was over she might well retreat behind her wall of distant civility.

It did not signify. Diana had learned long ago that she was not like other ladies, that she was to be denied the life they led. And so she had made a life for herself, as best she might. And in truth, not all of the neighboring gentry spurned her, though a number did. For Diana Rustin, twenty-six-year-old spinster, quasi-midwife, and great granddaughter of an earl, was not at all the thing.

* * *

Diana held the brace of candles high as she made her way down the unfamiliar stairwell. She had not wanted to leave the baroness, but she knew that if she merely sent the housekeeper, the duke would worry overmuch. And though things were not progressing all that well, she did not think there was cause for worry—yet.

Lady Rossmore had already looked pale and fagged to death two hours ago when Diana had entered her chamber, explaining her father's absence and her own presence. And before the young baroness could reply, a terrible pain had gripped her, and she had grit her teeth and squeezed the hand of her maid. And Diana had come forward to massage her stomach and tell her to scream all she wanted to. When the pain subsided Lady Rossmore had smiled wanly and rasped her thanks for any assistance Miss Rustin might render. But thus far the babe was not ready for any assistance, for all it was causing its mama undue pain.

Now Diana rapped lightly at the library door and entered at the duke's call. He rose and looked hopefully at her. She closed the door behind her and set down the brace of candles.

"No, Your Grace, there is no news yet," she said quietly. "But Lady Rossmore is holding up well and—"

"But—but why are you here? Should you not be with—"

"Yes, of course, Your Grace, but she'll keep a minute. Her maid and Mrs. Stebbins are with her. I merely wanted you to know that all was well." She kept her voice deliberately light. There was no sense oversetting the duke yet. He looked as ragged as any husband she'd ever seen. His chestnut hair looked unkempt, as if he'd run his long, thin fingers through it many times. His piercing, tawny eyes looked red with fatigue and narrowed with concern. He had removed his coat and cravat, and his tall, whipcord lean frame looked no less powerful for all his dishevelment. Indeed, she found the sight of him in his shirtsleeves oddly disconcerting.

His eyes seemed to be assessing her sharply. Did he not believe her? "I see," he said at length. "It is taking rather long, is it not? Her pains started earlier in the day, but she wasn't certain, as it *was* weeks early."

Diana sighed. "Yes. It *is* rather long, but first babes are known for that, Your Grace." She smiled softly; but it was an

13

effort, and she realized how fatigued even she was becoming.

Perhaps the duke realized that as well, for he gestured toward a chair and offered her a drink.

She declined, saying she wished to get back straightaway, and suggested he engross himself in a good book, as there was naught else he could do. And then she made her way abovestairs once more.

Adam must have dozed, slumped over in the baron's leather wing chair, for he was next aware of a hand on his shoulder, nudging him gently. Before he swam fully to the surface of wakefulness and opened his eyes, he thought it must be the doctor's daughter. She had come to tell him he had a nephew. But then he remembered a certain look on her face and doubted she would nudge his shoulder. He opened one eye, and in the dim light could make out a stout, motherly form. There was nothing motherly about Miss Diana Rustin. He opened the other eye, then forced himself to sit upright.

"Your Grace," said Mrs. Stebbins in her high-pitched voice, and he struggled up from the chair, still not feeling fully awake.

"What news, Mrs. Stebbins? What time is it? Is Georgie all right?" He was running his fingers through his hair as he spoke, then trying to right the dishevelment of his shirt. Something about the housekeeper's expression made his hands go very still. Suddenly he was very much awake.

"Tell me, Mrs. Stebbins," he said soberly. "Tell me what is wrong."

Mrs. Stebbins lifted a plump arm to dab at her eye with a handkerchief. "'Tis half after two of the morning. Miss Rustin sent me to tell you that—that Lady Rossmore is holdin' her own, but—but she's havin' a bad time of it, Your Grace." She sniffed into her handkerchief.

"Why? What—"

"The babe—the babe is turned, you see." She whispered the words, as if they were forbidden. Adam was not certain he understood.

"Turned?"

Mrs. Stebbins colored. "The—the feet are—are first, Your Grace," she mumbled.

14

"Oh, my God!" he uttered, suddenly understanding all too well. He knew little enough of childbirth, but he did know the child's head was meant to come first. This was a complication that could result in the death of the child, or—or worse.

He felt the blood drain from his face. "I've got to go up there!" he said urgently, reaching for his coat.

"Your Grace, please." The housekeeper put a hand to his arm to stop him. "There is naught you can do up there. It is better if—"

"What the devil can the doctor's daughter do?" he growled.

"She—" Mrs. Stebbins lowered her eyes—"she is going to try to—ah—turn the babe around."

"Dear God!" The duke felt his eyes nearly pop from his head. She was going to—the implications of it were mind-boggling, and terrifying. Was such a thing possible? And how did Miss Diana Rustin know—

He hadn't noticed Mrs. Stebbins step away to pour him a drink, but he accepted it readily enough. Nor did he hear her slip from the room as he downed the brandy in one gulp and then resumed pacing the floor. The housekeeper was right; there *was* nothing he could do for Georgie. If it had been his wife up there, he would have forced his way in, if for nothing more than to hold her hand. But she was not his wife, and much as he loved the little sister he had helped to raise, he did not belong with her now.

But it was agony to be relegated to the relative comfort of the library whilst Georgie was suffering so, and agony to have only his thoughts for company. He did not welcome those thoughts. He did not want to think about what Diana Rustin was attempting to do, and what the consequences could be if she failed.

All of England had been tragically reminded of the dangers of childbirth just months ago when Princess Charlotte had been delivered of a stillborn child and then herself died. The entire nation had been plunged into mourning and the Regent had been inconsolable. Adam had pushed the tragedy from his mind all night, but now, with Georgie in such peril, it intruded chillingly on his thoughts. No! he screamed inwardly. That would not, *could* not be her fate! She was only twenty-two years old. He did not want to think about the fact that the princess

15

had been only twenty-one.

Adam had been like a father to Georgie after their own father died when Adam was one and twenty. Georgie had been a girl of twelve and had come to Adam whenever their mother's harshness had been too much for her.

And she had come to Adam when Edward, Baron Rossmore, had asked to pay his addresses to her. Their mother had been opposed to the match—surely a duke's daughter could do better than a mere baron with only a single seat in Yorkshire. But Georgie had claimed that her affections were very much engaged, and Edward showed every evidence of being equally besotted. And although Adam had a healthy cynicism toward matters of the heart—indeed, he believed love within the married state very rare—he had given his consent.

He wondered now if he had done the right thing. Something was very wrong with the Rossmore marriage. Georgie had refused to speak of it, but Adam knew she had been devastated by Edward's departure less than two months before the expected time of her confinement. He had anticipated returning within three weeks, but still Adam knew he would not have gone merely because the Ministry asked him to. He had gone because he had needed to get away.

And now Georgie's life hung in the balance, and the man who less than two years before had declared his love for her was nowhere to be seen. Adam had sent word to him, but he might well have been on his way home at all events. The weather and the fact that Georgie had been brought to bed at least three weeks early no doubt accounted for his absence. Adam had to believe that, else Edward was a bounder.

Edward, come home, Adam called silently. You should be with her now. It was not a brother's place.

"Your Grace." It was a soft, husky voice this time, and there was no hand nudging him. He opened his eyes, fully awake straightaway. He got to his feet. "Miss Rustin! What—"

She smiled a tired half-smile, but a smile none the less. "You have a fine nephew, Your Grace."

"And Georgie?" His body was rigid with tension.

The smile faded, just a bit. "Lady Rossmore is resting now.

16

She is . . . comfortable, but very weak. I—I fear she lost a great deal of—of blood."

"What are you saying, Miss Rustin?" he asked tautly.

She tried to stifle a sigh. "I think she will be all right, Your Grace. We needs must watch her—for fever and to see that she does not—er—hemorrhage. But she is strong. I believe she will pull through."

"And the child? You—you turned him?" He still had not relaxed his stance.

"Yes, and a feisty little fellow he is. He will lead his mama a merry chase, I make no doubt."

Adam relaxed perceptibly. "Thank you, Miss Rustin. I cannot thank you enough. May I go to see her now?"

"Yes, but I caution you, she is sleeping. That is the very best thing for her now. Er, Your Grace?"

"Yes?"

"Do you know when the baron means to return? She is—ah—quite overset that he is not here. I cannot help but think his presence would aid her recovery."

It was the duke's turn to sigh. He feared she was right. "He is expected any time now. I sent word to him, but of a certain the weather has delayed him. I am persuaded he meant to be here for the confinement, Miss Rustin." He felt compelled to add this last. Whatever problems plagued Edward and Georgie were not meant to be bandied in public.

Miss Rustin's look was an odd, knowing one, however, and her words were no less odd. "I know that, Your Grace. I did not mean to imply otherwise." It was the certainty in her voice that perplexed him, he decided, and sought to shift the subject by asking the time.

It was near to five of the clock, Miss Rustin replied, and only then did he realize that she herself must be near to collapse. He insisted she sit by the fire, and he stoked the dying embers to revive it, then offered her a drink. He went to the sideboard to pour two glasses. His hand went instinctively to the brandy decanter but stopped midair. One did not offer brandy to a young lady, even a sometime midwife. What did young ladies drink? Lemonade, he supposed. Ratafia, perhaps? No, not young ladies who delivered babies.

"Ah—what would you care to drink, Miss Rustin?" he

finally asked.

She opted for sherry and then asked if she mightn't have some biscuits as well, as she was quite famished. He offered supper, or breakfast instead, but she declined both, pleading the need to sleep.

And it was then that it occurred to him that she would indeed have to sleep here at the manor, improper though it was. For in her present state, Georgie did not qualify as chaperone. Still, there was no help for it. It was dark, and the snow was still falling; Adam had no idea if the roads were yet passable. And even if they were, Diana Rustin was looking more exhausted by the minute. She was in no condition to go anywhere. He could only hope her father arrived before the gossip mill got word of her presence here.

He poured sherry for her and another brandy for himself. He'd had far too much already, but it had been a hellish night. When Mrs. Stebbins came in response to his summons, he requested scones and biscuits, and asked that a guest chamber in the south wing be made up for Miss Rustin. The south wing was well away from the family wing and his own chamber, and he thought perhaps to thwart some of the gossipmongers.

But Miss Rustin thwarted *him*, saying that she wished to be within easy calling distance of the baroness's chamber. "Even the dressing room will do," she concluded, but he was having none of that. She was not some damned lady's maid!

He told the housekeeper to prepare the Oriental Chamber instead. It was the room his mother always stayed in and was only three doors down from Georgie's suite. Unfortunately his own chamber was off the same corridor. The thought that such might be the case seemed not to trouble Miss Rustin.

He waited until Mrs. Stebbins had returned with a plate of scones and biscuits and butter before sitting in the leather chair across from Miss Rustin.

He sipped at his brandy while she nibbled delicately at a buttered scone. One flake caught on her pink lower lip. He watched, fascinated, as her tongue darted out and curled downward to retrieve it. The lithe movement of that little tongue made his body tighten in ways he wished it would not. He forced his eyes lower, away from her face, but that was worse. She filled out her blue woolen dress all too well!

18

Dash it all! Whatever was wrong with him? This was no time to be thinking what he was thinking! Nor was she the sort of woman one ought to be thinking such things about! Which brought him back round to the room arrangements.

"Miss Rustin, surely it has occurred to you that my chamber is in the family wing. Have you never a thought for your own reputation? Could not one of the maids have been sent to the south wing to get you if the need arose?"

She took a sip of her sherry, then dabbed at her lips with a serviette. "As to that, Your Grace, her own maid would not have been able to leave her and would have had to summon another, and send *her* to me. Too much time would be wasted, would it not? And I do consider Lady Rossmore's health far more important than that elusive quantity known as reputation."

There was no twinkle in her eyes, no bemusement in the curve of her mouth. Nor was she huffing and puffing self-righteously, in the way of Evangelicals and bluestockings and others of definitive, exceptionable beliefs. No, Miss Diana Rustin was merely quietly stating a deeply held belief. She was most definitely out of the common way. Still, he wondered if she truly understood the consequences of all of her actions.

"I appreciate your concern for my sister, Miss Rustin. But your reputation—"

"Your Grace, I learned long ago that people will condemn where they will, quite often unfairly. One may live the most circumspect life and still be made to suffer, you see." She sighed almost imperceptibly, and he saw once again that sadness, that weary resignation, come and go fleetingly in her eyes. How had she suffered? he wondered, for surely she had. She looked down at the sherry glass in her hands. "And so I decided long ago that I would not live my life in fear of tattlemongers. I would not try to please an unpleasable world. I would please myself." She raised her eyes, and the bemused sparkle was back in their deep blue depths. Extraordinary, he thought, that she pleased herself by delivering babies. "Does that shock you, Your Grace?"

"Everything about you shocks me, Miss Rustin," he murmured without thinking, and wondered exactly how else she pleased herself while ignoring the gossipmongers. Certainly she did not spend all of her time engaged in midwifery!

He ruthlessly cut off the wholly improper speculations which followed rapidly upon that thought and pulled himself back to matters at hand. "You said my nephew was feisty, and you do not seem overly concerned about him. Yet he came quite early, and I was given to understand such children are often sickly."

"And so they are, Your Grace, but the child is quite big and—well—I tend to doubt he was very early at first stop."

"But of course he was! Why, your very own father was quite clear that—well—I mean to say, would not Georgie have known—er—" He paused, wishing he had never started.

"All of that is true, Your Grace, but you see, a doctor bases his judgment on the size of the—ah—well on the date of the last—" Adam scowled at her, and she paused, then tried another tack. "Well, you see," she went on, and he was certain her lips were twitching, "it is possible for a woman to have seen her—"

"Ah, Miss Rustin, I withdraw my original question."

Adam had left Miss Rustin to finish her scones and had gone up to check on his sleeping sister and his nephew, who was also sound asleep. He returned to the library, meaning to convey Miss Rustin to her chamber and then betake himself to his own to sleep as well.

He found her curled up in her chair, head on the arm rest, those luxurious curls atumble, eyes closed. Miss Rustin was quite definitely asleep. Recalling her reaction to his touch, he whispered her name, then called more loudly. She did not stir. Very gently he put a hand to her shoulder and shook her. "Miss Rustin. Wake up, Miss Rustin."

She murmured something incoherent and shifted about a bit, but remained very much asleep. Most of her face was hidden from him, and he could not resist stroking the black curls from her cheeks. How soft they were; how utterly beautiful she looked in sleep. And how vulnerable. He wondered again at the cause of the sadness he'd seen in her eyes and felt a wholly unaccustomed surge of protectiveness, as if he wanted to spare her from further sadness.

Which, he told himself, was exceedingly ridiculous. He hardly knew the lady, and what he did know told him she was well able to look after herself. Probably a typical, managing female if he was not far off the mark, like his mother and even his sister.

But she did look adorably disheveled, he mused, and resisted the urge to plant a kiss on her temple as he whispered in her ear and very gently nudged her awake.

Diana heard her name whispered, felt the hand at her shoulder, and sank more deeply into the cushions. And if somewhere in the recesses of her mind she knew she ought not to permit that touch, she was much too befuddled with sleep to vouchsafe any objection. Besides, she rather liked that touch. It was soft and warm, and the voice accompanying it was deep and resonant and equally as warm. And then that hand stroked her hair and face and that voice whispered in her ear. And suddenly the warmth of comfort became a very different, fiery warmth; suddenly, she knew very well who it was.

She stirred, but did not open her eyes. For if he knew she was indeed awake, she would no longer be at liberty to savor these lovely sensations. So for one long, forbidden moment, Diana Rustin pretended she was a woman like other women. She pretended she was entitled to a woman's feelings, entitled to become a gentleman's wife, entitled to curl up in his library on a cold, snowy night and have him gently wake her and lead her abovestairs to a shared chamber.

But, of course, fate had decreed that Diana Rustin was not entitled to any such thing. And indeed, she had made her peace with it all, had found a measure of contentment in her life. Now, however, as she slowly opened her eyes and gazed into the strong, aquiline face of the Duke of Marchmaine, she had the uncanny feeling that contentment would prove most elusive for some time to come.

Chapter 2

"Please, miss, do wake up! She's in a bad way, her ladyship is!"

Diana awoke to a hand jostling her blankets and the urgent whisperings of a maidservant. As soon as the words penetrated Diana's sleep-befogged mind, she sat bolt upright in bed. The draperies had been drawn aside; the outside world was a swirling mass of white. Clearly no one, not Papa nor the baron nor the duchess, would arrive today. It was all up to Diana.

She took only a moment to smooth down her dress and tie her hair back in its ribbon, and then dashed after the maid down the corridor to Lady Rossmore's suite. Lady Rossmore was lying against the pillows, her blond hair twisting out of its braid, her face excessively pale.

She smiled wanly at Diana's approach. "Miss . . . Rustin," she rasped, attempting to lift her hand from the coverlet.

Diana took the hand as she sat down in the gilt-edged chair at the bedside. "Diana," she corrected softly. "But you must not try to talk. We will take care of you, and you have a wonderful, healthy new son."

Lady Rossmore's eyes welled up. "Thank you . . . my son . . . Diana. I . . . too weak to suckle. Get . . . wet nurse."

"You'll be right as rain in a day or two, Lady—"

"Georgie," she interrupted.

Diana hid her surprise. "Georgie. You—" She stopped as the baroness squeezed her hand tightly. "What? What is it?"

"Promise me," she whispered, her gray eyes fierce, "you . . . take care of . . . my son and . . . Edward."

"No! Georgie! You must not talk like that! You will be fine."
Frantically Diana felt her brow. "You have no fever. That is a
very good sign."

"Blood. So much blood. Even now—"

"That is quite normal," Diana lied. "We will change your
linen, and then you must rest. Your son needs you, Georgie,
and your husband loves you."

Georgie shook her head, and two huge tears tumbled down
her pale cheeks. "Edward does . . . not . . . want me anymore.
It is . . . you . . . promise me you—"

"Georgie," Diana interrupted in a soothing voice, trying to
mask her surprise. "There is naught but friendship between
the baron and me. I do not know how you conceived any
notion—"

"Servants . . . saw him . . . kiss you."

Oh, dear God! Diana thought. What must she have been
thinking all this time? Georgie's hand was limp in Diana's now,
as if she'd expended all her energy. And she probably had, but
her mental state concerned Diana at least as much as her
physical.

"Georgie. Do not talk—you need to rest. But listen to me,"
Diana said urgently. "Edward loves you. I have heard him tell
Papa so any number of times. There are some . . . things that
disturb him, things you must discuss with him when he
returns. If he did not love you, he would be indifferent to those
matters. As to that kiss, it meant nothing. He was merely
overset. It is *you* who fill his thoughts, Georgie."

"He went away," she whispered miserably.

"Georgie, I cannot pretend to know very much about
marriage, but Papa says every wedded couple must work out
their differences in the first years. Now come, we can talk more
when you are feeling more the thing. I will check your linens
now, and then we will give you your son to suckle. You must
try—it will help the bleeding, you must know. And then you
will rest. And no more of this extracting of unnecessary
promises," Diana finished softly, and rose to turn down the
coverlet.

As she did so her head turned slightly. Out of the corner of
her eye she caught a glimpse of tousled chestnut hair, a white
shirt not fully tucked into brown pantaloons, and scowling

23

tawny eyes. She blinked and straightened up, but when she looked again he was gone. God in Heaven! How much had he heard?

Having settled the baroness comfortably, at least for a time, Diana made her way back to her own room. There she found a maidservant who informed her that breakfast, and the Duke of Marchmaine, awaited her in the breakfast parlor. Given what had transpired minutes ago, this intelligence somewhat discommoded her. The maid helped her wash, smooth down her dress, and fix her long black hair as best she might, then guided Diana to the breakfast parlor.

The sideboard was heaped with hot, aromatic dishes that reminded her of how very hungry she was. Her appetite was effectively squelched, however, by one look at the duke's smoldering face. His hawklike, aristocratic nose might have been carved of marble. And his tawny eyes burned with fury, which was quite obviously directed at her.

Nevertheless he greeted her with a clipped, "Good morning," to which she mumbled a response. Then he rose and held a plate out to her, that she might choose from among the heaping dishes. She filled her plate without having any notion of what she put on it; her thoughts were churning on other matters entirely. The first was what on earth she would say if the duke questioned her about her conversation with Lady Rossmore—Georgie. By the look on his face she could only guess that he'd heard a far sight too much. How would she ever explain it? The other matter that occupied her mind to the exclusion of her breakfast was the duke himself.

She knew him by reputation to be a rakehell who had successfully evaded the matchmaking mamas, including his own, through some ten years on the Town. He was said to have a penchant for drinking, pursuing lightskirts, brangling with his mother and—of all things—designing houses. He was most assuredly not thinking about houses right now. He looked like he was thinking about Diana, and ways to strangle her, after he'd got the truth from her. But oddly enough, his obvious ire, his threatening stance, did not frighten her; indeed, it troubled her only in as much as she did not want to discuss its cause.

24

What *did* discommode her, however, was his proximity, and her reaction to it.

Neither of them had said a further word, but now, in the daylight, she was aware of him in a way she had not been last night. The full impact of his great height, his lean, muscular form, shown to perfection in his tight pantaloons and bottle green coat, his masculine scent, all hit her with a wholly unaccustomed force as he stood not two feet from her and watched her every move. The sensations thus engendered were not entirely unlike those she'd felt last night when he'd grasped her shoulders. But this time he had not even touched her! The thought was most disconcerting. When her plate was full, he took it from her to place it on the table before seating her. He signalled to a footman to pour her coffee, and then dismissed the man. They were alone.

He resumed his seat at the head of the table, to her right. She waited for him to speak, but he did not. He picked up his fork and speared a piece of sausage. She did not know if she could eat and so ventured a sip of coffee. Minutes went by. He ate with jagged movements, fueled, no doubt, by his anger. She had not touched her food. He swallowed a piece of toast.

"Eat your breakfast, Miss Rustin," he commanded curtly. "I have it on good authority that you are quite famished, and I take leave to doubt that three scones several hours ago would have done much to mitigate that condition."

She raised her eyes to his, searching for a bit of humor, and found none. She sighed and folded her elbows on the table. He was in the right of it; she *was* famished. But she could not eat whilst he looked dagger points at her. "Your Grace, if you mean to ring a peal over me, I pray you will do so now and be done with it. Then I shall eat my breakfast."

She thought his lips twitched, if only for a moment. She caught a glint in his tawny eyes, though he masked it straightaway. "The matter I wish to discuss can wait until we adjourn to the library," he said imperiously, then added in a voice much less controlled, "Now, eat your breakfast, Miss Rustin!"

She ate, or at the least made an attempt to do so, and then all too soon he was leading her into the library. He seated her before a cheerful fire wholly at odds with the prodigious frown

25

that had descended onto his face. He began to pace before her.

"If you are wondering just how much I heard, Miss Rustin," he began quite without preamble, "let me assure you that I heard quite enough."

She raised her chin a notch. What right had he to eavesdrop?

"And," he went on, "lest you think to turn the tables by accusing me of eavesdropping—" she blinked and he almost smiled in satisfaction—"it will not fadge, Miss Rustin. You see, I had come to look in on my sister, and paused at the door when I saw that you were with her. When I realized just what you were speaking of—"

"You should have turned right then and exited her chambers," she interjected, rising from her seat. She had got to brazen it out. "Forgive me, Your Grace, but with intention or not, you were eavesdropping on a private conversation."

Absolute fury suffused his face as he stalked to her, coming to stop but a foot away. He towered over her, his jaw rigid with tension, his tawny eyes riveting her to her place as surely as if his hands held her there. They were extraordinary eyes, she thought irrelevantly. Deep and piercing and intelligent. Cat's eyes. Only not the pussycat variety. More like the cat that stalked the jungle. A panther, perhaps. His body was like that, too, long and lithe and powerful. And just now he looked ready to pounce. Still, she stood her ground.

"And you, Miss Rustin," he said with quiet, deadly calm, "have committed the far more grievous sin of intruding between husband and wife. To wit, seducing Edward when his wife was incapacitated by her approaching confinement."

Her eyes flashed. She wanted to lash out and . . . and plant him a facer, as Papa would say. But, of course, she did no such thing, merely stamped her foot and clenched her fists and fairly spluttered in her fury. "I did no such thing! And you, sir, have no right to speak to me in such a manner. Furthermore, I take leave to tell you that none of this is at all your concern. Now, if you'll excuse me . . ."

She whirled away from him, but Adam was having none of it. Without a thought for her reaction when he'd touched her last night, he reached out and grabbed her wrist, pulling her forward. She would have fallen against him had he not righted

26

her. Those eyes, dark, velvety blue eyes, had flashed fire just moments ago. Now he watched the fire recede and that wariness that he recalled from last night take over. He thought fleetingly that he would have liked to explore that fire. Fire, after all, took many forms. Another time, he chided himself. Now there was another matter at hand. Literally.

Her pulse jumped where he held her wrist, and his hand felt altogether too warm at the contact. He could have sworn she felt the warmth, too. Did that account for that wariness, the . . . uncertainty in those deep blue eyes? He felt her entire body stiffen, as it had last night, and wondered what it was about his slightest touch that caused this reaction. But this time he did not let her go. And if he had expected increased anger, and fire, because he'd so detained her, he was disappointed. She merely, without moving, withdrew from him, somewhere into herself, and tilted her beautiful oval-shaped face up in an attempt, he supposed, at haughtiness.

But what he saw on her pale face was not haughtiness, nor aloofness, which he was certain she sought to cultivate. What he saw was . . . vulnerability, blast her! He did not want to see that.

With effort, he recalled himself. Those big blue eyes did not change the damning testimony he'd had from Georgie's own lips. "Everything about my sister, especially in the absence of her husband, is my concern," he said. "And whether he seduced you or vice versa is of no moment. The result is the same." He stared down at those velvety blue eyes and felt nearly sick at what she'd done. She tried to twist free of his grasp; he merely tightened his hold. If not, he was like to put his hands to her neck. How *could* she? And then another thought occurred to him, and the sickness rose like bile in his throat. "When you spoke last night of pleasing yourself, I had no notion that *this* was what you meant," he drawled contemptuously. Her eyes flared at that and her mouth fell open, but he went on, his ire mounting with his words. "Tell me, Miss Rustin, did you come here last night because you felt guilty? You'd taken Georgie's husband and now—"

"Ooh!" she exploded, yanking her wrist from his grasp and darting away to put the width of half the room between them. "I'll not listen to such vile words another moment! You are

27

odious in the extreme to say such things! I came here because she needed me and Papa was not available. And as to the other, there is naught between the baron and me." She drew herself up, and he thought her delicate chin quivered. "Good day to you, Your Grace. This is a rather large house. I trust we can contrive not to encounter each other again. I shall leave the minute the snow clears sufficiently." With that she sashayed toward the double mahogany doors.

The duke watched her progress, watched the sway of her beautifully proportioned hips beneath the form-fitting wool merino dress, watched her eyes flash once more as the heightened color on her cheeks spread and the dark curls danced about her face. And then he brought himself up short; the little witch had probably snared Edward in just that way, with her devastating combination of vulnerability and fire.

He sprang into action, fairly leaping toward the doors and slamming his hands against both just as she reached for one of the knobs. She gasped and whirled round, her eyes wide with a shock that was quickly masked. He had her well and truly cornered, one hand on either side of her head, his body just inches from hers. A pulse beat at her throat, and her breathing seemed erratic; but he was certain, once again, that it was not fear he saw in those deep blue eyes. Not fear, that is, of having aroused his ducal anger, nor fear of physical harm. It was that wariness again. He was not, he assured himself, becoming intrigued by it. And the throbbing of his own pulse, the blood that beat too rapidly in his veins, was due to anger, nothing more. It had naught to do with the fact that if he shifted slightly, his entire body would be pressed against the lush one he had cornered, and naught to do with the ebony curls trying to escape their ribbon. Nor had it to do with the red lips pursed now in vexation. He did not want to tug the ribbon from that hair and see how far the locks would fall, any more than he wanted to kiss those lips. All he wanted was to hear the truth from those very lips, and then he would dismiss her with all the disdain she deserved.

He *was* a panther, she thought. No other creature could have leapt so silently, so effortlessly to the door to block her exit. He had cornered her, his prey, and was gazing down at her with an intensity the like of which she'd never seen. She really had ought to be afraid of him, she told herself as her eyes travelled his long, lithe length. He was obviously a very dangerous man, fiercely angry with her, and she was utterly alone with him. But she was not afraid. Despite his anger, despite the fact that, though he was not even touching her she knew he could overpower her in seconds, she was not afraid. She knew what it was to be overpowered, hurt physically, by a man. And every instinct told her the Duke of Marchmaine would never do that. But there were other kinds of hurt, emotional kinds. She had suffered those, too, and had vowed long ago never to be vulnerable to such again.

That was why she told herself that the warmth she'd felt when he'd touched her last night, and again just now, must surely have been caused by the blazing fires to be found in the Rossmore grates. And the pulse beating so strangely at her throat must needs be due to her anger at his horrid accusations. It had naught to do with the fact that the panther held his whipcord lean body just inches from hers, that there was strength etched into every plane of his face and a magnetism that exuded from him and seemed to envelop her.

She would *not* let it envelop her! No more would she stoop to defending herself against those odious accusations. Let him ask Edward if he was so inclined to meddle!

"I have not dismissed you yet, Miss Rustin," he said in a low growl that quite effectively snapped her out of her reverie. "And you shall not leave here until I have the entire truth from you. And lest you think to evade or gammon me, let me remind you that I have naught else to do this day, save check on Georgie, and that no one is like to interrupt us. The staff know their business well enough without me, and we are not likely to have visitors this day, are we?"

Her eyes flew to his at this last, and then to the French doors. The snow was still coming down in swirling masses of white. And it was then, as the duke hovered just inches from her, seeming to press her back into the mahogany doors without ever touching her, that the full impropriety of the situation hit her. Georgie could hardly be considered a chaperone in her present state, and there was no one else in the house save servants. It was obvious that Diana could not leave, and equally obvious, as the duke had intimated, that neither

Papa nor anyone else would be able to reach Rossmore today. Diana had told Marchmaine the truth last night when she said she concerned herself little with the proprieties, for such concern had availed her little in her life. But suddenly, as Marchmaine glared down at her with that disconcerting intensity that sent ripples of warmth through her, she was very concerned indeed! And then she chided herself for being a ninnyhammer. There was no warmth coming from this man. Only anger and those wretched accusations. And her chief problem of the moment was not one of impropriety but of escaping the duke's presence without telling him what he wanted to know. For the entire episode was simply too private, and too humiliating, for all concerned. She could not speak of it.

"You may start talking, Miss Rustin," he commanded silkily, but she heard the steel beneath his words and girded herself for one more try.

"Your Grace, do try to understand. This is not your concern, nor mine, really. It is between Edward and Georgie. It would be most unseemly for us to discuss it."

His jaw clenched. "What is unseemly has already been done, Miss Rustin," he said repressively, then abruptly dropped his right hand from the door and swept it toward the sofa and chairs flanking the chimney grate. "Sit down, ma'am, and do not try my patience by attempting to leave again."

He pivoted to give her room to move, keeping his left hand firmly splayed across the juncture of the two mahogany doors. She sighed heavily. There really was no hope for it. She walked with what dignity she could muster to the leather sofa and seated herself at its edge. The duke followed in his silent, pantherlike way and folded his long, lean frame into the wing chair adjacent to the sofa.

Diana took a deep breath and stared down at the hands in her lap. Forgive me, Edward, she whispered inwardly, and then began.

"This is not, as I tried to tell you, my story, but Edward's and Georgie's. But if you would have it, well—to begin with you must know that Edward and Papa are friends. This despite the difference in their ages and despite the fact that—well, he was used to decline Papa's dinner invitations, because

30

Georgie did not wish to come." She met his gaze and was not surprised to see his brow rise in question. She smiled ruefully, deciding she might as well tell him; he would find out soon enough at all events, and this was hardly the worst of it. "I am afraid I am not considered quite the thing by—er—some of our neighbors. I am not received by everyone, you see, and Georgie—"

"I take your point, Miss Rustin. Go on," he interjected impatiently.

"Very well, but I did not mean to imply that I harbor any ill feelings toward her, for indeed, I do not. Georgie's sensibilities are—er—her prerogative, after all. Well, at all events, Edward would occasionally come after dinner to pass an evening with Papa. But about a year ago, the visits became more frequent. I would, of course, leave them to their gentlemen's talk, but gradually Edward began asking me to stay." She paused and stared at the flames in the grate.

"He said—he said he found my company restful. I didn't say much, just sat by the fire doing my embroidery or pouring out tea, but he made the comment more than once that—that Georgie was not a very restful woman. I was not comfortable taking part in the conversation, but more and more he drew me in, addressing remarks to me. It was as if he felt that as a woman I had ought to be able to understand another woman. And he desperately wanted to understand Georgie." At this she met his eyes again. The chestnut brows were arched in a frown, but she took a breath and determined not to be cowed by him. She would hold his gaze and tell the truth; she had done naught that was wrong, after all.

"I heard him avow many times, Your Grace, that he loved her. But he said that she was no longer the sweet girl he had courted and wed. She was . . . different."

"In what way, Miss Rustin?" he prompted, seemingly at his ease. But Diana detected the tautness in his face, even underlying his words.

She went resolutely on. "She had become demanding, he said, complaining frequently about the agedness of the house and—and using a shrill tone with the servants, even with him."

"And did not Edward attempt to put a stop to this?" The

31

duke had crossed his long legs, propping his elbows upon them and bringing his long tapered fingers together in a steeple.

"He said he did, but—ah—his exact words were that Georgie was so busy finding fault with him that she had no time in her day left for seeing her own faults."

Adam cursed inwardly. He did not like what he was hearing. No, not a jot. Yet he knew it was possible. He'd seen Georgie and Edward together enough to know that. Still, did not all newly married couples have their differences? And just what had Miss Rustin to do with all this?

"He began to despair, Your Grace, to feel that matters could only worsen."

"Surely things cannot be as bad as all that," Adam interjected crossly. "They have only been wed nigh onto two years, after all. And Georgie has been . . . enceinte a good part of that time. Surely Edward knew enough to make allowances for that. Besides which, Miss Rustin, I fear we are far off the mark. None of this excuses—"

"Your Grace," she interrupted firmly, "if you will allow me to continue."

He glowered at her but inclined his head in acquiescence. Let her have her say. Then he would—

"He began to despair because—" she paused, and he watched her take a deep breath, then shift her deep blue gaze to the fire once more. "Because he said she was becoming more like her mother every day," she finished in a rush.

He almost gasped. How dare she speak so! It was no wonder she could not meet his eyes, no wonder a blush had risen to her pale cheeks. She did not speak further, and neither did he. The only sound in the library was the crackle of the fire. He could feel a vein throbbing at his temple as he gazed at Miss Rustin. Edward was right about one thing. She *was* restful. She was, in fact, despite the shocking statement she'd just made, the picture of serenity as she sat with hands delicately folded, big round eyes on the dancing fire. The skin of her oval-shaped face was smooth, flawless. It would be soft to the touch, he knew, and warm. Ah yes, very warm.

Hellfire! What difference did it make *what* her skin felt like? He *would not* stray from the matter at hand! But even as he tugged his mind back to that very matter, he wondered if

Edward had touched her face as he kissed her, and if he'd touched—No, dammit! He would not think of it. He told himself it did not signify, and that the only emotion he was feeling just now was anger—at Edward, Miss Rustin, Georgie, and . . . at his mother. But the latter, of course, was nothing new. At all events, the thought brought him back around to Miss Rustin's last statement.

It was an impertinence for her to speak so! And yet—he sighed inwardly—he *had* asked, no—demanded, that she speak. And he did not for one minute suppose she had made that up. No, it was unfortunately all too likely that Edward had said that very thing. The truth was that no man could abide the formidable, overbearing Duchess of Marchmaine. But that Georgie should be trailing in her path! Adam had seen signs himself and had hoped he was mistaken.

"Are you acquainted with my mother, Miss Rustin?" he asked at length.

"Yes." She still did not meet his eyes.

"And do you agree with Edward's assessment?" Why was he asking her that? Her opinion surely did not signify!

"I am sure it is not my place to say, Your Grace," she replied. Good, he thought, she knew her place.

And yet he heard himself repeat, a trifle less calmly, "Do you agree, Miss Rustin?"

"Please, Your Grace, it is not my concern and—"

"Look at me, Miss Rustin," he commanded and when she complied asked more forcefully, "do you agree that my sister is becoming more like my mother every day?"

Miss Rustin sighed. "Yes, Your Grace, as does Papa."

What Dr. Rustin thought did not signify, Adam told himself; he did not even know the man. As to what Miss Rustin thought . . . damnation! It did signify. He did not know why, but there it was. Perhaps it was because her opinion corroborated what he himself had been noticing. Noticing and hoping he was wrong. Georgie was becoming the shrew their mother was. Much prettier, to be sure, but a shrew nonetheless.

Still, that did not exonerate Edward and Miss Rustin. When he said as much to her, she stiffened, ever so slightly. "I do not wish to be exonerated, Your Grace. I have done nothing wrong." Adam fairly growled at her to go on with her story.

She slipped an elbow up onto the armrest of the sofa. He wondered if she was as relaxed as she appeared. "One night some weeks ago, Edward appeared at the house quite overset. He and the baroness had just had a dreadful row, by no means their first. It began with Georgie insisting that the cook here at Rossmore be replaced."

"Mrs. Brownlow? But I was given to understand that she's been here nearly all her life!"

"So she has, but Georgie contends that Mrs. Brownlow is a mere rustic, that her palate and repertoire are not nearly sophisticated enough. She wishes to hire someone from London, preferably a Frenchman."

"Good God!"

"Yes, well, it seems matters deteriorated from there into a set-to about Edward's manner of dress here in Yorkshire."

"What the deuce is wrong with the way Edward dresses?"

"She—ah—thinks it far too informal. Rustic, if you would."

"What the devil is rusticating for if not—oh, never mind," he snapped. Those red lips of hers were beginning to curl in amusement. There was nothing amusing about any of this! "Go on!"

"Papa calmed him down and suggested he make clear that she had no say in either matter, that he was the man of the house and she would do well to remember it."

All well and good, Adam thought, but wondered if Edward was capable of standing up to Georgie in a fit of temper. Certainly his own father had not been up to quelling his mother. His father had simply retreated further into himself, until one day he'd simply given up, or so Adam had always felt. The old anger at his mother, and at his father's untimely death, rose in him. Ruthlessly, he suppressed it. Now was not the time.

"And what did *you* say, Miss Rustin? Surely you did not agree with your papa?" he asked mockingly. What woman would, after all?

"I have always believed that a man must be a man in his own home, Your Grace, though not a tyrant. I merely suggested he tell her that his own manner of dress was *his* concern, just as

34

her wardrobe was *hers*. A cook, however, *is* a woman's concern. But here there are extenuating circumstances. I felt he needs must tell her that Mrs. Brownlow's loyalty to the family was such that she could not be turned off, that her cooking was adequate, and that they must make the best of it."

"Would *you* accept such a dictum from *your* husband, Miss Rustin?" he asked pointedly.

Her gaze did not waver from his. "I have never . . . had a husband, Your Grace, but yes, I would."

Perhaps it was the calm conviction in her voice that made him believe her. He wondered why a woman with such uncommon good sense, coupled with such loveliness, had never wed. And then he recalled that if she'd never had a husband of her own, she apparently had taken someone else's.

Scowling, he asked, "Did Edward take your advice?"

"Yes. He came back the next night to report that Georgie had flown into a rage and—ah—" she blushed as she went on—"had locked her door to him."

Damnation! Matters were as bad as his deepest fears. He turned his anger at Georgie onto Miss Rustin. "And so now I begin to see everything. There you were, all sympathetic understanding, waiting with open arms—"

"I will not be insulted, Your Grace." She spoke quietly, and stood up, forcing him to do the same.

"Pray continue," he said gruffly, though he knew he would like the next part least of all. She did not resume her seat, but went to stand at the window, turning to face him. He moved to the fireplace and propped a hand on the mantel.

She went on. "That night Papa was out, gone to see about a sick child. I told Edward as much, assuming he would not come in. He never had when Papa was not home. But he was most overset and said he would only stay a few minutes. I assented, and he told me of this latest happenstance. I recall that we sat in the parlor, the width of half the room between us. He was staring into the fire. He spoke of Georgie when they first met, how he had loved what he took for spirit, but which had turned into a strident willfulness that he feared he could not live with. He had tears in his eyes. I did not know what to say, did not see how I could help him."

She paused and turned to gaze out at the snow. Adam did not

35

say a word, knew this was not the time to interrupt her. "It was when he rose to leave, and I to see him out, that he—he turned to me, and put his hand to my cheek, and told me I was very lovely."

Adam told himself the clenching of his jaw at hearing this was for Georgie's sake. It had naught to do with his own desire to—

"And then he—he leaned forward and—and kissed me. I was so surprised that at first I did not think to resist, and before I knew what he was about, he had his arms around me, and that was when I pushed him away. And then poor Edward was mortified and apologized profusely, saying he meant no insult. He left the house straightaway, and the next morning a note was delivered, addressed to both Papa and me. It simply thanked us for our hospitality, said that he had not meant to impinge on it, and that he was accepting a diplomatic commission on the Continent. He was certain it was the best thing that he could do at present, for all concerned."

She pivoted back round. "And that is all, Your Grace. No seduction, no liaison. Simply a lonely, distressed man who had a momentary lapse and looked for comfort in the wrong place."

Adam lowered his hand from the mantel and straightened his stance. He sauntered toward her as he spoke. "I see, Miss Rustin. Very simple and very possible. And, indeed, I have little doubt that it is true, up until that last night. And while I will own that the picture you paint *is* plausible, yet I can paint a different scenario entirely."

She lifted her chin and met his gaze squarely. He stood now just two feet from her, trying to keep his mind on what he meant to say, not on the picture in his mind's eye of Edward taking her in his arms. "I can imagine Edward coming to you all overset, needing comfort, knowing he should not stay if your father was not home. And you, the picture of sympathy, understanding, offering to make tea for him and suggesting he come in for just a bit. I can imagine you listening to his story, which ended with Georgie's locked door. And then, at the door, it could have been your arms snaking up about his neck, assuring him that you would never lock *your* door, that your papa would not be home for hours, that, indeed, he was quite often from home . . . and poor Edward, in the state he was in,

36

having no strength to resist your lures . . ." He heard her sharp intake of breath and smiled humorlessly. "Oh, yes, Miss Rustin, I can paint a different picture entirely. And truth to tell, it might not have been his last night at home, might it? It might have been weeks before he left that he began to visit you regularly. And perhaps the guilt finally caught up with him."

Without quite realizing it he had moved a step closer to her. She still held his gaze, but he knew she did so with difficulty. He thought a flicker of pain crossed her eyes, but then it was gone and they were steady once more. She was either very brazen or very brave.

He caught her chin between his thumb and forefinger, gently. "Do you not agree that my scenario is quite plausible, Miss Rustin?" he uttered silkily.

He felt the pulse at her throat flutter; she did not move. If she stiffened again, it was imperceptible. He wondered if she would issue another fiery denial, or perhaps seek to appease him by using her wiles on him. She swallowed hard and her eyes searched his face. And then she shocked him utterly by saying, "It is your privilege to believe what you will, Your Grace. Indeed, I am not surprised that you doubt me. 'Tis no more than I expected."

Blast! She was making him feel a veritable cad, when it was *she* who was in the wrong! Her eyes once more flickered with pain, pain that he told himself he did not want badly to erase. Her little chin felt warm and soft beneath his fingers. He told himself he did not want to stroke his fingers upward to feel the smoothness of her cheeks beneath him. Nor did he want to kiss her, to taste what Edward had tasted. . . . Abruptly he dropped his hand. Only then did she step back.

"There is one thing more you should know, Your Grace," she said in her husky voice. "Once, a very long time ago, a man hurt me. Rather badly. I was nineteen years old. And now, seven years later, I tell you that I have never again given a man the power to hurt me. And I never shall. So, believe what you will, and say what you will. It matters not a whit to me. And now if you'll excuse me, I shall go to Georgie."

With that, she turned and glided gracefully, silently, from the room.

Adam cursed volubly as soon as the doors closed behind her.

He pounded the fist of his right hand into the palm of his left. He was bristling with anger! He paced the floor and punched his palm again. He was seething! He ran his hand jaggedly through his hair. He was furious at Miss Rustin, Edward, Georgie, his mother, himself . . . even, however ludicrous, at the unknown man who had once hurt Miss Rustin, very badly.

Bloody hell! What a coil! He stared out at the snow-blanketed gardens, clenching his teeth. The devil of it was that he did not know *what* to believe! Whatever the servants had seen and reported to Georgie had been enough to convince her that Edward no longer cared for her. Surely a single, fairly innocent kiss would not have engendered such a notion. There *had* to be more to it than that!

Yet Miss Rustin did not seem a deceitful woman. She almost had too much dignity. And she had known suffering. That much he believed; the sadness lurking in her eyes would have told him that even if her own words had not. She had vowed never again to let a man hurt her. Would that not mean keeping her distance from all men? Might that not account for the fact that she was some twenty-six years old and unwed? But then, why would she make an exception with Edward? Surely her sympathy and understanding would not extend that far.

And then he recalled her own words about pleasing herself and not being overly concerned with proprieties. Adam rubbed his hand along his nape. Had he been correct, after all, when he accused her of "pleasing herself" in this manner? Was Edward merely an amusement, a man she could dally with but not allow to touch her heart?

It was hard to see the seemingly vulnerable Miss Rustin, who stiffened at his *own* touch, in such a role. And yet, the lady had a saucy side as well, and a face and form that could lure a man if he were not careful—

Damnation! He did not know *what* to believe! But one thing he knew very well. His first loyalty was to his sister. It was not to a woman he'd just met—no matter how deep and velvety her eyes, how flawless her skin, how lush her hair. . . .

He cursed again, and again, as the snow fell in relentless, endless swirls.

Chapter 3

Diana forcibly stilled the shaking of her body as she made her way unsteadily toward Georgie's rooms. She would not, *could not* think about what had just transpired in the library. Not now. Not yet. She must attend to Georgie; that was, after all, why she was here.

She found the baroness awake, her brow cool to the touch, though she was lying listlessly upon the bed. She was not bleeding excessively, and the listlessness troubled Diana far more than the absence of fever encouraged her. She tried to engage Georgie in conversation, but the baroness would say naught but to ask Diana once again to procure a wet nurse. Indeed, Georgie's maid asserted that her mistress showed little interest in feeding her son.

Diana left Georgie's suite most perturbed, but once inside her own room, Georgie's image faded from her mind and another took its place. An aquiline face with intense, tawny eyes and a long, lithe body that exuded the grace and power of a panther. And it was now, as she recalled the way those eyes had pierced her, the way that panther's body had stalked her, that she began to shake again.

She sank down onto the red and gold canopied bed as her body shuddered with memories and mortification over the hour she had spent with the duke. How could she have told him what she had? To have spoken of the episode with Edward was bad enough, but she'd had little choice in that. It was the other that truly horrified her. To have told him that a man had hurt her—dear God, what had come over her? She *never* spoke of

Robert, no matter how obliquely.

Why? Why had she spoken of him now? She wrapped her arms about herself, suddenly chilled. She was very much afraid that she knew the answer. It was not to convince the duke of aught that she had spoken, but to convince herself. To remind herself. She had spoken of the man who had once hurt her because . . . because for the first time in seven years she had met a man who, if she were not careful, might also hurt her very badly. She *would* be careful! She would let no man close enough to touch her heart. There was no choice. She had survived that time with Robert, just barely. She would not survive a second time.

She did not want to think of that time, but the memories rushed forward, blurring her vision with tears. Robert. Tall, blond, handsome Sir Robert Easton. They had met at an assembly in York, had been smitten with each other straightaway. He danced divinely, and Diana could still picture the way his blue eyes crinkled with ready laughter. But for the first time, she found that she could not conjure a picture of the rest of his face. She supposed it was because she'd not thought of him in many months.

Still, it was odd. She frowned now, trying to picture him. But somehow the image that came to her mind's eye had features far too angular, hair too dark. She shrugged and wiped away her tears. It was just as well. It was long past time that his image faded.

And indeed, it had been years since she'd grieved his loss. And even longer since she'd realized he was not worthy of her love, that she'd loved an illusion, or perhaps merely been infatuated with one. No, she had not missed Robert all these years. But what had lingered was the terrible feeling of humiliation that had come when he jilted her. That and the knowledge that he had done what any other gentleman would have done upon learning of Diana's past. For her fate had been sealed one cold winter's day in the woods behind her father's house. She had been twelve years old.

But she would not think of that, nor of the words Robert had uttered the day he cried off from their engagement. Words that meant not only the end of that betrothal, but the end of hope that there might ever be another.

No! She would not think of any of it. It was all water under the bridge. None of it signified. Diana had made a new life for herself, and she would, as she always had, make the best of it.

And that meant, just now, being very careful. She had never had to be careful around other men. But she knew, after less than twenty-four hours' acquaintance, that the Duke of Marchmaine was different. His touch warmed her when the touch of other men left her cold. His eyes burned with an intensity that bespoke hidden, unknown passions. There was a power, a magnetism about him, that she had never before sensed in any man. The duke's mere proximity caused her pulse to trip and her stomach to flutter.

But it was his touch—she swallowed hard and put a hand to her nape, massaging nervously—that she needs must avoid at all costs. It was a rather lowering thought, but while she might resist the compelling intensity of his eyes, the disturbing strength of his panther's body, she did not know if she could resist the heat of his touch.

She'd felt the warmth the first moment he'd put his hands to her shoulders last night. Warmth unlike any she'd ever felt, even with Robert. Instinctively, she'd recognized the danger to herself and had stiffened so that he released her. But each time he touched her—her wrist, her chin—it became harder to stiffen, to steel herself against him. And yet she must. It was the only way to survive.

Word had come to her that the duke was awaiting her for luncheon, and good manners bade Diana obey the summons. At all events, she was no coward and had no intention of hiding out for the duration of what looked like a blizzard. She would simply, she decided, see that they discussed little more than the weather and the state of Georgie's health.

The duke seemed to have come to the same resolve. For though he searched her face with far more intensity than she liked when first he sat down, he kept the conversation safely upon the snow and the impassable roads. Yet as they ate Mrs. Brownlow's cold glazed ham and brussel sprouts, Diana sensed a certain tautness in him, a remoteness evident despite his air of civility. And though she put it down in part to his concern for Georgie, she could not deny his pique at her after this morning's encounter. He still did not believe her, or at the least, was not certain *what* to believe.

She told herself it did not signify. That she could not help wondering what it would be like to bask in the favor of this tall, powerful man, she put down to excessive weakness on her part. She had never enjoyed the full favor of any man save Papa, and she never would. Nor did she need any such!

It was not until their places were cleared and a bowl of fruit placed before them that the duke spoke of Georgie.

He leaned forward, his serviette crumpled in his hand. "I am concerned about my sister, Miss Rustin. She is not feverish— I thank God, and you, for that—but she is most pale and lethargic. I am not familiar with the condition of women after birthing children, but still, Georgie's state seems excessive, does it not?"

Diana sighed. "I will not pretend to you that I do not share your concern, Your Grace. She has lost a great deal of blood, as you know. I would expect her to be pale, and tired. But this lethargy—well, I am persuaded it comes from her great distress. She—she refuses to suckle the child." She shook her head and put her hand to her nape, her head and voice lowered. "It is almost as if she has given up."

The duke cursed softly. She raised her eyes. "The suckling is not only essential for the babe, Your Grace, but it would help her as well. It contracts the—er—well—I mean to say—" The duke scowled at her, but she doggedly went on. "It would help stop the—ah—bleeding, you see."

"Damnation! Can you not speak to her of this? Surely if she were to understand—"

"Your Grace, if you will pardon me, what she needs to understand is that her husband cares for her. It is not I who can assure her of his devotion. If you had—had believed what I told you this morning, then perhaps *you* could. As it is . . ." She shrugged and let her voice trail off.

Marchmaine began paring an orange with a savagery that made her fear he would slice his fingers apart. "Regardless of *your* role in this, Miss Rustin, from what you tell me, Edward's devotion *is* very much in question. It would be rather difficult to assure her of something I am hard put to believe myself.

42

Better perhaps to persuade her that her son needs her. Surely a mother's natural instincts will take over once she holds the child." He finished paring the orange and set the knife down. "You look doubtful, Miss Rustin. Have you a better notion?"

There was no taunt, nor even a challenge in his voice. Amazingly, despite this morning's wretched encounter, he seemed to want her opinion. "I do believe that people can change, Your Grace. Perhaps Georgie can be convinced that she can, if she sets her mind to it, win her husband's devotion again. I am persuaded he does truly love her."

He looked dagger points at her. "I have my doubts about the latter, but as to people changing, I take leave to tell you, Miss Rustin, that you are rather naive. People do not change . . . at the least, not fundamentally."

He looked grim as he separated the wedges of the orange. It looked sweet and succulent, but he made no move to eat it. He clenched his fists on the table and shifted his gaze to the window, seeming to have gone off inside of himself. She heard herself say, very softly, "You are thinking of your mother."

His eyes flew sharply to hers. His bleak expression was all the confirmation she needed. "And I am thinking of *my* mother," she added. He quirked a brow in question. "She died when I was a child, you must know, but Papa still speaks of her with great affection. He quite adored her, you see, but he once told me that their first few years together were rather difficult."

"And after that? What changed?"

"According to Papa, it was Mama. One day she simply decided she'd had enough of brangling and dissension and determined to become a loving wife. And so she did."

The duke laughed cynically. "Your papa was telling you a Banbury tale, my dear. No woman could accomplish such a feat, nor would wish to. A woman simply assumes her husband is the culprit in every set-to, and goes about trying to change him."

Diana heard the bitterness in his voice and imagined he was thinking of his mother again. She cocked her head, considering. "Perhaps you are right in the ordinary way of things, Your Grace, but Mama had a very good teacher. My grandmother, Papa's mother." The duke leaned back in his chair, skepticism

43

evident on his face. Diana went on. "She had a very calming presence. Papa was one of four sons, you must know, and it was said that when the boys would set up a riot and a rumpus, she had only to enter the room for everyone to settle down happily at some quiet pursuit."

"And your grandfather?" The corners of his mouth lifted in what might have been a smile.

Diana grinned in fond memory. "Grandpapa was a veritable lion who roared his way through life. But with Grandmama he was a pussycat. He was quite unashamedly besotted. I think Mama saw them together and decided that was what she wanted."

"And you, Miss Rustin? Are you like your mother or your grandmother?" he asked so softly that his voice was almost a caress. A very warm caress.

Suddenly Diana wondered how they had come to be discussing *her* instead of Georgie. She looked into his eyes and felt his warmth engulf her. She did not want to be engulfed by his warmth. Quickly, she looked down at the hands in her lap. "I—I am told I have the look of my mother."

"But you have the nature of your grandmother." It was a statement, not a question. She did not know what to say. The silence between them was charged; unwittingly, she raised her eyes to his once more.

He was regarding her with his usual intensity, his tawny eyes warm, but there was another element she could not quite place, but which she was certain accounted for the blush she felt overtake her. He broke the contact by turning his attention to the orange on his plate. He pulled apart the wedges and picked one up. To her amazement he extended his hand toward her. "Would you care for a piece, Miss Rustin?"

She looked at the plump orange wedge nestled in the palm of his long, tapered hand, and knew she ought not to take it. "Hot-house oranges are very rare and especially sweet," he said coaxingly.

She lifted her hand to his and grasped the orange. Her fingers brushed his warm palm, and for just a moment she felt his hand curl up slightly, as if to enclose hers. But then his hand relaxed, and she was left to wonder if she had imagined the slight movement. Yet the rush of warmth she felt was surely not imagined. She did not meet his eyes and quickly scooped up the orange slice and brought it to her mouth.

Adam watched her take a delicate bite out of the juicy orange wedge and wondered what had come over him. Why had he offered it to her, and in that manner? And why was he watching as if transfixed as her pink tongue darted out to take the fruit into her mouth, as her lips curled in appreciation of its sweetness, as she pushed the remaining piece into her mouth and chewed and swallowed it? Cursing himself for a fool, he looked down at his plate, took another wedge and popped it into his mouth. Still, his eyes strayed back to her as she dabbed at the corners of her mouth with the serviette. There was a small piece of orange pulp on her lower lip. He shocked himself with the intensity of his desire to wipe it off for her. Or kiss it away.

Blast! What was wrong with him? His pulse was accelerating; he was acting like some moonstruck halfling. Yet he was certainly not moonstruck, and he was no halfling, was in fact, one and thirty. And she . . . she was a woman who had come between Edward and Georgie. She was a woman whose reputation was questionable, but perhaps not questionable enough for him to pursue her in a manner that his body was telling him to. So what the devil was he doing?

He was to ask himself that very question hours later, as he wondered why he had offered her a second slice of the orange from his hand, and a third, and a fourth. And to wonder, with even more perplexity, why she took each and every one.

Diana spent the afternoon in two rather unsuccessful pursuits. The first was an attempt to become interested in several books she borrowed from the library. The second, and far more distressing, was an attempt to interest Georgie in her son.

When the child cried, a maid would pick him up and give him over to his mother. The baroness would dutifully put him to the breast, but in so desultory a manner that the child hardly suckled and resumed his crying. The baroness seemed not to have the strength to lift a glass, nor the interest in becoming stronger herself nor helping her son to do so. Even given the difficult birth, such listlessness and indifference were most unnatural. It was all, Diana feared, to do with Edward. And on that head she felt herself to be in a devilishly awkward situation.

Nonetheless, she felt she needs must try, again and again, at the least till Papa arrived. She freshened up for dinner—indeed, there was little to do, since she had not a change of clothes—and returned to the baroness's suite. The child was crying again, and she took him from the young maidservant who was holding him. Georgie appeared disinterested, and so Diana sat down in a gilt-edged chair next to the bed. She rocked the baby—whose mother still had not give him a name—and cooed to him until he stopped crying. To Diana's amazement he opened his eyes and stared at her with an awareness she'd never seen in a newly born babe. He was a beautiful child, despite his still-wrinkled face, with a mop of hair the same blond as Edward's. She felt, and resolutely repressed, the now familiar pang that always struck her when she held other women's babies. Held them and knew she would never hold her own.

She tore her eyes from the child, knowing she must concentrate on Georgie. "He is so beautiful, Georgie. He will have the look of his father, I make no doubt."

"Yes," came the terse, whispered reply. Georgie's head was turned away from her, and the babe.

"The baron will be so happy to come home to the sight of his wife holding his son."

"No. I—"

"I think he will fall in love with you all over again, Georgie."

At that Georgie turned her head. Her eyes were moist. "It is . . . too late," she rasped, and then turned her head once more.

She would not say another word, nor respond to Diana, and within a short while Diana realized she had fallen asleep. But the babe was not asleep, was nestled contentedly in her arms, and she gave in to the temptation to hold him a few minutes more. She murmured to him and stroked his pink cheek and inhaled his baby smell and told herself these stolen moments were enough.

Adam had decided to look in on Georgie once more before dinner. He was becoming more concerned by the hour. She was not responding to him, her maid, Miss Rustin, nor even to the child. He knew her body was in a weakened state, but he agreed with Miss Rustin that it was her affliction of the spirit that was the more perturbing now.

But when he padded silently into Georgie's bedchamber, having been admitted by her maid, his thoughts did not linger long on his sister. For a quick glance told him she was asleep, and his eyes were drawn instead to the gilt-edged chair at the bedside.

Miss Rustin sat there, in the same blue dress she'd worn for nearly twenty-four hours, looking fresh and beautiful and utterly serene as she held his nephew in her arms. She was cooing to the child, smiling at him, seeming almost to communicate with him. She was quite oblivious of Adam, who stood just inside the doorway. The child's eyes were open. He made some gurgling noise, but otherwise remained still, quite content. And yet the maid had told him the baby had not been fed in several hours.

Adam thought about what Miss Rustin had said about her grandmother and smiled to herself. And then the image before him seemed to change. Miss Rustin's blue merino wool dress became a soft, flowing peignoir, her ebony curls were released from their ribbon to fall softly about her shoulders, and the child's hair changed from Edward's blond to a chestnut color. His own color.

And then the child, rather than staring up at her, began suckling—

Dear God! The image shocked him, sent bolts of heat through him. Where the devil had that all come from? Miss Rustin would never have his child, of a certain not his heir. Dukes of the realm did not beget heirs of doctor's daughters, least of all those of questionable honor and reputation. Nor did he wish any such thing! He blinked, forcing the image to shift back again to the woman in the blue dress.

He knew it would be best if he left the room without making his presence known, but he could not seem to move his feet. And then she looked up and their eyes locked. He felt a jolt, as if some current had passed between them. She flushed, in the manner of one caught in some improper pose. She made to rise.

"No, stay," he rasped. "I—I did not mean to disturb you."

47

And indeed, he had no desire to, for she looked as content as the babe. She was a woman who should have her own to hold, he thought, and wondered about the man who had hurt her so badly that the only babies she held belonged to other women.

"I'll put him down in a minute," she whispered. "I was trying to talk Georgie into taking him, but she—"

"Yes, I know," he said softly. "Join me for sherry in the Red Saloon in quarter of an hour, will you? Dinner will be ready after that."

She nodded, and smiled, that wide and lovely smile he'd noted when she first arrived. It was a smile that of a certain would have left a string of broken hearts behind it, had she been so inclined. He knew she was not; she would not let a man near enough. That is, he reminded himself, not any man except Edward.

Damnation! How near *had* she allowed him? He needed to know, he told himself, for Georgie's sake. And, now he thought on it, was that air of contentment Miss Rustin displayed the result of holding *a* baby, *any baby*, close? Or was it that this was Edward's child? Was she pretending, wishing it were her own? No! It was impossible. Edward was merely a diversion for her. Nothing more. The train of his thoughts infuriated him. For Georgie's sake.

He should simply have met her in the dining room, Adam thought. Why had he subjected himself to an extra half hour of her company, to watching her slowly, gracefully, glide across the carpet of the Red Saloon toward him? Why was the sight of her in that same damned blue dress doing things to him that the sight of dampened petticoats beneath a flimsey, fashionably cut gown did not?

Hellfire! He didn't *want* to want her. She was, by birth, a lady—not of the nobility, perhaps, but gentry nonetheless. The kind of woman a duke didn't marry *or* dally with. Not, of course, that he would consider marrying anyone, for he wouldn't. Let his bachelor friends desert him one by one; *he* would not go near the parson's mousetrap. This latest business with Georgie and Edward merely strengthened his long-held resolve on that head.

48

She stood before him now, and he handed her a glass of sherry as he greeted her. He was careful that their hands did not touch, for her sake, he told himself. And then the thought rose unbidden that gentry or no, she had, by being here unchaperoned, relinquished the right to call herself a lady. And besides, if Edward had had her, was she not, then, fair game? Or would that, in an odd sort of way, be poaching on another man's preserves?

Bloody hell! The whole notion made him nearly ill. He gulped down his sherry and then made an attempt to respond to the inane remark Miss Rustin had made about the weather. What the devil was she doing to him?

And then, because he was angry with her, with himself, because his glass was empty, he said something he never, in a saner moment, would have. "You ought to have babies of your own, Miss Rustin, instead of helping other women have theirs."

She blanched, and nearly spilled her drink. He took the glass from her and wanted to bite his tongue, but once having started, he had got to finish. He refilled both their glasses and ushered her to the adjacent red wing chairs.

"I meant no insult, my dear," he said in a softer voice. "'Tis merely that the babe looked well on you. I will not ask why you have never wed since I believe you intimated the reason earlier today. But I think it a deuced shame." He watched her color rise and wondered if he had only made things worse.

She gulped her sherry, then quirked a brow. "I have no such scruples about questioning *you*, Your Grace, since you have told me naught about yourself. Why have *you* never wed? If for no other reason than to get an heir, I should have thought—"

"You are impertinent, Miss Rustin," he interrupted, but felt his lips twitch. "But . . . touché, nonetheless." He sipped his sherry, having no intention of answering. It was his experience that women abhorred silences. If a man simply held his tongue, a woman would invariably start prattling, usually about herself.

But Miss Rustin did not seem uncomfortable in the silence. She merely regarded him steadily over the rim of her glass. And, unaccountably, it was *he* who began to speak! "I have a perfectly unexceptionable heir, as it happens, a second cousin.

And so I feel no particular compulsion to wed. Of a certain I can think of no other reason to do so." He tried to keep the bitterness from his voice. This was a subject that simply was not open for discussion. She opened her mouth to reply, and he forestalled her. "It is quite different for a woman, however. Whatever your fears are—"

"What are *you* afraid of, Your Grace?" she brazenly blurted.

"Miss Rustin!" This time *he* nearly spilled his drink. He slapped it down on the side table and stood up, towering over her. She really was the outside of enough!

Amazingly, her deep blue eyes began to twinkle up at him. "I apprehend fully that you are a duke of the realm," she began calmly, then rose as well, forcing him to step back. She sauntered to the chimney grate, then pivoted to face him. "And as such you expect not to be questioned. But on very short acquaintance you have contrived to engage me in discourse of a highly personal nature, to ask—no—*demand* answers to questions of matters quite private. And so I am persuaded you cannot fault me for merely taking a leaf from your own book."

He strode to her, trying to maintain his anger in the face of such audacity, despite the soft huskiness of her tone, despite the charming picture she made framed by the fire, despite the fact that she was probably right. "Hoist on my own petard, am I?" he quizzed.

She merely inclined her head in acknowledgement, her lips curling with a hint of mischief.

"It is not a question of fear, Miss Rustin," he heard himself say, "but merely that what I have seen of the married state does not commend it to me."

"I cannot decide if you are afraid that you will marry a woman like your mother or afraid that you will make the mistakes your father undoubtedly made," she countered, blithely ignoring the fury that began to suffuse his face.

"Miss Rustin, you go too far!" he fairly shouted, clenching his fists to keep them from her pretty little neck. "*If* I were to wed, I do assure you I should have no difficulty choosing precisely the right sort of woman—one of impeccable manners, unexceptionable breeding, and suitable biddability! As to my father, he was an exemplary man in all ways. How dare

50

you, who never even made his acquaintance, cast aspersions on him!"

He watched her swallow hard. All traces of amusement fled her face. "I am sorry," she rasped. "I own you are right; I spoke out of turn."

Adam blinked. He had not expected so rapid a capitulation, such genuine contrition. He was not certain he was comfortable with it. Her entire face, her demeanor, seemed to change . . . "Of couse, I did not know him," she went on. "'Tis only that . . . well, it seems to me that difficulties in a marriage are never to be laid solely at one person's door."

"What do you know of my parents' marriage, Miss Rustin?" he demanded sharply.

She shrugged slightly. "Edward alluded to certain—ah—and besides, it seems rather obvious, knowing—ah—"

"Never mind, Miss Rustin!" he snapped. "But did you not tell me that your father attributed the success of his marriage to your mother—er—changing? Would that not mean to say she was responsible for the difficulties as well?"

She clasped her hands at her waist. "Well, yes, but it is a bit more complex than that. I drew my own conclusions from all Papa told me. But that is neither here nor there. I—"

"And those conclusions?" he prodded, wondering why he cared. Why was he engaging in this absurd conversation at first stop? What did it signify what Miss Diana Rustin thought about marriage in general, or any one marriage in particular? Adam propped an arm on the mantel and awaited her answer.

She had cocked her head as if considering what to answer. "I believe," she said at length, "that Mama changed in part because Papa would not tolerate what he once called her waspish behavior. And in part because he responded so warmly to every overture she made. He truly loved her and—"

"I take your point, Miss Rustin," he said too harshly.

"Have I spoken out of turn again? I am sorry. Perhaps one cannot generalize, after all. I—" She paused and tentatively put a hand to the sleeve of his chocolate brown coat. "You loved him very much, did you not, Your Grace?"

He felt her warmth even through the layers of his clothes. It was the first time *she* had touched *him*, and for a moment he forgot about whom they were speaking. His eyes caught hers

51

and held them. He watched the pulse at her throat flutter and felt his own breathing alter. And then she seemed to catch herself. She lowered her eyes and made to lift her hand away from his sleeve.

Without thinking he covered that delicate hand with his. It was warm and soft, and he told himself he ought not to enjoy the feel of it so much. Just as he told himself, with equal futility, that he ought not to let his thumb gently graze back and forth on the underside of her wrist.

"Yes, I loved him," he replied at length, "and he, the poor devil, loved my mother, at least at the beginning. Which is why I believe love within the married state is simply a well-promulgated myth, Miss Rustin."

She raised her eyes again, but made no further attempt to move her hand. "And yet you believed Georgie and Edward to have made a love match," she uttered softly. Her voice was calm enough, but the pulse at her wrist was anything but. He noted that for the first time she had not stiffened against his touch. He wondered if she realized it. His thumb traced gentle circles over her tender skin as he tried to recall what she had last said.

"That elusive, tender emotion does not seem to have lasted very long for Edward and Georgie, does it?" he reminded her. "And if you would be honest, my dear, you would admit that your notions do not differ all that much from mine. If you truly believed love was to be found in the wedded state, I am persuaded you would have long since overcome your fears and entered that very state. Of a certain there would have been no dirth of suitors."

To his utter amazement and horror, her eyes filled with tears. She tried again to pull her hand away; he held it fast. "Your Grace, I should like to—ah—terminate this discussion now." She bit her lip and blinked back the moisture pooling her deep blue eyes. "Indeed, I find I am not hungry, after all, and so—"

"I am certain Mrs. Brownlow's cooking—quite excellent despite what Georgie says—will tempt back your appetite," he said quickly, softly. "And, my dear?"

"Yes," she whispered. Her hand relaxed again beneath his.

"I do have a name. I should like you to use it." He hardly

recognized the odd note in his voice.

A bit of the sparkle came back into her eyes. "Very well. And—ah—Marchmaine?"

"Yes?"

"I am not your dear."

He grinned, and wondered whence came the absurd notion that she had just issued a challenge. It was no such thing! He had got to keep his distance, for any number of reasons.

And so he told himself, over and over, as they shared a dinner of sauteed pheasant, rump of veal and minted green peas, and made sure, by mutual unspoken consent, not to let so much as their pinky fingers brush against each other.

Chapter 4

Diana tossed and turned in her bed, watching the snow fall relentlessly outside her window. She prayed it would stop in the night; she was playing with fire here at Rossmore with the duke. She did not know how much longer she could endure this.

He said outrageous things to her, chided her and ordered her about as if he had the right to do so, believed the worst of her. She ought to be repelled by him. And yet, when his eyes held hers, she could not look away. When he stood close, her own limbs lost their ability to move. And when he touched her— dear God! Tonight she had not even pulled away, had, in fact, touched him first!

Whatever was happening to her? She fell at last into a restless sleep, and awoke, miraculously, to a blaze of sunlight. One look out the window told her that the snowdrifts were taller in places than she was, but still, she took heart. If the storm was over, then the roads should be passable on the morrow. Perhaps she might even return home this afternoon. Of course, she would have to be certain Georgie was all right. . . .

She rose and went to the washstand, but then turned as a flash of color caught her eyes. There, on the bench at the foot of her bed, lay a dress of deep magenta. She went to the bench and saw that it was a lovely morning gown of jaconet muslin, with a full skirt, long loose sleeves and a tight, nipped-in bodice. She lifted it up and discovered, hidden beneath it, a beautiful, filmy, lacey chemise.

54

How lovely of someone to realize how much she would welcome a change of clothes! she thought. And then she felt herself flush with the knowledge of just who that "someone" must be. The garments must belong to Georgie, but she was in no condition to have thought to send them here. A maidservant must have brought them, but only one person could have given the order to do so. Oh, dear! Had the duke explicitly instructed that undergarments as well as the dress be brought? Had he seen the chemise? Surely not, she thought, and then mentally shook herself.

It was not like her to be so missish! What difference did it make *what* Marchmaine had seen? Rake that he was, it was undoutedly not the first lacey chemise he had seen. As for her, she'd been wearing her own clothes for two days. The thought of new ones was a temptation she could not resist.

She was in the midst of dressing when a maid, the same one as yesterday, came to help her. "Aye, and 'tis a near perfect fit," the girl bubbled, "just like I told His Grace 'twould be. Course, you fill it out a bit more, and the mistress be a might taller, but othergates you and her ladyship be of a size." She proceeded to stitch up the hem rapidly, despite Diana's protestations that the delicate fabric might be ruined.

"Makes no never mind," the garrulous servant went on, "for her ladyship's maid said as how the mistress don't care none for this color. But on you 'tis near perfect, I'd say, miss."

Diana thought the gown a bit tight across the bodice, but not unflatteringly so. And she assured herself, as she glanced in the looking glass, that it mattered not a whit that the vibrant magenta brought out the deep blue of her eyes and creaminess of her skin. Papa thought she looked good in everything, and there was no one else whose opinion signified in the least!

She made her way to Georgie's room as soon as the maid had pinned up her hair. Georgie still showed no signs of fever, and the bleeding had lessened a bit. But her lethargy had not. She repeated her request that a wet nurse be found, and no amount of gentle remonstration made the slightest difference.

Diana knew well that ladies of quality often hired wet nurses, simply to allow themselves more freedom. But Georgie was here in the country, not in London in the midst of the social whirl. To Diana's knowledge, she had never expressed to

Papa her desire for a wet nurse. Diana was persuaded it was her extreme distress that had prompted the request. Still, once the roads were passable, Diana knew she would have to comply with Georgie's wishes. For these first hours of his life, the babe had been able to draw enough nourishment from the small amount of suckling he did. But in a day or so it would not be enough.

Diana sincerely hoped, for Georgie's sake, that a wet nurse would not be necessary. That would enable Georgie to retreat further from her son, from life. Diana was very frightened of that, and had little notion of how to deal with it. Oh, Papa, she cried inwardly, hurry to Rossmore, please.

Marchmaine rose as she stepped over the threshold of the breakfast room. A footman closed the door behind her. She and the duke were alone.

It was the way he moved, she decided, even more than his long, lean proportions, that reminded her so much of a panther. He had come out of his chair, and now sauntered toward her, with the jungle cat's lithe grace, and with the same underlying, coiled tension. He was, like the panther, a predator. She would do well to remember that.

His tawny eyes, as always, were far too penetrating, and she let her gaze sweep his length as he stepped close to her. Today he wore a form-fitting coat of Devonshire brown and buff doeskin pantaloons that hugged his thighs. She felt the oddest constriction in her throat and jerked her eyes upward.

And that was when she realized that he was subjecting her to a very thorough scrutiny of his own. His eyes collided with hers, and what she saw there caused her breath to catch in her throat. She was not a child; she had seen that look on a man's face before and had known what it meant. Known and run as far away as possible. For she did not want to see desire in a man's eyes. Not for her.

And yet this time she could not run, could not even move.

Adam could barely breathe, and cursed himself again for behaving like a moonstruck halfling. If he'd known she'd look this way in that damned dress, he'd never have suggested Georgie's maid find Miss Rustin a dress at first stop. Not wishing to disturb her sleeping mistress, the maid had suggested this dress, as Georgie did not care for it. Adam

56

recalled seeing her in it once; it had not been at all flattering. Adam supposed he'd thought it would be equally unflattering on Miss Rustin. Which would have been all to the good.

Unfortunately, he could not have been more wrong. The deep magenta color had overwhelmed Georgie's delicate blond prettiness. But it only enhanced the luster of Miss Rustin's deep blue eyes and dark hair, the pearly luminescence of her white skin. And while the dress fell in graceful folds on Georgie's wispy frame, on Miss Rustin it clung. Almost indecently. Why, it delineated every lush curve, and with its oh-so-thin fabric, the blasted dress was practically an open invitation!

But she was issuing no invitations. At the least, not to him. He still did not know of a certain if she'd issued one to Edward. Damnation! Until he did know, he had got to remember that she might well be the lady she claimed to be. He could not, as he longed to do, stroke the smooth whiteness of her cheeks, the soft roundness of her breasts. . . . He swallowed hard and forced his eyes above her neck. And then, for the first time, he noticed the dark smudges under her eyes.

Unwittingly, his right hand came up, and his fingers brushed the delicate skin beneath her large round eyes. "You did not sleep well," he said, breaking the silence between them.

He knew, by the slight gasp she gave, by the look in her eyes, that she'd felt the same warmth he did the moment his skin touched hers. It was the same every time. He did not understand it. He did not like it.

He did not remove his hand.

"No," she rasped. "Indeed, I did not. I—I was concerned about Georgie, you must know."

His eyes held hers. Yes, he thought, she *was* concerned for his sister, regardless of what had happened with Edward. He had to believe that, else she was a superb actress. But was that *all* that had kept her awake? He was concerned for Georgie, too, but that was not all that had kept *him* awake. It was thoughts of what the sight of Diana, the feel of her, did to him.

"You did not sleep well, either, your—Marchmaine," she said in her husky voice.

His thumb moved ever so gently to caress her cheek. "I, too, was perturbed about Georgie."

Now it was her turn to swallow hard. He doubted she was thinking of Georgie at this moment, any more than he was. Her skin was so soft, her deep blue eyes wary, as always when he came too close. But she did not move, did not protest. He did not even think she was breathing, and of a certain not regularly. But then, neither was he. His eyes moved to her mouth, to her full lips, slightly parted.

Don't do it, Marchmaine, he told himself, even as he began to lower his head.

"We'll find out soon—what the devil!" came a booming voice just as the door burst open.

Adam jerked his head upright and lowered his hand. Miss Rustin's eyes went wide with shock, and she stumbled as they both whirled round to face the door. Without thinking, he put a hand to her waist to steady her.

"Diana?" boomed that voice again, this time in question. It came from a middle-aged man whose black hair was only lightly sprinkled with gray.

"Adam! What the deuce has been going on here?" Edward demanded, looking shocked, even outraged. Suddenly Adam felt his own surge of anger.

"I might ask you the same, Edward," he said tautly. Edward's flush told him his brother-in-law knew very well what he was talking about.

"Papa? Edward?" Miss Rustin rasped, her color high. Adam still did not lower his arm from her waist; she was none too steady on her feet. "How—however did you get here? The snow—"

"I found Edward at the Horsefeathers Inn. He was prepared to wait another day until the roads were passable, not knowing there was any urgency," Dr. Rustin explained. "Instead we commandeered two horses and—"

"How is Georgie?" Edward interrupted. So, Adam thought, he'd finally gotten round to asking about his wife. True, the two men had only burst through the door moments ago, but it seemed much longer than that. And Edward had been glaring at Adam and Miss Rustin the whole while. That and his delay in asking about Georgie answered Adam's own burning question all too well. He felt a sick pain in the pit of his stomach.

58

"You have a son, Edward," Diana said, smiling for the first time.

Edward did not smile. "Georgie?" he queried.

"Sleeping," Diana replied, and Edward's handsome face relaxed into a smile. Dr. Rustin, too, relaxed his rigid stance, a little.

"When was he born?" Edward's eyes were on Diana.

"Monday night—er—Tuesday morn, actually," she said.

"And you've been here all that time, Diana?" Rustin asked quietly, his eyes, the same dark blue as his daughter's, darting from her to Adam and back. It was then that Adam realized that his arm was still about her waist. He abruptly lowered it.

"Yes, Papa. There was no way I could leave in the storm." She squared her shoulders. "And besides," she went on, "Georgie needed me."

"What do you mean?" Edward started forward. "Is something wrong?"

"I'm persuaded she will be fine, now you are here." Miss Rustin took a step closer to Edward.

"Now I'm—why? What is wrong?" he demanded, then shifted his gaze. "Adam, what is wrong with Georgie?"

"She is in a weakened state, Edward," Adam replied, "but there is no reason for her not to recover." Edward frowned. "It really is a rather long story, and I think we'd all best be seated."

It was then that Edward remembered his manners and introduced Adam and Dr. Rustin. Adam advanced toward the doctor, but as they shook hands they eyed each other warily. Adam had the distinct impression that Rustin was silently telling him they had unfinished business. And he knew exactly what, or more precisely, whom, that business was about.

Edward unwittingly obliged the good doctor, for when Adam ushered everyone to the table, suggesting they fill their plates before any further discourse, Edward demurred. He excused himself, saying he wanted to see his wife and child and would return shortly for a full account.

As soon as the door had closed behind him, Rustin turned to his daughter. They were all standing next to the table. "I shall go up to see the baroness myself in a few minutes, and I'll wait until Edward returns for a report on the delivery. But first—" he paused and looked pointedly from Adam to his daughter and back. The fine lines at the corners of his blue eyes bespoke a man who smiled readily. He was not smiling now. "First, are you all right, Diana?"

They were not the words Adam had been expecting. An admonishment about proprieties, a demand to know what had been going on, but not this. What did he think—that Adam had ravished his daughter?

"Yes, Papa, I am fine." Her voice was whisper soft, but her gaze was steady, her hands clasped loosely at her waist.

Rustin frowned and stared piercingly at her. She lifted her chin a notch. Damn the man, was he trying to intimidate her? "Dr. Rustin," Adam interjected sharply, "I can assure you that nothing untoward occurred be—"

"I know that, Marchmaine." Rustin's gaze shifted to him for just a moment. "For I know my daughter. But that is not what I was asking."

Adam blinked as understanding dawned. Rustin trusted, and understood, his daughter. Uppermost in his mind was not concern for her reputation, but for her emotional state. He had walked in on a scene that might have been mistaken for the sort of closeness that Miss Rustin obviously avoided. The doctor meant to protect his daughter from hurt. Adam knew he would do well to remember that.

He did wonder, however, how much Rustin knew of the business with Edward. And just what *was* the business with Edward? Adam still was not certain.

Rustin was still piercing his daughter with his eyes. "Papa, truly, I am right," she reiterated. Rustin relaxed slightly, at the least enough to fill a plate from the sideboard and take his place at table.

They had all three just begun to eat their kippers and eggs Benedict when Edward returned. He took only a piece of dry toast and a cup of coffee before seating himself at the head of the table.

"She looks so pale, even in sleep. And the babe is fretful. What happened, Diana?"

Adam listened as Miss Rustin recounted the story of the difficult delivery to Edward and her father. All the while, he tried to discern whatever undercurrents there were between her and Edward, but failed utterly. Whatever was between

60

them was not being allowed to come to the fore now. Miss Rustin's voice was strong and steady, and though Edward himself grew pale in the telling, the doctor kept nodding in approval of what she had done.

She paused and took a sip of her coffee, but when she resumed her narrative, her voice was noticeably less steady. She had come to the part about the child's position before birth.

"Oh, my God," Edward blurted, paler than ever.

"It was breech, Papa, and I knew I had got to do something."

"What—what did you do?" Edward rasped.

"I—I turned him," she said simply.

Edward looked like he might very well swoon, but Rustin smiled faintly, as if his faith in his daughter had been justified.

"Was she in . . . a great deal of pain?" Edward's voice was shaky.

Miss Rustin nodded reluctantly. "It was not easy for her, Edward, and she lost a good deal of—ah—blood. But still, she had ought to be feeling a bit stronger now."

"What is wrong, Diana?" Rustin asked, setting down his fork.

Miss Rustin sighed. Her eyes met Adam's for a brief moment before she hastily looked away. He found himself wishing he could help her.

"She is still very weak, and more than that, quite lethargic. She—ah—does not wish to suckle the babe, and in truth has taken little interest in him."

"But she always said she did not want a wet nurse," Edward interjected, a deep frown marring his wide brow. "That is, until the Season. I did promise to convey her to Town this year."

"I had thought as much, Edward," Diana said quietly, "and despite her weakness I am persuaded she could suckle him if . . . if she wished. I have tried to encourage her, but . . ."

Her voice trailed off and she looked down, clearly uncomfortable. And with good reason, Adam thought cynically. Just how would she answer the questions certain to come now? Edward, however, surprised him by remaining silent. Perhaps he suspected the cause of Georgie's present state and did not really wish to discuss it. But he would have to, dammit!

61

It was Rustin, seated next to his daughter, who finally broke the silence. "Diana, what are you not telling us?" he asked gently, his blue eyes narrowed in concern.

Miss Rustin raised her eyes; her gaze met Adam's. He caught his breath at what he saw in those blue depths. She looked so vulnerable, so discomfited at what she had to say. Damnation! Could they not see what they were pushing her to? But he could not say aught. To do so would be to reveal his own knowledge and the intimacy of their conversations that might only make matters worse for her. He contented himself instead with a faint smile and a warm look of encouragement in his eyes. She nodded almost imperceptibly, and he knew she'd understood.

Only then did she shift her gaze to Edward. When she finally spoke her voice was a mere whisper. "After the birth she asked me to—that is, she did not think she would . . . live. And—and when I assured her that indeed she would, she did not seem to—to want to. She asked me to take care of her son and—" She paused and took another sip of her coffee, despite the fact, as Adam noted before, that her cup was nearly empty. He sat back and wondered at his own concern for her. It was her own damned fault she was in this ticklish predicament at first stop, was it not?

"She asked me—" her voice was barely audible now—"over and over to . . . take care of her son and—and you, Edward. She seems to think—that is—I cannot convince her that there is naught—ah. . . ." Adam watched her color rise, as did Edward's. If Edward had not fully comprehended before, he did now. He was fairly squirming in his chair. As well he might!

Edward glanced around uneasily. "Diana, are you saying that Georgie knows—er—"

"Papa, Marchmaine," Miss Rustin interrupted, "I—ah—do think it would be best if Edward and I discussed this in private."

"No!" exclaimed a chorus of three male voices simultaneously. Adam recognized his own as one of them. He'd be damned if he'd allow her to be private with Edward again.

Perhaps her father knew what had happened and was of like mind. But what of Edward? Did he not trust himself alone with her? The notion infuriated Adam.

"Your papa has a right to hear this," Edward said quietly. His face, usually so affable with soft lines, handsome blond brow and clear hazel eyes, was a picture of misery. Over Diana or Georgie? Adam wondered, and then Edward turned to him. "But perhaps, Adam, as this does not—er—concern *you*, you would be good enough to—"

"Like hell I will!" Adam growled, throwing back his chair and lurching upright. He began to pace the floor in front of the sideboard. "That's my baby sister lying up there, wanting to die because her husband no longer has a care for her, because the servants saw you with Miss Rustin, told her of the liaison—"

"What liaison, dammit?" Edward exploded, bolting from his chair as well. "There *is* no liaison! If the servants saw anything it was one—er—innocent embrace. Which was entirely my fault. I'll not have you besmirching Diana's good name by inferring otherwise, Adam. And I might ask you, once again, what has been going on in this house between *you* and—"

"There is *nothing* going on, Edward!" Adam snapped. "Not even an oh-so-innocent kiss," he added mockingly.

"The cozy scene we interrupted upon entering this very room looked anything but innocent," Edward retorted hotly, grasping the back of his chair tightly.

"As, I am certain, did the scene at the Rustin's door look to the servant who witnessed it," Adam drawled.

Edward looked dagger points at him. Was his anger on Georgie's behalf or Miss Rustin's? Blast it all! He still did not know. *Could* that kiss have been exactly what Miss Rustin had said?

"Gentlemen," Rustin interjected, his eyes, amazingly, crinkling in what might have been amusement. What the devil did he find to be amused about in all this? "You put me in mind of two dogs gnawing at the same bone. Might I remind you that the—ah—bone is not at issue. It is Lady Rossmore who is. Diana, what do you suggest is to be done now?"

"It is up to Edward, Papa." She looked up at Edward. "You must convince her of your devotion. No one else can do that. And I—I think you must explain why—why you left. But she must come to understand that you mean to stay and—and work out your differences once she is well. You—you do mean

63

to do so, do you not?" she concluded softly.

"You know I do. As do you, Rusty. 'Tis only Adam here who needs to have his mind removed from the Haymarket," Edward chafed.

Adam clenched his fists, advancing on Edward. "Now see here—"

"Gentlemen, please!" Rustin rose and went to stand between the two men. Adam subsided, and Rustin turned to his daughter. "Diana, do you go up to the baroness. I shall follow in but a moment."

"But—"

"Go," he said softly.

She nodded, and without a word, but with one last uncertain glance at Adam, rose and left the breakfast parlor.

Adam stared after her. "Is she always so obedient?" he murmured, before he'd thought better of it.

Rustin's lips twitched. "Hardly. You do not know my daughter very well, do you? If you did, you would—"

"How did you know about what happened between— between Diana and me?" Edward blurted, his entire body stiffly erect. "Did Georgie tell you?"

Adam sighed, poured himself more coffee and resumed his seat. "No. I overheard Georgie talking to her, and then I questioned Miss Rustin."

The doctor took his seat across from Adam once more and fixed him with a disconcerting blue gaze. "You forced her to tell you about that night, and then you did not believe her."

"Oh, hell," Adam muttered, and downed half the contents of his coffee cup. "I was angry. At Edward, Georgie, her."

"It is as I said. You do not know my daughter very well," Rustin put in quietly. He broke off a piece of blueberry muffin and put it in his mouth.

Adam shook his head. "I know her well enough to have realized that it—it did not make sense. But I—I suppose I was not thinking clearly. I was livid at the mere thought of Edward touching—that is—" He paused, wondering what the hell he'd been about to say. Rustin must have been wondering the same thing, for he was regarding him with those bemused eyes again; but there was something more in his gaze. It was as if he were hearing something beyond Adam's words, something Adam

64

had not meant to say. Adam was suddenly very uncomfortable. "Well, Georgie *is* my sister, after all."

"Just so," Rustin concurred, chewing the rest of his muffin.

"Oh, hell," Adam muttered again. So, Miss Rustin had been telling the truth. There *was* naught between her and Edward. He felt a sense of relief wash over him, followed almost immediately by a distinct sense of frustration. She was not Edward's, nor was she Adam's for the asking. She was a virtuous woman, blast it all! He glanced up at Edward. He, too, wore a bemused expression. "Why don't you sit down and finish your breakfast, Edward?" he snapped ungraciously.

Edward complied, his lips curling as he seated himself and reached for the marmalade. "I take it that last gracious remark was in the nature of an apology, which *I* will graciously accept," Edward said genially, liberally coating his now cold toast. Adam made a mental note that he owed Miss Rustin an apology, but as for Edward—

"You *did* kiss her, Edward," he pointed out.

"Yes," Edward countered soberly, "and as penance for that I have missed the birth of my child."

"I'm sorry." Adam reached out and put his hand to Edward's shoulder.

Edward nodded, and as Adam removed his hand a gleam lit the other man's eye. Edward took a bite of the toast. "We still have the matter of your time here alone with Diana to deal with, Adam."

Adam sighed, and shifted his gaze to Rustin. "You have my word that nothing untoward occurred, and well—as you have said, you know your daughter. But if you feel she has been compromised, I will offer for her, Rustin."

The doctor smiled while Adam held his breath. He'd had no intention of marrying, ever. True, Miss Rustin might be the antithesis of his mother, and he might want her, rather much, but he had no wish to wed her. Was he about to lose the freedom to follow his own path?

"I appreciate that, Marchmaine. But if you know my daughter at all, you know she would never hear of it. And, much as it is my fondest wish to see her happily settled someday, yet I do not think this is the way."

Adam waited for the sense of relief to overtake him, but it

was curiously absent. He felt instead a pang of some emotion, almost akin to disappointment. But that, of course, was ridiculous!

"Very well," he heard himself say, "but if for some reason you should change your mind, Rustin . . ."

"Thank you. Edward, you can contrive to see that your servants keep mum about the past days, can you not?"

"Of course. I will have a word with Stebbins this morning. No one else will be traveling today at all events, I daresay."

Rustin nodded, took a sip of coffee, and rose. "Well, then, I shall go and see the new mother now. You can follow in a short while, Edward. You must start to mend your fences straightaway."

"I know, Rusty," Edward replied gravely. The two men shook hands and the doctor turned to Adam.

He extended his hand. "Marchmaine. I am honored to meet you."

"No," Adam demurred, taking the outstretched hand, "the honor is truly mine, Rustin."

"Call me Rusty, why don't you? Nearly everyone does."

"Very well, Rusty. And I am Adam. Too few people call me that."

Rusty grinned and then exited the room, his medium-sized frame erect, his step that of a much younger man.

Adam smiled in his wake and turned to Edward. "Quite a man, isn't he?"

"Yes. And his daughter is quite a woman. Adam, I—I do not want to see her hurt. I know you have no disposition to marry. You must keep your distance, old chap."

Adam frowned. "I have no intention of hurting her. And you are, indeed, one to talk. *You* could have hurt her all those weeks ago—"

"No, for we were merely friends. Nothing more. I made a mistake, which she understood. And if she explained it to you—Hellfire, Adam! Must we go through this again?"

"No. No, I know what you are saying."

"I cannot hurt her, Adam, but *you* can. I saw—"

"For pitysakes, Edward! I have told you there is naught—"

"Adam. I am not blind and I am not stupid. She was hurt once, a long time ago and—"

"What do you know of that?" Adam demanded tautly.

Edward shrugged. "Almost nothing. Of a certain she's never spoken of it. Rusty mentioned it once in passing. But it explains why a woman who looks like that, a woman of her sweet nature, has reached the age of six and twenty yet unwed. All I'm saying is that Rusty and Diana mean a great deal to me. They are good friends. Have a care, Adam."

Adam regarded his brother-in-law with a frown. He had ought to say, "Of course, I understand. I will keep away from her." But he couldn't. The devil of it was that he *did* understand, but he could not promise to stay away from her. "I mean her no harm, Edward," he said at length.

Edward stared at him for a long moment and then reluctantly nodded. Adam shifted the subject; fair was fair, after all. "What are you going to do about Georgie?"

Edward ran his hand through is blond locks. "Devil if I know. Adam, you've got to understand. I love her. I've always loved her. But she—she makes it very difficult."

"I do know, for I . . . know my mother."

"Ah," Edward said bleakly, "then you *do* understand."

"Yes, and if I might suggest . . ." Edward lifted a brow in question. "Have you ever heard Miss Rustin speak of her mother and grandmother?" Edward shook his head. "Ask her about them. And then, well, perhaps she can talk to Georgie. Once you convince your wife of your own—er—"

"I take your point, Adam. By the by, when is my esteemed mother-in-law due to arrive?"

"Any day now, I'm persuaded." Adam grimaced as he spoke. "The roads had ought to be passable by the morrow, and I make no doubt she is already on her way."

"Charming," Edward said sarcastically, and then the two men grinned in perfect amity. Edward rose, saying he would go up to Georgie, and added as he stood in the doorway, "Then again, perhaps it will snow again tonight."

Yes, Adam thought, picking up his toast, once he was alone. If it snowed again, his mother would not be able to reach Rossmore Manor. Nor would Miss Rustin be able to leave. What? He dropped his fork. Where had that thought come from?

But he knew. If it did not snow, she and her father would

leave Rossmore on the morrow. And Adam would have no reason to see her again. He had no intention of marrying her, or anyone. He could hardly pretend to be courting her. He could go to see Rusty and she might be there, but that would hardly be the same. He wanted to be private with her. To talk to her. To touch her. To . . . kiss her. Only to kiss her. Surely one kiss would not hurt her. She was not, despite whatever fears she might have, repelled by him. Of that he was certain. But after today she would be gone. There was only today, and he suspected that Rusty would be watching her, and Edward would be watching *him*.

Hellfire and damnation! He picked up his fork once more and stabbed at his cold eggs with a vengeance.

Chapter 5

The idea came to Adam as he strolled to the library. He meant to work on the plans he was drawing up for Edward for the renovation of the east wing of Rossmore. He always worked in the library, Edward preferring the smaller, more private study as his personal sanctum. Adam had not looked at the plans since Georgie was brought to bed. But now, he thought, was a good time. He was always happiest when working, and it would take his mind off Miss Rustin, Georgie, his mother. . . .

At all events, there was little else to do just now. According to Mrs. Stebbins, Edward was still with Georgie, as was Rusty. Miss Rustin, it seemed, had retired to her room.

Miss Rustin. He paused just outside the library door as the idea took hold in his mind. He *did* need to apologize to her, after all. Surely neither her father nor Edward would cavil at that. He crossed the threshold and strode to the huge mahogany desk neatly ensconced in the bay window of the library. He would not wait for her to wander belowstairs of her own accord. She might not do so until luncheon, and then, of course, there would be Edward and Rusty. And the day would pass all too quickly.

He only had today, and he simply had got to be private with her, to speak with her, one more time. He scribbled a note and summoned a footman. Once the man departed, he turned his attention to the new stairwell he was designing, but his ear listened all the while for a certain feminine footfall just outside the door.

In the event, it was not a footfall he heard, but a soft knock.

She did not wait for his answer but opened the doors, slipped inside, and closed them again. She stood with her back to the doors, hands at her waist. He rose and went toward her. She was so beautiful; had he ever thought her anything but? Her skin was soft, white, flawless, her hair dark and lustrous, her form rounded and womanly and perfect.

He saw a look of uneasiness in her eyes, however.

"You should not have summoned me, Your Grace," she said in her husky voice.

"Then, you should not have come," he responded silkily, coming to stand just a foot before her.

She flushed, a delightful shade of pink. "You are right. I— I'll go."

She started to turn back round, and he reached out and grabbed her hand.

"No, no. Come, my dear, I wish to speak with you. Come to the fire."

No! Diana told herself. Do not go to the fire! It was . . . it was too dangerous.

This morning had been bad enough, what with Edward accusing her with his eyes of untoward behavior with the duke, and the duke accusing her far less subtly of untoward behavior with Edward. And then Marchmaine confusing her utterly with his warm and encouraging looks as she went through her difficult narrative.

What could he want now? She had ought to leave. His hand was warm, oh-so-warm and large and enveloping as it held hers. His voice was deep and rich and compelling. He was so large, his broad shoulders encased in the Devonshire brown coat that set off his chestnut hair and tawny eyes perfectly.

He led her to the hearth. Why did she not pull her hand away? Why did she allow him to lead her? He stopped and turned her to face him. His hands moved to grasp her upper arms gently. Why, oh, dear God, why did she feel such heat beneath his touch? Surely it must just be the fire in the grate. . . .

"I owe you an apology, Miss Rustin," he began without preamble. Her eyes, widening with distress, met his.

"No, please, I—I had rather not discuss it."

"I'm afraid I must insist," he said gently. She did not want

70

his voice to be so gentle. "I know it was not easy for you this morning. And I did not help any with my . . . accusations. I know they were unfounded, my dear, and I am sorry for them."

His eyes were warm, intense as always, and she felt her own begin to prickle with moisture. *Now* he was sorry; now he recanted his accusations. Because of the others. He had not believed *her*. Why was she never worthy of a man's trust? Why was she so tainted? She turned away, lest she disgrace herself with tears, and pulled out of his grasp. She went to one of the tall south windows, wrapping her arms about herself and gazing down at the glistening white gardens below. "Th-thank you—" she paused and swallowed the lump in her throat— "for your apology. I—I did not enjoy this morning. I only hope that—"

"You are overset," he murmured into her ear, startling her utterly. She had not heard a sound as he crossed the room. A silent jungle cat, she thought, not for the first time.

"No, I—"

"Yes, you are." He turned her round and lifted her chin with his forefinger. She bit her lip. She *would* not cry. His eyes, the color of brandy, she decided, were far too penetrating. "You are overset because I did not believe you at first stop. That it was only after speaking with Edward and your father that I—"

"Please," she pleaded, feeling a betraying tear trickle from her eye and down her cheek. She tried to turn her head, but he would not allow it. He held her chin firmly with his right hand as the fingers of his left came up to brush away the tear. How could such large, powerful hands be so gentle?

"In truth, I suppose I did believe you, deep down," he said, the timbre of his voice soft and soothing and eminently masculine all at once, "but I did not want to."

"Why?" she rasped.

"I suppose I did not want you to be . . . innocent." He leaned closer. His fingers stroked her cheek.

"Why?" This time her voice was threadbare.

"It complicates things." He lowered his mouth. Dear God! Was he going to kiss her? She could not allow it; she could not move away.

71

"I—I do not understand," she breathed.

"And furthermore," he went on, quite as if she had not spoken, "I did not want to believe that Georgie had become what she had, nor that Edward had . . . turned to you in a moment of weakness." He brushed a lock of hair from her brow. His touch was feathery light, but her skin burned in its wake. It seemed to her that his mouth loomed closer and closer as he spoke. She must not stay! She knew she mustn't, yet she could not will her feet to move, nor her head to turn.

"'Twas far more comforting," he went on, "to believe Edward had been lured by a temptress."

"B—but I am not a temptress."

He chuckled softly, a low, intimate sound that came from deep in his throat. "Oh, yes you are, my dear. You may not have lured him—" his hand wrapped itself around her nape even as his deep, husky voice wrapped her in a seductive warmth—"but you are . . . most definitely . . . a temptress."

She opened her mouth to issue another denial, and that was when his lips took hers. Softly, gently, ever-so-lightly. She felt warmth and comfort and a most incongruous sense of security. And a tingling sensation, as if some current were passing between them. And then he deepened the kiss, pulling her closer, his lips becoming more demanding, his tongue seeking entrance into her mouth.

The tingling became a jolt, the warmth a searing heat. She stumbled and put her hands to his chest to steady herself. And to push him away, she told herself. But her hands clutched at his jacket as she parted her lips, and then her teeth. . . .

Dear God! he thought with what little rational sense was left to him. The heat of her, the softness—it was more than he'd ever imagined. She was opening for him, kissing him back. His body was on fire. He'd kept his hand at her nape, the other dangling at his side, afraid to frighten her. But now he could not help himself. . . .

The moment he wrapped his arm about her waist she pushed at him, jerking her mouth away. He let her go, keeping a grip on her elbow until she steadied herself. The movement of his hand had frightened her, broken the spell, as he'd intuitively known it would. He cursed himself for a fool, even as he realized it was just as well. What the devil had he been about at all events?

72

His breathing was labored as he fought to bring his heated body under control. She seemed to be fighting the same battle, her color high, her body trembling, but she would not meet his eyes. He reached for her, meaning only to offer a reassuring touch of his fingers on her cheek, but she whirled round and pressed her brow to the cool window. She wrapped her arms about herself, and he cursed again, silently.

He'd had no right to kiss her; she was a lady and he was sparking fires he could never extinguish. No! That was not precisely true. The fires had been sparked the moment he saw her, the moment his hand touched her in the most casual of gestures that first night. But he *had* fanned the fires, dammit! And had not been able to keep himself from doing so.

And she—her abject posture now told him she was regretting their embrace. He was certain her response was out of character for her. She was probably reflecting on that now, wondering what had come over her. He thought he knew, but the answer would not comfort her, nor could they do aught about it.

He stepped closer to the window and gently turned her to face him, then dropped his hand. She still would not meet his eyes. He did his level best to ignore the way that blasted dress of Georgie's hugged her breasts, clung to her hips. . . . He took a deep breath. Virtuous woman she might be, but he'd be damned if he'd tell her lies, or allow her to do so. "I know that propriety demands that I apologize," he said huskily, "but I find I cannot do so." At that she raised her eyes in surprise. The corners of his mouth lifted slightly. "For I am not sorry at all, you see." She blinked. "And if you would but admit it, neither are—"

"You overstepped your bounds, sir," she interrupted, the shakiness of her voice belying her raised little chin. "You had no—"

"Ah, but Miss Ru—Diana, you enjoyed it as much as I did," he murmured, his eyes twinkling.

Her eyes flashed. "You, sir, are no gentleman!"

"Did you not enjoy it, then? Am I so far off the mark?" He did his best to look chagrined.

She bit her soft pink lip, and he watched the play of emotions march across her face. He knew the exact moment she admitted the truth to herself and strove mightily not to let a flicker of satisfaction show on his own face.

She sighed deeply. "You are monstrous unfair, Marchmaine."

"Adam."

She sighed again. "Very well. Adam. You are most unfair. I cannot possibly answer such a question." She twisted her hands at her waist.

"And why, pray tell, is that?"

"Because if I answer 'yes,' I should be shockingly brazen. And if I answer 'no' . . . I . . . ah—" She looked away from him.

Adam put his fingers beneath her chin and turned her head back. "And if you answer 'no,' Diana?" he prompted softly.

"I—I should be a liar," she whispered.

He could not possibly keep a trace of satisfaction from his eyes now. It was all he could do to keep from lowering his lips again. He prudently lowered his hand instead.

"Do not look so—so—wretchedly pleased with yourself, Adam. 'Tis merely that you—you took me by surprise."

"Liar." He was grinning now. He really could not help himself. Her lips were pursed quite adorably in vexation.

"And—and besides, I—I've never been kissed like—like that before."

"I know that, Diana, and—"

"You—you know? You mean you could tell?" She colored, and her eyes widened in a chagrin he knew was not feigned. "Oh, dear. Did I do it so very badly, then?"

He coughed. "Er—no. You—you did it very well."

He could have sworn she breathed a sigh of relief. He held his hands rigidly at his sides, lest he give in to the temptation to grab her and show her just how well she did do it.

"Oh. I—thank you for that," she said ingenuously, her lovely lips curling enticingly.

Dear God, was this the same woman who just days ago had shrunk from his touch? But then he recalled that on their very first meeting he had noted that she could be very saucy, or very solemn. It was the saucy Miss Diana Rustin who stood before him now, and she was deuced hard to resist.

He took a step forward; she moved back, putting one hand

up as if to ward him off. "Now, Adam, you must know it *was* most improper of us to—to do that. You *do* understand that it must not happen again, do you not?" She sounded as if she were trying to convince herself as well as him.

He closed the space between them and lifted his hand to brush a wayward black curl from her cheek. "This from a woman who does not care a rush for proprieties?" he murmured.

This time when she stepped back, he watched her retreat even further, within herself. He'd seen her do it before. This was the solemn Diana, the vulnerable one. "It is, in truth, not a matter of proprieties, Adam. You must know that," she said with that quiet dignity which he somehow knew masked old hurts. And it occurred to him that while the saucy Diana filled him with the desire to kiss her senseless, this Diana made him want to enfold her in his arms and protect her from hurt. Jarred by his own thoughts, he was not certain which desire was the more dangerous.

"I—I may be without experience," she went on, "but I am not a child. What we . . . were doing—well—that sort of thing can only lead down one of two paths. Neither one is open to me. I—I hope you will forgive my . . . lapse in decorum."

Adam's eyes flickered. How could she blithely reduce what had passed between them to a "lapse in decorum"? But he kept silent as she continued.

"I will own that we have had a somewhat shaky start, but perhaps from now on we may be friends." With that, she extended her hand, clearly expecting him to shake it.

Good God! He'd never been "friends" with a woman in his life! Did she really think, after that exquisite "lapse in decorum," that he could begin now? But as he searched her velvety blue eyes, wide now with distress and a kind of pleading, he recalled her other words, that neither path was open to her. Nor could he take her down either path. For she was not the stuff of which mistresses were made. And he was not disposed to marry. Though why she would not marry elsewhere. . . . No, he did not wish to think of that.

He realized with a start that she was still standing with her hand extended. Friends, he thought incredulously. Did she not know that was impossible? But seeing no choice, he took the small, delicate hand in both of his.

"Friends," he whispered, even as his wayward eyes devoured her soft lips.

Friends, Diana thought, swallowing hard and trying to ignore the heat that coursed through her, from the hand that he held down to her very toes. Whatever had possessed her to say such a thing? She could be Edward's friend, Georgie's, but Adam's? No, she was not so naive as to think she could ever be Adam's friend. And he did not believe it either, if the warm look in his eyes signified at all. It would be best, she knew, if they never saw each other again, once she left Rossmore. She told herself she did not feel a wave of sadness at that thought.

Slowly, she pulled her hand from his, assuring herself she did not feel immediately chilled. "I—I suppose I had ought to go to Georgie now," she said for lack of anything better. She sidestepped him and moved toward the center of the book-lined room.

"Yes, I suppose," he echoed, and wondered at the doubt in his own voice. Surely she needs must leave; they had said all there was to say. And yet, instead of ushering her out, he heard himself add, "But—er—perhaps not just yet." He came toward her, and she quirked a brow in question. "That is, perhaps you had ought to give Edward and her a bit more time together. And then, well, I do think you can help them, if you are willing."

"I?" He was too close; Diana backed up, trying to appear nonchalant. Just hours ago he believed her to be the problem and now. . . . She backed into a leather sofa and skirted it, then glided toward the huge mahogany desk in the bay window.

He had stopped at the sofa, but the intensity in his eyes reached across all the space that separated them. "Yes, you, my dear," he said. "Tell each of them what you told me of your mother and grandmother. That, at the least, will be a start for them."

He watched her shrug nervously and back up along the side of the desk. He told himself he would not follow. He would merely engage her in conversation; it might, after all, be the last time they conversed alone together.

"If you truly think I ought to do so, then of course I shall," she replied. "But I—I know so little of marriage." She sounded

76

so sweet, so vulnerable, and he found himself moving again.

He *was* a silent cat, she thought; in a flash he stood before her. "I am persuaded you know a good deal more than the rest of us, Diana," he said softly.

She did not know what to say. His words confused her utterly, and his stance—dear God! He stood so close that his breath caressed her cheek. Quickly she darted back and glanced down, seeking some distraction. The desk was strewn with drawings and mathematical computations. It took a moment for their importance to register in her mind.

"Adam, these—these are architect's plans, are they not?"

"Yes, they are," he said tautly. Her eyes shot up in surprise at his sudden change of tone. His face was shuttered, his stance almost defensive. But that made no sense.

Most curious, she glided behind the desk and scanned its contents. The plans appeared rather complex, but most of the lines and numbers meant little to her. And then her eyes alighted on two penciled, watercolored sketches of a portion of Rossmore Manor. An interior and exterior view of the east wing. She recalled Edward saying it was in sad need of renovation. She also recalled the gossip that the Duke of Marchmaine dabbled in architecture.

She looked up at him again. He had not moved. "These are your plans, are they not?" she asked quietly.

"Yes." If possible, he grew more taut. She did not understand it. She supposed she had ought to leave, but that would mean brushing past him in the narrow space between the wide desk and the window bay.

Instead she looked down again at the drawings. "The gossips are wrong," she murmured.

"I beg your pardon?" His voice was curt.

She met his gaze. "I'd heard that you dabble in architecture. And while I know little of the art, yet I have seen plans before." She cocked her head. "You are not a dabbler, are you, Adam?" she asked softly.

Was it her imagination, or did he relax his stance just a bit? "No."

"You are, in fact, very serious about this, are you not?"

Again, he relaxed slightly. "Yes."

"And you are very good." This was a statement, not a

77

question, and it nudged a half smile from him. He leaned against the side of the desk.

"Now, how would you know that, Diana Rustin?"

She smiled in return. "I do not lay claim to any specialized knowledge, you must know. But I do remember seeing the plans of Arden Chase when Sir Horace and Lady Hartcup were engaged upon the renovation of their kitchens. Have you met Lady Hart?"

"I don't believe I have."

"Well, you'd remember well if you had. She is quite an original." She grinned. "At all events, 'twas some three years ago, and I recall her wringing her hands over the architect's inability to contrive a space for a second backstairs leading from the kitchens to the formal dining room. She ended up, at Sir Horace's suggestion, designing it herself. And then the architect wrung *his* hands."

Adam stepped closer, a corresponding grin splitting his aquiline features. Dear Lord, but he was handsome, she thought, and forced herself back to the matter at hand.

She lowered her gaze and pointed to the two watercolored sketches. "These put me in mind of Lady Hart and her backstairs. Edward once said that it would be a devil of a task to contrive a safe staircase to fit the narrow space available in the east wing. Everyone knows the current one is much too steep, and rickety besides. But you seem to have solved the problem quite handily. Unless—unless I am reading this incorrectly?"

"No. You are correct," he replied, coming to join her behind the desk. "I did not wish to destroy the original look of the house any more than necessary, and I disliked Georgie's idea of demolishing several guest chambers to create a grand, sweeping stair."

"And so you have repeated molding and balustrade patterns found in the rest of the house, and, if I do not mistake the matter, you've removed that second-floor balcony."

"Yes." He leaned forward, rummaging for a particular sheet of intricate line drawings. "You see, even though the space is narrow, 'tis not unworkable. 'Tis only that visually it appears so small. I hope to create a sensation of spaciousness by the removal of the balcony and the installation of a barrel-vaulted ceiling."

"Which repeats the ceiling design in the entry lobby of the main wing," she put in.

He smiled, a relaxed, engaging smile that seemed quite unlike him. And then, at her prompting, he went on to explain the other renovations he planned for the east wing. She listened, but did not trouble to try to comprehend every word of his rather technical explanations. Rather she watched him—the excited gleam in his eyes, the animation on his face. She suspected this was a side of the Duke of Marchmaine that few saw, and she felt quite honored. She also suspected that his happiest hours were spent poring over his drawings and executing new ones.

When he finished speaking she said the first thing that came to mind. "The renovations will be wonderful, Adam. Did I know more about architecture, I should be in a position to say they will be brilliant. But surely it will not take all that long. What will you do next?"

She saw a flash of pleasure in his eyes. It was followed by a quickly masked flicker of pain.

"I shall continue my plans for my own seat, Damerest Hall," he replied, his eyes on the desk as he arranged the drawings in neat little piles. " 'Tis a rambling Elizabethan mansion much in need of work. 'Tis in Marchmaine, in the Plain of York, you must know."

She heard the pleasure in his voice as he spoke of his principal seat. But she did not wish to be distracted from the topic at hand. "The Plain of York is meant to be very beautiful. As I am persuaded is Damerest Hall. But when that is finished, what will you do?" she asked quietly.

She could sense him stiffen beside her. He still did not meet her eyes. "There will always be some friend whose seat is in need of renovation," he said with a faint edge of bitterness.

Diana frowned, perplexed. "But surely that will not—"

"Earlier, you called architecture an art," he interrupted, gesturing toward the drawings and then finally meeting her gaze. "Most people would call it a science, a mathematical science."

She shrugged. "And to some it is. Certainly to Lady Hart's architect it was. He was most at home with his numbers and straight lines. But you—forgive me if I am presumptuous—

79

but it seems to me that for you it is an art. You conceive a picture in your head, and then draw it. Making it fit into mathematical computations comes last. Am I so far off the mark?"

He smiled again, a warmth lighting his tawny eyes as he gazed down at her. "You—you have hit the mark exactly, Diana," he breathed, a note of wonder in his voice.

Without thinking she put a hand to his forearm as it rested against the desk. She felt the heat of him through the sleeve of his brown coat. Dimly she realized she had ought to remove her hand, but she did not. "You are a visionary, Adam. That is why I think you need to be designing buildings of your own, not merely renovating other people's designs." She saw the pain flicker in his eyes again and felt immediately contrite. "I'm sorry. I have been presumptuous again and I—"

"No!" He reached out with his thumb and forefinger to stroke her cheek. His touch sent little points of heat radiating throughout her body. She had all she could do to keep from clasping his hand, to hold it more firmly against her face. And then she wondered whatever was wrong with her.

"You could never be presumptuous, Diana. 'Tis only that I have other responsibilities, you see." She heard the sadness in his voice and ached for him. "Life is never so simple as we wish it, my dear, is it?" His eyes held hers, piercing them deeply.

"No," she echoed softly, somehow knowing that they were speaking of much more than architect's plans, "life is never so simple."

"Adam are you—oh!" exclaimed Diana's father. Adam cursed inwardly as he lowered his hand from her cheek. Hadn't they played this scene before? Rusty advanced farther into the room. "I knocked, but—er—apparently you didn't hear me." Adam expected a fierce scowl to accompany the words, but Rusty's blue eyes looked pensive, even a bit bemused as they went from Adam to Diana, then down to the desk, where Diana's hand still rested on his forearm.

"No, P-Papa, we—ah—did not hear you," Diana uttered, belatedly taking her hand from his arm. Adam knew an insane urge to grab it and put it back. "We were discussing the—the—"

"The plans I've drawn for the renovations here at Rossmore," he finished for her.

"I see." Rusty's words hung in the air, as if he did not see anything at all. But it seemed he was not angry about the little tête-à-tête he'd just interrupted. If anything, he appeared confused, his eyes searching his daughter's face, silently questioning.

"How—how is Georgie, Papa?" she asked.

Rusty smiled faintly. "She'll do, if she gets over these fool notions of hers. You did well, Diana. Very well."

"Thank you. I—I suppose I had ought to look in on her," Diana replied, her gaze darting from Adam to her father.

"Yes, why don't you, Diana," Rusty said, before Adam could open his mouth.

With a rather strained smile for both men, Diana silently left the room. For once in his life, Adam found himself tongue-tied. What could he possibly say to this man to justify having been private with his daughter again? To justify the fact that his hand had been caressing her soft, smooth face—again?

He swallowed and found his voice. "Rusty, I—"

"I came to find a book, don't you know," Rusty interrupted. "Hope you don't mind."

"Of course not. Rusty, 'tis not—that is, nothing—I mean to say—" Adam sighed, appalled at his unprecedented inability to string three words together. "We *were* discussing these plans, you must know."

Rusty's gaze met his, and Adam was shocked to find the blue eyes twinkling. "I do not doubt that for a minute, Adam," he said. "And quite an intriguing discussion it must have been. For I did knock rather loudly, you must know."

Oh, Lord, Adam thought. Whatever was the man thinking?

Chapter 6

Diana was just rounding the corner to the great stairwell when Edward came upon her.

"Diana!" he said with genuine pleasure. "I was just now coming to look for you."

"I was about to go up to Georgie," she responded. "How do you find her?"

Edward sighed. "Very . . . weak. She—she is asking for you, but I thought to have word with you first. In the morning room, perhaps?"

Diana nodded and allowed Edward to lead her down the wide corridor to the sunny blue and yellow morning room. He sat her down on the yellow chintz sofa and took the adjacent wing chair.

"At first stop, I want to thank you, Diana," he began, "for everything. For my son, for Georgie's life."

"No, please—"

"Hush, my dear," Edward smiled faintly. "You must let me have my say. And since the child's birth, I know you have done everything you could for them. But more than thanking you, Diana, I must—" he paused and took a breath. Diana knew what was coming and wished she could forestall him, but she could not. Knowing Edward, he would not rest easy until he'd said his piece. "I must apologize for what happened on that last night before I left. And for any subsequent . . . awkwardness you may have endured because of it."

"Oh, Edward." She leaned forward and spoke earnestly. "'Tis not necessary to thank me. I was but doing what needed

82

to be done. I am only sorry that Georgie had such a difficult time of it, and that you were not here. As for that last night, I understood all along what it signified, and you needn't feel aught of remorse on my account. It is with Georgie that you must make your peace, Edward."

He sighed deeply and ran a hand through his blond hair. "I know, Diana. I know full well." He rose and went to the chimney piece, leaning against it as if he had not the strength to support his own weight. She swivelled to face him. "But 'tis easier said than done," he went on.

She did not speak, merely looked at him expectantly. After a moment he took a deep breath and continued. "She is so weak that I feared to tire her by speaking overmuch. But I believe—I hope—that I persuaded her that I have not—er—formed an attachment elsewhere." He looked down into the fire blazing in the grate, avoiding Diana's gaze. "She is very grateful to you, Diana, and bears you no ill will."

"I am glad. Perhaps—if you would like—she and I might become friends."

At that he raised his eyes and smiled faintly. "Yes, I should like it above all things. Adam—Adam seemed to think you—you might help us. Though why you should wish to, when neither of us deserve it, is quite beyond me. But he said I needs must ask you about your mother and grandmother. I do not know what he meant by that. I only know that—" He paused and sighed again, and pushed himself away from the mantel. He went to one of the draped windows, and stood erect, hands clasped behind his back as he stared out at the white gardens.

"I only know," he went on, "that while she may understand that—that there is naught untoward between you and me, she has no notion of why I—I went to you that night, or any other. 'Twas something she refused to listen to months ago, and now I fear to overset her in her weakened state."

"You are probably in the right of it, Edward," Diana said softly. "Today is not the day to speak of such things. But I am persuaded she will gain her strength back rapidly, now you are here. And very soon she will want to know these things, and you needs must tell her."

Edward stared at her bleakly. "And do you truly think it will make aught of a difference if I do?"

83

And that was when she repeated to Edward what she had told the duke about her family. "And so, you see," she concluded, "I do believe matters *could* change, if Georgie were determined upon it."

Edward sighed heavily and rubbed his nape. "I hope to God you are right, Diana. For I could never become the silent, ineffectual man Georgie's father became. I would—God help me, but I would leave her first."

Diana rose and went to him. "She loves you, Edward," she uttered softly. "Let us hope it never comes to that."

He nodded, and asked Diana to tell her story to Georgie. Diana smiled her acquiescence, but just as she made to take her leave, Edward stopped her.

"There is one more thing I would say to you, Diana." His voice was gentle as he began walking her to the door.

She lifted a brow in question. "Adam," he began tentatively, then took a deep breath. "Adam is a good man. I have great respect for him. But he—he is not disposed to marry, my dear. I only tell you this because I care about you and I—I do not wish to see you hurt."

She smiled, desperately trying to keep all emotion from her eyes. He was not telling her anything new, after all. And even if the duke *were* hanging out for a wife, she did not qualify. "Oh, Edward, you needn't worry about me. I know full well the duke's feelings about marriage. Indeed, I am no more disposed to that state than he. We have merely struck up a friendship these last days, having had our concern for Georgie in common."

Edward looked skeptical, but as she held his gaze unwaveringly, he finally nodded and let her go.

She breathed a sigh of relief when she'd closed the morning room doors behind her. Then she squared her shoulders and made her way to Georgie's rooms.

The babe was asleep, but Georgie's eyelids fluttered open as soon as Diana came in. "I owe you an . . . apology," she said softly.

Goodness, Diana thought. That was the third one today. This was all beginning to sound like a Cheltenham tragedy. "Truly, Georgie, 'tisn't nec—"

"Yes, it is. I wronged you and you have done so much."

84

"Georgie, please," Diana replied, sitting down at the bedside chair and taking the baroness's hand, "do not tire yourself. 'Tis enough said about that. I shall be glad if we can be friends now."

Georgie smiled tremulously. Diana noted that her long silky blond hair had been brushed and tied back. There was a bit of color in her cheeks. "I should like that," she said, then paused, a look of uncertainty crossing her brow. "Edward—Edward says he—he loves me."

"Of course he does. I never doubted it." Diana squeezed her hand in reassurance.

"But I—I make it difficult for him," Georgie added sadly, her voice barely audible.

"Did he tell you that?"

"Not today. But once—once before. Diana, I—I don't know how to go on. I do not understand what—oh, Diana! I am so afraid he'll leave me again once—once I am well." Georgie's face was twisted in distress. Diana thought it was too soon to tax her strength with such talk and set about to soothe her.

"Georgie, I know so little of marriage. But—but I do know a bit about men. And I know Edward. I am persuaded there *is* a way for you both. But for now, you must rest and regain your strength. And then . . . there is your son."

"Yes. I truly *do* want to feed him, and Edward would—would like me to. He—he wants me to name him as well."

Diana smiled. "And have you thought of a name?"

"I was thinking of—of William Edward. My father's name was William."

"That is a lovely name, Georgie. But—ah—might I suggest Edward William instead?"

"But William was my father! Surely—"

"But Edward is your husband, Georgie," Diana interjected quietly, and then patted the baroness's hand and left the room.

Luncheon was a relaxed affair. Edward reported that Georgie was in better spirits and then announced, with a note of wonder in his voice, that she had decided to name the child Edward William. They would call him Ned.

Amidst the good wishes that greeted this pronouncement,

Diana felt the duke's probing eyes on her. She met his speculative gaze with a look of pure innocence. If he actually wondered if she'd had any part in Georgie's decision, well, it was best she keep her own counsel.

Papa brought the conversation round to the weather and the state of the roads. Surely some of the snow was beginning to melt, and perhaps he and Diana had ought to try to return home this afternoon. She was surprised at the vehement objections that greeted this suggestion. Adam was adamant that the roads, even if passable, would not be safe. Edward feared that Georgie was not yet out of the woods. And so Papa, after casting a rather odd look about the table, agreed that there would be no more talk of departure until the morrow.

Diana told herself that she did not feel relief at this pronouncement.

Adam betook himself to the library after luncheon, intent on working on his designs. But every time he looked down at the paper-strewn desk, he heard Diana's voice, praising his work, asking what he meant to do next. And following immediately upon the remembered soft huskiness of her voice came her image, floating before his mind's eye when it should have been intricate line drawings he was seeing.

She was beautiful, he mused, with her white skin and raven-dark hair, her velvety blue eyes, and that mouth . . . a mouth that smiled with sweet and gentle innocence, yet had opened for him with explosive passion.

Good God! He bolted upright from the desk, pacing and trying to calm his rapidly heating body. She was out of reach, any man's reach, but especially his, for myriad reasons. He would do well to remember that. He needs must sit back down and devote himself to work. Tomorrow she would be gone from Rossmore Manor, and he could relax.

But he did not sit back down. He stood at the wide bay window, one hand pressed to the cold glass, his eyes staring out at the frigid blanket of white that covered the garden below.

Diana found herself unaccustomedly restless. She supposed

it had to do with not being in her own home, where she had her own chores and routine to occupy her. But deep down she knew it was more than that. She had requested writing materials—indeed they had been brought to her here in the morning room—but she found she had no desire to catch up on correspondence. Edward had put the music room at her disposal, but she had yet to sit down at the pianoforte. Furthermore, at home, she did not feel the need to occupy herself every minute of the day. And she could not remember when she had last felt this wretched restlessness. She paced the carpeted floor of the morning room, trying to make sense of it all.

Papa sat nearby in a powder blue wing chair. He appeared engrossed in a collection of Greek plays; but every so often he would lift his head, and his eyes would follow her. She stopped pacing and went to stand at the window. She did not wish Papa to ask questions she could not answer.

It was not a moment later that his voice broke the silence.

"Perhaps, if you are bored, Diana, you might wish to look for a book in the library."

She whirled round to face him. "The library?" No! she thought. Adam would likely be there. She did not want to be private with him. "Ah, no, Papa. I would not wish to disturb Adam. He is working there, you must know. And besides, I do not much feel like reading."

"Ah," was all he said, and she turned back to the window. "Would you like to talk about it?" he asked gently after a moment.

She turned more slowly this time, schooling her face to a bland expression. "Talk about what, Papa? Oh! You mean the snow. Why—"

"Diana," he chided with a smile that reminded her he had not just fallen off a turnip wagon.

She sighed. "I collect you are referring to the fact that I have been wearing a path in this lovely Aubusson carpet this half hour and more." She smiled faintly. "I am merely restless, you must know. I am persuaded it must come from—ah—the snow, and having been obliged to remain indoors for so long. Perhaps I ought to have a walk in the garden." Her smile brightened as the idea took hold. "Yes, I shall have a walk. The sun has been shining all day. Perhaps there is a path or two by now."

Diana watched her father arch a very skeptical brow and give her a look that said he knew he was being gammoned. He did not believe the snow had aught to do with her present mood. Undoubtedly he was right, but she did not care to delve too deeply into the matter. And the notion of a walk *was* most appealing. Papa, dear man that he was, did not question her further—merely advised her to bundle up and try to borrow a warmer pair of boots than the thin leather half boots she was wearing.

Mrs. Stebbins did contrive to procure her an old pair of boots, not much thicker than her own, but which came all the way up to her knees. With those and her warm, full cloak and fur-lined gloves, she was ready to brave the gardens.

Despite the sun, she shivered as she stepped outside. She drew her cloak tightly round and gingerly stepped forward, seeking solidly packed snow.

She avoided the huge drifts, and though several times she stepped into a soft mound of snow and sank to the tops of her knees, for the most part she walked on firmly packed snow. In some places the snow had begun to melt, but rather than create pathways, it had simply iced over. These patches, too, she avoided, and realized that travel today would, indeed, have been an unnecessary risk. Yet she told herself this restlessness would not gnaw at her if she were back home at Three Oaks Cottage.

He saw the claret cloak first, a splash of color against the endless white snow. And though the hood shielded her face, he knew very well who it was. He wondered how long she'd been out there; it must be wretchedly cold. Stay where you are, Marchmaine, he told himself. And he did. For four long minutes. And then he decided that a blast of cold air was just what he needed to clear his head.

"Oh, my goodness me! You startled me!" Diana gasped, fairly jumping from her boots a short time later when he came

88

round a snow-covered hedge to face her.

"I'm sorry. I did not mean to." He hurried toward her, grasping her lightly by the shoulders. "Are you all right?"

"Yes, of course. I—I—simply was not expecting anyone."

"No, I don't imagine you were. But I saw—that is—I was working and felt the need of some air." He dropped his hands, and she took a step back.

"I, too, felt the . . . need of air."

Her nose and cheeks were red from the cold. The sun notwithstanding, it *was* rather bone-chillingly cold, and the wind seemed to pick up even as they stood there. The "need of air" must have been rather extreme for her to subject herself to such discomfort. Had she been as restless as he?

He resisted the urge to move close to her again, to share his warmth. "Yes," he said finally. "You *have* been confined awhile. 'Tis nearly two full days since you—you've been here." He heard the tension in his own voice and knew it came from what he did not say. Was it only two days since he'd met her? He wondered if she heard his silent question.

Her deep blue eyes were solemn, unfathomable. "Yes," she echoed softly. "It—it somehow seems much longer. I—I mean to say it—"

"I know, Diana," he interjected gently.

"So—so much has happened."

She looked away as soon as she said the words, and he knew then that she was not speaking of the birth of his nephew. But they had ought to be speaking of that—that and nothing else. He opened his mouth, intent on some comment about the child's health, or Georgie's, when suddenly the sky darkened.

Diana shivered, her eyes meeting his again as she drew her cloak more closely round herself. Her lips seemed to turn blue. A wave of remorse hit him. It was, undoubtedly, because of him that she was out here, nearly freezing. . . .

Without thinking he brushed her soft lips with his fingers. "You're cold, Diana. Your lips are blue. Come inside now." She closed her eyes for a moment and shivered anew. This time he did not think it was from the cold.

"Pray do not . . . do that, Adam," she murmured, opening her eyes and tilting her head back just enough to break the contact with his fingers. He frowned, lowering his hand. "It—

it only makes things worse," she rasped, then quickly looked away from him. He knew she was not speaking of the cold or the color of her lips.

He sighed heavily. "How long have you been out here, my dear? Too long, I'll wager. Now, come, there's a cheerful fire in the library."

No! she thought frantically, her eyes unwittingly meeting his again. She did not want to go with him to the library. Did he not understand that the fire was quite hot enough, right here in the snow? Every time he touched her. . . . He reached for her elbow, and she sidestepped him. Did he not feel the heat between them? Or was it that he was simply not discommoded by it? The thought was a lowering one, and made her more determined than ever to put some distance between them. He was standing much too close. She could smell his clean, masculine scent. She could feel his breath, grazing her cheeks, warming her despite the rising wind. No, it would never do.

Resolutely she stepped farther back, carefully avoiding a snowdrift. "Truly, Adam, I am not that cold. I own I've not even been here two hours. Do you go—"

"Two hours! Good God! 'Tis long enough, I should say, to catch your death."

"No, I—"

"For pitysakes, Diana, look at the sky!" Adam snapped, directing her gaze upward. "It may well snow again," he said without thinking, and their eyes locked with a jolt, both realizing, simultaneously, the implication of more snow. More days of enforced confinement, together yet apart. . . . His eyes moved over her face and came to rest on her soft, full lips. Lips in need of warming.

"Adam, do you go inside," she finally said, a bit breathlessly. "I shall stay—"

"Dammit, Diana! You're like to contract chilblains!" he exploded, knowing he was likely overreacting but unable to help himself. That she preferred freezing out here to allowing him to warm her infuriated him. "I vow you do not have adequate boots, nor gloves, and your insistence upon remaining here is the height of foolishness!"

"My gloves are fur-lined," she said with dignity, "and Mrs. Stebbins was kind enough to lend me a perfectly adequate pair of boots. My feet are not in the least cold, you must know, so you may cease playing nursemaid and I—"

"Playing nursemaid is the last thing I have on my mind, Diana, as you know deuced well," he growled in an undertone, then wondered what the devil had come over him. He advanced toward her, but restrained himself from touching her by clenching his fists.

Then he recalled what else she'd said. He frowned prodigiously. "What do you mean, your feet are not cold? Even mine are, and I've been out here but a few minutes."

"Well, then perhaps *your* boots are not adequate, Adam," she retorted, her blue eyes gleaming. He knew he was seeing a fleeting glimpse of the saucy Diana. "As for me, *my* feet are exceedingly comfortable. Indeed, I hardly feel them at all!"

"Hardly feel—damn and blast it all, Diana! Do you not realize—Oh, never mind! Come along!" He felt his eyes bulge with fury that he dimly realized was misplaced. He grabbed her elbow and unceremoniously propelled her to one of the rear doors.

He meant to let her go soon after they were indoors, but not three yards into the narrow rear corridor, she stumbled. Her face twisted into a grimace.

"Hellfire! What have you done to yourself?" he demanded, turning to face her and putting his hands to her shoulders.

She lifted her little chin. "Nothing. You may be sure I am quite well. Now, if you'll excuse me, I shall retire abovestairs."

"Bloody hell," he muttered. "'Tis your feet, is it not?" Her lip quivered in answer. She did not look as if she could walk two more steps, let alone several flights of stairs. And he was a bounder for being angry with her.

Swiftly he moved to take her up in his arms. But she read his intention and fairly jumped out of his reach. "No Adam! I—I can walk."

His eyes met hers. The gleam was gone; the solemn Diana was back. She did not want him to hold her, and he knew her reticence had naught to do with proprieties. She would rather endure pain than— He cursed inwardly, but knew there was no help for it.

"Very well, but you're coming with me to the library," he finally said firmly.

She did not demur and allowed him to take her elbow once more as they slowly made their way to the library. Her jaw was clenched from pain, but she said not a word. She faltered several times, and leaned more heavily against him, but he did not make the mistake of offering to carry her.

But once behind the closed library doors, her control slipped. She fell back against the sofa with a groan, making no effort to hide the pain from her face. He cursed inwardly and drew a chair and ottoman up to the fire.

"Come to the fire," he said gently, and drew her up, letting her lean against him as he guided her to the chair.

He tried to ignore the soft feel of her, the sweet scent of her, to think only of her injured feet, and the fact that if he did not get her warm and dry she was like to become ill. Somehow he slipped the cloak from her shoulders and settled her into the tapestried chair.

"Adam, you needn't—"

"Hush, Diana." He sat down on the ottoman, facing her, and pulled her right foot onto his lap. He could tell as soon as he touched the thin, worn leather boot that it was woefully inadequate, but the look of pain on her face made him refrain from saying so. Nor did he comment, beyond a barely audible curse, when he saw the tears in the seam just next to where her little toe would be. The boots were sodden, and he knew her feet were frozen, but not so numb as they'd been outside. The pain, he imagined, would get worse before it got better.

Very gingerly, he pulled that first boot off, and looked up sharply at her sudden intake of breath. She remained silent, however, so he bent his head to the task of rubbing some warmth into her toes. But her thin woolen stockings were quite soaked through. He quickly removed the other boot and then gently suggested—no, commanded—that she remove her black stockings as well.

At that her eyes rounded in indignation. "I shall do no—"

"Diana, I do not believe you have a missish bone in your body. Now come down off your high ropes and do the sensible thing. We have already, perhaps, saved you from frostbite and the loss of several toes, but you are still fair on your way to chilblains, not to mention an inflammation of the lungs."

"Adam, I am not like to—"

"*Now*, Diana," he said firmly, and without another word rose and went to stare out of one of the windows.

When he turned back moments later, she was sitting comfortably in the chair, her legs propped on the ottoman, her magenta skirts draped across her shins. It was a modest enough pose, to be sure, but she hadn't dragged her skirts down to cover every possible patch of smooth white skin. No milk-and-water miss was Miss Diana Rustin. He permitted himself an appreciative glance at a pair of trim, shapely ankles and two very small, very dainty bare feet. And he might have smiled, but for the ugly red color of those feet. At the least, they did not appear swelled yet, but one never knew what damage could be done in a short time. He frowned, and then realized that the sodden stockings were nowhere in evidence.

His lips twitched as he held out his hand. "They need to dry, Diana," was all he said.

Reluctantly, she produced the stockings from behind her back. "Adam, I am persuaded I shall be right as rain in a trice, merely by sitting here before the fire. You needn't fuss. I take leave to doubt anyone has ever contracted chilblains after less than two hours in the snow."

Her color was high, and the words came out in a rush as he took the wet stockings from her. She seemed far more discomfitted at his touching the stockings than his seeing her bare feet and ankles.

He filed that rather interesting notion in the back of his head, then turned away, so that she would not see the telltale curving of his lips. He wrung the moisture out of the stockings and hung them from the mantel before turning back to her.

"And I take leave to inform you, ma'am, that you would be wrong." He sat back down on the ottoman, gently setting her feet on his lap. "Even one hour is quite sufficient, particularly when one's boots afford little more protection than a pair of satin slippers!" He kept his tone light, to distract her from his gentle probing of her feet.

Nonetheless, her body went rigid at his touch. "Please, Adam, this—this isn't necessary. You—you really had oughtn't to—ah—"

He quite ignored her words, his hands engulfing her cold feet in their warmth. "Does it hurt very much?" he inquired softly.

"No! That is, they do hurt but—but not where you—ah—I mean to say . . ." Her voice trailed off, and she squirmed, refusing to meet his eyes.

"Relax," he murmured, gently massaging her toes and suddenly understanding very well what she meant. She was feeling that extraordinary warmth that always leapt between them whenever they touched. He was feeling it as well, and enjoying every minute. Still, he felt obliged to put her at her ease as his large hands moved from her toes to the tops of her feet. "Your feet need warmth, Diana, and that is what I—"

"Not that kind of warmth," she blurted, and then her eyes flew to his. She flushed a deep crimson; surely she had not meant to acknowledge what was between them. And just as well, he knew, since there oughtn't to *be* anything between them.

Diana was mortified. How could she have said that? How had he disarmed her so much with a mere touch on her foot? But it was no mere touch, and she knew it. It was a caress, soothing and gentle, yet so heated that her entire body felt warmed. And there was that tingling sensation that went straight to the pit of her stomach. Dear God, what was happening to her? She wanted to lie back, to let his hand slide from her foot to her calf. . . .

The direction of her thoughts jolted her, and she gave herself a firm mental shake. She tried to pull away, but he held her firmly.

"'Tis either this—er—warmth, or my valet's special chilblain remedy, my dear," Adam said in a voice laced with amusement.

He watched the play of expression across her face, as her discomfiture gave way to an answering bemusement. Her lips curled, and one finely arched black brow lifted. "You are quizzing me, Adam. A gentleman's gentleman concerns himself with boots, not what is in them. Why, no self-respecting valet—"

"Do not cast aspersions, Diana, on the very worthy Hampton. His odd assortment of remedies has served handily any number of times. This particular recipe calls, I believe, for seven onions fried in hog's lard, and then pressed—"

"Please, no more," she interrupted, smiling for the first

94

time. "I collect that your—er—remedy—is by far the preferable."

He nodded smugly. "Indeed it is. Now, would you kindly relax? Your . . . limbs are quite rigid enough to snap."

She obeyed, and a moment later a contented sigh escaped her as he continued his ministrations, this time on her heel and ankle. She slid farther down into the chair, inadvertently assuming a most languid pose. And as he warmed her, he felt himself grow more and more heated, until he feared that *he* would be the one rigid enough to snap!

He had ought to stop. Surely he had done enough. Her feet were not quite so red. But no, he had not even touched the arches and balls of her feet. Gently he brought his finger to the underside of her right foot.

"No!" she squealed, suddenly squirming and trying to twist away. He frowned and kept working on her foot. "Adam, no!" she repeated, and then went off into a paroxysm of . . . of giggles!

She twisted and turned, trying to escape him, but he let her go only long enough to grab the left foot. She howled; she couldn't stop giggling, and Adam couldn't stop the wolfish grin that suffused his face.

She was ticklish! Self-contained, saucy-solemn Miss Diana Rustin was ticklish! For some reason the knowledge delighted him, and he couldn't help wondering what other parts of her lovely anatomy were similarly sensitive. He felt his loins tighten at the mere thought, and at the flushed, delectable, dishevelled picture she made.

"No! Please, stop, I—I can't take any more!" she spluttered between giggles.

And so he stopped, and bitterly regretted in the next moment that he was a heartbeat too late.

For as his hands left the sensitive bottoms of her feet, and began to stroke the other parts, to soothe her, and as she murmured contentedly, "Mmm, yes, much better," another voice entirely pierced the warm and cozy air surrounding them.

"Well, I never! How *dare* you, Adam? By all that is holy—this is an *outrage!*"

Adam cursed volubly under his breath and forced himself

95

not to move. It was the outside of enough! This was the third such interruption today. But the intruding voice was not booming, merely strident. And it was not masculine, but feminine. And though the figure of a shocked, middle-aged person once more marched into the room, the eyes were not twinkling, but blazing.

He knew she could see him clearly, but could see only Diana's legs and feet. Bare feet. Diana strained to rise from the chair, but he squeezed her ankle reassuringly and held her firmly in place. Her health was more important than any outraged sensibilities.

The stout, formidable female form strode to within three feet of him but did not trouble to walk round and peer at the occupant of the tapestried chair. Apparently two bare feminine feet were quite damning enough.

Adam did not rise, but continued his soft massage as his eyes met those of the intruder.

"Hello, Mother," he said with a calm he was far from feeling. "It is customary, I believe, to knock on closed doors. Perhaps you will be good enough to await me in the morning room. I shall be there in a trice."

"I most certainly will *not* leave this room!" she declared. "Have your wits—not to mention your manners—gone a-begging?"

Adam sighed. There really was no help for it. "Then, do sit down, Mother," he said resignedly. "I am not in a position to rise just yet."

And that, he knew, was true in more ways than one. For if he was not yet finished warming Diana's feet, *she* had warmed *him* to a point where his mother would have true cause for the apoplexy!

Chapter 7

"And I most certainly will *not* be seated," the Duchess of Marchmaine huffed, "whilst you entertain your *cher amie* in your own sister's house!"

Diana gasped. Even for the arrogant duchess, that was a bit much. If Adam was not holding her feet, if she were certain they would not buckle did she try to stand, she would have risen, excused herself with dignity, and exited the room. As it was, she could only listen to the duchess continue, "You have truly crossed the line this time, Adam, and—"

"And you are about to do so as well, Mother," Adam interjected menacingly. Diana marvelled that he could face down his mother with such aplomb. "I believe you remember Miss Diana Rustin?"

The duchess inched forward, her strong nose high in the air, and peered down at Diana. She lifted her chin. "Yes," she sniffed, "and I have always suspected, as I told Georgina, that she was no better than she should be."

Diana gasped again. She was sure she blushed. But she could not utter a single word, so dumbfounded was she at such blatant rudeness. Adam, however, had no such difficulty. He was still holding her feet, and she could feel the anger rise in him like a physical thing. His jaw clenched and his piercing amber eyes blazed. He was going to explode! But she did not want to come between Adam and his mother.

In that split second before he spoke, she leaned forward, to stop him somehow. But he shook his head almost imperceptibly before very gently setting her bare feet down on the ottoman. Then he rose and drew himself up.

"I will assume, Mother, that an arduous journey has rather addled your tongue, else surely your natural good manners would not permit you to speak so," he said forcefully. Diana did not know which she admired more—the way he stood up to his mother, or the way he kept a tight leash on his own temper. For despite his relatively civil words, she could see that he was in a towering rage. But though she was most gratified at his chivalrous defense of her, it pained her to be a bone of contention between them.

She thought that perhaps if she *could* rise and excuse herself, the situation might defuse itself. But she feared that her feet, still in some pain, would betray her. Besides, Adam and the duchess were glaring at each other, quite as if she were not even there.

"Have you forgotten whom you are addressing, young man?" the duchess demanded imperiously, her ample bosom fairly heaving in indignation.

Diana's eyes flitted back and forth between mother and son as they faced each other, palpable hostility between them. Though Adam was tall and lean and his mother of medium height and rather stout, their features were similar. Each had deep, piercing eyes, the duchess's dark brown to Adam's tawny, and each had the same strong jawline and aristocratic, aquiline nose. But while on Adam the angular features looked handsome, bespeaking a man of rare strength, on the duchess they merely looked harsh. Diana wondered if the woman ever smiled.

A ghost of a smile, a mirthless one, crossed Adam's face now. "I have not forgotten for a moment, ma'am, to whom I am speaking," he said at length with a thinly veiled sarcasm Diana was certain the duchess missed. "Miss Rustin has injured her feet in the snow. She can barely walk, and I am trying to prevent her from becoming ill and contracting chilblains. And by the by, Mother, Miss Rustin is the one responsible for saving Georgie's life and that of your grandson."

"Grandson?" For the first time the duchess looked nonplussed, her dark eyes widening. "Do you mean to say 'tis true? She was brought to bed?"

Adam's eyes narrowed, and he took a step closer to his

mother. "Do *you* mean to say you have been in this house these many minutes and have not yet inquired about Georgie?" he asked in a voice of deceptive softness.

The Duchess of Marchmaine recovered quickly. "Well, of course I meant to ask *you*," she retorted indignantly. "That is why I came here straightaway, not troubling even to talk to the servants. And after that harrowing ride in the carriage—well— why else would I have risked life and limb if that dreadful proprietor at the Horsefeathers Inn had not told me Georgie's time had come? But when I arrived, what did I find? Not—"

"Carriage ride? You came in a *carriage?*" Adam interjected. "God's teeth, Mother! The roads are treacherous! How could you—"

"I will *not* have that manner of language from you, Adam! Pray, how else did you expect me to travel? Surely not on a *horse* in this weather and dressed as I am!" She gestured toward the elegant dove gray travelling costume she wore.

Adam shook his head. "I cannot conceive that you persuaded your coachman to—"

"Well, you may be certain it was not easy," she proclaimed, belatedly pulling off her gloves and sinking into a wing chair just several feet from Diana's own.

Adam resumed his place on the ottoman and again slid Diana's bare feet onto his lap. His fingers began to work their magic once more. Diana tried to pull her feet away, but he would not relinquish them, giving her a brief but reassuring look. She fancied she knew just what he was thinking; his mother's sensibilities had already been outraged, and so he might just as well see to Diana's comfort. His eyes shifted to his mother, who glowered at him. Adam met her gaze with a bland one of his own, and Diana decided it was the better part of valor for her to say nothing at all.

At length the duchess went on. "I own I shall be obliged to do something about Peter Coachman, Adam. He forgets his place. At first he actually had the cheek to *refuse* to drive me anywhere today! But I had been forced to sit out the storm in a most wretched, ramshackle inn some degree south of here, and I would *not*, once the storm abated, pass one hour further in that place!" She shuddered as delicately as her solid form would allow. "Not but what the Horsefeathers was much better. What passed for nuncheon was a disgrace—but still, I might have remained there for the day had not the proprietor informed me that Edward and the doctor had bolted from there this very morning because of Georgie! And what a riot and a rumpus did Peter Coachman set up over venturing out yet again! As if it were any great distance, and as if I would ever consent to being away from my only daughter's side at a time like this!" She punctuated her statement by removing a frightfully long hat pin from a rather enormous hat of gray *velours épingle*.

Diana noted that her fervent rush to her daughter's side seemed to have come to a halt at the library door. She had not yet inquired about Georgie, nor made a push to see her. Diana caught Adam's gaze for a moment; he rolled his eyes in exasperation. That, she supposed, was better than the barely veiled hostility of minutes before.

"And what does that incompetent coachman do, Adam," the duchess continued stridently, "but contrive, on such a short trip, to break the axle or somesuch on my *new* travelling carriage. Why, we fairly had to limp up the drive!"

"What the devil? You mean to say—"

"Oh, but that is not the worst of it, Adam! That fool coachman stopped right in the middle of the icy, narrow roadway as soon as he heard something 'snap,' so he says, in the axle. And so the groom driving the luggage coach was obliged to swerve, to avoid a collision, you must know, and in so doing, overturned the entire coach!"

"The devil you say!" Adam erupted, setting Diana's feet aside and bolting up.

"Are you trying to tell me you set out this afternoon with *two* carriages?" he shouted, towering over his mother. "Do you not realize you were risking life and limb—yours and those of your servants—by venturing out at all? Could you not at the least have left the luggage coach at the inn for another day?"

The Duchess of Marchmaine looked genuinely taken aback. "Why, Adam Damerest! What an odd notion! I don't believe I've *ever* travelled without proper luggage and retainers in all my born days. I'm much too old to start now. Not but what my two very best portmanteaux are no doubt ruined beyond bearing, lying out there still in all that snow."

"Lying out—" Adam spluttered. "Do you mean to tell me you left an overturned carriage in the—"

"Well, of course I did! And left two grooms to deal with all that luggage. Not but what I was obliged to take my maids up with me, for they were wailing and blubbering and like to have the vapors. Well, and what else could I do, Adam? I could not very well right the carriage myself, you must know!"

If it was at all possible for the formidable duchess to look helpless, she did at that moment. Adam glared at her with a mixture of ire and disbelief. "I do not suppose you have as yet sent anyone of the Rossmore servants back to the luggage coach, have you?" he drawled.

The Duchess of Marchmaine took umbrage. "I should say not, Adam! I came to you straightaway. My first concern was Georgie, after all!"

Diana stifled another gasp. She had the urge to shriek and to giggle all at once. Her eyes flew to Adam's. She could not tell if he was about to explode with laughter or wrath. But his eyes met hers, and in that instant's communication she knew they were both thinking the same thing. His mother had been here a full half hour at the least, had ranted about Diana and the servants and incompetence and impropriety, but not once had she truly asked about Georgie. It was hardly a laughing matter, but Diana supposed, when one was obliged to deal with such an odious person regularly, laughter was healthier than constantly smoldering and erupting with rage.

And so Diana was much relieved to see Adam's lips twitch as he stalked to the bellpull and yanked it. A charged silence ensued as they awaited Stebbins.

The duchess finally broke it by clearing her throat and saying, "You *did* say I had a grandson, did you not, Adam?" So, she was human after all.

Adam smiled for the first time since his mother's entrance. "Yes, Mother. A robust baby boy, born in the wee hours, Tuesday morning."

"How perfectly splendid!" Her lips curled in what might have been taken for a smile, but she quite ruined it by adding in her usual toplofty manner, "It is always fortuitous when a woman fulfills her duty and presents her husband with an heir straightaway. Oh, dear!" Her lips turned down now in a frown.

"Edward must not have been here in time for the birth, was he?"

"No, Mother. No one was here except—"

A discreet cough from the doorway interrupted Adam's words. He went to confer with Stebbins in the matter of the luggage coach, leaving an awkward silence behind him. Diana did not try to fill it. The duchess was virtually ignoring her existence, and so she settled back to wait upon events.

However, curiosity got the better of the formidable duchess, belated though it was. "The duke made reference to your having saved Georgina's life. Surely he was mistaken and meant your father." It was a statement, not a question, and Diana noted, in addition to the lofty tone of voice, the deliberate use of Adam's title. She smiled inwardly at the woman's attempt to dictate the parameter of Diana's relationship to her son.

"Well, I do not know that I saved her life in as much as—"

"In as much as God presumably has a hand in such matters," Adam finished for her, striding toward them. This time he stood next the hearth, leaning one hand on the mantel. "However, it was Diana who delivered the babe, and it was a rather difficult birth."

The duchess's eyes bulged. Her hand went to her bosom. "Miss Rustin del—surely you jest, Adam! Such a thing is unheard of!"

Diana could have sworn Adam was enjoying himself. "Yes, well, I believe you have heard of it now," he countered dryly, his lips curling. "The babe was turned, you see, and without Diana—"

"And just where was the doctor?" The duchess's eyes blazed.

"Delivering Mrs. Caldwell of twins, er—over in Midvale, you must know."

Adam's twinkling eyes met Diana's. She lifted a bemused brow, as if to remind him that he'd had nearly the same objections as his mother just two days ago. He inclined his head almost imperceptibly, his eyelids slowly coming down, as if to say, "touché." But when he opened his eyes again, they regarded her with a certain warmth that seemed to say, "two days is a very long time." She felt her cheeks grow warm.

"How dare Dr. Rustin be off in Midvale of all places!" The

102

duchess's ranting voice effectively broke their silent communication. "Why was—turned? Did you say the babe was *turned?*" She sat bolt upright in her chair, Adam's earlier words apparently having just registered. She was obviously very good at hearing only what she wanted to. She looked from Adam to Diana. Both nodded. The duchess turned rather ashen; then with one hand clutching her bosom and the other actually pointing at Diana, she went on, "And *you* are the one who . . . who . . ."

"Yes, Your Grace," Diana replied softly.

Suddenly the duchess pulled both hands back to her lap. Her color returned. "I do not believe it!" she exclaimed.

She rose majestically from her chair. "Such a thing is not possible! Why, you—you are the doctor's daughter! You are not even wed!"

Diana forced herself to rise as well, her feet notwithstanding. She could not allow Adam to continue speaking for her. She swayed a little and clutched the back of the chair for support. Much as she hated to admit it, he had been right—her feet hurt like the very devil. She tried not to let the pain show on her face. "Nevertheless, Your Grace, that is exactly what happened," she said quickly but firmly. She noticed Adam surreptitiously moving toward her as the duchess impaled her with a baleful eye.

"You, miss, are impertinent!" Her Grace declared, then whirled to Adam. "And *you* are little better. I see I shall have to speak to Georgina. I shall have the truth from her in a trice. She—she *is* all right, is she not? You did say her life was—was saved?"

"So, Mother, you have finally asked the most important question of all," Adam drawled. Then pointedly sidestepping her, he put his hand to Diana's elbow. "Come, Diana, I know you are in pain. Do sit down."

Not until she was once more ensconced in the chair, her feet on the ottoman, did he turn to his glowering mother. "We believe Georgie will be fine, Mother. She is very weak, though, and needs a good deal of rest. She lost quite a bit of blood, you see."

"Dear God!" She looked genuinely stricken. "And to think that wretched storm kept me from being here. At least

Edward—oh, Lord! *He* was not here either, was he?" Adam shook his head. "Well, I own it was very badly done of Edward to have hightailed it to the Continent at such a time! My poor Georgina! No mama, nor husband, nor even the doctor! Thank God *you* were here, Adam! You and—oh! Oh, dear! It is just as I thought. You both were here, alone—"

"Hardly alone, Mother. The house is full of servants, not to mention Georgie!"

The duchess put her nose in the air. "Georgina can hardly have acted as chaperone when—"

"Oh, for pitysakes, Mother!" Adam erupted, his fists clenched at his sides. "If I had turned Diana away Monday night, as *propriety* demanded, Georgie would more than likely be *dead* by now! Would that have been better?" His entire body was taut with rage; but then he turned briefly to look down at Diana, and he seemed to relax, a certain warmth creeping into his eyes. That and a rueful admission that he was well aware that he *had* almost turned her away.

The duchess drew herself up, a rather absurd gesture since she was a full head shorter than her son. Her eyes flitted from Adam to Diana, to the mantel and back to Adam. "None of which explains what two black stockings are doing dangling from the mantel!" she pronounced in a huff.

Diana bit her lip to keep from moaning in sheer mortification. She did not move; Adam would likely stop her, and the last thing she wished to do now was call attention to herself. She had rather the floor would open up and swallow her. As that did not happen, she merely lowered her head, certain her face was beet red.

"They are drying, Mother," Adam said in a hard voice, "as should be perfectly obvious. I did not want Miss Rustin, who is a *guest in Edward's house*, along with her father, to suffer chilblains or inflammation of the lungs. I believe I had already made that clear."

The duchess paled visibly beneath the steel in her son's voice. She had not missed the admonishment it held. In as much as this had been one of the most awkward interviews Diana had ever had to endure, she would have been less than human had she not felt a twinge of pleasure at his unqualified support. How different was he—a man she'd known a scant two days—from Robert, who'd purported to love her all those years ago!

"Well," the duchess said with an arrogant lift of her chin, "I am certain my maid awaits me in the Oriental Chamber. I shall freshen up and then go to my poor daughter straightaway!"

"Yes, Mother, do," Adam replied, and now Diana thought she saw a glint of amusement in his amber eyes. "But—er—I gave Stebbins orders that the Queen Anne Room be readied for you."

"Whatever *can* you have been thinking, Adam? You know very well I *always* occupy the Oriental Chamber!"

"Yes, but it is occupied now," Adam replied mildly.

"By whom?" his mother demanded ominously.

Diana decided she had been silent long enough. "By me, Your Grace." She ignored the older woman's look of outrage, as well as Adam's frown. "It was necessary for me to be as near as possible to Georgie in the nights, you see."

The Duchess of Marchmaine narrowed her eyes, as if considering the validity of Diana's claim. "This," she pronounced finally, "is the outside of enough! Good afternoon to you, Adam, Miss Rustin!" And with that she marched proudly, regally, from the room.

Diana breathed a sigh of relief, and then did not know whether to laugh at the woman's pomposity, or cry for her own humiliation. She did realize, however, that by addressing her directly for the first time at the end, the duchess had made a major concession. And so when Diana caught the hint of amusement in Adam's eyes, she allowed her lips to twitch. His curled. She smiled. He grinned. She chuckled. He laughed.

Then abruptly they both sobered. "I'm sorry," Diana said. "'Tisn't the least funny. But it was either that or—or cry."

"No. You must never let her make you cry!" Adam came to sit once more on the ottoman. "But you are right, of course. 'Tis not funny at all. I was thinking of Edward, poor devil. I do not think he has a chance."

His bleak eyes met Diana's. She had no answer for him. The Duchess of Marchmaine, Georgie's mother and mentor, was simply an odious woman. To be wed to anyone at all like her would be a trial for any man.

And suddenly, as he bent to examine her feet one last time,

105

Diana thought she understood why Adam Damerest had never wed.

Having satisfied himself that her feet were looking a bit better, Adam had left Diana briefly with the admonition not to move. A maid had come to her with fresh, dry stockings and a pair of soft, comfortable slippers. And then Adam had returned to lend her his arm for the trip back to her room. Feeling had returned full measure to her feet, and they did hurt, though not nearly so much as they might have. And so, at the door to her chamber, she'd turned to him. "Thank you for saving me from my own foolishness, Adam. I do realize now that this could have been a good deal worse."

He had released her arm and now smiled down at her. "Apology accepted, my dear. You will oblige me please by not trying to come down for tea. Stay here and rest those feet. I'll have your tea sent up to you."

She had acquiesced gratefully—she hadn't relished taking tea with the duchess at all events. And indeed, by the time the dinner hour approached, she was feeling much more the thing. She was attempting to twist her long black locks into a semblance of order when her usual maid entered. The girl carried a deep green gown and a note from Adam. In it he informed her that they'd decided not to dress for dinner, she and her father not having evening clothes with them. But as Adam suspected his mother would ignore that agreement, he was sending along another of Georgie's gowns for Diana.

She smiled as she read the short missive. How very thoughtful of him! He hadn't wished her to feel discommoded in the presence of his mother. She appreciated his gesture immeasurably, but unfortunately she could not wear the gown. While it might flow quite elegantly from Georgie's wispy form, on Diana it clung and plunged most indecently. With a sigh, she set aside the lovely gown and donned the magenta day dress once more.

Adam raised a brow when she entered the Red Salon, where sherry was being served. Edward stood in conversation with Papa, and the duchess had not yet arrived, and so Diana glided to Adam. He handed her a glass of sherry and looked quizzically at her. "The green gown is lovely, Adam, but I could not possibly wear it," she said without preamble.

"Whyever not? Georgie, I assure you, was more than happy to give it to you."

She smiled at him, thinking he looked decidedly handsome in the brown coat and buff pantaloons he'd worn all afternoon. "I am most grateful, but, well, Georgie and I are not—er—made in the same way, you must know, and—"

She paused as a devilish gleam lit his eyes. He began a slow and pointed perusal of her person. She felt her cheeks flush and took a gulp of the sherry. "What I mean to say—ah—"

She paused again. A wolfish grin suffused his face now, and she felt her flush receding and her own lips twitching. "Well, not to put too fine a point on it, Adam, if I'd worn that gown, your mama would have had all her suspicions confirmed."

"Whatever do you mean?" His expression had turned suitably sober.

A tinkle of laughter escaped her. "Odious wretch! You must know precisely what I mean. In that gown I should indeed have looked like someone 'no better than she should be,' like a—a—bit of muslin, painted Haymarket ware—and—and—"

"I do take your point, my dear," Adam interjected, a bark of laughter escaping him.

It was then that the duchess entered, wearing a rather hideous evening gown of purple silk brocade. Her sharp eyes swept unerringly to Diana and Adam, engaged in their tête-à-tête in the corner. Her forbidding look told Diana there would be no more laughter this night.

In this she was correct. The duchess had a most unique talent for setting everyone's hackles up within a very few minutes. This despite the beautifully laid table, sparkling with crystal and gleaming with the finest cream and gold porcelain. Edward and the duchess sat across from each other, at the head and foot of the table, with Diana next to Papa and across from Adam.

"'Tis a pity you could not have been with your wife at such a crucial time, Edward," the duchess said between delicate spoonfuls of barley soup. Diana watched Edward's jaw clench. "Not but what you could have been much help, of course, unless you'd conveyed her to London where my personal

107

physician might have attended her." She took a sip of her wine. "Not to cast aspersions on *your* skills, Dr. Rustin," she continued with cloying sweetness, "but here in the country you cannot possibly garner as much experience as in the city."

"Indeed?" Papa queried. Diana recognized his pique but thought it tempered with a bit of amusement. "Well, curiously enough, Duchess, I *have* delivered a fair amount of babes in the last thirty years. But it hardly signifies, does it, since it was *Diana* who saved the baroness's life."

The duchess's brown eyes flared. "Well! I am persuaded that if—"

"Mother, how did you find Paris?" Adam interjected quickly.

The duchess lifted her nose a trifle. "Paris is an exceedingly beautiful city. I always say 'tis a shame it was given to the Parisians. And, of course, the journey back here was appalling."

And so it went. She addressed not a word to Diana, for which Diana was most grateful. In truth, she thought it the better part of valor to say little. Adam began a discussion of the Rossmore renovations with Edward. He included Diana and her father in the discourse upon the design of the banister for the new stairwell and the alterations required to accommodate the barrel-vaulted ceiling.

Unfortunately, the stuffed turbot did not hold Her Grace's attention for long, for she launched herself into the conversation. "Are you still amusing yourself with those drawings, Adam? Surely you should have been finished by now. Rossmore Manor, while I own quite pretty, isn't all *that* grand, after all." Good God, Diana thought as she watched Edward's eyes narrow, Adam's fingers tighten on his wine goblet and Papa look as if he'd rather be anywhere but here. Did the woman not realize what havoc she wreaked with her wretched tongue?

Obviously not. The duchess merely assumed that she was correct in all things, and that it was her right to say so. None of the men at table seemed at all surprised, although that did not lessen their discomfiture. A vein throbbed at Adam's temple. His aquiline nose flared slightly as he fought for control of his temper. "On the contrary, Mother," he said with icy civility,

"Rossmore is a fine example of Palladian architecture, and the integrity of the house must be preserved carefully."

"By replacing one narrow stairwell with another?" Her Grace queried with a raised brow, and Diana could hold her silence no longer.

"I have seen the plans for the renovation of the stairwell, Your Grace, and I can assure you they represent quite an ingenious, graceful use of the available space," she ventured.

The duchess turned to her for the first time, with a cold smile that did not reach her eyes. "Oh? And are you as well versed in architecture as you are in . . . midwifery, my dear Miss Rustin?"

Edward nearly choked on his wine. Papa gasped. Diana felt herself flush, whether from anger or sheer embarrassment she did not know. But she rallied herself. "Not at all, Your Grace. After all, architecture is an art which requires special talent and study. Midwifery, on the other hand, merely requires experience, some training and a willingness to disregard the proprieties in favor of more important matters."

This time Edward did choke. Papa coughed. Adam frowned. The duchess sent her a withering glance, her ample bosom rising and falling in indignation. "You seem to have quite a talent for disregarding the proprieties, do you not, Miss Rustin?" she countered disdainfully.

This time it was Adam who spoke. "I believe Miss Rustin is a woman of many accomplishments, Mother, including a willingness to learn new things, a sense of aesthetics, and a sense of priorities!"

Papa spluttered into his wineglass. The duchess looked dagger points at her son and then turned her baleful brown gaze onto Diana. Taking courage from Adam's unequivocal defense, which she had not expected after her last remark, Diana smiled graciously at the duchess. "Perhaps, Your Grace, you have not had the opportunity to truly study Adam's plans. I am persuaded you would be most impressed if you did. I own Lady Hart would have had a great deal less difficulty with *her* renovations had she engaged Adam for the plans."

"Winifred Hartcup is an eccentric!" Her Grace declared with lofty contempt, as if that were quite the definitive statement about the entire matter.

Adam gritted his teeth. It was Papa who countered, "Yes, perhaps so, Duchess, and quite a delightful one, I must say."

"I look forward to making her acquaintance," Adam said pointedly, his jaw relaxing just a bit.

Diana admired the strength of character that enabled him to put the duchess in her place whilst keeping within the bounds of courtesy and filial duty. Still, her remarks about his architectural endeavors *were* rather cutting, and Diana wondered how he endured it.

Edward was not quite as adept at control. It was during the fourth remove—a round of veal garnished with fresh vegetables—that Papa extended to Edward his compliments to the cook.

"Yes, I own you may be right, Dr. Rustin," the duchess concurred. "The veal *is* passing fair, if one has naught better with which to compare it. This *must* be the work of Mrs. Brownlow, Edward, is it not?" Edward nodded tautly. "Just as I thought. Georgie has been most remiss. Any hostess worth her salt would not consider employing such a hopeless provincial. I cannot think—"

"Mrs. Brownlow has been here longer than I have, Duchess, and here she will remain!" snapped Edward, setting his fork down with a clatter.

Her Grace pushed her plate away with a huff, and silence reigned until a footman entered bearing the dessert trifle.

Diana was never so happy to see a meal end, nor ever so relieved that the gentlemen decided to forego the tradition of leaving the ladies alone whilst they partook of port and cigars. She felt as if she'd been through a war of sorts, for surely lethal words had been volleyed. And she simply could not bear another skirmish.

Good nights were said quickly, and publicly. There was no time for a private word with Adam, which, of course, was just as it should be!

The bright sun was at odds with Diana's gloomy mood the next morning. She and Papa would be leaving today; there was no longer any reason to stay. She knew it was for the best, and yet . . . and yet she could not bear the thought that she might

110

never see Adam again. They would go their separate ways and life would go on. It was all for the best.

She resolved to put a cheerful face on it as she donned her own blue merino wool dress and made her way belowstairs.

Breakfast was a far more pleasant affair than dinner had been, the duchess never emerging from her chamber before noon. Edward stayed only a short while, wanting to get back to Georgie, who, he reported, had spent a restful night and appeared stronger. Papa had already seen Georgie and agreed that she appeared much improved, as did little Ned, who was suckling vigorously. But Papa warned Edward that Georgie still had need of a great deal of rest.

Adam seemed pensive, despite his attempts to make conversation. His eyes rested far too often and far too intently on Diana for her peace of mind. She assured herself she would not miss the penetrating gaze of those tawny eyes.

After breakfast Diana went to say a few words to Georgie. And then she joined her father, Adam, and Edward belowstairs. It was time to leave; there was no reason to delay. Nor did she wish to, she reminded herself. Delay would only mean having to see the duchess again. Circumstances had brought Diana here; she did not belong here. Of a certain she would stay away whilst Her Grace was in residence. After that, Diana hoped she and Georgie might pick up the threads of their tentative friendship.

As to Adam, it was best that they'd not had time again to be private, was it not? They had said all there was to say, had they not?

Edward said a heartfelt farewell. Papa went outside to see about the carriage; his horse would be tied behind. Diana made to follow, but Adam detained her with a hand on her arm. She felt his warmth, even through the folds of her cloak. She couldn't bear it; it was a warmth she would never feel again. She looked down at the hand and back up at him, silently imploring him to remove it. He obeyed, and she told herself it was for the best.

"Diana, I have not had the opportunity to apologize for—for my mother's behavior. I—"

"Adam," she interrupted him, looking up into those compelling tawny eyes, letting her own eyes scan his

111

handsome, hawklike face. She wondered when, or if, she would ever see him again, for she did not imagine he would stay very long, now his mother was in residence. She swallowed the lump in her throat and told herself it was for the best. "Adam, you need not apologize. You are not responsible for the words of another. And besides, I—I think it is you who bear the brunt of it."

How on earth, he wondered, did she know so much about him, understand so much, in the space of so little time? He doubted she would return whilst his mother was here. Indeed, he did not know how much longer *he* could endure. Would he never see Diana Rustin again? "Never" seemed so final, and yet, in all the times he'd come to visit Georgie since her marriage, he'd never met Diana. He very well might not have, had it not been for extraordinary circumstances, and it was doubtful they would meet again.

Which was as it should be! he reminded himself. And yet, he had never seen eyes such a deep, velvety blue, never felt skin as soft and smooth, nor kissed—dear God! What the devil was wrong with him?

He told himself to back away from her; they stood two feet apart. Instead he moved closer. Slowly, he lifted his hand.

He was going to touch her, she thought, perhaps stroke her cheek. She mustn't allow it; she could not move. She remembered the feel of his large, gentle hand on her bare skin and lowered her lashes. She heard him sigh and lower his hand. She looked up and she knew he'd fought an inner battle. She told herself the outcome was for the best.

It shocked him that he ached so much to touch her, even for a moment. And for that reason he hadn't. But he could not for all the world have prevented his next words, for all he had not planned them.

"Your father means to come check on Georgie and Ned every day. Come with him," he urged softly.

"No, I—I do not think I ought—"

"Oh, but you must," he insisted, a gleam suddenly lighting his eyes. "At the least, whenever you can. After all, Georgie will want to see you, to speak with you."

Diana met his gaze. Yes, she thought, Georgie might wish, despite the presence of her mother, to see Diana. But the light

112

in Adam's eyes, the warmth in his tone, told her he was not only speaking of Georgie. Oh, Adam, she thought as she acquiesced, we are playing with fire, and I am the one likely to be burned. This was *not* at all for the best, and yet she felt as if she'd been given a reprieve.

And Adam thought, as he watched the Rustin carriage lumber down the snow-covered drive, that the fire was already burning him, and he hadn't the least idea of how to put it out.

Chapter 8

Diana busied herself with household chores for the better part of the day. But when she had finished meeting with the housekeeper, caught up on her correspondence, taken lunch with Papa, and mended all the linens she cared to for the day, she found herself unaccustomedly at loose ends. She and Papa were seated before the fire in the library, he with his newspaper, she with a piece of needlepoint that she hardly touched. The late-afternoon sun filtered through the sheer blue curtains of the two large windows to their left.

"Do you want to talk about it, Diana?" Papa's gentle voice jarred her in the silence of the room.

"Talk about what, Papa?" she asked with studied nonchalance, picking up her canvas and needle.

"My dear," he said, peering at her over the newspaper, "this is your papa sitting across from you, not some over-eager swain you wish to fob off. If you wish not to speak of it, I understand, but do not think you can gammon old Rusty into believing there is nothing wrong."

Diana blinked back the sudden moisture in her eyes. "I am fine, Papa, truly. I am no longer a frightened child in need of comfort, nor a heartbroken young girl needing a shoulder to cry on. I am a woman fully grown, and I—I should know better." She swiped at a wayward tear. "'Tis nothing, really. Nothing happened, and I shall be—"

"Perhaps you ought to give it a chance, Diana. He is very taken with you and—"

"Papa," she stopped him, "he is a duke, and I am a doctor's

114

daughter. We are worlds apart."

He folded the paper onto his lap. "And is that the only problem?"

"Of course. What other—"

"Not every man is Robert Easton," he interjected gently.

Diana gave up all pretense of doing the delicate needlework before her. She blinked rapidly, willing the gathered moisture in her eyes to recede. "Oh, Papa, we have been all through this before. There are some women meant to wed, and some not. And truly, I have made my peace with it."

Diana watched the play of emotions flit through her father's eyes. She knew all the things he wanted to say, and didn't, being the dear man he was, because they'd all been said before. Finally she heard his soft sigh of resignation.

"Very well, my dear. You *are* a grown woman, and I shan't interfere. I know you made your peace with it." He picked up his newspaper and buried himself behind it, for all intents and purposes having terminated the conversation. But Diana waited; she knew him well.

"All I *will* say," came a suddenly gruff voice from behind the paper, "is that you don't look very peaceful now."

And there, Diana admitted to herself as the day lengthened, was the very crux of it. Adam Damerest had cut up her peace.

She took tea with Papa, but he was called out after that. She ate a solitary dinner and spent the remainder of the evening alone, all of which gave her time to think. Too much time.

It was hard to believe that after all these years, a man had been able to shake her from the peaceful cocoon she'd spun for herself so long ago. But Adam had, and now there was naught she could do but wait for the discomfitting feelings to pass. She did not know how long it would take. No man had ever engendered within her such warmth, such affinity, such a sweet and tingling coursing through her body. No man had ever kissed her so, discomposed her so. She must stay away from him, yet she had agreed to visit Georgie. Perhaps if she waited a few days before returning to Rossmore, these strange feelings would begin to subside. And when she *did* visit, she would keep her distance from Adam. She had no other choice; as she and Adam had tacitly agreed, there was no future for them. She could not be his mistress; she could not be his wife.

115

It was not only the difference in their stations, although that was part of it. It was that she could not be *anyone's* wife. A strange man whose face she could hardly recall had seen to that, and lest she forget, Robert Easton had driven the point home seven years ago.

She sat now curled up in a wing chair before the fire in her bedchamber. She did not know the hour, only knew that Papa was still out and that she could not sleep. Nor could she hold the painful memories at bay any longer. And so she did not try, but let them pour over her, reminding her why she must keep her distance from Adam Damerest, Duke of Marchmaine.

She had been twelve years old on that cold bleak October day. She'd been playing in the woods behind Three Oaks Cottage, enjoying the sound of the yellow and brown and red leaves crunching beneath her feet. She'd wandered farther than she realized; the cottage was barely visible now. She started to walk back, stopping every now and then to watch a squirrel cart nuts to his hideaway, to watch a bird gather twigs.

And then she heard the sounds. A crunching of leaves, but the tread too heavy to be any of the small creatures who frequented these woods. It was not late; she doubted either Papa or Mrs. Barrett, the housekeeper, would be looking for her. She caught a glimpse of a large man through the curtain of trees. She noticed a battered hat and a thin coat that seemed inadequate to the coldness of the day.

Her first thought was that he was lost; after all, no one had reason to be here. And so she stepped forward until he was within hearing distance and asked him if that was indeed the case.

The man did not answer, but his small, ferretlike eyes took on a very strange look as he moved closer to her. His eyes were all Diana could recall now about his face, that and a certain redness to his nose. She spoke again, but he only grunted in response. His unwillingness or inability to speak frightened her more than his appearance. She took a step back; he advanced quickly toward her and began tugging at her cloak. Her first thought was that he was cold, that he wanted the warm cloak.

He did not want the cloak, but by the time she realized that it was far too late. She ran, but he caught her easily. She struggled but could not prevent him from throwing her to the ground, tearing at her clothes. He was a very big man and she was small and delicate. Even as she fought him she knew she could not stop him. Even as she screamed she knew there was no one to hear.

She was twelve years old and she was terrified. Diana shuddered now at the memory. She had not known what this rough, foul-smelling man wanted from her. His dirty hands were pawing at her skin, touching her in places that—And when she finally understood what it was he really meant to do to her, she began to moan, and cry uncontrollably. The pain was unbearable; she felt as if he were tearing her body in half. She shrieked, and then suddenly everything went black.

When she came to, she was alone, broken and bleeding on the cold, hard ground. She lay there whimpering, wanting to die, for a very long time, until the cold seeping into her very bones grew too much for her. She staggered to her feet. And that was when she realized that he *had* taken her cloak, after all.

Diana sighed now and drew a handkerchief from the pocket of her dressing gown and dabbed at her wet cheeks. It was rare that she allowed that scene to replay in her mind. But when she did, she did not try to stop the tears that trickled out.

She settled back into the wing chair and allowed herself to remember the rest of it.

Mama had been gone two years by then. It was Papa who cared for her, Papa and dear Mrs. Barrett, who made certain not another soul ever found out what had happened.

Diana's body healed surprisingly quickly. Her mind and heart were slower to heal, but heal they did, though she'd never have believed it possible that terrible October day. It was all Papa's doing. He spent countless hours with her, holding her and soothing her and explaining about men and women. He told her that the man in the woods was little more than an animal, that few men were like that. He made her understand that what had happened was not her fault, that she was beautiful and worthy and good, and that someday a man would come along who would love her and marry her and teach her all that was wonderful between a man and a woman. For that which transpired between a man and a woman in the marriage

117

bed was the most beautiful experience on God's earth, Papa said.

And Diana believed him. She never forgot what happened, but it stopped haunting her, stopped making her fearful. She realized one day that she was happy and whole; she could go on with her life. And when Papa told her the man, who had been run to ground because of the cloak, had died in an alehouse brawl, Diana was able to put it entirely behind her. Or so she thought.

The years passed. Diana grew to womanhood, and Papa began taking her to the assemblies in York to meet suitable young men. She went with the same excitement as every young girl. She wanted to make a love match. She did not fear the marriage bed, in truth did not think of her past much beyond knowing that she would have to tell her husband-to-be about it before the wedding. Papa assured her it would not make a difference to a man who loved her, and she believed him.

Sir Robert Easton was the embodiment of her dreams. They met the summer of her nineteenth year, and it took only two months for Robert to make his offer and for Diana to joyfully accept. And that very night, when he offered and she accepted and he kissed her for the first time, Diana completely forgot about the evil man in her past and what she had got to tell Robert.

He was away for three days after that, and so she could not tell him; but she did not trouble overmuch about it. It had to be said, but Robert would smile and take her hand and gently tell her that it made no difference. It was all in the past and had naught to do with them now. In the meantime the news of their betrothal travelled all over Yorkshire, and Diana went about in a haze of bliss.

And then Robert returned and she told him. But he did not smile. He did not take her hand. And his words were anything but gentle. Diana shifted in the wing chair now, her eyes burning as she stared into the fire. She recalled that afternoon as if it were yesterday.

Robert's face had gone rigid with tension at her words. She could feel him withdrawing from her, even though he did not move.

"This changes things," he said tautly.

118

"What—what does it change, Robert? I do not understand," she said softly, reaching her hands out toward him.

He did not take her hands. He stepped back and went to stand at the open window of the front parlor. He turned to face her, hands behind his back.

"You must see that it makes a difference, Diana. You are not—that is, my family is an old and noble one. Our lineage is impeccable. Please try to understand, my dear, that I cannot mar the purity of my ancient bloodlines with—"

"Mar the purity?" she echoed with dawning horror. "Robert, what—what happened was not my fault. Surely you—"

"I am sorry, Diana," he interrupted, shaking his blond head. "If I had only myself to consider, perhaps—well, but there is my family. I cannot do it."

She felt a sense of panic rise up in her as she began to see she could not sway him. In a last attempt, she threw pride to the winds and ran across the room to him. She put her hand on his arm and tried to keep her voice from quivering. "Robert, three days ago you—you held me in your arms and told me you love me. And I love you. I am still the same person I was then. How can you throw away all that we—"

"Please, Diana," he said calmly, too calmly. He lifted her hand from his sleeve. "Do not make this harder than it is. I truly wish it were otherwise, my dear, but I know my duty and I cannot shirk it. As it was, there was some talk in the family about you being a doctor's daughter, but your own charm and the fact that you *are*, after all, the great granddaughter of an earl quite scotched that objection. But this—this is something else entirely."

"B-but no one need know," she whispered, knowing that she was virtually begging but that she could not live with herself did she not try to do all she could to sway him.

"But *I* would know, Diana. I would always know that I was not the first."

This time it was not a wave of panic that overtook her, but nausea. *Now* she truly understood. "'Tisn't really your family at all, is it, Robert? 'Tis *you*. Your—your manhood cannot bear this knowledge."

"'Tis all of the above, Diana," he said wearily, then turned

119

to stare out the window. "I will, of course, allow you to be the one to cry off. Even though 'tis only been three days, word has spread about the countryside, and I sent an announcement to the *Gazette*. I'll—I'll send a retraction. And of course, I shall never repeat a word of this conversation."

Diana stepped back from him, feeling cold tentacles wrap themselves around her heart. "Very well," she heard herself say quietly, with an attempt to salvage her pride. She nudged her chin up, determined not to cry in front of this man who had suddenly become a stranger.

"I wish there were another way," he added. Did he, she wondered, but knew it did not signify. Nothing did. "As it is, I—ah—you may put it about that we decided we should not suit."

She merely nodded, not trusting her voice. He stared down at her, his eyes warm for the first time since she'd told her story. But he made no move to touch her. She did not know what she would have done if he had. Part of her yearned for him to reach out to her, to relent, to take back what he had said. Yet the coldness had already seeped into her heart, and part of her wanted never to see him again.

The choice was not hers. After what seemed endless minutes he whispered, "Goodbye, Diana."

She did not know how she managed the requisite, "Goodbye, Robert," but she did. He turned and left the room.

She never saw him again.

Diana swiped at her cheeks now with the handkerchief again, remembering it all as she stared into the fire. She had stood alone in the middle of the front parlor once he'd left. The day was overwarm, but she'd felt cold and clammy. And then suddenly she'd begun to shiver uncontrollably. She'd sunk to the carpet, and there Mrs. Barrett had found her and called Papa. The two had gotten her into bed. Mrs. Barrett had undressed her, and Papa had come with his black bag.

But there was nothing wrong with her, physically, and nothing in Papa's bag could fix what *was* wrong. She told Papa the whole, and as he had once before, he held her and soothed her and told her she was good and beautiful and worthy and that she would one day find the right man. Robert had obviously not been that man.

120

And Diana felt soothed and comforted by his presence; but she was not a little girl anymore, and she knew Papa was wrong.

She might be good, she might even be beautiful—enough people had told her so—but she was not, and never would be, worthy. Robert's words played themselves over in her mind. "You may put it about that we decided we should not suit . . . should not suit . . . should not suit." What he had meant was that *she* would not suit. She was not suitable, nor ever would be. She was tainted. And she cringed as she recalled his other, damning words, "I would always know I was not the first."

No man could ever be the first for her, and she finally came to understand, that warm summer day, that she could never marry.

In a way this whole episode with Robert was worse than what had happened when she was twelve. Oh, there was no physical violence this time, but there was a dreadful sense of betrayal that left a gaping hole in her heart. For Robert *had* betrayed her, declaring his love and then reneging.

And what made this far, far worse was that as a child, despite what had happened, she'd been left with hope. She'd eventually been able to put it behind her. But now she knew there *was* no hope, and she would never entirely put it behind her.

For she came to understand in the succeeding days, as she wandered silently about the house and gardens, seeing no one, that Papa had not lied to her. He had told her the truth as he'd known it. *His* truth. He had been passionately devoted to Mama and would have stood by her no matter what. But Diana had met many men, had seen many married couples together. And she suspected that most men were governed more by pride than love. Most men were like Robert, not like Papa.

And never again would she give a man the opportunity to hurt her so badly. Diana stood now and walked to the fire, stoking it gently with the poker. She had made that vow seven years ago, and she had kept it. She had cried her heart out all those years ago, and grieved for her lost love even as she realized that she'd never really known him at first stop. She'd loved an illusion. Eventually she had recovered her equanimity, although there was always a certain cold, empty feeling

121

in her heart that never quite left her. She had gone on with the business of living. She had not gone again to the assemblies at York. She had not flirted, nor encouraged any young men who came her way, despite Papa's entreaties. She had made a life for herself, different, of a certain, than the one she'd envisioned as a young girl, but a rewarding, peaceful life nonetheless.

And no one, no man, had succeeded in cutting up her peace. Until now. Dear God, she must not let this happen! She must stay away from Adam Damerest. Only heartache awaited her if she followed the path toward the Duke of Marchmaine. She had got to remember who and what she was. She had got to stay away from him.

Diana did not accompany her father to Rossmore Manor the next morning, despite his best efforts to persuade her to do so. When he returned home midday to take luncheon with her, he reported that Georgie was still weak but not looking quite as peaked. He also said that "everyone" had asked for her and that Georgie, especially, seemed most eager to speak with her. Diana felt her heart begin to sink, even as her mind began inventing excuses as to why she could not go. But she knew the excuses would avail her naught when Papa added that Edward had invited them both to Sunday dinner.

That was two days hence, and Diana knew there was no hope for it. For whilst she might make some excuse not to accompany Papa on his rounds tomorrow, she could not be so rude as to refuse a direct invitation. Edward was her friend, after all, and she suspected Georgie wanted to become one. Then there was her promise to Adam. So she would go on Sunday, have a long, comfortable cose with Georgie, and avoid being private with Adam. And then she would not return until she knew he'd left Rossmore. It was the only way.

Papa spent the afternoon in Midvale visiting Mrs. Caldwell and her twins, and Diana made the rounds close to home. The sun shone, melting the snow, and Diana found herself wishing for another storm. Then, perhaps, she would not have to go. . . .

And she told herself, as she made an almost frantic effort to keep busy and avoid excessive rumination all day Saturday, that she was not looking forward to Sunday. She did not miss Adam Damerest, his smiles, his frowns, the warmth of even his most casual touch. And she told herself, when she awoke to bright sunlight on Sunday morning, that she did not feel a brief surge of joy that it had, indeed, not snowed these two days past.

Neither she nor Papa made it to church that morning, there being several emergency calls to attend to. She went to see the two Porter children, who had taken a chill whilst playing out in the snow, and Papa went to minister to old Mrs. Conniston's rheumy joints. The morning passed quickly, and Diana told herself she did not feel a sense of anticipation as the carriage made its way over the partly melted snow to Rossmore Manor. She had *not* missed Adam, she reminded herself.

They were merely friends of brief acquaintance; had they not agreed upon it? There would be no warmth in his tawny eyes when he greeted her. She would not allow him to touch her. She would smile and murmur platitudes and spend as much time closeted with Georgie as possible.

It was evident as soon as Stebbins admitted them that all was not well at Rossmore. Stebbins' smile of welcome was forced. Two maids scurried about as if afraid of their own shadows. There was a palpable tension in the air, its source made quite obvious by the shouting coming from the morning room.

"Damnation, Mother!" Adam's voice exploded from behind the partially opened door. Stebbins looked chagrined. Diana froze. Papa's lips twitched. None of them moved as Adam went on. "It was the outside of enough for you to invite Lady Truesdale here. That is not why I agreed to take you to church. Georgie is hardly up to visitors and—"

"None of which stopped you from inviting that ridiculous Winifred Hartcup," the duchess interrupted waspishly, "nor, I might add, that doctor and his daughter!"

"Rusty and Diana are close friends of mine," Edward said tautly. *"They* are welcome any time."

"And as to Lady Hart and Sir Horace, I included them, even though I had just met them, because they were standing *right there* when you were gushing all over Lady Truesdale. Besides, Lady Hart is quite charming. That Truesdale woman is a viper," Adam said disdainfully. It was clear he was fast losing patience with his mother, and with it his customary civility.

123

Diana wondered how much the duchess had pushed him to bring him to this pass.

Stebbins at that moment seemed to recover himself and took a step forward. But Papa forestalled him and took Diana's arm. "Chin up, my child. Here we go."

Papa's unfailing good humor was contagious, and she found herself sternly repressing a chuckle as they pushed the door open.

"And," the duchess was saying, "as to allowing Georgie to speak to that doctor's daughter—" The duchess's mouth froze, quite open, as the subject of her disparaging words appeared at the threshold.

"Do go on, Duchess," Papa said genially, "you mustn't let us stop you. Good afternoon, Edward, Adam."

Edward's face was red as he came forward to greet them. Adam followed, but there was a decided gleam in his amber eyes. He shook Papa's hand and then turned to Diana, taking her gloved hand and raising it to his lips. She did not want to feel that jolt at his touch, nor the heat of his lips even through the barrier of her gloves. But she did.

"Welcome back," he murmured softly, but the warmth in his eyes said, *I'm glad you came.*

"Thank you," she uttered in return, but her eyes were pleading, *Please do not look at me that way.*

He released her hand, and Papa turned to greet the duchess. "You've been eavesdropping!" she exclaimed in umbrage.

Edward gasped, but Papa chuckled softly. "No, dear lady. I fear it was rather that *you* were shouting."

This time it was the duchess who gasped, and Diana made haste to inquire after Georgie and Ned.

"Ned is doing quite well," Edward replied, "and Georgie is better, but she has been somewhat—ah—" He paused, glancing at the duchess.

"Agitated," Adam finished for him, frowning at his mother.

Oh, dear, Diana thought. Her Grace had obviously not brought peace and harmony with her. And now she meant to visit Lady Truesdale upon them as well. Adam was right; the woman was a viper. And her son Percy was worse. Diana shuddered inwardly as she remembered her last encounter with that rather repulsive libertine. She sincerely hoped neither meant

124

to make an appearance this afternoon.

Luncheon was the same tense affair that she supposed all meals taken with Katherine, Duchess of Marchmaine, were. Few people, few matters pertaining to the running of Rossmore Manor, escaped her barbed tongue. The excellent glazed ham and the hapless Mrs. Brownlow were no exception. It was obvious that the issue of the cook was far from over. Edward gritted his teeth when Her Grace brought it up, and Papa neatly changed the subject.

After luncheon they all retired to the family drawing room, and Papa excused himself to go to see Georgie. Edward made a valiant attempt to play the gracious host, but the duchess sorely tried everyone's patience. And when Stebbins appeared, needing Edward's assistance upon some household matter, Edward barely tried to hide his relief at having the excuse to leave.

That left Diana, Adam, and Her Grace. For several moments the silence was palpable. Diana glanced at Adam, standing at the carved and gilt chimneypiece. Today he wore a bottle green coat that fit superbly on his long lean frame. His doeskin pantaloons stretched tautly across his thighs. . . .

She swallowed hard and forced her eyes upward. He met her gaze, the expression in his tawny eyes telling her he wished his mother at Jericho. For one fleeting moment so did Diana; then she reminded herself it was best this way.

It was Diana who broke eye contact, turning in time to see an almost malevolent look on the duchess's face. Adam must have noted it as well, for he launched into a spirited conversation about his nephew's probable eye color and purported attempts to smile. Diana agreed that the baby's eyes did indeed look the same shade of gray as Georgie's, but demurred upon the matter of the smile.

"For what seems to be a smile at this very tender age is more often than not a disturbance of the belly, you must know," she said with a twinkle in her eye.

Adam grinned. "Ah, but our Ned is most precocious. Is that not so, Mother?"

The duchess, sitting ramrod straight on a Hepplewhite chair that looked far too delicate to hold her ample weight, smiled in a manner that puckered her thick lips and left her eyes cold.

"Of a certain Miss Rustin must know better, Adam dear. After all, *she* is the midwife, not I." Her tone implied all the ignominy usually attached to that profession, her withering glance all the disdain reserved for any common lightskirt.

The woman was so odious that Diana decided she simply could not take her seriously. Adam, however, did. Though her eyes were still fixed on his mother, Diana could feel Adam's anger rising. She turned to see his fists clench and a vein throb at his temple. He stalked from his stance at the mantel toward where she and the duchess sat at right angles from each other, on either side of the rococo sofa table. How had he, in the space of less than a se'nnight, become her champion? It seemed impossible, and yet there it was. And much as she did not wish to be a bone of contention between mother and son, Adam's reaction warmed her, far too well.

"Mother," he growled, towering over the large woman in her stiff, olive green bombazine dress, "I am certain—"

What he was certain was never revealed, for, providentially, Papa put his head in at that moment to inform Diana that Georgie was asking for her. He did not linger, but walked on down the corridor, murmuring something about returning shortly. Diana jumped up, never so grateful for an interruption. The close proximity of her chair to that of the duchess, and Adam's stance directly in front of the two, made it necessary for Diana to brush between him and the ivory damask sofa before making her way to the door. She paused, expecting him to step back to give her a wider berth. For a moment he did not move, and she realized that he did not want her to go. His hold on his temper was tenuous at best, and it came to her in a flash that it was only her presence that kept him from unleashing it.

At length he stepped back and allowed her to sidle past him. "Excuse me," she murmured, and made her way to the door. But he followed her. She turned just before the door, and he stopped a foot away. His stance effectively blocked his mother from Diana's view.

She met his gaze, trying to convey without words that it was all right, that he needn't be in such a taking on her account. But still the vein throbbed at his temple. His long, lean panther's body was taut with tension.

"Adam, what *were* you saying?" the duchess demanded from behind him. Adam ignored her; the only indication that he'd heard her was the clenching of his fists. Diana felt the overwhelming urge to soothe him, to calm him. A look was not enough, yet she was afraid to touch him. She did not want to feel his warmth, and besides, it was not her way to reach out and touch a man, any man, except Papa.

Nonetheless, her hand rose and settled gently on Adam's forearm. She saw the startled look on his face and followed his eyes as he looked down at their joined arms. She felt his heat and closed her eyes as it coursed through her. And she felt the rigid tension of his muscles ease. She opened her eyes and raised them to his. The intensity of his gaze caused her breath to catch in her throat.

"I—I must go to Georgie now," she stammered.

He smiled faintly; the vein no longer throbbed at his temple.

"Adam!" snapped the duchess.

Again he ignored her. He covered Diana's hand with his large one for the briefest moment. "It's all right now. Go," he whispered.

And then he opened the door for her.

Diana was shaking once the door had closed behind her. Her instinct had been right; her touch had calmed him. Oh, dear! She did not want to have such ability, such . . . power. She had been told before that she had "healing hands," but there was an added element here, even if she could not say precisely what, that made her most uncomfortable.

And worse, Adam had known exactly what was happening. He had been surprised, perhaps, but not at all discomfitted by what was, indeed, a brazen overture, made in the presence of his mother, of all things! He had, now she thought on it, actually been pleased. And he had stood thusly with her for what seemed endless minutes, but must only have been seconds, and received and reacted to her wordless communication.

The intimacy of the entire scene, his mother notwithstanding, overwhelmed Diana, and she had to stop and take several deep breaths before ascending the stairwell to the family apartments.

Adam had watched her leave the family drawing room and

127

wondered if she was as shaken as he by their encounter. Never had a woman had such an effect on him. He'd known desire before, but never had it been stimulated so subtly. Mere proximity to Diana in her modest, form-fitting dress of plum-colored Kerseymere, with her elusive scent, mysterious and yet utterly feminine, would have been enough to heat his blood. But when she'd reached out and put her delicate hand on his arm, he'd wanted to pull her close and hold her firmly, his mother be damned!

It was more than desire; he knew it, and it worried him not a little. He'd wanted, needed, to protect her from his mother. He'd never felt the need to protect a female before, with the exception of Georgie.

And he'd never before missed a woman in her absence. He was restless by nature, quite content to flit from one woman to the next, never regretting for a moment the passing of each through his life. But he'd missed Diana these few days past. He'd missed her and did not like the fact one whit.

And then there was the other matter, which shook him perhaps the most of all. Her touch had inflamed him, but it had calmed him at the same time. He had felt his anger slipping away, felt the muscles in his chest and neck and arms relax, even as another part of him had tightened painfully.

Dear God! She was a complication he did not need, for many reasons. One of those reasons, he realized, had risen from her chair and walked toward him, gazing at him with a very odd, speculative look in her dark brown eyes.

"She is a guest in this house, Mother, a friend to Edward, Georgie, and me," he said quietly, with steel beneath his tone. "I find your innuendoes unconscionable, and I would have them cease."

She drew herself up. "Adam, can you not see her for what she is? Do you not see she means to trap—"

"That is enough, Mother!" he barked, and stormed from the room without a backward glance.

Chapter 9

Diana found Georgie sitting up in bed, attired in a frothy pink bed jacket and looking decidedly fretful. Or, she amended, perhaps Adam's word—"agitated"—was more apt. Little Ned was gone from his cradle, and Georgie would say only that Edward was with him in his own chamber. Why Edward had not stayed with Georgie whilst he spent time with his son went unexplained, as did the reason for Georgie's agitation.

They spoke of her health—her slowly returning strength, how often she had ought to get up and walk about—for several minutes. And then the conversation turned to platitudes. Diana knew of a certain that Georgie wished to speak of more, but she could not draw the baroness out.

Edward, carrying the child, entered the room as they were speaking of the likelihood of more snow in the next se'nnight. And that was when Diana realized exactly what was wrong. Edward smiled briefly at Diana. Then he set the blanket-swathed babe down gently in the cradle at the foot of the four-poster bed.

"He's sleeping," Edward said rather curtly to his wife, his jaw barely moving, his mouth tight.

"Yes," she replied coldly, her face shuttered but her hands, fidgeting with the bedclothes, belying her outer calm.

"Well, I'll leave you two, then," Edward said, casting a meaningful glance toward Diana before striding from the chamber.

Diana almost breathed a sigh of relief when he left; the tension between the baron and baroness had been palpable. It was clear Edward wanted her to say something to his wife. She supposed she had ought to speak to Georgie of her mother and grandmother, but one did not simply launch into such discourse out of the blue. Diana had got to wait for Georgie to broach, once again, the topic of her difficulties with Edward. She had alluded to them in those first hours after Ned's birth, but now Edward was home, and her mother was here, and she mightn't wish to speak of it at all.

But she did. After just a few moments of pulling threads from her comforter and looking everywhere but at Diana, Georgie suddenly heaved a sigh that sounded much like a stifled sob.

"I don't know what to do, Diana. Edward and I have had the most dreadful row. Again. I would not dream of burdening you with my—my personal troubles, except that you and your papa are trusted friends of the family. And besides, Adam keeps telling me I needs must speak with you."

Diana smiled and pulled her chair closer to the bed. "I fear Adam gives me too much credit. I know only what my observations, in the course of my work, show me, and what I learned from my family. But I have never been wed. There is much I do not know."

Georgie laughed mirthlessly. "Yet being wed almost two years has not afforded *me* any special knowledge. If anything, I am more confused now than when I was a bride." She looked away and lowered her voice. "Then I thought that if we loved each other, it would be enough."

She turned her head back, and now her eyes were moist. "I cannot seem to do anything right anymore. I missed him so much when he was away, and he is home less than a se'nnight and we've already come to dagger points several times."

"This is a difficult time, Georgie. You have a new babe, your strength is at a low ebb, there are visitors . . ."

"Yes." She lowered her eyes. "I fear Edward does not like Mama very much."

That, Diana thought, was rather an understatement. She searched for the right words. "I believe your mama can be . . . difficult."

"*I* do not have any problems getting on with her."

Diana took a deep breath. "I know that, Georgie. I believe it

130

is the—ah—gentlemen who find her a bit . . . trying."

Georgie bit her lip. "I daresay you are in the right of it. She and Adam are forever at loggerheads. And Adam tells me—for I do not recall—that Mama and Papa were the same. Diana, I—I do not want Edward and I to—to brangle all the time. But somehow we are either in the midst of a set-to, or trying so very hard to avoid it."

"What—what happened today, Georgie?" Diana asked after several moments.

Georgie shrugged. "'Twas a little thing, really. I merely commented that I liked the way Adam looked in his pantaloons, that they are all the crack now and that I did wish Edward would be a bit more fashionable."

"Ah."

"Truly, Diana, he looks the veritable rustic in those britches of his. Of course, they are completely declassé in London—well, except for formal evening attire, that is. But even in the country it is not at all the thing. Mama travels all about, visiting in the best country houses, you must know, and she says—"

"Er, Georgie, forgive me, but I do not think Edward would be much impressed with your mama's observations of country house dress."

Georgie sighed. "I fear you are in the right of it once again. Why, Edward flew into a veritable pelter when I so much as mentioned it! It is most provoking, you may be sure. He is setting up a riot and a rumpus over a mere trifle."

Diana took another deep breath. She did not know why or how she understood the matter; but somehow she did, and she needs must choose her words carefully. "But do you not see, Georgie, that to Edward 'tis not a mere trifle at all. To him it seems that you are putting the opinion of others above his comfort."

"But it would please me so very much if—"

"Georgie, my grandmama once told me that a woman's primary concern in marriage must be to make her husband happy. And that he in turn would make *her* happiness the most important thing in the world to him. Can you say, in truth, that it is of Edward's happiness that you are thinking when you suggest he set aside his britches for pantaloons?"

Georgie narrowed her gray eyes. "No," she admitted at length, then pursed her lips petulantly. "I suppose I hoped my husband would wish to please *me*. But you are saying that *I* must yield. I suppose you will say the same in the matter of Mrs. Brownlow as well." Diana smiled ruefully, and Georgie sighed. "Must we of the fairer sex *always* be so . . . so submissive, then? I do realize we owe obedience to our husbands, but I have not gainsaid a direct order. Must I never think for myself? I do hope I have more spirit than that!"

Diana shifted uncomfortably in her chair. "I have no experience in such matters, Georgie, but I do not believe it is a matter of—of being submissive. My mama and papa were at loggerheads for many years, you must know. Then, to hear Papa tell it, Mama went to Grandmama—Papa's mother—for help. For she could bear the dissension no longer, you see."

"But what could your grandmama have done?"

Diana smiled and told her something of the natures of her mother and grandmother. "So you see," she went on, "Grandmama was a woman of unusual serenity. Everyone adored her, especially Grandpapa. But she was quite spirited, if memory serves. She was never afraid to speak her mind, yet it was she who taught Mama that—that she alone had the power to completely change her marriage. Not by being submissive, Georgie. Papa would never have wanted a submissive wife."

"What—what did your mama do?" Georgie asked hesitantly. Diana was not certain she wished to hear the answer.

"She made a decision not to brangle with Papa any longer. To please him, to put his comfort and happiness above all else. It was not submissive, for 'twas *her* decision, you see. And Papa told me that once she did that, *he* wanted only to please *her*! They were used to have the most famous rows over an old chair that sat in the front parlor. It was Papa's favorite but was sadly threadbare, and Mama wanted to send it to the upholsterer to be refurbished. But Papa liked it well-worn, with the cushions all soft and molded to his frame. And he refused to part with it even for a few days. I was very young, but I do remember once, after some high-born lady had paid a morning call, Mama angrily proclaiming that she would not entertain another guest in the mortifying presence of Papa's chair!"

"Diana, do you not think your Papa was being a trifle unreasonable?"

"Oh, yes," Diana agreed cheerfully. "But you see, the chair was much beside the point. Papa simply wanted to know that he and his comfort were more important than the opinion of Lady Whoever-She-Was."

"Rather like Edward and his britches?" Georgie ventured reluctantly.

"Yes, I think so," Diana concurred. "And Mama, I do assure you, got exactly what she wanted in the end. One day she told Papa she understood how much he liked the chair as it was, and that she would no longer trouble him about refurbishing it. Papa told me that within a se'nnight, after determining that she really meant it, he told her over breakfast that he thought a mauve velvet would look especially fine on his chair."

Georgie brushed moisture from her eyes. "I—I understand what you are trying to tell me, Diana. Perhaps Edward would react in like manner. I do not know. But it all seems—forgive me—but it seems rather childish on the part of those who purport to be the stronger sex."

Diana chuckled. "I have watched enough women struggle in childbirth, and seen their husbands' reactions, to seriously doubt which is the weaker sex. But that is neither here nor there, Georgie. You must decide what you want. Do you want harmony, and Edward's love, or do you wish to uphold what you believe to be right and reasonable?"

Georgie twisted the comforter that lay across her lap. "It would not be easy," she murmured.

"No, I imagine not."

"I think Mama has always upheld what is right. Or what she believes is right."

"Yes. I am persuaded that is so."

Georgie's eyes filled with moisture. "Papa died when I was twelve, but still I recall the wretched brangles he and Mama were used to have. And even more, I remember Papa's long and sullen silences. I do not want a life like that." She swiped at the tears gathering in her eyes. "But—but Edward is not always right, you know, nor reasonable," she added with a touch of defiance.

"No, I don't suppose he is," Diana concurred calmly.

133

"Yet you are saying that *I* must yield!"

Diana shrugged. "It seems to me, in my limited experience, that with gentlemen it is simply the most expedient way." She took Georgie's hand and grinned. "And you must remember it does not mean you shan't get exactly what you wish in the end."

Georgie grinned back and squeezed her hand in return. "You—you will not tell Edward of our conversation, will you?"

"I would not dream of repeating it to any gentleman of my acquaintance," Diana replied gravely.

Georgie burst into giggles. "Oh, Diana, I am going to like having you as a friend. Very well, indeed."

Diana had insisted that Georgie lie down and rest, and then made her way belowstairs. She was quite pleased with the way her talk with Georgie had gone and hoped her new friend would be able to change how matters stood between herself and Edward. Diana knew *she* had done all she could.

She realized, as she descended the last few steps to the main floor, that it was undoubtedly time for Papa and her to leave. Luncheon was over, and they had each seen Georgie. Yet Diana did not want to leave, and she knew very well why, even as she berated herself for the reason. She and Adam had naught of a personal nature to discuss; they had no reason, and no right, to be private with each other. He had asked her to return for a visit, and so she had done. But the visit was over.

Or so she thought. Once on the main floor, she turned in the direction of the family drawing room, where everyone had previously been gathered. But it was through the double doors of the morning room that she heard voices. She recognized the duchess's voice and Papa's, and caught the murmur of others. She hesitated in the corridor. Not a moment later Stebbins appeared, smiling warmly at her as he stepped forward silently to open the double doors that she might enter.

Her eyes went immediately, unerringly to Adam. He stood at the hearth, a decided frown creasing his brow. He looked up at her entrance, and for just a moment his tawny eyes danced as he raised his brows in exasperation, then surreptitiously let his gaze sweep the room. Diana's eyes followed his.

Papa and Edward, still unaware of her presence, lounged in the matching powder blue wing chairs to the right of the hearth. On the yellow chintz sofa facing the hearth sat the duchess in her olive green dress and Eleanor, Lady Truesdale, in a dove gray carriage dress. Between them sat Lady Truesdale's daughter, Lucy, a young lady just out of the schoolroom. Diana's heart sank, even as her eyes continued scanning the room. As she feared, Lady Truesdale's son, Sir Percival, stood in the window embrasure, facing them all. His arms were crossed at his chest, and his handsome face bore the look of practiced ennui. He was immaculately groomed, as always, in a coat of navy superfine and a pristine white shirt. His sandy hair was meticulously combed, and his light gray eyes, so like his mother's, were cold.

They had always been cold. She and Percy had long known each other but had not met all that frequently as children. And on those brief occasions his pale gray eyes had conveyed all the disdain he felt for one of lesser station. But then she'd grown up, and the look in those eyes had changed. They had become predatory, very interested, but just as cold. She shuddered inwardly as she recalled the one time, many years ago, when she had been unfortunate enough to find herself alone in a corridor with Percy. He had backed her into a corner, and though he hadn't done more than stroke her arm, he'd made it clear with his words and his pale eyes exactly what he wanted of her.

His intentions had not been honorable, and she remembered how cold his touch had made her feel, how repulsed she had been.

It came to her in a flash that Adam's intentions were also not honorable, yet she was certainly not repulsed by him. Of course, Adam's intentions were not exactly *dis*honorable either, but she knew marriage to her, were *she* so inclined, would be out of the question for him. She might be the great granddaughter of an earl, but she was also a mere doctor's daughter and, far worse, something of a midwife. Clearly she was not an eligible partí, and Adam had made it plain that he was not hanging out for a wife. But when he touched her, she did not feel cold at all. Her eyes now sought him out again, and

135

she flushed at the thought of just what he did make her feel.

Thankfully, no one else seemed to have noted her presence, and as polite conversation continued, she moved silently forward. Adam pushed himself away from the mantel; but in that moment Percy's eyes shifted, and he espied her.

"Ah, Diana, you've come to join us," Percy said effusively, striding toward her. She caught Adam's frown out of the corner of her eye, and was aware of Edward and Papa rising, but none could reach her before Percy.

He took her hand and brought it to his lips. She felt that same shudder of repulsion his touch always engendered, but this time she did not try to repress it. Adam was watching, and for some reason she did not wish him to think she welcomed Percy's attentions.

"Good afternoon, Sir Percival," she said with formal civility, and caught the tightening of his smile. He disliked her use of his title, preferring the informality they had shared as children. But they were no longer children, and though she still thought of him as Percy, she refused to call him that.

Adam felt himself relax slightly at Diana's formal greeting of Truesdale. Adam had never cared for Truesdale and cared even less for his familiarity toward Diana. But at the least she did not return it. If Adam was not much mistaken, she fairly recoiled when Truesdale took her hand and pressed his lips to it. Adam told himself he was relieved at her reaction because he did not want her to join the ranks of Truesdale's flirts. He did not want her to be hurt. It was not, he reminded himself, that he was jealous. After all, they were merely friends. . . .

Truesdale seated her in the Queen Anne chair to the left of the sofa, then proceeded to draw up a stool and position himself next to her. Edward and Rusty resumed their seats; Adam gritted his teeth. Everyone greeted Diana, and then Lady Truesdale shifted the conversation back to the fascinating topic of the latest styles in men's cravats.

Adam reluctantly retired to the mantel. He abhorred these sorts of gatherings, where one was obliged to do the pretty with people one disliked. Watching Diana squirm under Truesdale's pointed looks only made it worse.

His gaze flicked to Lady Truesdale. Slightly shorter and rather thinner than his own mother, she had a drawn, disdainful air about her colorless mouth. Her somewhat sparse hair was a silver blue, her chin firm and pointed, her gray eyes as pale and cold as her son's. As a mere baronet's widow, she would, he was certain, have been awed by his mother's superior rank in London. But here in this remote corner of Yorkshire, Lady Truesdale considered that she reigned supreme. That Georgie was of a higher rank and Lady Hartcup of an equivalent one did not deter her from this belief. Georgie was simply too young, and Lady Truesdale was certain the Truesdale wealth and holdings far exceeded those of Rossmore. The fact that the parish bore the name Rossmore and not Truesdale irked Lady Truesdale almost as much as it pleased Adam's mother.

As to Lady Hartcup, neither Eleanor Truesdale nor the duchess took her very seriously. Lady Truesdale had once referred to her as "that dithering, meddlesome matchmaker," and his mother had always decried the fact that Winifred Hartcup had "no regard for her own consequence, let alone anyone else's!"

Adam knew that Lady Hart, as she was affectionately referred to by many, was considered the premiere matchmaker in all the north country. Diana spoke highly of her, and Adam had been quite charmed upon meeting her for the first time this morning. He hoped to have the opportunity to further his acquaintance with her during his stay at Rossmore.

Lady Hart had chosen not to visit today, perhaps out of consideration for Georgie's delicate state. Lady Truesdale, of course, had had no such scruples. She had, in fact, inquired after Georgie and the heir in a most perfunctory manner, before beginning her usual gossip about acquaintances and fashion. But there was a difference in her manner today, and it had taken several moments for Adam to apprehend what she was about.

She and the duchess had an uneasy friendship at best, each constantly trying to outdo the other. Today, however, Lady Truesdale's manner toward his mother was most amicable, and just short of gushing toward *him*. That had made Adam rather suspicious, as she was wont to be guardedly polite and deferential toward him. His mother, much to Adam's disgust, seemed completely disarmed. Good God, Adam thought. Did his mother not see how devious Lady Truesdale was? For Adam had known straightaway that the woman wanted something. And though he might have considered the two dowagers equally unpleasant and difficult, it was borne home to him that Lady Truesdale, with her ability to charm, was quite the more dangerous.

As to what the woman wanted, Adam had discerned that just before Diana's arrival. Eleanor Truesdale's daughter Lucy was just come of age. She was a rather comely little thing, except for the somewhat vapid look in her eyes. Lady Truesdale, when she had finished extolling the unexceptionable Lucy's virtues, had said she meant to convey her to London for the Season. But then she'd turned to Adam and pointedly asked how long he meant to stay at Rossmore. And that was when Adam had known his suspicions were correct—Eleanor Truesdale very much wanted to avoid the bother and expense of the Season. She wanted to procure a husband for dear Lucy right here in Yorkshire, in Rossmore Manor in point of fact.

And so Adam had casually replied that he would no doubt be taking his leave rather soon, as there were pressing matters calling him home to Damerest Hall. Lady Truesdale's mask of sweetness had slipped a trifle, and the duchess had eased the ensuing tension by launching into a discussion of the many varieties of knots for gentlemen's cravats.

Diana's arrival had altered the tension in the room, but not eased it. Lady Truesdale greeted Diana in a dismissive tone, and seemed to regard Percy's obvious interest with an indulgent eye and a barely suppressed smirk. This infuriated Adam, as he understood its cause. For Eleanor Truesdale assumed and accepted that her son merely had dalliance on his mind. She did not at all care for the looks that passed between Adam and Diana, however. And before Adam could forestall her, the woman turned to Diana.

"I understand you are quite the heroine of the week, dear Miss Rustin," she said sweetly, and then went in for the kill. "My congratulations! Oh, but so perturbing it must have been for you to be snowbound here for days, all alone with the duke. Whatever did the two of you *do* for all that time?" she cooed.

Diana paled visibly. Rusty looked like he might have the apoplexy. Adam glared at his mother. How *could* she have spread such gossip after what Diana had done for Georgie? And when in blazes *had* she told Lady Truesdale? They'd not been private today—

A trill of laughter from Lady Truesdale interrupted his thoughts. "Pray do not look so perplexed, Marchmaine. 'Tis all over the neighborhood that Miss Rustin came to the baroness's aid when her Papa was not about. And that Lord Rossmore and Dr. Rustin were seen at the Horsefeathers Inn days later, asking for news of the baroness. So very . . . brave you are, Miss Rustin."

"Yes, she is, Lady Truesdale," Adam countered tautly. "'Twas a difficult birth and she saved Georgie's life. *So* brave and lovely is Miss Rustin, in fact, that I have offered for her. But alas, the good doctor refused, feeling his daughter's reputation to be above reproach. We were, after all, in a house full of servants, not to mention my sister, Baroness of Rossmore." Adam's eyes rested for a moment on Diana. She was doing her damnedest to hide her shock. Of course, Rusty would not have mentioned his offer, wanting to save Diana further distress over the matter. It had been a rather off-handed offer at all events, and Adam, relieved at having his gallantry refused, had not mentioned it to Diana either. Perhaps they had both done her a disservice. "Be that as it may," he went on, "the doctor is aware that my offer still stands. Do you imagine there are minds pretty enough here in Rossmore to create a scandalbroth out of such meager ingredients, dear Lady Truesdale, thereby changing the good doctor's mind?" he finished smoothly.

He knew, without looking, that Diana had regained her color, that Rusty and Edward were silently applauding, and that his mother was furious.

"I cannot think of anyone who would do such a thing, Marchmaine," Lady Truesdale said stiffly. "But I am pleased to note that you are a marriage-minded man. You have been a bachelor for so very long, have you not? Surely 'tis time for you to think about setting up your nursery."

Adam clenched his teeth. His eyes flew to Diana's. She was biting her lip, and he knew she understood his pique. But he was surprised when she spoke up. "I should not be too sure, dear Lady Truesdale; not everyone is disposed to wed. I know *I*

139

am not, else I should have done so years past. I have my work, you see. As for His Grace, his generous offer to me notwithstanding, he once told me that he has a perfectly unexceptionable heir—a second cousin, I believe—with whom he is quite satisfied. And I do know he plans extensive renovations of Damerest Hall. I am persuaded they will keep him in Yorkshire at the least through the summer. And I do not know if there will even *be* a nursery there for years!"

Adam almost applauded. She was truly magnificent in her dress of Bishop's blue, her ebony locks dancing about her face, her deep blue eyes shining as she spoke so earnestly yet subtly on his behalf. He was most grateful, but wished she hadn't. Lady Truesdale looked livid, and his mother's ire intensified. Damnation! Diana did not need their enmity.

"But you know what they say, Eleanor," his mother put in, looking dagger points at Diana and then smiling at Lady Truesdale and Lucy, "no man is of a marrying mind until he meets the right woman. That is the way it was with my dear late husband, and the way it was with Edward."

Edward wisely did not cavil, and conversation thereafter drifted to a second-hand rehash of Lady Hart's annual Valentine's Ball, just over a fortnight ago. For one reason or another, none of them had been able to attend, but his mother and Lady Truesdale seemed quite certain of the details over which they passed negative judgment.

Adam was thinking that it was long past time that the Truesdales left when Lady Truesdale turned to him. "Marchmaine, would you do Lucy the honor of conveying her to see Georgie? She does so want to see the babe, you must know," she said ingenuously. As ingenuous as a serpent, he thought disgustedly.

Rescue came from two quarters. "I'll take her," Edward volunteered. "'Tis time I went up to my wife at all events."

Lady Truesdale opened her mouth to reply, but Rusty forestalled her. "I'm afraid I must be the one to disappoint your dear daughter, Lady Truesdale. Georgie is still in need of a great deal of rest. I cannot allow her to have visitors just yet."

"Well then," Percy Truesdale said, rising languidly, "we shall have to return for another visit." He took Diana's hand again and gazed down at her so pointedly as to leave no one in

140

doubt as to whom he really meant to visit.

Adam was very glad to see the last of them, and equally glad when his mother retired abovestairs to rest before dinner.

He and Edward, Rusty and Diana sprawled comfortably in the morning room in the wake of the others' departure. They seemed to breathe a collective sigh of relief. At first no one spoke, and then they all spoke at once about what a trying hour that had been.

At length Rusty stood. "Diana, I need to be leaving as well. But first I'll go check on Georgie once more."

Adam's mind was suddenly racing. He needed to speak with Diana. She'd been avoiding his eye since the others had left. He could not let her go without—

"Edward, why do you not go with him?" he suggested nonchalantly. "You did say it was time you went to her, did you not?"

Edward frowned, but Rusty, after a look that was a little too pointed, urged him to come along. Adam did not want to think of Rusty's motivation in leaving him alone with Diana. Every one of them knew it was highly improper, and yet no one was stopping it. Edward followed Rusty out without a backward glance.

"Adam," Diana ventured, "I do not think—"

"Diana," he interrupted, having closed the door behind Edward and Rusty, "we need to talk."

He guided her back to the hearth and seated her in one of the powder blue wing chairs. He took the other. The sofa, he knew, was not a good idea. "At first stop, I want to apologize."

She blinked. "For what?"

"When I told Rusty I would offer for you did he wish it, and he demurred, I—I let it go at that. It was proper, I suppose, that I speak only with your father. But somehow it does not seem right. The—the choice should have been yours."

She was sitting back in the chair, a picture of calm and repose, her hands clasped gracefully in her lap. And yet her beautiful face was alive with expression. Forced cheerfulness warred with distress. He could have sworn her eyes misted over for just a moment before she spoke.

"Now, Adam, I thought we were friends. Surely you needn't play the gallant with me! I appreciate the honor of your offer,

141

but we are all agreed, are we not, that 'tis not necessary. And you know very well that I do not care a rush for—for proprieties, and that neither of us is disposed to wed." The words had come out in a rush, the lightheartedness ringing false. And the hands in her lap no longer looked quite so graceful. They were, indeed, twisting in agitation.

Without thinking, he covered her hands with one of his. "Nonetheless," he said softly, "my offer stands."

She bit her lips, shaking her head, and looked down at their hands. Suddenly the air in the room changed, became charged with a new kind of tension. He recognized it for what it was, but did not, as prudence demanded, release her hands. He was not ready to give up their softness, their warmth.

Her eyes met his, and locked. "I—I think I'd better—ah—go," she rasped.

"Yes," he uttered.

She stood, and he rose with her. He had released her hands but stood very close. "There is one thing more," he said. "I—I appreciate what you said at the end, but truly, my dear, you should not have done. I fear you have made two powerful enemies."

Her pink lips curled. "You may rest assured, Adam, that neither was my bosom friend before. Besides, did you not realize where that Truesdale woman was headed? You did not seem overly smitten with the estimable Lucy, but that would not have stopped Eleanor Truesdale. How could I allow her to foist Lucy on you? The girl, I am persuaded, is a veritable peagoose. Unless—she *is* very pretty. Adam, have I misread—"

"No, no, Diana. You have read it all most astutely." Adam smiled and ran his forefinger down her cheek. She closed her eyes momentarily, as if savoring the sensation. He, too, savored it. "But I do not need you to protect me, my dear."

"But you protected me!"

"That is not at all the same. I am a man and you are a woman." His voice had grown deeper, though he had not meant it to. His hand lingered at her face, now grazing her chin with his knuckles, though he had not meant it to.

"I—I know that, Adam." Her voice was a whisper. His eyes searched her face, then swept down over her body, lush and rounded though properly covered by her high-necked, high-

142

waisted dress of Bishop's blue velvet. He took a step closer. He could feel her warmth, smell the elusive womanly scent that was exclusively hers. He wanted to let his hand slip to the nape of her swanlike neck. He wanted to pull her close, to kiss her. . . .

He cleared his throat and made himself drop his hand. He thought she sighed almost imperceptibly. Had she been holding her breath? Had she known what he was about? One look into the blue depths of her eyes told him she had, and that the sigh was not one of relief. She knew his dilemma, and shared it. What was right and what one wanted were not always the same thing.

Yet for all that, neither of them moved. He did not know where his next words came from; of a certain he had not planned them. "Speaking of a man and a woman, I suggest you stay clear away from Sir Percy Truesdale, my dear."

Diana stiffened and pulled away from him; surely it was not for him to say such things to her. She went to the window and stood there, staring out at the denuded garden, hardly seeing the patches of snow that glistened in the sunlight. Did he not realize that by his statement he had assumed a familiarity to which they were not entitled? She had not wanted to come here, had not wanted to be private with him. And yet he had orchestrated both. He had stood so close to her, touched her, made her body ache with the need to have him kiss her, hold her. And then he had spoken to her in a manner highly inappropriate, for he was neither male relation, nor betrothed, nor husband. Nor would he ever *be* any of those things. It was almost cruel to speak—

"Diana?" he inquired, following her.

She looked up. "Adam, you must not tell me that. You are neither my father nor my betr—"

"I am aware of that," he snapped. "For pitysakes, I spoke out of concern for you. The man means you no good."

"I am not a fool, Adam. I know that. But that is much beside the point. You do not have the right to speak to me of such things!"

I want the right! screamed a voice inside him. Adam blinked, shocked at his own thought. He did not wish to wed and neither did she. And at all events, dukes of the realm did not marry

143

doctor's daughters, and that was an end to it. But why was she so overset about his cautionary words? "My dear," he began, gently grasping her upper arm, "I—"

"No, Adam," she said quietly. "I am not your dear." She pulled away and walked slowly to the door.

He strode after her, reaching her just behind the sofa. "Diana, whatever is wrong?" he asked, taking her by the shoulders and turning her round. To his horror he saw that her eyes were wet.

"Oh, Adam. You are no more child than I am. You must know precisely what is transpiring here. We—we are playing with—with fire." Her voice had become lower, more halting. "And I—I cannot bear it, Adam." A tear trickled from the corner of her eye. She sniffed. "Please let me go. I shall not come here again."

"I'm sorry," he said huskily, and could not keep himself from pulling her close and placing a chaste kiss on her brow. Oh, Lord, why could it not have been simple? Why could she not have been the sort of woman of which mistresses were made?

But she wasn't. He drew back from her and dabbed at her face with his handkerchief. She kept her eyes lowered. "You are right, of course," he said at length. "But Georgie needs you, I believe, and I—well, I beg you will have pity on me." At that she met his gaze.

His lips twitched. "Pray do not condemn me to staying here without at the least having your visits to look forward to." She shook her head. "Then, I shall visit you and Rusty at Three Oaks, though I daresay your coming here will occasion less comment. After all, you are coming with your papa to see Georgie."

"Oh, Adam," she sighed. "You must know—"

"I agree that we—we must not be private again, Diana. But surely you cannot cavil at an unexceptionable visit. You did say we were to be friends, did you not?" he coaxed. "And friends see each other and talk with each other, do they not?"

"Yes," Diana breathed, and did not add the obvious, that one's friends did not grasp the other's shoulders in just that way, nor let his fingers graze the other's cheek, nor cause the other to feel little ripples of warmth and pleasure at his very touch. She did not say any of it, for he knew it as well as she. Just as he knew they were playing with fire.

"Very well, then," he replied. "Until tomorrow."

She nodded and did not ask the question on the tip of her tongue, "To what end, Adam?" For she knew the answer.

There *was* no end. None except heartache.

Chapter 10

True to her word, Diana came every day with Rusty for the next se'nnight. And, true to his word, Adam did not again seek to be private with her. But when she was not there, he thought of little else but *being* private with her. Talking with her, touching his hands to her cheek, touching his lips to hers. And in the darkest reaches of his increasingly sleepless nights, he thought of touching a good deal more than that. And then he would pound the pillow and feel himself sweat despite the cold night air. And he would wonder what the devil was wrong with him.

Never had a woman so invaded his thoughts, his sleep, his very dreams! There was, he assured himself, no reason for this one to do so. She was merely another female, one of many who had and would pass through his life. The only difference, he told himself, was that she was unattainable.

But that was not the only difference. And he knew it very well. For she was unlike any female he had ever met, and he had not the slightest notion of what to do about her.

In the meantime there were certain disturbing undercurrents in the Rossmore household that he did not like one whit. And there were certain tensions that were so overt as not to qualify as undercurrents at all. There were the intent looks Edward cast his way each time Stebbins announced the arrival of Doctor and Miss Rustin. There were the dagger points his mother looked at him every time he addressed a remark to Diana, even in a roomful of people. Once, as he helped her up next to her father in their carriage, he turned back to see his mother's brown eyes staring quite malevolently at Diana. The

146

fierceness of that gaze shook him.

And then there was the matter of the servants. The duchess travelled as always, with two grooms, a coachman, her personal maid, and a maid of all work. The latter, a hapless girl who docilely followed orders, was responsible for seeing to her mistress's laundry, and, in general, to her every whim and comfort. As such, she dutifully contrived to poke her head into every nook and cranny of backstairs life at Rossmore. It was she who reported that the sheets were not aired "sufficiently" before being put on the beds, that the bottoms of certain pots were blackened, that the parlor maids were neglecting to dust the lower rungs of the chairs.

The duchess, of course, reported such infractions to Mrs. Stebbins. The kindly housekeeper was, as far as Adam could determine, quite at a loss as to what to do about problems she considered rather trivial or nonexistent. So whilst she fretted, Adam's mother, as the days went on, worked herself up into quite a taking.

It was Sunday, and Adam feared that matters would come to a rather explosive head very shortly. It had been a trying day. He had demurred when his mother asked his escort to church, and she had left rather miffed. She returned in unaccustomed good spirits, however, and would only say, by way of explanation, that she'd had a lovely chat with Eleanor Truesdale after the service.

Her good humor did not prevent her from wreaking havoc between Georgie and Edward just after luncheon. Edward had come storming down to the library to relate the incident to Adam. Apparently the duchess had gone to speak to Georgie about the laxness among the staff and Mrs. Stebbins' failure to remedy the matter. Edward had walked in to Georgie's chamber in the middle of the discussion, and Georgie had informed him of the various infractions of the staff. Georgie had assured Edward that it was for the sake of *his* comfort that she wished matters corrected. Whereupon Edward, knowing full well from whence such accusations had come, flew into a pelter. He paused at this point in his recital to Adam and stalked to the window, running his hand through his hair. "My comfort! Good God, Adam, who the devil does she mean to gammon? Georgie does not give a straw farthing for *my* comfort. All she cares about is pleasing her benighted mother! Oh! I do apologize, Adam. I know she's your mother as well, but the woman's impossible."

Adam could only nod grimly, and Edward went on with his narrative. He told Georgie not to trouble herself overmuch with "his" comfort. And then he reminded her, in rather stern tones, that Mrs. Stebbins had run Rossmore for years with no problems, and that there would be no problem now if "certain persons" did not see fit to interfere in matters which were none of their concern!

At this juncture the duchess began huffing and puffing in umbrage, and Georgie reminded Edward that "Mother is our guest, after all." That set Edward's teeth on edge, and he glowered at the duchess until she left the chamber in high dudgeon. He then had a few choice words for Georgie before he, too, stormed out.

Georgie apparently cried her eyes out until Diana and Rusty arrived for their daily visit. It was Diana who calmed Georgie down. Adam would have given a great deal to know what Diana had said to Georgie. But he was prevented from getting near Diana by his mother, who monopolized his time by giving him her own, very different, version of the contretemps.

Despite the tumult, Adam was certain today was only a skirmish and that the major battle was yet to come. He did not exactly know what he could do to prevent it; it was not his house, after all. The duchess, of course, was *his* mother, but bitter experience had taught him that she heeded no one's word but her own.

And so when Edward came to him again, just before dinner, to report that Mrs. Stebbins was in tears and threatening to quit, Adam offered him the best advice he could. He suggested Edward either ask the duchess to leave Rossmore, or instruct Mrs. Stebbins to agree to everything the duchess said and do nothing. Edward had sighed and nodded reluctantly and added, "And Georgie?" To that Adam had no answer but to suggest Edward wait until Georgie had recovered more of her strength.

That was when Edward made his two announcements. The first was that Rusty had deemed Georgie well enough to venture belowstairs for one meal a day. Adam greeted his pronouncement with mixed feelings. He was pleased his sister was recovering so well, but he feared an explosive battle was imminent. And what better time than mealtime with everyone present?

The second announcement was that Rusty would only be coming every other day or so to look in on Georgie. Adam said nothing, kept his face expressionless, whereupon Edward grinned and said he'd invited Rusty and Diana to tea on Wednesday.

Adam did not trust that grin at all.

Katherine, Duchess of Marchmaine, was fuming. Edward was most disrespectful, Adam showed supreme indifference to her feelings, and Georgina had turned into a watering pot. And that doctor's daughter continued to visit and turn the head of her son, who was in danger of making an utter cake of himself.

Katherine smiled into the looking glass as her maid curled her hair and pinned it into place. At the least *that* she could do something about. The wheels had already been set into motion. Of course, she herself would have thought of something similar had Eleanor Truesdale not stolen a march on her. And Katherine had seen no need to improve on Eleanor's quite excellent plan.

Not that she was enamored of the idea of having Lucy Truesdale for the next Duchess of Marchmaine. Lucy was, after all, merely the daughter, and now sister, of a baronet, decidedly plump in the pocket though he be. But she *was* a comely girl, and pretty-behaved, and one who knew her duty. She would make a biddable daughter-in-law. She was well-bred, and her training had been rigorous. She was fully prepared to become a nobleman's wife.

And though Katherine might, had she had her druthers, have preferred the daughter of another duke, or marquis or earl—well, she comforted herself that Lucy was a damn sight better than that doctor's daughter!

And there, of course, was the rub. Katherine had never seen Adam look at a female, either eligible or not, the way he looked at Diana Rustin. And *she* was most definitely *not* eligible! Why, she was no better than she should be! Katherine shuddered delicately at the thought of just what the gel did with her days. That she was even permitted into polite company merely

149

affirmed what Katherine always said about the hopeless provincials in this godforsaken north country.

But Adam, though he might deny it, appeared in a fair way to developing a dangerous tendre for the gel. If he would merely offer her a carte blanche and be done with it, Katherine would not mind at all. Adam, however, seemed to have taken leave of his senses. Rather than offer her a slip on the shoulder, which was no more than she deserved, he'd offered marriage! Thank heavens Dr. Rustin had refused. Katherine did not understand why, but she was taking no chances that either he or that daughter of his would change their minds. Katherine had got to take matters into her own hands. She had got to protect Adam and the purity of the Damerest lineage.

Eleanor, bless her scheming little heart, had offered the way. And after all, Katherine reasoned, she'd given Adam ten years in which to find himself a proper duchess. He'd not done so, and his time was up.

The plan was very simple, really. Diana Rustin must be permanently discredited in Adam's eyes. And who better to accomplish that than Lady Truesdale's dear son, Percy? Percy had long had his eye on the doctor's daughter. His intentions were, of course, not at all honorable, but Eleanor was persuaded the gel's refusal was merely a way of being coy and upping the ante. A female of her station could do very well for herself with Sir Percy Truesdale.

And so Eleanor meant to give a ball, within just a few weeks. A ball where Adam would lead Lucy out for the first dance, and a waltz. A ball where Percy would be given the opportunity to be private, very private, with Diana Rustin. By the time Adam found out about it, Miss Rustin's reputation would be in tatters. And while Adam gnashed his teeth, Lucy would be there to charm and comfort him. And, if necessary, Lucy would lead him into the garden, where she would become hopelessly compromised. . . .

Ah yes, Katherine mused as she straightened her toque and dismissed her maid, it would answer very well. And once Adam was properly settled, she and his wife would be able to scotch any lingering nonsensical notions Adam might still harbor about pursuing architecture as more than a mere gentlemen's avocation. After all, he would be setting up his nursery, and the duke and duchess would need to take their rightful place in London society. There would be no time for those silly drawings of his.

Now, Katherine told herself complacently, the only remaining problem on the horizon was to teach Georgina how to run a proper household. For that simple task she need not wait for anyone to throw a ball. *That* could be accomplished by week's end, she was certain!

The battle royal came, as Adam had feared, the very next day at luncheon. Yet when it was over, Adam was left with the notion that perhaps there was hope, after all.

Edward had carried Georgie down the stairs, and she looked quite lovely in a full-skirted mint green dress of jaconet muslin, her blond hair pulled back softly. Edward's eyes strayed to her often across the table in the small family dining room, but there was a cloud of pain in his expression. Yesterday's contretemps had not been forgotten.

The duchess and Adam, across from each other at the two sides of the table, completed the intimate company. It was Georgie's first time belowstairs, surely cause for celebration. Their mother had other ideas, however.

"I do not care for this soup. And truly, I hardly consider Scotch barley broth a proper appetizer for—what did I hear was to be served—ah, yes, mackerel pie and saddle of mutton. This soup rather reminds me of something one is served in a second-rate inn. I should think an eel soup would have been more the thing. Do you not agree, Georgina?"

"Well, I—ah—" stammered Georgie, who had been partaking quite heartily of the Scotch barley soup.

"The soup is quite excellent," Edward remarked firmly, "and a great favorite here in the Dales."

"Yes, I rather like it myself," Adam put in.

Georgie said nothing.

His mother proclaimed the mackerel pie too dry, the creamed asparagus insipid and the mutton overcooked and too simply dressed for the sophisticated palate. Edward grew more tense, and Georgie more silent.

"Georgina, are you feeling quite the thing?" the duchess

inquired between bites of the supposedly overcooked mutton.

"Yes, Mama," Georgie mumbled.

"You do relieve my mind," the duchess replied, "for you've said nary a word at table. You must not forget your duties as hostess, even if we are *en famille*."

"Yes, Mama."

"And you must not forget, Duchess," Edward put in, "that Georgie still has not got her full strength back."

The duchess lifted her chin. "I am well aware of that. Perhaps she ought to come down to tea instead of nuncheon these next two days. I daresay tea will be less strenuous. And we are to have company for tea on Wednesday. I am persuaded you'll like that, Georgina. I understood that Edward invited Dr. Rustin—" she paused, imbuing the name with just a hint of disapproval, not mentioning Diana at all, and glaring ever so briefly at Edward—"and so I took the liberty of inviting the Truesdales as well."

Georgie smiled wanly and Edward clenched his jaw. "In light of Georgie's weakened state I do wish you would confer with me next time, Duchess, before extending the hospitality of this house," he stated repressively.

Adam watched his mother's eyes widen. "Well! I naturally thought that in my own daughter's home I—and besides other company had already been invited and so I merely assumed—"

"Dr. Rustin and his daughter are hardly company," Adam interjected tautly, unable to stop himself, "as you know full well. Why, they are here nigh every day at all events and—"

"I am *well* aware of that, Adam," his mother said pointedly.

Adam bristled. "The point is that their presence will not tax Georgie overmuch."

"Neither will the Truesdales', I am persuaded," the duchess insisted. "Georgie has always enjoyed Eleanor's company, have you not, child? And Lucy is such a dear."

"Yes, Mama," Georgie mumbled. "Lucy is quite—ah—pleasant—but—but I do tire easily and—"

"Of course you do, my dear. But it *has* been a fortnight, after all. You mustn't pamper yourself overmuch. I hardly think an hour in company—"

"I do wish, Duchess," Edward interrupted, his smooth blond brow furrowed, "that you would refrain from making assumptions about what is best for *my* household!" Edward's fingers clenched the stem of his wine goblet tightly. Adam knew he was making a Herculean effort to keep a leash on his temper.

The duchess's ample bosom heaved, the buttons of her black bombazine dress threatening to pop right off. She looked to Georgie for support that was usually forthcoming. But, to Adam's surprise, Georgie said not a word and kept her eyes glued to her plate as she concentrated on spearing her asparagus. His mother knew better than to look to *him* for support; they'd been at loggerheads for years.

And so she pivoted to face Edward squarely. "I never thought to hear such lack of filial devotion from you, Edward. I had thought you wanted me to feel welcome in this house."

Edward muttered a curse which Adam hoped only he could hear. "Of course, I wish you to feel welcome, Duchess. But 'tis a far cry—"

"I have never cared for your manner of addressing me, Edward," she said stiffly. "Perhaps if you called me 'Mother,' as I long ago requested, then—"

"I believe I made it clear, long ago," Edward countered in steely tones, "that my mama passed on to her reward many years ago and that I could not imagine *anyone* taking her place."

Georgie looked ill. Adam's mother had the light of battle in her brown eyes. Quite deftly, with a caustic comment about dust on the chandelier, she shifted the subject to the laxity of the staff.

"Now you are becoming stronger, Georgina," she said, "it really is time for you to take a firm stand in household matters. You needn't follow Mrs. Stebbins about with a broom, you must know. Summoning her to your chamber should do nicely. As to Mrs. Brownlow, well, I hope you are finally persuaded there is no hope there."

Edward's spoon clattered to his plate. "Duchess, you go too far!" he shouted.

"Edward, please!" Georgie pleaded.

"Dammit, Georgie, I've had all I can take of this!" Edward barked. "If your mother is so dreadfully discommoded by staying here, then perhaps it is time she packed her bags and left!"

The duchess gasped. Georgie's eyes welled up. Adam,

clenching his napkin in his fist, turned to his mother. "Can you not see, Mother, what havoc you are wreaking in other people's lives?" he ground out bitterly.

"How dare you, Adam!" she countered, brown eyes flashing. "And *you*, Edward, to be so ungrateful when all I've—"

"Mama, please." Georgie's voice, soft and pleading, brought everyone up short. Her words were usually, "Edward, please," as they'd been a moment ago, for she was always trying to appease her mother. To Adam's knowledge she'd never said, "Mama, please." They all stared at her, and she took a deep breath. "Mama, I am sensible of the fact that the staff may have—have become a bit lax of late. It is only to be expected, I think. After all, toward the end of my confinement I was not up and about much, and they were one and all more concerned with bringing me sweets, or hot water, or extra blankets, than in dusting the bottom rungs of the chairs. And then there was the excitement of the birth and their concern for my health. And since then, well, everyone *is* in something of a dither. But—but after all, 'tis not every day the House of Rossmore produces an heir. I—I fully intend to—to see to matters once I get my full strength back, Mama, but—but I should appreciate it if you would wait and allow *me* to be the one to do that."

Adam heard his mother's sharp intake of breath. Georgie must have heard it as well. Her hand went nervously to her spoon, which she picked up and clutched tightly, but she went doggedly on. "As to Mrs. Brownlow—" she paused and, taking a deep breath, lowered her eyes. "I do agree, Mama, that her—her repertoire is not quite the thing for the most sophisticated palate. But—but we are not in London, and we are not entertaining the Regent. Mrs. Brownlow has been here most of her life and . . ." she paused again, and her voice became little more than a whisper. Yet no one stirred, and they could hear her very well. "And I should like to please Edward in this, Mama. I should like Mrs. Brownlow to stay, and I should like there to be no—no more discussion of the matter."

Absolute silence greeted what was, for Georgie, an extraordinary pronouncement. Adam felt his lips twitch and had to keep from grinning. Edward was gazing at his wife in wonder, and the duchess looked thunderous.

Georgie finally raised her eyes and glanced at their mother. "Mama, please try to understand," she mumbled.

"What I understand, daughter," she said ominously, "is that you have no more notion of filial duty than your brother or your husband!" She threw her serviette down onto her plate. "Never have I been made to suffer such Turkish treatment! And in the home of my own children! The ingratitude and unseemly behavior of all of you is simply not to be borne!" And with that, her entire body quivering with fury, the duchess stormed out of the dining room.

Georgie stared at Adam, then Edward, then burst into tears and ran from the room. Edward bounded after her, calling her name over and over. Adam calmly finished his claret, grinning all the while. Perhaps there was hope for this family, after all. And he silently thanked Diana. For without knowing any particulars, he was certain she'd had more than a little to do with Georgie's new-found courage and good sense.

And he admitted to himself that he missed Diana, and wished that she were here, or that he had the freedom to simply go and visit her. How he would enjoy recounting today's brouhaha and then attempting to coax from her precisely what she'd said to Georgie. He could just see the soft womanly smile that would curl her lips as she demurred with some moonshine about not knowing aught about the married state. She had the most tempting lips. . . . No, Adam! he admonished himself, and downed the rest of his claret.

The duchess, mercifully, kept to her chamber all day. Adam wondered, fleetingly, if she would take Edward's suggestion and simply leave, but a moment's reflection told him such would not be. She would not be so easily routed, and besides, whatever would she tell Eleanor Truesdale?

Georgie, according to the servants, who gossiped quite vociferously and unabashedly, spent the entire afternoon weeping copiously, but as Edward stayed with her all the while, Adam decided that was a good sign.

He gave them their privacy until just before dinner when he felt the need to see for himself how Georgie was, and to speak with Edward.

155

Georgie was dry-eyed by now, sitting up in bed whilst Edward and Ned sat together, quite absorbed with each other, at the foot of the bed. Adam chatted with them for a time, and then drew Edward into the corridor to have a word with him.

Adam expressed his concern that the little tea party planned for two days hence did not auger to be very pleasant. Edward, well aware of that, concurred immediately with Adam's suggestion that adding Sir Horace and Lady Hartcup to the company might help. If Georgie's energy appeared to be flagging, Edward would convey her abovestairs, straightaway. And Adam's further suggestion that the Hartcups and Rustins be asked to come half an hour *before* tea produced a decided grin from his brother-in-law.

Neither thought it necessary to enlighten the duchess, who, at all events, did not come down to dinner.

Tuesday dawned dark and dreary and cold. Light snow flurries fell all morning, and Adam hoped it would clear, rather than turning into a storm. For Diana and Rusty were meant to come this afternoon. Besides, he did not wish their little tea party, set for the morrow, to be cancelled.

As it was, the snow did not let up, nor did it worsen, and Diana and Rusty arrived straightaway after luncheon. The duchess still had not made an appearance, and Adam was beginning to think she would not emerge until tea time on the morrow, which suited him quite well.

Rusty went up to see Georgie first, and Adam cornered Diana, beckoning her into the library. She tilted her raven-capped head sideways and gave him a crooked smile that said, as effectively as words, "I thought we agreed not to be private with each other."

His only reply was to take her by the elbow and nudge her inside with a whispered, "I must speak with you." Once the door was closed he drew her to the fire and stood with her before the hearth. He looked her up and down; he could not help himself. She wore the same blue merino dress she'd worn the night they'd met. It brought all the memories of that first meeting back forcefully. Now, as then, he thought she looked delectable in the form-fitting dress. Now, as then, he wondered how long her dark hair was, and longed to plow his fingers through the shining locks. Now, as then, he fought to keep his hands to himself.

Diana fancied she knew exactly what Adam was thinking as his eyes devoured her. Why was she not insulted? Why did she not fall into a ladylike swoon? Why had she come in here at first stop, knowing beforehand what a mistake it would be? Why did he have to look so . . . so strong and indomitable and handsome in his doeskin pantaloons and chocolate brown coat? And why had she missed him so much when it had only been two days since she'd seen him?

His tawny eyes were on her lips. She forced herself to speak. "Adam, you—ah—wished to talk with me?"

Adam cleared his throat and took a step back. What the deuce was wrong with him? Again he was behaving like a moonstruck halfling. But there was no moon, he had not been "struck," and he was no halfling! He quickly seated her, and himself, in adjacent chairs, and recounted the story of yesterday's contretemps. She chuckled with him at the end, agreeing wholeheartedly that though Edward and Georgie still had some way to go in resolving their differences, yet a turning point of sorts seemed to have been reached.

Then his expression sobered. "Thank you, Diana. I know that you—"

"I? Whatever can you mean, Adam?" she asked, rising and going to the window. "I have done naught."

"Somehow I knew you'd say that," Adam replied, and followed her to the window. Her back was to him, but it seemed to him that she was fighting back tears. "Diana?" he queried.

She sniffled. "Pay me no heed. I am merely being foolish. I am very happy for them, Adam. I—I do think they will go on together quite well."

She could not say, even to herself, why she was suddenly crying, except perhaps that her ability to help someone else underscored her inability to help herself. Whatever understanding she might possess would never be applied to her own marriage. She felt his hands come up to grasp her shoulders and stiffened herself against his warmth.

"Do not do that, Diana," he murmured in her ear.

"Do not do . . . what?"

157

"Do not fight me. I only want to hold you a few minutes, like this. Surely there can be no harm in that. Relax."

Diana shook her head, even as she felt her body relaxing against his arms and, as he pulled her closer, fairly melting into his warmth. She sighed inwardly, knowing how dangerous it was, yet allowing herself just this moment. Her back was pressed to his strong, hard chest. Her entire body vibrated with an exciting awareness that she'd never felt before. And yet at the same time she'd never felt so relaxed, so safe.

Adam inhaled her mysterious, feminine scent and savored the feel of her in his arms. She was warm and soft, and he had no right to this and yet he could not let her go. Her neck was long and white and graceful, and it was all he could do to keep from bending his head and pressing his lips to that vulnerable spot where nape met shoulders. . . .

"Whatever did you tell Georgie to give her such . . . courage, Diana?"

He could feel, rather than see, her smile. She turned her head slightly so that he could see her profile. "Now, Adam, they are women's secrets. You cannot ask me to reveal them," she said smiling mysteriously.

He chuckled softly and allowed one hand to creep up to the base of her nape, where his thumb, almost of its own volition, began idly stroking the soft, white skin. He felt his body grow heated at the feel of her bare skin, while his mind was thinking that a woman with such secrets had ought to be wed.

He didn't realize he'd spoken this last aloud until she pulled away from him. She put the space of several feet between them and turned to face him, wrapping her arms about herself. She lifted her chin. "Adam, I believe we went over this a long time since. I tell you again, there are some women meant to marry and some women not. I am not, and truly, I should not care to discuss this again."

She looked and sounded utterly composed, yet there was an almost unnatural stillness about her that belied her outer calm. She was the solemn Miss Rustin now, but he knew her too well to be put off. He stayed where he was, but his eyes met her deep blue ones and held them.

"I beg to differ with you, Diana," he said softly, and unwittingly took a step closer. She moved back, toward the

158

window. Still their eyes were locked. "You are a woman of great charm and rare understanding." He stepped closer, again. Her next step put her flush against the window.

"Surely such qualities, did I possess them, might be of—of use in many . . . situations. One need not be wed to—"

"No, perhaps not." He came to her now and put a hand to her cheek. It was smooth, warm, slightly flushed. "But there is more to it, Diana. You are a woman capable of great passion." She shook her head; he ignored her. "And as it is perfectly obvious that you are not a wanton, one can only conclude that you are rather more disposed to wed than not."

"No," she whispered. "You are wrong. You do not know—"

"Yes, I do," he breathed, and did not let her finish. He did not allow his thoughts, his better sense, to intrude. He merely did what he was longing to do, and, gently taking her face in his hands, brought his lips down onto hers.

Diana had known what he was about, had seen the look in his piercing eyes as he moved inexorably closer to her. She had known and seen and had allowed it to happen. And now she felt the gentleness of his hands on her face, the warmth and firmness of his lips pressing hers, swallowing her words and causing a forbidden tide of warmth to rise in her body. Only a taste, she told herself, a moment's joy to savor and remember all the dark, lonely nights of her life. She would not let this kiss go so far as that other. . . .

His tongue was pushing at her teeth; instinctively she parted them. His tongue met hers. Her heart beat wildly, her blood pounded. His hands wrapped themselves around her, and that was when she came back to her senses. She pushed at him, jerking her mouth from his.

"For God sakes, Diana," he rasped, hardly aware of what he was saying, his body shaking with need. "Don't fight me. You want this as much as I do!"

He sought her mouth again, his arms tightening around her back.

"No!" she whispered harshly, twisting free of him. "I *have* to fight you, Adam. I have to!"

She ran from him, from the room, leaving him cursing after her. He cursed her for an innocent temptress, and himself for an utter bounder.

159

Chapter 11

Diana had wanted to cry off from tea at Rossmore Manor on Wednesday. Any excuse would have done, except that Papa would have questioned her closely and she did not wish him to think aught was amiss. In truth, of course, everything was amiss. She had not wanted to pull away from Adam yesterday. She had wanted him to go on kissing her, touching her. There was something about his touch, his nearness, that drew her in the way of a moth to a flame. It was more than his heat, and the answering heat he called up in her. It was some sense of rightness, of connection, that she felt with him whenever they were close.

But it was not right, and there could be no connection. . . .

It was bitterly cold on Wednesday, the skies an unremitting gray and the ground covered with the fresh layer of snow which had fallen yesterday. Her misgivings notwithstanding, when afternoon came Diana found herself walking with Papa up the stone steps toward the front portico of Rossmore. Stebbins admitted them and took Diana's cloak and Papa's great coat.

Papa went to see Georgie and reported that she seemed much improved and in better spirits than she had been in some time. To Diana, Georgie confided that Edward had been most attentive since Monday's contretemps, and had, quite without Georgie asking, suggested that they hire a French cook for the London house! Diana was most pleased for her, but felt obliged to remind her that the road would not always be so smooth.

"Goodness me, I know!" Georgie concurred, rolling her

The Publishers of Zebra Books Make This Special Offer to Zebra Romance Readers...

AFTER YOU HAVE READ THIS BOOK WE'D LIKE TO SEND YOU 4 MORE FOR *FREE* AN $18.00 VALUE

NO OBLIGATION!

ONLY ZEBRA HISTORICAL ROMANCES "BURN WITH THE FIRE OF HISTORY" (SEE INSIDE FOR MONEY SAVING DETAILS.)

MORE PASSION AND ADVENTURE AWAIT... YOUR TRIP TO A BIG ADVENTUROUS WORLD BEGINS WHEN YOU ACCEPT YOUR FIRST 4 NOVELS ABSOLUTELY *FREE*
(AN $18.00 VALUE)

Accept your Free gift and start to experience more of the passion and adventure you like in a historical romance novel. Each Zebra novel is filled with proud men, spirited women and tempestuous love that you'll remember long after you turn the last page.

Zebra Historical Romances are the finest novels of their kind. They are written by authors who really know how to weave tales of romance and adventure in the historical settings you love. You'll feel like you've actually gone back in time with the thrilling stories that each Zebra novel offers.

GET YOUR FREE GIFT WITH THE START OF YOUR HOME SUBSCRIPTION

Our readers tell us that these books sell out very fast in book stores and often they miss the newest titles. So Zebra has made arrangements for you to receive the four newest novels published each month.

You'll be guaranteed that you'll never miss a title, and home delivery is so convenient. And to show you just how easy it is to get Zebra Historical Romances, we'll send you your first 4 books absolutely FREE! Our gift to you just for trying our home subscription service.

BIG SAVINGS AND FREE HOME DELIVERY

Each month, you'll receive the four newest titles as soon as they are published. You'll probably receive them even before the bookstores do. What's more, you may preview these exciting novels free for 10 days. If you like them as much as we think you will, just pay the low preferred subscriber's price of just $3.75 each. *You'll save $3.00 each month off the publisher's price.* AND, your savings are even greater because there are never any shipping, handling or other hidden charges—FREE Home Delivery. Of course you can return any shipment within 10 days for full credit, no questions asked. There is no minimum number of books you must buy.

4 FREE BOOKS

TO GET YOUR 4 FREE BOOKS WORTH $18.00 — MAIL IN THE FREE BOOK CERTIFICATE T O D A Y

Fill in the Free Book Certificate below, and we'll send your FREE BOOKS to you as soon as we receive it.

If the certificate is missing below, write to: Zebra Home Subscription Service, Inc., P.O. Box 5214, 120 Brighton Road, Clifton, New Jersey 07015-5214.

FREE BOOK CERTIFICATE

4 FREE BOOKS

ZEBRA HOME SUBSCRIPTION SERVICE, INC.

YES! Please start my subscription to Zebra Historical Romances and send me my first 4 books absolutely FREE. I understand that each month I may preview four new Zebra Historical Romances free for 10 days. If I'm not satisfied with them, I may return the four books within 10 days and owe nothing. Otherwise, I will pay the low preferred subscriber's price of just $3.75 each; a total of $15.00, *a savings off the publisher's price of $3.00.* I may return any shipment and I may cancel this subscription at any time. There is no obligation to buy any shipment and there are no shipping, handling or other hidden charges. Regardless of what I decide, the four free books are mine to keep.

NAME

ADDRESS   APT

CITY   STATE   ZIP

(   )
TELEPHONE

SIGNATURE   (if under 18, parent or guardian must sign)

Terms, offer and prices subject to change without notice. Subscription subject to acceptance by Zebra Books. Zebra Books reserves the right to reject any order or cancel any subscription.

GET
FOUR
FREE
BOOKS
(AN $18.00 VALUE)

AFFIX
STAMP
HERE

ZEBRA HOME SUBSCRIPTION
SERVICE, INC.
P.O. Box 5214
120 BRIGHTON ROAD
CLIFTON, NEW JERSEY 07015-5214

eyes. "This morning I made the most dreadful error. Edward seemed in such a pleasant humor, you see, and so I suggested that today, as we were having guests, he might consider donning a pair of pantaloons. He does have several, you must know, and I *said* that I realized he would not wear them all the time, but—well! Diana, he near to tore the roof down railing at me about how he would *not* be told what to do and how to dress in his own house! Then he stormed out, and I did not see him for two hours."

"Oh, dear. Georgie—"

"I know." Georgie nodded her blond head ruefully. "And when he returned, it was to spend time with Ned and not with me. But I remembered your papa and his chair, and so I said that I have finally come to realize that—that it *is* his prerogative to wear what he wishes and that his comfort is most important to me. And then I vowed I would not make mention of the pantaloons again."

"And what did Edward say to that?"

"Why, his mouth dropped open, and then he smiled in a way I haven't seen for a very long time."

Diana grinned. "I am very happy for you, Georgie."

"Well, I shall try. And perhaps he'll surprise me and wear the pantaloons, after all."

But when Edward came in not a moment later to carry his wife belowstairs, he was wearing a pair of creme-colored Kerseymere britches. Georgie bit her lip, then glanced at Diana and finally shrugged. Then she smiled at her husband and insisted she could walk well enough on her own. But Edward said he would not hear of it and scooped his wife up effortlessly. Georgie seemed quite content to settle in his arms as Edward carried her from the chamber.

Diana followed them into the corridor and gazed after them wistfully until she became aware that she was the object of a piercing stare. She turned, and Adam sauntered down the corridor toward her. He was wearing a bottle green coat, gold waistcoat and buff pantaloons, all of which fit him far too well.

She swallowed. "Hello, Adam," she said quietly, schooling her face to a neutral expression.

"Hello, Diana. Please accept my escort down to tea, as Edward seems to have his hands full." He smiled, his tawny

161

eyes regarding her intently, and drew her arm through his.

There seemed no avoiding him. The corners of her lips curled. "I daresay he does, in more ways than one."

"That's better."

"What is?"

"Your smile. You will need it, and your sense of humor, this afternoon." He patted her hand as he gazed down at her.

"Oh, dear. That bad?" she asked, chuckling.

"Let us just say our little tea party may be rather . . . interesting. There will be the Truesdales—my mother's guests, of course—and then Sir Horace and Lady Hartcup. Oh, and their two houseguests as well. My mother was apparently not best pleased about all the additions to the guest list, but the servants' grapevine has it that she *will* put in an appearance. 'Twill be her first since Monday's brouhaha, you must know. Oh, and there is one other little matter which has just now got her dander up."

He had been grinning throughout his little speech, but when she asked the cause of this latest upset, his expression became suitably grave. "It seems the Rustins and the Hartcup party were invited for one half hour before Lady Truesdale and her offspring. And no one thought to inform the duchess so she might relay the change in time. Can you conceive who might be guilty of such an oversight?"

They had reached the main floor. Diana looked up at him, caught the gleam in his amber eyes and let forth a cascade of giggles.

An imperious clearing of a throat brought them both up short. They turned, and there stood the duchess, glowering at them both.

Adam was not in the least discomposed. He merely squeezed Diana's hand as it rested in the crook of his arm, and then said genially, "Well met, Mother! Shall we go in to tea?"

He extended his free arm to her, and her eyes widened. Diana could see the indecision in them, as the duchess debated whether to share Adam's escort with Diana or to walk unaccompanied behind them. With a lift of her chin, she took the proffered arm, and the three of them proceeded to the morning room.

Georgie was already there, seated on the yellow chintz sofa, with Edward propped on the sofa arm to her left. Georgie's head was turned up toward him, and she was reclining back in her seat. But as soon as Adam, Diana and the duchess entered, she sat bolt upright, and Edward jumped up from his perch. Before any of them could be seated, however, Stebbins announced the arrival of Sir Horace and Lady Hartcup and their guests.

Adam watched Winifred Hartcup glide into the room on a cloud of purple chiffon, her husband at her side, her guests closely behind her. Sir Horace was tall and thin, with a shock of white hair and gray-green eyes that twinkled down at his wife. Lady Hart was, Adam thought, a rather beautiful woman, for all she must have seen more than fifty summers. Her hair, light brown streaked with gray, was piled high atop her head in a most extraordinary series of coils and twists. Her green eyes sparkled with warmth and a lively intelligence that he suspected missed nothing. Now she swooped down on Georgie to offer her felicitations, and then turned to the assembled company to introduce her guests.

Mrs. Millicent Weeksgate was a petite, pink-cheeked lady of middle years and an abstracted air. "Dear Millicent is a writer of Gothic tales," Lady Hart explained, patting the lady's hand and drawing her forward. Mrs. Weeksgate appeared quite flustered as each gentleman was presented to her. But her pink cheeks turned almost crimson upon being introduced to Rusty.

"Gothic tales? How very fascinating, Mrs. Weeksgate," Rusty said, smiling to put her at her ease.

"Oh, yes," Lady Hart put in, "dear Millicent has been writing for some five years now, ever since her dear husband departed this life, is that not so, Millicent?"

"Yes, I—"

"And I do believe there is a *doctor* in her current story, is there not, dear Millicent?"

"Dear Millicent's" cheeks were flaming by now, but her slate blue eyes seemed to light up as she said to Rusty, "Yes, indeed. My heroine is in great danger, you must know, and the doctor is the very *key* to the plot, for only he knows the secret of her birth!"

"Ah," Rusty uttered, his blue eyes gleaming. "And is the doctor a miscreant or a man of honor?" he asked, leading her to

163

a pair of mahogany chairs to the right of the hearth.

Adam did not hear Mrs. Weeksgate's reply, but he turned to see a most intriguing smile playing at the corners of Lady Hart's mouth. Why, she's matchmaking, he thought and threw her a bemused look that let her know he knew it. She schooled her expression immediately to one of bland innocence, and proceeded to introduce her second houseguest.

Signor Antonio D'Orsini was a dapper, middle-aged Italian gentleman with intense black eyes and silver-tinged black hair. He was, it seemed, an acclaimed portrait painter who had recently completed Lady Hart's portrait. "It was unveiled at the Valentine's Ball—oh, I'm so sorry you all missed it, but I do understand, what with Lady Rossmore's blessed event in the offing—well, and the portrait is quite magnificent, much more so than its subject, I do assure you. And Signor D'Orsini received so very many offers for commissions that he has not yet made up his mind which to take. And so, of course, Sir Horace said he might stay with us at Arden Chase in the meantime. Is that not so, dear heart?" She turned to place a hand on her husband's sleeve.

He gave the hand a squeeze. Adam noted the affectionate display with interest.

"Of course, Win, my love," Sir Horace said, gazing fondly at her.

Adam had the distinct impression that though a man of few words to his wife's garrulous nature, Sir Horace was not a man to live under the cat's foot. Something about the looks the couple exchanged told him that. Lady Hart had meant what she said. The decision about who was welcome at Arden Chase *was* Sir Horace's.

Signor D'Orsini greeted the men with a bow and the ladies with a flourish. He took the hand of each in a lingering caress and murmured effusive compliments. Georgie giggled; the duchess lifted her nose in a gesture of studied indifference. Diana appeared amused, but Adam was not. He had met these Latin Lothario types before. In truth, no woman was safe around them. But any attempt on Adam's part to speak or help Diana retrieve her hand was forestalled by Edward, urging everyone to be seated. It was not Diana whom Signor D'Orsini led to one of the powder blue wing chairs, however, but the duchess. The portrait painter then sat in the adjacent wing chair and engaged his mother in conversation, a rather bemused look in his eyes.

A bit surprised, Adam glanced at Diana, whose eyes danced as she met his gaze. Adam frowned and seated Diana across from his mother in a side chair next the hearth. He took up a stance close by at the mantel. Next to Diana in the Queen Anne chair sat Lady Hart; Sir Horace stood behind her, his hands on the back of the chair. To Lady Hart's right sat Georgie and Edward on the sofa, and Adam noted that Edward had made certain that he was seated between Georgie and D'Orsini.

Rusty and the authoress of Gothic tales appeared still to be in a discussion of that lady's latest literary endeavor. D'Orsini was irking Edward by asking whether he'd had Georgie's portrait painted yet.

"Such an enchanting subject would the baroness make!" exclaimed the Italian. "As would her mother," he added gallantly, turning to the duchess.

She ignored him and addressed herself to Lady Hart, seated across the sofa table from her. "Winifred dear, such a lovely dress. Is it new? I own I can never tell with you, for you do tend rather to favor purple, do you not?"

"Indeed, I do, Katherine. Actually, I wear it all the time, except when I'm wearing lavender, that is," returned Lady Hart congenially.

"*All* the time, Winifred?" the duchess inquired with lofty disbelief.

A peal of laughter escaped Lady Hart. "Yes, Katherine dear, for I own 'tis my very favorite color."

"And while my Winifred would look lovely in any color," Sir Horace put in, stroking his wife's left cheek with his forefinger, "she looks especially beautiful in purples and violets." Now he let both hands come to rest on her shoulders, and Lady Hart slid her left hand up to clasp his.

Adam marvelled at this second and more pointed public display of affection between husband and wife. And then Sir Horace did the most extraordinary thing. Millicent Weeksgate made a comment about the exquisite purple gown Lady Hart had worn for her portrait, and how it made the green of her eyes look so deep and mysterious.

165

"Indeed," Sir Horace murmured, smiling at Mrs. Weeksgate, and quite nonchalantly raising his wife's hand to his lips and kissing it.

Adam blinked. He did not think he'd ever seen a man kiss his wife's hand in public. Such was reserved for decidedly non-connubial flirtations. And yet Lady Hart seemed not the least discomposed, as if it were a frequent and most natural occurrence.

No one else of the company seemed to think so. Adam's gaze swept about the room. Georgie looked shocked, Edward mildly so, but then he turned a hungry gaze onto his wife. D'Orsini looked amused, the duchess was outraged, and Rusty's faint smile looked approving. It was the expression on Diana's face that shocked Adam, however. She looked . . . envious; there was no other word for it. And Adam once again wondered about the long-ago man who had hurt her so badly that she shunned the married state.

She was easily the most beautiful woman here, Adam thought. Georgie was a pretty bit of fluff, a blond confection. His mother, if one wanted to be kind, might be called handsome. Millicent Weeksgate was sweet-looking. And Lady Hart had the striking beauty that a man could not help but admire. But it was Diana, with her white skin and raven locks, her big, velvety blue eyes, her wide and gracious smile, her aura of serenity, who drew a man inexorably to her. That was not to mention her prefectly proportioned form, covered but not hidden now in a round dress of royal blue silk. And not to mention the passionate nature that bubbled just below that utterly composed surface.

Oh, Lord, Adam groaned inwardly, and forced his attention to the discussion now ensuing about Lady Hart's recent Valentine's Ball.

It was a yearly event, much anticipated in the north country. Adam had heard of it—indeed, who in Yorkshire had not? But having met Lady Hart for the first time just over a se'nnight ago, and at all events being in the habit of spending most of the coldest months at a series of house parties, he had never attended the ball. He found himself rather intrigued as he listened to the discussion of the Valentine Lottery, which was reputed to be "Fate's" way of making matches amongst all of the single people of Lady Hart's acquaintance. The match between her own niece, Alexandra, and the nabob Viscount Weddington seemed to be Lady Hart's greatest coup this year.

Mrs. Weeksgate, having just arrived several days ago, had missed the festivities, as had the Truesdales, who'd been visiting in Shropshire. It appeared Lady Truesdale was not eager to have Yorkshire's premiere matchmaker taking her offspring under her wing. Signor D'Orsini had apparently declined to be included in the lottery, which Adam could well understand. He was obviously not a man disposed to wed. No one made mention of the Rustins' absence from the ball, but Adam knew well it was an event Diana would assiduously avoid.

Conversation shifted to the subject of the weather and the likelihood of more snow, and then onto the birth of little Ned in the midst of a blizzard. Lady Hart, unlike the duchess and Eleanor Truesdale, thought Diana quite the heroine. Diana flushed and, as usual, downplayed her role. Adam smiled warmly at her until he felt Lady Hart's gaze on *him*. He met those green eyes and decided they were much too penetrating for comfort. He was almost relieved when Stebbins announced the arrival of the Truesdales.

Winifred Hartcup watched Eleanor Truesdale make her grand entrance. The gentlemen rose, dear Horace introducing Millicent and Signor D'Orsini this time, and there was a bit of reshuffling as everyone found seats once again. The new arrangement rather intrigued Winifred.

Eleanor's daughter Lucy now sat on the sofa next to Georgie, with Edward propped on the arm to his wife's left. Georgie seemed a bit uncomfortable, as if her husband's close proximity was somehow not seemly in public. How extraordinary, Winifred thought.

Signor D'Orsini, the dear man, had yielded his wing chair to Eleanor, and had pulled up an upholstered bench to sit between her and Lucy. He then proceeded to work his Latin charm on both of them. Lucy blushed rosily, and Eleanor patted her silver-blue hair. Quite amazingly, the duchess, who had not at all cared for Signor D'Orsini's attentions herself, seemed miffed at the lack of them now.

Winifred's eyes continued to scan the room. Dear Rusty was

still engaged with Millicent upon some literary discussion. It was rare that anyone could keep Millicent conversing that long; she was wont to retreat quickly into her own world of heroes and villains and damsels in dire danger. And Rusty, well, Rusty had been alone far too long. She watched his blue eyes crinkle in a smile. Ah, she thought, her hunch had been right. But she was not certain if aught could be brought about whilst Diana remained unwed.

Dear Diana. Winifred did not know why she shunned the wedded state, but it assuredly had naught to do with lack of masculine interest. Why, one need only look at the duke, and the dreadful Percy, and the way they were vying for her attention, to know that. But for some reason Diana kept herself aloof. Winifred had discussed it with Horace any number of times and had concluded that the dear girl must have had her heart quite shattered by her broken betrothal all those years ago. Winifred had tried to interest Diana in a parade of young gentlemen over the years. But though she had been unaccustomedly unsuccessful, she refused to give up. If ever a woman was meant to be wed, it was Diana Rustin.

Winifred's eyes shifted to her left, where dear Horace now sat on a bench, just a bit behind her. She was able to see Diana, still seated a few feet away, quite clearly. The duke retained his stance at the mantel, but Percy had commandeered a gilt-edged chair much too delicate for him and wedged himself between Diana and the hearth. He had effectively cut Diana off from the duke, who was looking dagger points at him. Percy's interest in Diana was long-standing and wholly dishonorable. Winifred dismissed him for the reprobate he was, knowing that Diana was much too clever to be taken in. The duke's interest in Diana—for such it seemed to be, given the intent looks he'd been casting her way this half hour and more—was another matter. Winifred did not entirely understand it. He was not, by all reports, hanging out for a wife. And if he were, marriage to a mere doctor's daughter was like to give Katherine the apoplexy. Clearly he was not tied to the apron strings, but Winifred wondered if he would so defy family tradition. . . .

She did not know, but at the least she acquitted him of dishonorable intentions. He had the reputation of a gentleman, and appeared on good terms with Rusty. Besides, what she saw in the looks he gave Diana was not lechery, but a certain warmth, an attempt at shared communication. Winifred resolved, as the tea was served, to determine whether any of that was returned by Diana.

And so she watched and talked and listened, all the while drinking her tea. And, with the help of a murmured conference or two with dear Horace, she reached certain conclusions.

Despite the unwelcomed presence of Percy, the looks exchanged between Diana and the duke were very warm on both sides. That did not, of course, mean to say that aught would come of it. There was, after all, the great difference in their rank, the duke's reputation for having a roving eye, and the determination with which Diana clung to her spinster state. But clearly there were possibilities here; Winifred had never seen Diana look at any man in just that way.

Dear Horace quite agreed.

He also agreed that Rusty had been alone far too long, and that Millicent was quite lost without a man, for all she'd been widowed these five years past.

"A dinner party, perhaps, dear heart? To help move things along?" she whispered behind her teacup.

"An admirable idea, Win, my love," he concurred.

Of course, Winifred would have preferred a house party— so very *much* could be accomplished—but one could not very well invite those not an hour's drive away to a house party! Still, even with a properly organized dinner party a determined hostess could accomplish a great deal.

Quite satisfied with her ruminations thus far, Winifred turned her attention to the other occupants of the room. Katherine and Eleanor were each casting sharp glances at the corner of the room occupied by Diana, Percy, and the duke. And every so often they would have a whispered conversation. A bit *too* often, Winifred thought; their friendship was not *that* close. They were planning something, she decided, and whatever it was, she was persuaded she would not like it. The baleful looks Katherine cast Diana's way confirmed Winifred's guess that the duchess would be appalled did the duke decide to pay his addresses to Diana. No, Katherine did not approve of Diana. And Eleanor had long turned a blind eye to Percy's attempts to seduce Diana. That combination did not bode well, and Winifred knew she needs must keep her wits about her to foil whatever plot the dowagers were hatching.

She watched as Percy offered a plate of scones to Diana, using that as a ruse to lean close and whisper in her ear. Why, he was nearly nibbling on her very lobe! Diana went very still and pale, and the duke looked like he might snap his delicate teacup right into pieces! And then for some reason Winifred's eyes shifted across to the occupants of the powder blue wing chairs. Katherine was regarding the exchange between Percy and Diana with a faint smirk. Eleanor followed her gaze and then took a sip of her tea. Delicately replacing the cup in its saucer, she leaned toward the duchess. There was a lull in the general conversation, and, as Winifred was watching Eleanor's lips, she had no difficulty deciphering her words. "You see, dear, it will all work out just as I said it would. No need to trouble overmuch about it."

Winifred sighed inwardly, her deepest fears confirmed. They *were* hatching some scheme, and it looked as if Diana was to be their victim, Percy their weapon. It was easy to see why Katherine agreed to this—if Percy in some way ruined Diana, the duchess need not worry about her son paying court to Diana. But what had Eleanor to gain from this? Percy would be well occupied, of course, but he certainly did not need his mother to organize his affairs d'amour. The duke would no doubt be furious, and decidedly *un*occupied. He would be free—free for what?

Winifred's eyes swept the room, and she chided herself for her addled brain. Why had she not realized sooner? The question was, free for *whom*, and the answer was sitting on the sofa right next to Georgie. Eleanor wanted the duke for Lucy!

Well, that would simply never do! Winifred would need to find a few distractions for them. Perhaps for Lucy some young gentleman who would turn her empty, pretty head with compliments and who was of sufficient rank to satisfy Eleanor. Unfortunately, she doubted Percy could be distracted, and as to Katherine. . . . Her eyes moved from Katherine to Eleanor to Signor D'Orsini. And she wondered. She remembered a certain gleam in the dear painter's eyes when he first met the duchess. Winifred had not thought much upon it then. Katherine was such an overbearing woman that she could not imagine any man—but Signor D'Orsini was a very strong man. And she noted that even though he was conversing with Eleanor and Katherine both, his eyes kept drifting to Katherine. Winifred pondered the extraordinary notion that was beginning to take hold. Signor D'Orsini *was* an artist; perhaps he saw something that no one else did.

"No, Win, my love," Horace whispered in her ear.

How did the dear man always know what she was thinking?

"But is it not worth a try, dear heart? I promise I shall be excessively subtle."

He raised a brow. "Win, my love, no man in his right mind— oh, very well. I own you've hit upon even more harebrained notions in the past, and been successful. I shall wait upon events." And with that he sat back with a mischievous grin tugging at his lips.

The conversation was general now, something about the duchess's recent trip to Paris and the ordeal of her journey home. It was easy enough to shift the subject. "I must say, Katherine dear, that you are none the worse for wear," Winifred said. "Indeed, you are in splendid looks. Do you know, I believe Signor D'Orsini is right; you had ought to have your portrait done."

"Oh, no," the duchess demurred, and actually looked a trifle flustered. "I do not think—"

"Katherine dear, when was the last time you sat for a portrait? When you were a bride?" Winifred asked.

"Why, yes."

"Oh, my dear, that will never do. A woman needs must have another done once she comes into her full woman's beauty. That is what my dear Horace told me when he convinced *me* to sit. Do you not agree, Signor D'Orsini?"

The painter's lips twitched. "Indeed I do, dear lady."

"Oh, but, what a ninnyhammer I am! Signor D'Orsini has so very many offers for commissions that I do not know *when* he might get to you. And you are only visiting here, and so I do not suppose—"

"Well, then," the duchess interrupted, "perhaps as I *am* only visiting, and as you have not yet begun another portrait, Signor D'Orsini, you might consider doing mine straightaway." Not precisely a command, Winifred thought, but not precisely a question either. She wondered what Signor D'Orsini would do.

He looked with bemusement at the duchess, and then replied, "It would be my pleasure, Duchessa."

And so it was settled. Signor D'Orsini would move here to Rossmore as soon as might be arranged. Eleanor looked miffed, but Winifred was feeling quite pleased with herself.

She was less than pleased minutes later when Eleanor announced that she was giving a ball in a fortnight's time. Everyone present was to have a card, of course, and she did hope Georgie would be well enough to attend. A ball, Winifred thought. It was unlike Eleanor Truesdale to tax herself, not to mention her pocketbook, to give a ball in the provinces. Eleanor reserved such exertions for London. And then a look passed between Eleanor and the duchess, and Winifred knew that the ball was part of their scheme.

And as Lucy waxed enthusiastic about the profusion of flowers they were to have, and the acres of potted palms to create a garden effect, and that all the main floor salons were to be thrown open for their *huge* number of guests, Winifred watched Percy watching Diana. And she understood even more. Diana was to be led down the garden path at this ball. Somehow, the ball was to be the scene of Diana's downfall. Well, not if Winifred could help it!

After a hurried conference, sotto voce, with Horace, she made her own announcement. She was giving a dinner party in a se'nnight's time. Everyone must come. She hoped Georgie would be right enough, and she could stay the night if she wished not to travel twice in one day. Of course, she could bring little Ned if she wished. Georgie started to speak, but the baron interrupted, saying it would be up to Dr. Rustin, but that they much appreciated the invitation. So did everyone else; it seemed they all meant to come.

Oh, most excellent, Winifred thought, and was glad when it was time to leave. Her dinner party would need to be carefully planned; she must begin her cogitations immediately.

Adam breathed a sigh of relief when the requisite hour for tea was over. An hour, he reflected, could be an interminably

172

long time. And though it was over, the last of the guests having departed, Adam could still feel the tension in his body.

He had not enjoyed himself in the least. No, he amended, he had been quite amused at certain goings-on—Rusty's little tête-à-tête with Mrs. Millicent Weeksgate, Signor D'Orsini's attentions to Eleanor Truesdale and Adam's mother, Lady Hart's sharp eyes observing, her mind no doubt scheming. Whatever scheme she hatched, however, he did not doubt it would be fairly benign. She was a bit of a meddler, but she meant well. Unfortunately, the same could not be said of his mother and Lady Truesdale. They'd had their heads together a damn sight too frequently for his peace of mind.

And then there was Percy, blast his hide! His interest in Diana and her *dis*interest were painfully obvious. Even as the guests had waited for their wraps to be brought, Percy had cornered Diana with the intention of helping her on with her cloak. But Adam, having the advantage of knowing just *which* cloak was Diana's, had commandeered it from Stebbins and swept it round her shoulders before Percy could utter a word. For that simple act, Adam won from Diana a smile of gratitude that quite took his breath away.

But now his breath was back and uneasiness remained. He did not trust Percy to act the gentleman, to retreat when the object of his pursuit rebuffed him. When Adam had tried to warn Diana about Percy, she had reminded him that he had not the right to protect her. Well, Rusty did, but Rusty had appeared quite oblivious today to all but that pea goose of a lady author. Clearly, Adam would have to enlighten him as to Diana's need for protection. He would do it at first opportunity.

Such did not present itself for two days, however, and in the interim there were some rather interesting, if times unfortunate, goings-on at Rossmore.

The latter took the form of another row between Georgie and Edward. The subject was a nurse for Ned, and the slamming doors served to remind Adam that whatever progress had been made between the baron and baroness, they had a long way to go. Edward's old nurse arrived on Thursday morning to take over the Rossmore nursery, as she had decades ago. She was a round, pink-cheeked woman with a ready smile, and Edward

173

and the Stebbins and Mrs. Brownlow greeted Nanny Haycock with joy.

Adam's mother did not. Nanny Haycock had not been in residence two hours before the duchess declared that she was much too soft and wont to mollycoddle Ned and that with her the boy would never be fit to go off to school at the proper time. Edward thought this perfectly preposterous, and did not scruple to say so, but Georgie said that perhaps the matter needed more thought, perhaps they had ought to interview other candidates. Whereupon Edward declared that the position was filled and stormed off to his study. The duchess, in high dudgeon, ensconced herself in the morning room, and Georgie became a watering pot once more.

It was not a half hour following this delightful interlude that Signor D'Orsini arrived. With him came his valet, a mountain of luggage, several huge canvases, an easel and three boxes of painting supplies. Mrs. Stebbins showed him to a spacious chamber in the guest wing, and then he went in search of a room to convert into a studio.

He announced at luncheon that he had settled upon a small red sitting room in the guest wing. It had a big picture window and an eastern aspect, and he was quite in raptures about it.

The duchess was not. "Signor D'Orsini, I have never even *seen* such a room," she declared. "I own it will be most inconvenient. Surely you can find something a bit closer to the main part of the house."

Something like amusement flickered in the Italian's eyes before he inclined his head in a slight bow and replied, "Alas, *bella dama*, I have much regret for the great inconvenience to you. But no, I cannot find another studio. The lighting in this one—it is perfect, no?"

Adam watched his mother's eyes widen. He wondered when the last time anyone had so calmly denied one of her requests. She opened her mouth to speak; the artist forestalled her, his dark eyes holding hers with an intensity quite at odds with the softness in his voice.

"Ah, Duchessa, you will oblige me please by accompanying me to the studio straightaway after luncheon. I should like to do some sketching. Tomorrow, we begin in earnest."

The duchess looked nonplussed. Adam stifled a chuckle. Not

only had her thinly veiled command been denied, but she had, for all intents and purposes, just been issued a counter order. Adam could sense Georgie and Edward holding their breaths, awaiting her reply.

When it came it shocked everyone.

"You, Signor D'Orsini, are a most provoking man!" The painter raised one black brow. "Nonetheless—" she lifted her chin—"I shall accompany you."

Signor D'Orsini was the only one who did not stifle a gasp of surprise. He merely smiled very faintly, if a bit smugly.

Adam could not wait to relate it all to Diana.

Diana and Rusty arrived the next morning, and while Rusty went up to Georgie, Adam beckoned Diana into the library. She tried to demur, to remind him of vows he had no wish to recall.

"Please, Diana, I only wish to talk to you," he coaxed, and of course, she came.

It was not easy to keep to his unspoken resolve not to touch her. Her skin was so white against the raven curls framing her face, her eyes such a luminous blue against the deep plum color of her Kerseymere dress. And with her came that strange combination of fire and serenity that Adam was finding increasingly irresistible.

Nonetheless, he seated her on the sofa, himself in an adjacent leather chair, surely far enough away from her that he could keep his word. She laughed with him at his recounting of luncheon yesterday with Signor D'Orsini and sighed when he told her of Georgie's latest set-to with Edward.

"I think I shall suggest that she observe Lady Hart with Sir Horace whenever she can," Diana mused.

"Ah, you noticed that at tea, did you?" Adam asked.

She smiled that wide and gracious smile. "At tea, and countless times before."

"Well, better you tell her than I. She would bite my head off did I suggest she seek Edward's permission so frequently."

Her blue eyes danced. "But, my dear Adam, did you not note that Sir Horace refused Lady Hart nothing?"

He grinned and leaned forward, closer to her, and knew the moment he spoke that his next words were a mistake.

175

"And would you be a wife like Lady Hart, Diana?" He had only meant to tease, but of course she did not take it that way.

Her face became shuttered; he recognized the solemn Miss Rustin. "That is something I shall never know, shall I?" she said softly, and then excused herself to go see Georgie.

And Adam berated himself for what was, however unwitting, a thoughtless remark. But he cheered himself with the memory of her calling him "my dear Adam." It did not change aught, but it had been very nice to hear.

The sound of footsteps in the corridor reminded him of his resolve to speak with Rusty about Diana. It was, indeed, the good doctor he had heard, and he beckoned him inside the library. He settled them both near the hearth with snifters of brandy, and then began without preamble.

"Rusty, it is perhaps not my place to speak of this; but I do not know if you noted aught amiss at tea on Wednesday, and so I am taking the liberty of broaching the subject."

Rusty's black and silver brows rose in question, and Adam went on. "Sir Percy Truesdale was most particular in his attentions to Diana, and she was most . . . perturbed by them. And there is, I assure you, nothing honorable in those attentions."

Rusty took a slow sip of brandy. "And did you truly think, Adam, that I was unaware of these . . . attentions?"

"Forgive me, Rusty, but you seemed rather—er—pre-occupied."

"Ah. The delightful Mrs. Weeksgate. Well, my friend, distracted though I might have been, I did not fail to note my daughter's situation. Did I try to interfere, experience has taught me that I would only have succeeded in embarrassing her. For in truth, Percy and his most unwelcome attentions are a very old story. And while I would be remiss in my duty as parent did I not keep my eye peeled, yet I am confident Diana can continue to fob him off, as she has done these many years now."

"I do not doubt Diana's determination, nor your own concern, but if you will forgive me, I believe matters may so transpire as to require even greater vigilance. I am not certain what is afoot, but I suspect Lady Truesdale is plotting something rather unpleasant. Just—just watch Diana, Rusty.

She has made it plain that I have not the right to do so—"

"And she is correct in that, is she not?" Rusty interrupted, his eyes twinkling.

Adam slapped his glass down on the nearby table. "Yes, yes, but—Hellfire, Rusty! She needs more than your protection, or my concern. She is much too beautiful to be—that is, if it is not Percy, then it might be someone else!" Adam was becoming exasperated. Rusty did not seem to be taking this nearly seriously enough. It was Adam's fear for Diana that prompted him to blurt, "Dammit, Rusty, what she needs is the protection of a husband!"

"I believe I am able to protect her, Adam," he replied evenly. There was no humor in his eyes now.

"Yes, of course. I did not mean to imply—that is, even you must own that you cannot offer the same protection as a wedding ring. You cannot be with her at all times."

Rusty's face clouded over. Adam had the feeling that something beyond the present conversation suddenly overset him deeply. "That is true," he said heavily.

"Rusty," Adam went on after a moment, "she has made it quite clear that she does not wish to wed. She—ah—told me, some time ago, that she was hurt once, very badly, by a man." Rusty's eyes widened. "I do not know any particulars, nor am I asking, but perhaps it is time for her to overcome this reluctance and—oh, blast it all, Rusty! She is a beautiful, charming woman. 'Tis a terrible waste for her—"

"I know that, Adam. But she is a grown woman who knows her own mind. I have learned to respect that." He took another sip of the brandy and peered at Adam over the top of the snifter. "As for you, my friend, I know that you speak out of concern. But I must take leave to tell you that unless your interest in this matter becomes personal—and I mean *very* personal—then I do not wish to discuss this again. It really is *not* your concern, old chap."

And that, Adam thought ruefully, put him neatly in his place.

Of course, his interest was not *that* personal, he reflected once Rusty and Diana had left Rossmore. After all, he had offered and been refused, and that was an end to it. But still, he cared about her; they were friends, were they not?

She was in danger from Percy, and that aside, she was a woman meant to be wed. He poured himself another brandy and sat staring into the fire. That was when a little inner devil asked him how he would feel if Diana did suddenly take his advice and wed some handsome country squire or dashing captain of the guards. It took him only a moment's reflection, and he knew exactly how he would feel.

He would hate it. And what in bloody hell did *that* signify?

Chapter 12

Katherine, Duchess of Marchmaine, was not best-pleased to be making her way to Signor D'Orsini's "studio" this Friday morning. Yesterday, after nuncheon, they had had their first sitting, and it had been simply appalling! This puffed-up Italian painter actually thought that a commission to do her portrait gave him leave to order her about!

"Turn this way, *bella dama* ... lower your chin, *bellíssima.* . . . Smile for me, Duchessa."

Katherine did not understand most of the names he called her, but she was certain she would not approve of the half of them!

Now he ushered her into the studio, chiding her—chiding the Duchess of Marchmaine!—for being late.

"We must catch the very best light, *bella.* You must be on time, every day!" he exclaimed, seating her quickly in the red brocade chair that was to appear in the portrait.

And then he proceeded to twist her this way and that, scolding her as if she were a child did she so much as move a shoulder muscle. It was simply not to be borne! But when she tried to tell him so, in no uncertain terms, he threw up his hands, sending his pencil flying.

"No, no, no, Duchessa!" he exclaimed. "You must not speak, for I am working on the face now. I will make this portrait *magnífico* for you, *bella,* so that all will see the beauty and goodness of Katarina, Duchessa di Marchmaine." He had come round the easel to stand before her, and now his loud, dramatic voice softened.

"Now, come, you must help me, *bella*. I am trying to capture your mouth."

He put his pencil-smudged fingers to her chin and tilted it up. His fingers were calloused, and too warm, and she did not like them on her face. She was about to tell him so when his thumb stroked up to her mouth. "Let me see you smile, *bella*," he coaxed. She did not like the husky note in his voice. She did not like the fact that he was standing so close to her. She did not, as a rule, permit any man to come so close that his thighs were brushing her skirt, nor to put his hands on any part of her person.

"A soft smile," he was saying while his thumb, bold as brass, continued stroking the area around her mouth. It was most provoking to be obliged to sit still whilst he took such liberties, but she knew that if she moved, he would spend half an hour rearranging her in the chair. Instead she forced a smile so that he would step away from her.

This he did, smiling down at her and murmuring, "*Bene, bene.*" His dark eyes twinkled, and she was most grateful when he retrieved his pencil and went back to his easel. She stifled a sigh of relief. It would never do for him to know how much his proximity discommoded her, but the fact was that there was something about him. . . .

She did not understand it and pondered the matter as Signor D'Orsini went back to his sketching. His overly exquisite manner of dress and his melodramatic manner of expression had caused her, upon first meeting him, to dismiss him as a fop. Even today, as he worked, he wore a superbly cut claret coat, a black and gold waistcoat, and a starched cravat tied in the complex mailcoach. His black hair was slicked back, and surely that was a gentlemen's cologne that she smelled when he came close. But she was beginning to realize that he was no useless fribble. His extravagant manner hid, she very much feared, a quiet strength of purpose from which he would not be diverted. How else to explain his very polite but very definite defiance of her every wish? She was not accustomed to such Turkish treatment, and was already regretting having agreed to this foolish portrait.

But there was, if she would be honest with herself, more that perturbed her about the Italian. For when he had stood so close just moments ago, it had been his physical presence that discomfitted her. Was it because, despite his rather average size, he seemed possessed of an uncommon physical strength? Was it because of the breadth of his chest, or the fact that his thighs, encased in those shockingly tight pantaloons, seemed overly well-muscled? Surely a man of mature years ought not to be so—so well-formed. Yet despite the fine lines about his eyes and mouth that proclaimed his age near her own nine and forty years, he had the movement and form of a much younger man.

Katherine did not at all like the notion of being closeted with this man for days on end. She decided that she did not want her portrait done after all. But just as she was about to open her mouth and tell him so, he smiled at her. *"Bene, bene, bellissima.* You are doing very well," he said.

And she heard herself asking what *bellissima* meant.

"It means, 'very beautiful,' Katarina, Duchessa di Marchmaine," he replied in his deep voice.

It was merely Spanish coin, Katherine reminded herself. It meant nothing. She knew perfectly well she was not *bellissima.*

But she did not tell him she no longer wished her portrait done.

They worked again on Saturday morning and then went in to luncheon. Signor D'Orsini declared that he would sketch a bit more in the afternoon, and then he would show the duchess what he'd done thus far.

Georgina came down for luncheon and was in excellent looks. Adam appeared preoccupied; Katherine knew he'd spent the morning with his nose buried in those drawings of his. The doctor and his daughter were not present, thank goodness, though why her children found it necessary to discuss when next the Rustins would visit was quite beyond her.

She was pleased when the discussion turned to Lady Hart's dinner party and especially the Truesdale ball. Georgina was eager to attend both and speculated as to which of her ball gowns might fit her by then. Katherine offered several suggestions, and Georgina resolved to try on several of the gowns this very day. Edward saw fit to interrupt that rather

181

pleasant discourse to remind Georgina that it would be up to Dr. Rustin whether she could attend either entertainment.

"After all, Georgie," he said, "a ball is quite strenuous, and even a dinner party, what with the uncertain weather, may be unwise."

It was on the tip of Katherine's tongue to say that surely Georgina would be the best judge of her own strength, but Georgina opened her mouth to say it first.

She did not, however, say anything of the kind. "Of course, Edward," she replied instead. "I shan't do aught that Rusty deems inadvisable. And you, too, may tell me if you think I am overdoing my activity. I am sensible of the fact that until recently, my health was very much in jeopardy."

Edward smiled brightly across the table at Georgina. Katherine was astounded at such a statement, but decided to hold her peace.

She could not, however, keep silent when conversation shifted to little Ned and, inevitably, to his nurse. Edward fairly sang Nanny Haycock's praises, and Adam concurred, saying that she seemed devoted to Ned already. Georgie added that Nanny was very sweet, and that was when Katherine could contain herself no longer.

"Devotion is all well and good, children," she answered them, "but it can be misguided, you must know. And 'sweet' in a nanny is not necessarily a virtue. A child is never too young to develop bad habits. Why, I have seen the Haycock woman pick the child up if he so much as whimpers, even if he is well fed and warm! This, of a certain, does not auger well for—"

"Duchess," Edward interrupted, "I apprehend that you disapprove of Nanny Haycock, but I regret to say that the matter is not open for discussion. Nanny is here to stay."

Katherine felt her eyes flash, but Georgina again spoke before she did. "But, Edward, Mama does have a point that—"

"Damnation, Georgie!" Edward exploded with a complete disregard for manners or the sensibilities of women. "I am deuced tired of this! You cannot bear to hear Ned cry, and you are always most relieved when Nanny picks him up. You are completely in accordance with my way of thinking until your mother starts railing about the matter! I tell both of you ladies, I have had enough!"

How dare he, Katherine thought, trying to conceive a suitable set-down. She glanced quickly about the table. Georgina's lip was quivering. For pitysakes, was the girl to dissolve into tears again? Adam, blast that unnatural boy, was repressing a grin. He was seated across from her, and she could swear he was looking at Edward as if he'd like to applaud that ghastly little speech! But most surprising of all was Signor D'Orsini. He was sitting to Katherine's left, and she noted that his brows were drawn together in a frown. He looked decidedly miffed, and Katherine was most pleased that at least *someone* was piqued at the barbarous usage to which she was subjected in this house.

She opened her mouth to frame a suitable rejoinder to Edward, when she felt Signor D'Orsini's booted foot kick her. Startled, wondering how his foot had accidentally strayed several feet, she met his gaze. He shook his head almost imperceptibly and formed a "Shh" sound with his lips. Why, he was telling her to be silent! He had kicked her on purpose! She felt her hackles rise until she realized that he must mean to speak for her. It was rare that a gentleman did that for her, and she settled back to listen. But Signor D'Orsini did not speak for her, did not address Edward at all.

Instead he began asking Adam about the architectural changes he planned for Damerest Hall! Katherine was outraged! The audacity of the man! To silence her and then— Her hand fairly shook with rage as she reached for her fork. She quite forgot about the set-down she meant to give Edward, and concentrated instead on the choice words she would have to say to Signor D'Orsini as soon as they were closeted in that studio of his.

Quite unwittingly, she was distracted by the turn the conversation took. They were discussing details of the Elizabethan moldings and staircases at Damerest Hall—a tedious topic as far as Katherine was concerned—when suddenly Signor D'Orsini announced that he was considering the purchase of a small Elizabethan manor house in Derbyshire.

Katherine nearly choked on her wine. A foreigner, a painter, buying an Elizabethan manor? What was the world coming to? And was there no end to this man's impudence?

Adam watched D'Orsini lead his mother from the family dining room. Edward stood ready to help Georgie out of her chair. Over her head Adam and his brother-in-law exchanged a look of bemusement.

"A most interesting man," Adam murmured.

"Yes," Edward concurred. "I vow I cannot wait to see the . . . portrait that comes of all this."

Edward led his wife away before she could ask what they were talking about.

The one person Adam would have liked to discuss it all with was, of course, not there. He had not expected Diana and Rusty again today, and did not know if they would come on the morrow either. After all, Georgie was rapidly regaining her strength, was up and about for several hours each day. She did not need the constant vigilance of a doctor, or his daughter.

But Adam needed—No! He did not *need* to see Diana; he merely wanted to, in the way that friends liked to see one another. Besides, he was mindful of the fact that he had probably spoken out of turn to Diana *and* Rusty on Thursday—to Diana with his question about what sort of wife she would be, to Rusty about protecting her. Adam wanted, needed to make amends, and resolved to visit them at Three Oaks if they did not come here by Sunday afternoon.

It was, he told himself, the polite thing to do.

Katherine was in a huff, but she vowed to hold her tongue until she and the Italian reached the studio. She had no intention of amusing any lurking chambermaids. Signor D'Orsini had a firm grip on her elbow, and he seemed to be propelling her down the corridor. A glance sideways told her his brows were drawn together in that frown of his. He was angry. But surely not at *her*, Katherine thought. Why, *she* hadn't kicked *him* under the table, had she?

Once inside the studio, he ushered her straightaway to the chair and began arranging her head this way and that. He still had not said a word, but she could see that he was in quite a taking. She opened her mouth to speak, and he had the audacity to put his hand under her chin and push her mouth closed.

"We work," was all he said, and moved behind the easel.

Katherine was seething. She would choose her moment, and then she would tell this overblown Latin dilettante exactly what she thought of him. Then she would allow him to show her the preliminary sketch. If she did not approve, that would be an end to the whole matter. He could pack his bags and leave, and she would no longer have to put up with his high-handedness.

"Why do you make trouble between the baron and your daughter?" he asked, his hand never pausing as he sketched.

"I beg your pardon?" she said icily.

"I ask why you—"

"Yes, I heard you! How dare you say such a thing to me?" She pounded her fist on the arm of the chair.

"Be still, Duchessa," he commanded softly.

She resumed her position but gave vent to her outrage. "What is between my family and me is none of your concern!"

"Just as the matter of the nurse for the bambino is none of *your* concern, Duchessa." His pencil kept moving in small precise strokes.

"It most certainly is. Ned is my grandson!" she proclaimed heatedly.

"*Sí,* and he is much loved. He will be fine. I am not so certain about his parents."

"What are you talking about?" Katherine demanded.

Signor D'Orsini stopped sketching and eyed her pensively, as if deciding what to say. He sighed and picked up the pencil again. "You come between a man and his wife, Duchessa. This is not a good thing."

"I do no—"

"And you undermine a man in his own house. This is a grave—"

"I have had enough of your insolence!" she interrupted, rising majestically from her seat. "I shall not suffer another moment of such ill usage!" She lifted her chin. "I find I do not wish my portrait done after all."

Signor D'Orsini put his pencil down, smiling faintly, and wiped the smudges from his fingers on a cloth. "*Bene, bene.* It is good you get up now. I am ready for you to see the sketch. Then you decide."

Katherine knew she had ought to storm right out of the studio and this odious man's presence. But curiosity got the better of her. Head high, she walked round the easel to gaze at the sketch. Signor D'Orsini moved back to make room for her.

She stared, motionless, at the penciled visage that met her eyes. The woman who stared back at her from the canvas had all of her features and looked quite lovely. More lovely, in fact, than Katherine Damerest, Duchess of Marchmaine, had ever thought she was. But there was something wrong with the drawing, something profoundly disturbing, and it took her a moment to realize what it was. Even in black and white, she could see the sternness in the eyes, the harshness about the mouth.

Her hand went to her breast, where her heart was suddenly beating rapidly. "This—this is dreadful," she rasped, pointing to the canvas. "What have you done? This is not I. This is an insult!"

He shrugged. "I do not make judgments, Katarina, Duchessa di Marchmaine. I am an artist. I draw, I paint, what I see."

She drew herself up. "Then, your eyes fail you. Burn it, Signor D'Orsini. Your services will no longer be required!" She whirled round and strode for the door.

His voice stopped her. "Very well, Duchessa. Or, if you like, I could change it."

Despite herself, she paused, not a foot from the closed door.

"I thought," she said in a voice dripping with sarcasm, her back to him, "that you paint what you see."

"Sí, bella, I do. But we can change what I see, no?" She turned slowly round. He walked toward her.

"I do not understand."

"Come back," he said, gesturing her to the high-backed chair again.

She could not say why she obeyed and sat down. Perhaps it was curiosity; she had not the faintest idea what he was talking about.

"I ask you to smile," the painter said, standing directly in front of her, "and you give me what you saw on the paper. But

186

you do not like the smile. It is not a woman's smile."

"I smiled exactly as you told me to! Why, I even permitted you to paw at me and rearrange my mouth."

"Ah, but you see, *bella,* a smile comes from inside, not outside."

"I do not know—"

"You will permit me, Duchessa," he said softly, leaning down, "to show you, no?"

She eyed him warily, but nodded her consent. And before she knew what he was about, he lifted her chin, lowered his head, and put his lips to hers. Good God! Katherine thought in shock. This painter, this—this foreigner, was actually kissing her! His lips, far too warm and full, pressed hers. His tongue pushed her teeth apart. His—his—oh, dear heavens!

When at last he lifted his head, her body was shaking. She tried to summon up her very justifiable outrage, but instead felt stupefied.

"I—I—you are—are impertinent, Signor D'Orsini!" Her voice lacked its usual strength. "You had no right to do that. No one has *ever* kissed me in such a manner."

He lifted one black brow. "Then, I am sorry for you, Duchessa. But—ah—not even your own husband . . . ?"

The shaking had subsided; she felt more her own self. "Certainly not!" she said loftily. "The late duke always treated me as a lady. *He* was a gentleman!"

Signor D'Orsini's eyes danced as he looked down at her. "Then, I am sorry for you both, Duchessa. The bedchamber is no place for a lady and a gentleman, only for a man and a woman." His voice had taken on a very husky note; he was standing much too close to her chair, his thigh almost brushing her skirt. She told herself that her irregular breathing was due to her shock.

"I—ah—I am persuaded I should be—"

"Let us try that smile again, Duchessa," he said softly. "You have only to think about . . . what just transpired, and the smile will come."

She pursed her lips. "You are very sure of yourself, signor."

"Only sometimes, *bella.*" His hand went up to lightly graze her chin. "I merely follow my instincts. Shall we . . . try again, to see if my instincts are correct?"

187

She cleared her throat. "That will not be necessary."

He stepped back. *"Bene,* Duchessa. You give me a woman's smile, no?"

She did not know what sort of smile she gave him, only knew that she could think of little else but that kiss. And inevitably, however inappropriately, she could not help comparing it with her husband's kisses. The memories had dimmed over the years, but she recalled, now she thought on it, that William's kisses had been sweet at first, and later perfunctory, and finally nonexistent. As to what transpired in the bedchamber—well! It had always been a duty to Katherine. She had no idea what it had been to William; it was not something they discussed.

Katherine had certainly not minded when his visits to her chamber had ceased, and it had never entered her mind to seek a lover. Why on earth would she want to?

And where in heaven's name had such a thought come from?

She watched Signor D'Orsini, sketching intently, and wondered at the arrogance that allowed him to think that *his* kiss would change *her* smile.

"No, no, Duchessa!" he exclaimed suddenly. He wagged his pencil at her. "You do not think about what I ask you to think about."

How did he know—oh, never mind, Katherine told herself. And she allowed her thoughts once more to revolve around how she had felt just a few minutes ago. It was all, she told herself, for the sake of the portrait.

It was most odd, Adam reflected on Sunday morning, and he could hardly credit it. But he was certain that twice at dinner last night, a brangle had been avoided by a look cast at his mother by Signor D'Orsini. Adam was beginning to think his initial assessment of the artist fell short of the mark. He was clearly a man of unexpected depths, a man who would bear watching. He had further surprised everyone by offering to escort the duchess to church this morning. As Edward and Adam had had no intention of going, they had vouchsafed no objection to D'Orsini's escort. Strangely enough, neither had the duchess!

Adam wondered what Diana would—damnation! Adam

188

slapped his pencil down on the drawing he'd been unable to concentrate on. Why was he constantly speculating on her thoughts, her whereabouts, her reaction when he recounted things to her? Why was she in his thoughts at all? He had never before permitted a female to so invade his private time. Why now?

Oh, he wanted her more, he had to admit, than he'd ever before wanted a woman. He enjoyed her company, perhaps more than—well, and what did it signify? Nothing could come of it. Nothing at all.

Still, he had resolved to visit Three Oaks Cottage today, and he meant to do so, straightaway after luncheon.

She would not ask him. Diana would not ask her papa if he meant to go to Rossmore Manor today. If he went, he would surely take her, and if he didn't—well—that stood to reason, did it not? Georgie was on the mend. She did not require such vigilance on the part of her physician. Besides, they'd been there two days ago.

Had it only been two days? How could one person possibly miss another so much in such a short time? How ever had she, sane, sensible, serene Diana, come to such a pass?

She would see Adam at Lady Hart's dinner party, of course, and at the Truesdale ball, if he stayed here that long. But each encounter would only make the time of his final departure that much more painful. She did not comprehend the depth of her feelings. She did not recall missing Robert so acutely when they were apart. And yet, she had thought she loved him.

She did not love Adam. She couldn't; she wouldn't. So why did she think of him nearly every waking moment?

It had grown cold and bleak, and yet as the afternoon wore on, Diana could no longer abide the confines of the house. Wrapping her cloak about her, she stepped outside to amble down the winding front drive leading out from Three Oaks. She wondered if it would snow; it hadn't in days and the sky certainly threatened. And if it did snow, what would happen to Lady Hart's dinner party?

She heard the hoofbeats before she saw the sleek chestnut, or its rider. Her head jerked up, and she did not trouble to hide her smile of welcome. He looked wonderful, his chocolate brown greatcoat flapping in the wind, his thick hair tousled, his tall lean form erect in the saddle.

He drew up some three yards from her and dismounted in one fluid motion.

"Adam," she said softly, and had the nearly overwhelming urge to run into his arms. She checked herself in time, and told herself her heart was not beating faster as he approached.

It was fustian, of course, an absurd notion, but for one moment Adam had thought she was about to run into his arms. And he had been prepared to grab her, to lift her and swing her round and cover her mouth with his. Even now, as she stood demurely before him, wrapped in her claret-colored cloak, he ached to put his arms around her and pull her close. He wanted to bury his face in her neck and inhale her scent. He wanted— No! he told himself. He wanted to talk to her, and to Rusty. That was all.

"Hello, Diana. I—I came to see how you and Rusty are. I— is it not too cold out here for you?" He wondered at the awkwardness of his own tongue.

Her blue eyes began to dance. "I've got proper boots on today."

"Ah, well, then. Shall we walk, or—"

"No, no. Come to the stables and we'll go inside. You'll join us for tea?"

He smiled and nodded, feeling more in control of himself. Rusty looked momentarily surprised to see him, but greeted him genially nonetheless. They settled themselves in the front parlor before a cheerful fire, and when Diana excused herself to see about tea, Adam brought up to Rusty their previous conversation. Rusty brushed aside his attempt to apologize, and assured him that his concern was appreciated for the friendship it bespoke. But the odd look in Rusty's blue eyes said something else entirely. Something to the effect that he knew that friendship had had little to do with it. When Diana returned, Adam told himself he'd imagined that look. Conversation flowed easily over tea. Adam understood all too well why Edward had come here so often. The parlor was small

190

but elegant, the furniture delicately carved but surprisingly comfortable. And most of all, there was an air of peace and harmony about the room. Adam was not certain if it came from its inhabitants or its furnishings; he supposed a little of both. Or perhaps they were one and the same.

He watched Diana's fluid motions as she poured the tea and passed round a plate of scones and biscuits. There was a grace, a softness to her movements that many of the most polished ladies of ton could not hope to emulate. Her voice was warm, her smile achingly beautiful. Here in her own home he saw more clearly than ever the aura of serenity about her, one that beckoned a man to take his ease. How extraordinary was such a trait in a woman!

Diana was asking about Georgie and Edward. Adam was able to say quite truthfully that matters seemed somewhat improved but that part of it appeared to have to do with his mother.

"The duchess?" Diana asked incredulously.

"Do tell," Rusty murmured.

"I do not quite collect what is happening, you must know," Adam replied as he sipped his tea. "'Tis almost as if Signor D'Orsini has decided to—to take her in hand, so to speak. I have seen her several times open her mouth to speak, obviously in high dudgeon, only to close it at a look from the Italian. And when he decides 'tis time to return to the studio, she does not cavil."

"An interesting fellow, this D'Orsini," Rusty put in.

"What does Edward say to the matter?" Diana asked.

"We both feel there is more to this painter than meets the eye. For all of his Latin flair for the dramatic, the fellow plays his cards close to his chest. But whatever those cards are, so far we've no objections." He grinned and caught a dancing light in Diana's eyes.

There was more that he could say, about a certain look in his mother's eyes, one that he'd never seen before. About a certain current that seemed to pass between D'Orsini and his mother. He might be tempted to identify it were the woman anyone else, but the formidable Duchess of Marchmaine? Surely it could not be!

But Adam did not say any of those things, and strangely, it

191

was not Diana's presence that stopped him. It was Rusty's. With Diana he would have been quite comfortable—oh, no, he told himself. Such comfort would not do at all.

A serving maid came in soon thereafter with a message for Rusty. He read it and announced that he had got to go to see Amos Fontenay, near the village. The man could not seem to stop coughing, and his wife was certain he had the pleurisy or an inflammation of the lungs at the very least. Rusty did not seem unduly overset about the condition of Amos Fontenay's lungs, but drained his teacup and rose to leave nonetheless. He threw Adam a brief look which indicated that he, too, was expected to take his leave. Well, and so he must, Adam assured himself. It would be most improper to stay.

He glanced at Diana, and before she lowered her eyes he caught the look in them. She felt as he did—did not want him to leave, knew he must.

Why dammit? Why must he? If Edward could visit, why—oh, hellfire! He was no callow youth, and he knew deuced well why. Edward was a married man and could visit as a friend of the family. Adam's visits must be more circumspect, unless . . . unless he decided to—to court her.

But, of course, he did not wish to do any such thing. He was not, after all, disposed to marry. No female had ever held his interest long enough, and nothing that he had ever seen of the married state commended it to him. And yet, Diana was unlike any female he had ever met. And, now he thought on it, he *could* think of one thing that commended the wedded state to him.

He had thought at the time that the Earl and Countess of Debenham were a rare exception, but now he wondered. Nigel and Allegra had wed just months ago under somewhat havey-cavey circumstances. It was not a love match, nor would Adam have expected his friend Nigel to contract one. And yet, just weeks after their nuptials, Adam had seen Allegra gazing at her husband with a look of adoration such as Adam had not known a woman capable of. Nigel had seemed quite oblivious, but when his wife had run away, he became distraught, a man obsessed with finding the wife he realized he loved beyond reason.

The earl and countess had been reunited for months now,

but Adam had never thought to seek such happiness for himself. How many other women could there be who would look upon their husbands with such love?

Yet now he wondered. . . .

Fustian! he admonished himself. He did not love Diana, nor she him. . . .

Rusty excused himself to see about his carriage. Adam knew he had only moments to speak with her. She was seated on the sofa, just to the right of his chair, her eyes still lowered, her hands in her lap. If he reached out, he could cover her hands with his. Wisely, he did not. "Last time we spoke," he began without preamble, "I said something which overset you. I did not mean—"

"No," she interjected, raising her eyes. She recalled all too well his question about what sort of wife she would be. "I should not have reacted thusly. You were only quizzing me, after all."

He smiled at her, a smile that curved his mouth and lit his tawny eyes with warmth. "Well, then, if I am forgiven, I shall muster the courage to ask you to grant me the first waltz at the Truesdale ball."

Diana felt a rush of delight, mixed with relief. He had shifted from the awkward subject of their last encounter. He meant to stay for the ball. He wanted a dance, and of all dances, a waltz. She did not waste a moment's thought on the wisdom of refusing.

"I should be delighted to dance the waltz with you, Adam," she replied, trying to keep her voice light.

The warmth in his eyes became more intense. She suddenly felt a familiar tension in the room. He was seated to her left, in a tapestried chair that had always seemed quite large enough for Papa, for Edward, even for Robert. But Adam's tall, broad-shouldered form rather dwarfed the chair, emphasizing his strength. She thought of his arms about her, his body close as they danced the waltz, and knew that a most embarrassing flush was threatening to overtake her.

To cover her awkwardness, she blurted, "I did not know you were staying for the ball."

Adam's eyes danced. She was blushing quite adorably, and virtually squirming in her seat. He would give rather a great deal to know what images the waltz called to her mind. They brought more than a few to his, God knew. He had not, in truth, known that he meant to ask her. The words had simply just come out, for all he knew the whole thing was most imprudent.

Oh, devil take it! he thought. In for a penny, in for a pound. "And I should like the supper dance as well, Diana," he said by way of answer.

Her eyes blinked her surprise; her beautiful mouth smiled her pleasure. But she had time for no more than a nod before Rusty returned to say goodbye, and Adam was obliged to take his leave.

"I shall see you at Lady Hart's," he murmured as he bent over her hand.

"Yes," she whispered, and her hand trembled.

Rusty looked on, a most enigmatic expression in his normally clear blue eyes.

Katherine squirmed in her seat. Signor D'Orsini had fairly rushed her from the table at luncheon, and now he stood, sketching and erasing and muttering to himself.

"No, no, *bella*. I fear you have lost it—the smile I want. We must find it again, no?"

Her eyes widened. What did he mean, "find it again"? He moved round the easel and came to her in a trice.

"This time I think, Duchessa, you stand up. Like this, no?" He took her by the elbows and gently but firmly pulled her from the chair.

He did not release her once she was on her feet, despite her attempt to pull back. She hadn't realized that his hands were so strong. He was standing much too close to her. Why, his chest was almost touching her br—Well! It was most improper, and she meant to tell him so.

"Signor D'Orsini, I insist—"

"I think, *bella,* it is best if you do not speak," he whispered.

And then he kissed her! She did not want him to, but there was no escape. His hands held her, the position of his—his thighs trapped her, and the chair held her captive from behind. She tried to tear her mouth away, but one of his hands came up to grasp her nape to pull her mouth to his.

She could not fight him, and so Katherine Damerest stopped trying. Instead—she could not later say how it came about—she felt herself relaxing and—and enjoying the feel of his lips on hers. It was a mere kiss, and yet it was making her whole body feel odd—warm in places it was never warm, shaky in places that were always steady. And then she became aware that his hands were moving up and down her back, her sides, onto her breasts! Dear God! What was he doing? She had ought to stop him, slap him for such impertinence. But her body was becoming ever warmer, and with a will of its own, it swayed to him and clung.

It was he who broke the contact, taking her by the shoulders and gazing down at her with fiery black eyes. His breathing seemed heavy; her own was completely unsteady.

"You—you take liberties, sir," she rasped.

His eyes gleamed. "Yes," he said without apology.

"You—you will not do so again." Why did her voice not carry a tenth of its usual command and conviction?

"No?" he queried. Why was he smiling so? Why did she not administer the slap the blackguard so richly deserved? Why did her breasts tingle?

"You have no right to—to do what you did. You—I—I . . ." her voice trailed off; she felt confused, unsure of what she'd wanted to say. Her body was betraying her, acting most strangely.

She groped behind her for the arm of the chair and sank back, onto her seat.

"What is it, *cara?*" he asked in a gentle voice.

She wanted so much to rail at him, to put him in his place. But she had, after all, not fought him as she should have done. Mortified as the full realization of what had just transpired hit her, she could not meet his eyes. "I do not know what came over me. No one has ever—that is—I have never felt like this before. I do not understand, but I will not allow such—such a thing to happen again."

"I think you are right. You do not understand," he murmured and then lowered himself on his haunches until his eyes were level with hers. He drew her gaze and held it.

"You amaze me, Katarina, Duchess of Marchmaine. You

195

were many years a wife, and now many years a widow. And yet, I am thinking that you are very much an innocent." There was a kindly note in his voice; no man had ever spoken to her thusly, and she was hard put to hold on to her anger.

But she still had her pride. Squaring her shoulders, she said, "I hardly think the mother of two grown children may be called an innocent. And I fail to see what any of this has to do with my portrait."

"Ah, but then, you are not the artist," he countered smoothly, rising and moving back to the easel. "Smile for me, Katarina. I think you will like your portrait." He chuckled to himself. "Oh, yes, you will like it very well, indeed."

Chapter 13

Diana sat before the looking glass and put the finishing touches to her toilette. She felt quite calm, and after all, why should she not? She was merely going to a dinner party at Arden Chase. She and Papa had been there many times before. Lady Hart was a gracious hostess; it would be a lovely evening.

But it was not merely another dinner at Arden Chase, and Diana knew it well. Adam would be there. She sighed. It was utterly nonsensical, and unconscionable besides, for her to think of him so much. Why could she think of little else? Why had she changed her gown three times tonight before deciding on the plum-colored Turkish satin? It was a lovely gown, one of her favorites, with tiny puffed sleeves falling off the shoulder, matching satin buttons running from the corsage down the front of the skirt, and a border of roses at the hem. She wore her mother's ruby pendant and small matching teardrop earrings, and now she wound a satin ribbon through her dark hair.

She felt utterly feminine and knew she was in her best looks, except for the dark smudges under her eyes. She was not sleeping well, and refused to think of how much more difficult the nights would be once Adam had left Rossmore.

As it was, she knew she would be seeing far less of him, now that Papa had pronounced Georgie out of the woods. She'd gone with Papa to Rossmore on Monday morning, and he had declared Georgie quite fit enough to spend a good part of each day belowstairs. But when Georgie had asked whether she might attend Lady Hart's dinner party, Papa had looked doubtful. Despite Georgie's marked recovery, and Lady Hart's offer that she bring Ned and stay the night, he thought it prudent for her to remain at Rossmore. Edward seconded that, stating that they would all three stay home and reminding her of the uncertainty of the weather.

Georgie had looked disappointed, and opened her mouth to speak, but a glance at Diana had caused her to smile at Edward and nod her acquiescence. Diana hoped, now that the evening in question had arrived, that Edward and Georgie would enjoy what must be a rare private time together.

She and Adam, of course, would not have the opportunity to be private tonight, nor had they had private discourse on Monday morning. But they had, not for the first time, said things with their eyes that they'd had no right to say. She saw in his eyes a kind of hunger that he could call up in her with a mere touch of his hands. And she saw mirrored in his eyes her own knowledge of the futility of it all. She could not wed. He did not wish to, and even did he change his mind, a doctor's daughter was not an eligible partí for a duke of the realm. The latter was an unspoken barrier between them, and lest they forget, the duchess was there to remind them.

But it would never come to that. Their acquaintance would soon come to an end. Diana was persuaded Adam would return to Damerest Hall soon after the Truesdale ball. Meanwhile, she would enjoy this night at Arden Chase, and the ball, to the fullest. She would not dwell on her confusing, deepening feelings for Adam Damerest. She would not attempt to put a name to the heat her body felt in answer to his, to the pleasure in his company, to the urge to turn and speak with him at all hours, even though he was not there.

No, she would not put a name to such forbidden feelings. For that would only make it harder when word came to her, as it surely would one day soon, that the Duke of Marchmaine had departed the Yorkshire dales and gone home, where he belonged.

The weather was severe. Icy blasts of cold air assailed anyone unfortunate enough to lift his face from the folds of his coat, and the clouds were ominous. It was, Adam reflected, undoubtedly fortuitous that Edward had insisted he and Georgie stay home from Lady Hart's dinner party. Adam had anticipated snow all day, wondering whether any of them would be able to go. But other than a few flurries of snow this morning, the sky had remained clear, though bleak.

And so here he was, mounting the stone stairs of Arden Chase behind his mother and Signor D'Orsini and wondering whether the ominous sky would have kept any of Lady Hart's guests away.

And then they were inside the entry lobby, and the one guest who interested him the most immediately caught his eyes. She was just now relinquishing her claret-colored cloak to the butler, and then she turned and saw Adam. And smiled.

Was it that smile—wide and full of grace and unabashed pleasure at seeing him—or was it the gown she wore that caused his pulse to accelerate? It was not the sort of frothy confection Georgie would have worn, nor the sort of stiff, ornate garment his mother favored. It was a sleek, smooth plum-colored satin that hugged her curves and moved when she did. It was, in a word, utterly sensual, and his hands grew damp with the need to run them over—

He pulled himself up short, closing his mouth, which he realized was quite gaping open. He walked slowly to her, taking her hand, and reminding himself to release it after he'd pressed his lips to her gloved fingers. And then he forced himself to turn and greet the rest of the company.

I am not shaking, Diana told herself as Adam turned to greet Lady Hart. His mere touch did not straightaway flush the cold of the evening from her entire body. The admiring gleam in his eyes did not warm her to the golden glow of a summer's day. The sight of him in his forest green velvet coat and tight creme-colored britches did not cause her body to quiver and her mouth to go dry. She was no green girl to be so affected by a man; she was a woman fully grown, mistress of her emotions.

She schooled her face to bland serenity, and willed her wayward body to follow.

Winifred Hartcup surveyed her dinner table with supreme satisfaction. It was, of course, a pity the baron and baroness could not attend, but given the vagaries of the weather, she certainly understood. And from what she'd gleaned via the servants' grapevine, an evening to themselves might be just what the Rossmores needed.

As to the rest, matters seemed to be falling out quite nicely. Winifred had seen the heated look exchanged by dear Diana and the duke in the entry lobby. Only a nudge or two would be needed there, provided Percy could be kept occupied. Rusty had visited dear Millicent two times already, once to bring her a book of poetry and then to return one of her own Gothic tales, which Rusty had read with alacrity.

Even Winifred's third little project seemed, surprisingly enough, to be moving right along. The duchess's portrait was under way, and tonight Katherine was not at all her usual acerbic self. And she actually seemed flustered at finding out that Signor D'Orsini was to be her dinner partner.

They were fourteen at table, and Winifred was quite pleased with their placement. To her left sat the duke, with Diana beside him, then Rusty and dear Millicent. Between Millicent and Lady Truesdale sat the wealthy, retired nabob, Colonel Plunkett. The old gentleman lived a stone's throw from Arden Chase, and Winifred always enjoyed his company. Eleanor Truesdale found him a dead bore and was quietly smoldering over finding herself seated next to him. The fact that Sir Horace, at the head of the table, sat to her immediate left seemed not to mollify Eleanor in the least.

But much as Eleanor's obvious discomfiture amused Winifred, she had not invited the colonel merely to annoy the viperous Lady Truesdale. No, it was rather his houseguests, his niece and nephew, who had been of interest to Winifred. Her eyes continued round the table, and she decided her hunch on that head had been right.

Next to dear Horace sat Katherine and Signor D'Orsini, engrossed in a discussion which Eleanor was straining to hear. To Signor D'Orsini's left sat Lucy Truesdale, who simply would not do for the Duke of Marchmaine. Hence the man to Lucy's left, Captain James Plunkett, the colonel's nephew and heir. Eleanor would not be best pleased with the connection should such a match come about, but Lucy, who was painfully shy, could do a good deal worse. Captain Plunkett was amiable, dashing in his regimentals, and destined to be quite plump in the pocket one day. Best of all, he was drawing Lucy out, and the dear girl was gazing up at him with a rapt expression.

Winifred's eyes shifted to Horace. He, too, had caught the tête-à-tête between Lucy and the captain, and now he smiled faintly at Winifred, nodding almost imperceptibly. As always, she felt a little rush of pleasure at his approval of her little schemes. He always gave her the confidence to go on to the next one, and it was such fun to confide in him and share her little triumphs.

But she was not quite so sanguine about the last pair round her table. For next to Captain Plunkett sat his widowed sister, Mrs. Amelia Brixworth. A comely, voluptuous woman of some thirty summers, she had been left well provided for by her late husband and had no particular disposition to marry again. Winifred's sources had told her the lady was not averse to a little discreet dalliance, however, and the string of broken hearts she had reportedly left behind her in the few years of her widowhood led Winifred to believe she could well handle Percy. And Mrs. Brixworth, with her fiery auburn hair and her low-cut gown of coral silk, was just the distraction Percy needed.

Poor Percy, Winifred mused as she sipped her Madeira. He really was faced with a dreadful dilemma. He was seated between Mrs. Brixworth on his right and Winifred herself on his left. But while his eyes could not help feasting on the ample charms displayed so enticingly by Amelia Brixworth, his real quarry, Diana Rustin, was seated across the table. Like his mother, Percy was not best pleased with the seating arrangement. But for the moment he could do little more than glare across at Diana, engaged in a tête-à-tête with the duke, and console himself with his lascivious contemplation of Amelia Brixworth's dècolletage.

Oh, the joys of being a hostess! Winifred thought, as the oxtail soup was taken away and the dressed crab and truffled chickens were served.

Little tête-à-têtes gave way to general discourse. The duchess's portrait was discussed, and Eleanor Truesdale made it plain that she expected hers to be next. To the surprise of everyone except Winifred, Signor D'Orsini demurred.

He glanced at Katherine a moment before replying, "Who can say, Lady Truesdale, what I shall be doing next."

Eleanor Truesdale quickly shifted the talk to her ball, which would take place in a se'nnight's time. Lucy spoke animatedly about the planned decorations, and her own gown, and Captain Plunkett smiled indulgently. Then Percy asked Diana for the first waltz.

"Thank you, Sir Percival," Diana replied with great politeness, "but my first waltz is already bespoken."

"Well, then," Percy said smoothly, running his fingers over the rim of his wine goblet, "I shall have the second waltz. And the supper dance."

"I am afraid the supper dance is bespoken as well," Diana said calmly.

"And she has promised the second waltz to me," Rusty put in.

Percy, looking dagger points at Rusty and then at Adam, clasped the stem of his goblet so tightly that Winifred thought it might snap. Surprisingly, it was Amelia Brixworth who stepped into the breach.

"How fortuitous, Miss Rustin, that your dances are bespoken. I own Sir Percival has quite forgot, have you not, dear sir?" She put a hand to Percy's arm and pouted prettily. "'Twas whilst we were having sherry in the Purple Saloon before dinner. You asked *me* for the first waltz, *and* the supper dance."

Percy blinked for a moment in confusion but recovered quickly and smiled at her. "You are quite right, Mrs. Brixworth. I fear all the delicious food and superb wines have quite addled my brain. I shall be delighted with your exquisite company, my dear. As to Miss Rustin—Mother, are you planning a third waltz?"

"Of course, Percy, dear," Lady Truesdale called across the table.

"Excellent," Percy replied smugly. "Then, I hope, Miss Rustin, you will honor me with that."

Diana consented, her face admirably passive. Adam clenched his teeth. Mrs. Brixworth inched her bosom closer to Percy's plate. Winifred rang for the orange trifle.

It was during the consumption of the elegant sweet that

202

Lucy exclaimed, "Oh, look, 'tis snowing!"

A chorus of groans and "oh, my goodness, mes" greeted this pronouncement, as everyone craned their necks to see the steady stream of white flakes falling to the ground. The duchess and Eleanor thought to leave straightaway, before it grew worse, but the men disagreed, and it was Horace who made the final pronouncement. He walked over to one of the windows and peered out.

"Don't know but what it's been falling for hours, with none of us the wiser. I own it would be foolhardy to venture out now. Visibility is poor, and Lord knows what the roads are like. There's plenty of room here. My Win always keeps the guest rooms aired. Do all of you stay the night, and in the morning we shall see."

Dear Horace resumed his seat, and Winifred caught the glint in his gray-green eyes. She was to have her house party afterall. How perfectly delicious! Winifred savored a spoonful of the trifle, ruminating upon the most auspicious room assignments.

Winifred dismissed her maid and sat at her dressing table, absently brushing her hair. Everything was falling in just famously! Her guests were all bedded down for the night, or at the least, had been shown to their rooms, and Winifred was quite pleased with the impromptu allotment of guest chambers.

Percy was at the far end of the east wing, close to Mrs. Brixworth but far from Diana. The duke and Rusty had each been placed between Percy and Diana. Signor D'Orsini had his old room back and Katherine—

"Win, my love, where *are* you?" Horace called impatiently. "Come on now! I'm tired."

Winifred set her brush down and grabbed the purple velvet wrapper from the back of her chair. It would not do to keep Horace waiting. The dear man absolutely refused to go to bed without her, and insisted on going to bed as soon as he was tired. Winifred, of course, was never tired, especially when she was working on one of her projects.

She rose and glanced through the dressing room door into her bedchamber. That new upstairs maid had turned down her bed again. The dear girl was still maintaining the polite fiction that the Hartcups were respectable people who maintained separate bedchambers. Oh, well, the girl would give up soon enough, as the rest of the staff had done.

For, of course, the Hartcups were not respectable at all. In winter they slept in Horace's chamber, for the ornate bed hangings kept his four poster toasty warm. And in summer they favored Winifred's room, with its huge, airy window. But she could not recall a time, in more than thirty years of marriage, that they had ever slept apart. "Whyever would one want to?" Horace would have asked had she questioned him, and indeed, she had got to agree.

"Winifred!" he bellowed.

"Coming straightaway, dear heart," she sang out, and dashed through his dressing room into his bedchamber.

He was standing next the bed, his dressing gown unbelted over his naked body. The sight of him like this never failed to cause her heart to go pitter-patter. She herself wore a purple chiffon night rail, which Horace permitted out of concession to the cold. But in summer. . . .

Horace shrugged out of his dressing gown and climbed into bed, holding the blankets back so that she could climb onto the other side. He tugged the blankets over them and pulled her close.

"Mmm," she sighed contentedly. "You know, dear heart, I was thinking."

"About what?" he murmured, his mouth at her nape as he inhaled her scent.

"Well, I hope I've done the right thing. You know, I put Katherine in the chamber—"

"I know where you put her, Win, my love. Now enough. I do not wish to speak of any of them any longer. This is our time now."

"You are right, Horace, of course," she concurred, feeling her body relax as he turned her round and pulled her into the curve of his long, lean body, spoon fashion.

This was the golden hour, the very best time of day. Their time.

"They're all fools, the lot of 'em," Horace mumbled, nibbling on her ear. His hand cupped her hip, and Winifred

204

wriggled closer to him. "If they had a lick of sense, any of 'em, they'd go out tomorrow and find the nearest vicar to tie the knot." He kissed her nape.

"This is what life is all about, Winifred," he rasped, as his hand came under her night rail to rest on her belly.

She felt that familiar mixture of utter peace and rising heat. "I know, dear heart, I know," she whispered, and turned to take him in her arms.

Rusty could not sleep, and gave up trying. He belted the brocade dressing gown he'd found in his room, lit a taper, and made his way belowstairs. He would go to the library, to find a book to read.

"Oh! You startled me!" gasped a soft female voice as he entered the library.

"Millicent! Are you all right?" He set the taper down and walked briskly toward her. "I'm sorry. I did not mean to frighten you."

He stopped some three feet from her. She was wearing a silk wrapper, much too light for the frigid night air. "No, I—silly of me, really. I hadn't expected anyone."

She pulled the wrapper more tightly around herself, holding it closed at the bosom. She looked so soft and vulnerable and tiny. He hadn't realized how very small and delicately made she was. Her hair, flaxen streaked with silver, was down now, falling in soft waves about her face and pulled back with a ribbon. He wanted very much to loosen that ribbon and watch her hair fall free.

Instead he asked, "Could you not sleep, my dear?"

"No, Dr. Rustin. I—"

"Rusty." He smiled at her. Even by candlelight he could see her pink cheeks begin to flush. He stayed where he was, not wishing to scare her away.

"Rusty," she repeated softly. "I thought to come here and—"

"Are your characters keeping you awake again, Millicent?"

He finally coaxed a smile out of her. She ran her hands up and down her arms. "No, not this time. I—that is—"

"Are you cold, my dear?"

205

"Oh! Well, I—ah—'tis a very cold night, is it not?" She ran a hand through her hair. She was quite endearingly flustered.

He held out his arms. "Why do you not come here, and let me warm you, Millicent."

Her slate blue eyes grew round. "Oh, I couldn't! I mean to say—"

"I only mean to hold you, Millie," he said gently, and took a step forward. "Come."

She met him halfway, and he enfolded her in his arms. For minutes they said nothing. How long had it been since he'd held a woman thusly? She fit perfectly, her head coming just to his chin. She smelled of spring flowers. How did she contrive that in the midst of a snowstorm?

"Warmer now?" he asked after a time, keeping his arms firmly clasped round her.

"Oh, yes," she breathed into his shoulder.

"It is good to have someone to share the cold nights with," he said, and tilted her head up to his.

"Yes," she uttered softly.

Her lips looked sweet and pink. How long had it been since he'd wondered what a woman's lips would feel like, taste like?

"I've been alone a long time, Millie. Too damned many long, cold nights. I'm tired of it. How long have you been alone, my dear?"

"Five years," she whispered.

"Are you . . . tired, as I am, of being alone?"

She bit her lip, and nodded.

His eyes scanned her face slowly. He brushed her cheek and her brow with his finger. They'd met such a short time ago, but somehow, he'd known from their very first meeting exactly what he wanted. Still, he hadn't meant to say the next words, not yet. But now, holding her like this, he could not help himself. "I would be very honored, Millie, if you would come to me, and be my wife."

She blinked, and he saw the pleasure in her eyes before they narrowed. "B-but, Rusty, you hardly know me."

He chuckled softly. "I know enough. I know that you are sweet and good and lovely. I know that you need someone to take care of you, that you have a wonderful imagination and will never bore me, that you will warm my nights." His voice had grown husky, and he bent to touch his lips to hers, softly, ever so gently. When he withdrew, his voice was a bit shaky. "And I know that I could love you, Millicent."

Her eyes glistened with moisture. "Oh, Rusty, I think that I could love you, too."

"Could you, Millicent?" He grinned as she nodded. "I am glad, so very glad."

He kissed her again, a bit less gently, and when he stepped back he was a good deal more shaky.

"Will you come and sit with me now, near the window, and watch the snow falling? Then in a while I'll take you to your room."

Her eyes widened in consternation. He shook his head at her. "You ninny. I meant that I will see you to your door. But I am not ready to part with you just yet."

Millicent smiled at him, and put her hand in his and walked with him to the large bay window. He angled a love seat to face the window and pulled aside the draperies so that they could look out at the night. He draped an afghan across their laps; but it was still cold, and he pulled Millicent close, his arm about her shoulders.

"Cold?" he asked.

She looked up at him. "Oh, no, Rusty," she replied, eyes shining. "Not anymore."

"Not anymore." What sweet words they were, he thought, as they watched the snow fall steadily against the black sky. Rusty stroked her cheek with his free hand, and they began to talk, soft murmurings about their separate lives in the past and their hopes for the future together. Millie had a grown daughter, married and living in Kent. They would go to visit her as soon as the severe weather abated.

"What about Diana?" Millicent asked at that point. "Will she mind?"

Rusty did not even hesitate. "Diana will be delighted. She has been telling me for years that I had ought to do this. But I have never before been tempted."

Millicent giggled. "Neither have I. But truly, Rusty, Diana is a lovely girl, and I would not want to usurp her place as mistress of your household. Not but what I am persuaded she is much more efficient at running a house than I. Oh, dear." She sat bolt upright and looked stricken. "You really can have no notion of what you are getting into, Rusty. I am afraid I am rather a bit addlepated about domestic chores and—"

"Millie, Millie," he interrupted, pulling her back within the curve of his arm. "It is not your domestic abilities that . . . interest me. I have a housekeeper for all that." He tugged the ribbon from her silky hair and whispered in her ear, "I am marrying you for far more important reasons, madam."

He felt a shiver ripple through her and did not think it was from the cold. "And as to Diana, you needn't trouble about her. I make no doubt she will welcome you, and the shared responsibility. And besides, perhaps she herself, that is . . ."

His voice trailed off, and after a moment Millicent said, in her usual abstracted manner, "She and the duke seem rather . . . fast friends."

Rusty raised a brow. "So you noticed that, did you? Well, unfortunately matters for them are a bit more complicated than for us. For us, they are blessedly simple."

He took her hand and raised it to his lips, and thus they sat in companionable silence for several more minutes. And then he rose and helped her up, and escorted her abovestairs. The corridors were icy cold, and she clung to him for warmth; and he found that he liked that very well. So well, in fact, that he was loathe to let her go at her door.

He forced himself to release her, and kissed her brow. "As soon as the snow abates, I shall go find the vicar and have the banns posted. I do not wish to wait, Millicent."

She lowered her eyes. "Neither do I, Rusty," she mumbled, and then to his delight, stood on tiptoes and kissed him softly, briefly on the lips. Then she fled into her chamber.

James Rustin went to bed a very contented man.

Katherine was restless. She had tried reading, had had a maid bring her hot milk, had tossed and turned and plumped her pillows. But still she could not sleep, and had resorted to pacing her chamber.

She could not understand this unaccustomed sleeplessness. The evening had been rather pleasant—surprisingly so, since she did not usually enjoy provincial entertainments. And she could not fault the accommodation. Her chamber, though perhaps small, was well appointed with a canopied bed and furnishings in the Queen Anne style. A blazing fire had been awaiting her, the bed had been warmed, and a maid sent with nightclothes to help her retire.

By now the fire was little more than glowing embers, and a decided chill pervaded the room. The dressing room was colder still, but Katherine found herself lighting a taper and opening the wardrobe out of sheer boredom. She scanned its contents—an assortment of dressing gowns, night rails and slippers—obviously kept for guests who found themselves, as she now did, without luggage. Katherine closed the wardrobe doors, grudgingly granting that Winifred Hartcup was a thoughtful hostess.

And that was when she noticed the hitherto unseen door, wedged between the wardrobe and a highboy. Curious as to whether the door led to a sitting room or an anteroom of sorts, she picked up the taper and slowly turned the knob.

Before she'd got the door fully opened, she realized that a taper was burning on the other side. Her heart began to pound. Who was in here? Logic told her to close the door and stay on her own side, but curiosity got the better of her, as well as a bit of pique. Whoever was here did not belong here. Briskly she pushed the door open. And gasped.

He was standing at the window, peering out, clad in a dark velvet dressing gown. A quick glance told her this was no sitting room—this was his bedchamber!

He turned and smiled. "Ah, *cara*. I have been waiting for you," he said, and came forward to take the taper from her suddenly unsteady hands and to draw her inside.

"What—whatever do you mean, Signor D'Orsini? There must be some mistake. Surely Winifred did not realize—"

"Katarina," he interrupted, shutting the door behind him and possessing himself of both of her hands. "Lady Hart is a woman of great wisdom. I do not think she makes mistakes."

Katherine's eyes widened. "Signor—"

"My name is Antonio, Katarina. I have been listening to you prowl about your rooms for the last hour. I have wondered whether to wait for you to discover that door, or to go and get you myself. But I did not want to startle you."

The night air was cold, very cold, but her hands were warm, too warm. This was madness. "Ah, Si—Antonio, this is highly improper. I had best be going now."

"You cannot pretend you were sleeping soundly, Katarina. Do you not know why you could not sleep?" He brushed her cheek with his knuckle. His voice was deep and husky. Her silk dressing gown felt much too thin. Dear heavens, was it sheer? And her hair was down! He must think her a veritable wanton!

"I expect 'tis the strange surroundings," she said stiffly, pulling away from him.

"Katarina." His voice was soft, oddly compelling. She did not recall ever giving him leave to use her Christian name. Why was she using his? "I could not sleep either," he murmured. He was touching her again, his hands at her shoulders, his broad chest far too close to her bosom.

For the first time she realized that his dressing gown gaped open, and that—that there did not seem to be a nightshirt beneath it! Her heart began to pound again.

"It is very cold tonight, *cara.* Let me keep you warm. I will help us both sleep, no?" He bent his head and, before she could speak, took her lips in a soft, gentle kiss.

His tongue traced the inside of her lips, and she felt a tingling all through her body. She reacted instinctively, swaying to him, causing him to tighten his grip on her shoulders and attempt to force his tongue between her teeth. That was when she drew herself up, pulling her mouth away. He did not release her shoulders. Whatever was wrong with her? There could be no mistaking his intent. It was madness, all of it.

"You forget yourself, Antonio," she said, surprised at how breathless she sounded. "There is no portrait here, no need—"

"*Cara,* did you really think this was all about a portrait?" he asked in a tone, almost tender, that she had never heard before. It quite unnerved her.

"Well, of course. What else—"

"It is about you and me, Katarina. A man and a woman and the joy we can bring each other."

She swallowed hard. "I—I am a respectable woman."

He chuckled. "Of course you are. And I mean you no

210

disrespect. And no one else will know. It is between us. And indeed, if you—ah—enjoy our time together, I shall make you even more respectable."

"Antonio, what—whatever do you mean?"

"That I am rather respectable myself, *cara*. I do mean to buy that manor house in Derbyshire, you must know. And then there is the villa in Italy, left to me by my grandmama—"

"You—you have a villa in Italy?"

"*Sí, cara mía.*" He chuckled again. "Did you think that because I like to paint I was born in a briar patch?"

"I—no—that is, I did not think—"

"Good. Then, do not think now, Katarina. It is a time to feel." He dropped his right hand from her shoulder and let his long, artist's fingers graze her neck, her throat, and down to her breast.

She could hardly breathe. He was right. She could not think. She forced herself to speak. "I do not understand, Antonio. Why me? I am not—"

"But you are, *bella*. You are everything to me. Come to me now. It is time." He moved back some ten paces, toward the bed, and held his hand out to her. She looked at that hand and the bed, and was suddenly terrified.

"I—I cannot, Antonio. It has been so long. I have forgotten—"

"Ah, *cara*. It is like riding a horse, no? There are some things one never forgets." She shook her head, appalled to feel tears in her eyes. She never cried!

"Come to me, Katarina. I will bring you a woman's joy."

Two tears fell, trickling down her cheeks, and Katherine Damerest, Duchess of Marchmaine, held out her hand and stumbled forward.

Adam had known, from the moment he'd seen the snow falling and realized its implications, that he would not be able to sleep. In part it was having Diana under the same roof, only doors away, that was tormenting him. Of course, they'd spent several nights under the same roof when first they'd met, but now it was much worse. Now he knew her much better, and the wanting went beyond mere desire, to an ache that pervaded his

211

body, his mind, the very core of his being.

But it was not only Diana. It was Percy. Adam did not trust the fellow a stone's throw. He hoped Diana had a lock on her door and the sense to use it. He hoped Percy would take the bait of Mrs. Brixworth, which Lady Hart had so neatly dangled before him. But none of those things were certain, and Adam could not sleep.

He debated whether to check on Diana, which surely passed all bounds of propriety, or to listen at Percy's door, to make certain he was there, or to nonchalantly stroll down the corridor half a dozen times. For the moment he simply paced his room in his shirtsleeves and britches, listening for footsteps that did not belong outside.

Percy waited until the house settled itself into sleep. He sat drinking brandy and pondering his options. Amelia Brixworth, tempting morsel that she was, was available, and very willing, and only two doors away. Diana was farther, past, if he was not mistaken, the doors of her father and Marchmaine. Diana was not willing and for all intents and purposes not available. But he had wanted her for a very long time. And now she was within reach. He had even taken the precaution of bribing a servant to filch her key for him.

There was, however, the possibility that she might damn her reputation and actually scream. Which made him consider simply waiting for his mother's ball next week. The little charade she planned for him to enact, strictly for her own purposes, would do the job nicely. Of course, his mother did not know that he planned a little variation on her script, to suit *his* purposes. And there would be no one to hear the uppity Miss Rustin scream then.

But Percy did not want to wait. She had looked particularly delectable in that satin dress tonight, and far too occupied with Marchmaine. Percy decided that he had waited long enough.

He padded silently, barefoot, down the icy corridor. He carried no taper, not wanting to attract attention, but even in the darkness he knew where she was; he had counted the doors.

Chapter 14

It was pure fustian, Diana told herself. That the key was missing was a mere accident. She was letting her imagination run amuck; she was in no danger. True, the looks Percy had given her at dinner had been enough to make her skin crawl. But he had been looking at her in that manner for years. . . .

And if she would be honest with herself, Percy was not the cause of her sleeplessness. For the image that filled her mind as she tossed and turned in her bed was of a face far more dear, eyes far warmer, a mouth far more inviting than that of Percy Truesdale. 'Twas the face of a man she could not have, a man whose mere presence made her smile, a man who knew she had ticklish feet. A man who could make her want, despite herself.

She finally began drifting off to sleep, her candles burning low in their sockets, her mind swirling with forbidden images of the Duke of Marchmaine.

She was half awake, half asleep. The images were so vivid. She could actually see the door handle turning, slowly and silently. The door opened with nary a squeak. And then he stood there, at the threshold, a tall, dark silhouette only faintly illuminated by the guttering tapers. He did not carry a candle. He closed the door behind him and came forward slowly, his face completely shadowed.

Her blood began to pound. She knew she should send him away, knew in her heart of hearts that she did not want to. She did not move a muscle, only waited.

And then the spell was broken by a scuffling noise; he had bumped into the chair near the bedside. He let forth with an explicit curse, and suddenly Diana realized two things. She was not dreaming; she was quite awake. And the voice was not Adam's!

"Oh, my God!" she gasped. "You're not—you—get out!" She sat bolt upright in bed, yanking the covers to her chin.

Percy tossed the chair aside and laughed quite mirthlessly. "Little whore. Whom were you expecting as you lay there, eyes wide open, lips parted just so? Did you think I could not see?"

Of course, he could see, she thought wildly. The candelabrum stood on the nightstand, right next to her. She scrambled to the other side of the bed and jumped off, dashing for the nearest weapon to hand. It was the empty water pitcher from the washstand.

Percy advanced on her, and now she could see his face. He looked angry, and very determined. He came closer; she raised the pitcher.

"Put that down, Diana. I'm tired of playing your games," he growled. "We are going to play my way now."

He was just a foot away. He grabbed for the pitcher.

"No, damn you!" she screamed, and smashed it down on him.

She had aimed for his head; but he jerked aside, and she caught him on the neck and shoulder.

"Goddamn bitch!" he snarled as the pitcher shattered and he staggered back.

She sidestepped him, skirting round the bed, meaning to make for the door. But he grabbed her, one hand still at his neck, the other snaking around her waist.

"No!" she shrieked.

Suddenly the door burst open.

"Let her go, Truesdale!" Adam's voice was low and ominous with a barely controlled fury she had never heard from him before.

Never had she been so grateful for a voice. She jerked, but Percy held her fast. Adam raced into the room, and a second later Papa appeared at the threshold, clad in his nightshirt and carrying a brace of candles.

"What the devil!" he exclaimed sleepily, setting the candles down and coming forward.

214

Percy cursed volubly and let her go. Without thinking she ran straight into Adam's arms. She was shaking, sobbing, aware of Adam in his shirtsleeves, holding her tightly, aware of Papa's hand briefly touching her head. She clung to Adam for dear life. And then Papa dashed to Percy, grabbed him by the arm and sent his fist into his jaw.

"You bastard!" Papa roared, and Percy groaned and rubbed his jaw along with his neck.

"Enough, old man! She's not hurt," Percy muttered, as he tried to duck Papa's second swing. Papa caught him on the shoulder.

Adam had never known a rage like this. *He* wanted to smash Truesdale's face to a pulp. He wanted to kill him. But he had let Rusty take him on, for Diana needed Adam more than *he* needed revenge. He held her as if he would never let her go. She had run to him. With her father standing not two feet away she had run to Adam. That fact had not been lost on Rusty, but he had not appeared overly perturbed. Now as Percy stumbled against the bedframe, Rusty came back to them and patted her head and murmured soothingly to her as she nestled against Adam's chest.

Diana was still shaking. Now that it was over she realized how frightened she had been. He wasn't a stranger in the woods and she wasn't a little girl, but his intent had been clear. She burrowed deeper into Adam's chest.

And then Percy cursed again, having stepped on a shard of pottery.

"Goddammit!" he exploded. "My foot is bleeding! Rustin, haven't you got something to stop the bleeding? Christ, I think there's a piece of that blasted pitcher in my foot!"

"I shall call you out for this, Percy," Papa growled, quite ignoring Percy's bleeding foot.

"No, he's mine," Adam seethed with deadly menace.

"No!" Diana's voice was weak, but she forced herself to lift her head. "Please, I do not wish a scandal, nor do I wish either of you to be forced to flee the country, or worse, to be hurt."

Adam did not like it. He wanted to put a bullet through Percy Truesdale. But Diana's eyes beseeched him, and he did not want to overset her further. His gaze met Rusty's; the older man concurred.

"It is more than you deserve, Truesdale. And if you ever dare to touch her again, you'll have Rustin *and* me to deal with. I warn you that I am a crack shot. Now get the hell out!" Adam spat contemptuously.

Percy stared resentfully at the three of them and began to move toward the door. "Oh, and hand over the key, Truesdale," Adam added.

He heard the clink of metal as Truesdale tossed the key to the ground. "As you wish, Marchmaine," he drawled. "No need to get your dander up. I merely wandered into the wrong chamber. But—er—why do you not ask her whom she was awaiting. You did not exactly jump in fright when the door first opened, did you, Diana?"

Diana sucked in her breath and began to tremble. Adam tightened his hold on her as Truesdale sauntered arrogantly out the door.

When he'd gone Rusty let loose a string of expletives that shocked even Adam. "Diana, are you all right?" Rusty asked.

Adam remembered him asking that question once before, weeks ago. It pained Adam to recall that it was *he* whom Rusty had suspected might have hurt her then.

Diana lifted her head and slowly pulled out of Adam's arms. He was loathe to let her go, but had no choice. "Yes, Papa." She sniffed back her tears. "He had only just come. I—I was half asleep. When—when the door opened I, thought I was dreaming you see, and—"

"Diana, you do not have to explain anything," Rusty said, and held his arms out to her. "You have done nothing wrong." He hugged her and stroked her hair, and Adam was certain he had provided solace for his daughter many times before. What he did not know was what she had needed solace for.

"I—I hit him with the pitcher," she mumbled, stepping back and wiping her eyes, "but it did not stop him."

"Perhaps not, but that and your screams brought us running. You did very well, Diana," Rusty assured her, then added, "How did you know about the key, Adam?"

Adam shrugged. "I guessed as much. My room had a key. Lady Hart provided every amenity. I did not think she would forget such an important one. And I knew Diana would have used it if she'd had it."

216

"Thank you. Both of you," Diana said.

"Can you sleep now, child?" Rusty asked.

"I—I think so, Papa."

Rusty picked up the brace of candles and bent to retrieve the key. He handed it to her. "Be careful where you step, Diana. There are pieces of pottery all over this area near the foot of the bed."

She nodded, twisting her hands at her waist.

Rusty's eyes went from her to Adam. Rusty was going to leave, and Adam would have to go with him. Damnation! He didn't want to leave her. If he could just have a moment alone with her. . . .

Rusty bid his daughter a good night, kissing her on the brow. Then he looked Adam straight in the eye and said, "I'll wait for you in the corridor."

Adam blinked as Rusty disappeared through the door. He could hardly credit that he'd been granted a moment to be private with her. He would think about the implications of Rusty's action later. For now he could only think of Diana.

She turned away from him. "I *was* dreaming, or thought I was, when he came in. I did not—"

"Diana." He put his hands to her shoulders and turned her round. She kept her eyes lowered. He knew just what was troubling her. He would not ask about whom she had been dreaming, nor who she thought was walking through the door. For he thought he knew the answer. Nor would he ask the next question. If he *had* walked through the door, would she have turned him away? He did not think he wanted to know the answer to that.

"Look at me," he said softly.

She raised her deep blue eyes to him. And what he saw there took his breath away. Beneath the embarrassment at what Percy had intimated, he saw something far more devastating. He saw hunger, the same hunger that he felt, that neither of them could acknowledge. He saw the rapid pulse beating at her throat, and he thought he knew the answer to that question he dared not ask. He leaned closer, his lips hovering just above hers. She did not draw back, but parted her lips ever so slightly.

Hellfire! He wanted to kiss her so badly that his every muscle ached. He needed her; she needed him. But he had no right to fulfill those needs, nor was this the time; Rusty was waiting for him. And one kiss would never be enough. It would only make the hunger all the greater.

Steeling himself, taking a deep breath, he whispered to her, "You do not have to say anything more, my dear. I understand. Everything." And then he cradled her face in his hands. "Will you be all right now?"

She bit her lip and nodded, but he did not quite believe her. She was still shaken, her face pale even in the candlelight. She was so vulnerable, so beautiful. Dear God, he did not want to leave her!

It was not merely that her beauty stirred him, that the sight of her in the thin nightdress made his loins tighten now that the danger of moments ago was past. It was not merely that her raven hair was down, falling riotously, luxuriously about her shoulders and down her back, and that for the first time he could see just how long it was. It spilled down to her waist, and he longed to run his hands through it, to pull her close and to drink of her sweetness.

But it was more than that. Much more. He did not want to leave her alone, vulnerable, unprotected. He wanted to stay with her, to hold her, comfort her, take care of her. Never, ever had he felt this way about a woman, and he was shaken to the core by the depth of his emotions.

And with all that, he had not the right to more than this stolen moment with her. "Diana," he said urgently, "I want you to know that if you ever need help, now or any time, any place, you may come to me, or send for me. Do you understand?"

Yes, Diana thought, I understand. You are offering me all that you can, and I must accept it, for I have no right to more, nor ever will. Hold me, Adam, she cried silently. I need you to hold me.

"Yes, Adam. Thank you," she rasped, and felt the chill of the night as his hands slid from her face and he stepped back.

"Good night, my dear," he whispered, and then he was gone.

Adam closed the door behind him and unclenched his fists. It had taken a supreme act of will to leave her like that, without holding her again, or pressing his lips to hers. Yet he had feared that if he did he would never let her go.

Rusty was waiting for him. He had known, somehow, that Adam needed that time with her. But why had he granted it? No explanation was forthcoming, for the good doctor merely said, "Thank you, Adam. I do not know if I could have stopped the blackguard myself. I—"

"What are you talking about, Rusty? It was *you* who planted him a facer."

"It is *you* who is the crack shot, whose voice carries ducal authority. No, Adam, I am in your debt." Rusty sighed. "You were right, of course, when you said last week that I could not be with her all the time. But I should have heard the footsteps, or the door. I was sleeping so damned soundly—"

"Rusty, you cannot blame yourself. You had no way of knowing. But I—I feared something like this. I should have kept watch, should have been here sooner."

Rusty gazed quizzically at him. "Do you really think so?"

"Dammit, Rusty. Don't you dare tell me again that it is none of my concern."

Rusty chuckled softly. "Oh, no, Adam. I am not about to tell you that. Oh, no, not at all."

Adam pondered Rusty's words, and a good deal more, for the rest of the night.

Diana did not attempt to go to sleep straightaway. She locked the door and lit the candelabrum with fresh tapers. She donned a pair of slippers lest she accidentally step on a broken shard of pottery, and drew a chair up to the window. She pulled a blanket from the bed and wrapped it round herself against the chill of the night air.

And then, as the snow came down slowly, relentlessly, inevitably, she allowed herself to think. She had not wanted it to happen. She had admonished herself, fought herself against it, but it had happened anyway. Slowly, relentlessly, inevitably, like the snow of a Yorkshire winter.

She had fallen in love with Adam Damerest, Duke of Marchmaine.

If she hadn't known it before this night, or had known but hadn't wanted to admit it to herself, she could no longer deny the truth of it. When she had been in danger and the door had burst open, she had seen Adam, whom she had known a few short weeks, and Papa, who had raised her and loved her and comforted her always. And she had run to Adam. Instinctively, unequivocally, unabashedly. She had run to Adam, and felt a world of safety and comfort and caring in his arms. And when the danger was past, and especially when Papa had gone, she had felt something else. When he had held her by the shoulders, his tall, whipcord lean body, clad only in his shirtsleeves and britches, so close to hers, she had felt the heat of desire. And when he had taken her face in his hands, giving them the only closeness to which they were entitled, she had felt the pain of desire, and love, unfulfilled.

And so it would remain. She did not know how he felt about her. He wanted her, he had a care for her, but she did not know if he loved her. It was better that she not know, for it did not signify. That there was love between them did not change the painful reality that naught could come of it. She would not be his mistress; she could not be his wife, even did he wish to defy his mother and the traditions of his rank and station and wed her. It could not be.

Someday, long after he had gone, she supposed it would hurt less. For now she felt a pain far deeper than that of losing Robert. For she had been infatuated with Robert, and though his betrayal had stung, it had not left her with an aching void. But she loved Adam from the depths of her soul, and she would never feel quite complete without him.

At length, wearily, Diana climbed into bed and slept.

It was ten of the clock when Adam strolled into the breakfast parlor. He was not, it seemed, the only late riser, for though Sir Horace and Lady Hart appeared to be nearly finished, the remainder of the table was just filling up. It stood to reason, he supposed. The snow was still falling and there was no place to go.

Rusty was there, seated next to Mrs. Weeksgate. He whispered something in her ear, and the lady blushed. Adam repressed a grin. They were smelling of springtime and roses; he wondered if they even realized it yet.

Lady Hart certainly did; she exchanged a supremely smug

look with her husband. Percy Truesdale was standing at the sideboard, filling two plates. He sat down next to Amelia Brixworth, handing her a plate. He gave her a smile which did not reach his cool gray eyes. His face looked taut with tension. Mrs. Brixworth smiled back at him in the manner of the proverbial cat who'd caught its canary. It was not difficult to guess where Percy had gone after the debacle in Diana's room. Nor was it difficult to guess that Mrs. Brixworth's charms had not dimmed Percy's lust for Diana.

Captain Plunkett, seated next to Sir Horace, was downing eggs Benedict with gusto. His nephew sat beside him. Lucy, Lady Truesdale, and Adam's mother had not put in an appearance. Nor had Diana. Damn! He did not think she was by nature a late riser. Had she slept at all? Was she all right? Was she hesitant to face the company? Mercifully, it seemed that no one else had heard anything untoward last night. Was she concerned about that? How he wished he could go abovestairs to reassure her!

He was just filling his plate when Signor D'Orsini walked into the breakfast parlor. He looked about, seeming not to find what he was looking for, and came to fill a plate. There was a certain spring to his walk, Adam noted, that he'd never seen before. And his greeting was decidedly jovial, even for the normally effusive Italian. And what, Adam wondered, had put that decided twinkle in his dark eyes?

Adam seated himself next to Mrs. Weeksgate after exchanging greetings all round. A footman poured him coffee, then moved round the table to where Signor D'Orsini now sat across from Adam. Not two minutes later, a murmur was heard in the corridor. Adam looked up from his scrambled eggs and kippers to see his mother and Lady Truesdale stroll toward the doorway. It was incongruous to see the ladies in their evening clothes in the morning, but then, they were all similarly clad. With the exception, that is, of their hosts; Lady Hart was lovely in a flowing violet silk morning gown.

What was most incongruous about the languid stroll of the duchess and Lady Truesdale, however, was not their clothing, but rather the earnest expressions on their faces. Adam had no idea what they were discussing so intently, but he did not like it. Instinct told him it boded ill. A glance across the table told

221

him Signor D'Orsini liked it even less than Adam; the painter was frowning prodigiously. He rose, as did the other men, and held out the chair next to him. And then his eyes met the duchess's.

Adam watched his mother meet D'Orsini's eyes, register his disapproval, and look away. She murmured something to Eleanor Truesdale and then walked briskly into the room. He expected the duchess to spurn Signor D'Orsini's offer of the chair and give him a set-down with frosty eyes. Instead, she walked straight to the chair he held and gave him a shy smile. A shy smile! Adam had never seen the like before, and if he was not mistaken, there was a faint blush on his mother's cheeks. A blush! D'Orsini's answering smile was almost . . . gentle, and his dark eyes twinkled down at the duchess.

Adam had never seen a man look at his mother in that way; certainly, in his memory, his father never had. But then, his mother had never smiled in that way at his father. And there was something else different about his mother, he mused as D'Orsini seated her and then himself. It was something in the way she moved, held herself. A certain stiffness was gone, a certain harshness—

He narrowed his eyes and stared at the two of them across the table, their heads close together. It couldn't be, he told himself. It wasn't possible! And yet. . . . He caught D'Orsini's eye and raised a brow in question, his own eyes flitting to the duchess and back. D'Orsini returned a perfectly bland expression, and then Adam knew. He could not say exactly how, but he knew. The Italian had done it! Somehow, he actually had—

Adam grinned and raised his coffee cup to D'Orsini in silent salute. The artist tried valiantly to maintain his bland expression, but his lips twitched suspiciously. Adam did not release his gaze, and finally D'Orsini himself broke into a smile, and raised his own cup in acknowledgement.

Adam resisted the urge to applaud and yell, "Bravo!"

Meanwhile, Lady Truesdale had taken a seat next to Percy, and mother and son were engaged in deep discourse which had Eleanor Truesdale frowning. Was the blackguard telling his *mother* about last night? It hardly seemed credible, and yet Adam would not put it past— Lady Truesdale whispered

222

something to Percy and patted his hand. Percy smiled unpleasantly, like the lion who had just cornered the lamb. Adam did not like that smile at all.

Captain Plunkett sauntered in, just as Sir Horace and the colonel were leaving. The last guest to make her way into the breakfast parlor was Diana. She was still pale, and there were dark smudges under her eyes. She walked with her usual calm composure, but her velvety blue eyes were anything but calm. Adam cursed inwardly.

"Oh, Diana, good morning, dear girl," called Lady Hart cheerfully. "Come and sit here, why don't you?" Lady Hart blithely patted the empty seat to her right, the seat that happened to be next to Adam as well. Adam quirked his brow at his hostess for her transparent machinations and received a bland smile in return. Bland smiles seemed to be de rigueur this morning, but this time Adam was not amused.

Diana bent to give her father a kiss on the cheek before taking her seat. "Are you all right?" Adam whispered as he poured her coffee. He knew the question was foolish in the extreme; it was plain as pikestaff that she was not all right.

He thought he heard her expel a soft sigh. "Yes, Adam. I am fine," she uttered, and he knew she was lying. But it was not the expected apprehension that he heard in her voice, saw in her eyes. It was an ineffable sadness, and it cut him to the quick. For he suspected that it was not Percy who was the cause of it, but himself.

Only a few of the company still lingered over breakfast. Rusty and Mrs. Weeksgate had just left, taking Lady Hart's suggestion that they stroll through the picture gallery.

"Marchmaine, dear boy," Lady Hart said, "Horace and I have decided to embark on a new project of renovations. Parts of the south wing of Arden Chase are virtually crumbling, you must know. We want to rebuild it, and to create several new guest suites. We never seem to have enough, particularly during the Valentine's Ball. It does seem to get larger every year, I must own.

"Now tell me, dear boy, would you be of a mind to come with me and tour the south wing, and then adjourn to the library, to discuss it? After that you can decide whether to accept the commission. It will require some degree of artistry, I am persuaded, for the wing shall have to be enlarged, and we do not wish to destroy the original line of the house."

Lady Hart finally paused for breath. Adam did not have to look at his mother to know she was frowning; he could feel her displeasure. D'Orsini's eyes were alive with interest. Diana merely tilted her head at Adam, awaiting his reply. There was no one else in the room. He wondered if his hostess knew what she was doing by making this request in front of his mother.

"I am flattered that you should ask me, Lady Hart, and I shall be happy to accompany you and see what you have in mind. But you must know that I do not accept commissions. I merely do favors for friends now and again."

"Well, I would hope, Marchmaine, that you will count me among your friends. But I really could not allow you to embark upon such a project as a mere 'favor.' Oh, my goodness me, of course not! Especially not an architect of your caliber." She paused, and at his raised brow added, "I do my research, dear boy. No, you may give the money to charity if you like, but commission it shall be. Besides, my little bit of research tells me the Regent has suggested you design one of the new buildings he has in mind for London. *So* very exciting, is it not, and surely *that* would take the form of a commission!"

Dear God, Adam thought, where *did* she get her information? Diana looked surprised, and pleased. His mother looked neither. She knew about Prinny's offer because Adam had discussed it with her. He ached to accept it, but the duchess was outraged at the mere idea. Why, she'd acted as if he wanted to renounce his title and dignities and go take up residence in what she disparagingly called the Colonies. And so, because he was not certain he wanted yet another bone of contention with his mother, he'd yet to give Prinny an answer.

His mother's eyes now flashed with anger. "Winifred, surely you can understand that my son's respect for his own consequence would preclude the acceptance of a commission of any kind. A gentlemanly avocation is one thing, but—but the other is simply not done," she said self-righteously.

Lady Hart cocked her head, her expression reflecting bemusement. "Do you really think so?" she asked almost incredulously, then added, "Well then, Marchmaine, let us see if my little project stirs your avocational interest, shall we?"

Adam felt his jaw clench compulsively. He wanted to strangle his mother. She looked about to speak again, but this time D'Orsini's hand came up to cover hers in a gesture of restraint as he shook his head ever-so-slightly. Adam's respect for the Italian was rising by the hour. Why, he could actually become fond of the fellow!

"I should be delighted to accompany you, Lady Hart," Adam said decisively, and stood up.

"Splendid!" his hostess replied, "and do you come as well, Diana. You have such a fine aesthetic sense, dear girl. Katherine, Signor D'Orsini, you will excuse us?"

"Of course, dear lady," D'Orsini said gallantly, as he rose from his chair.

Adam noticed that his mother looked dagger points at Diana. She was in a fine taking, indeed, and D'Orsini was well aware of it. Just what would he do about it?

Katherine was furious—at Adam, Lady Hart, Diana, even Antonio D'Orsini. He sat next to her, calmly refilling their coffee cups, after the others had left, quite as if nothing untoward had occurred. "Antonio," she said at length, unable to endure the silence, "I simply cannot allow you to think that because of—of what happened between us, that I—I will allow you to govern my actions, or my speech."

Antonio sipped his coffee, toyed with a sweet roll, and then finally turned to her and took her hand. *"Cara,* why do you think *you* have the right to govern the life of another?" he asked softly.

"I beg your pardon!" She snatched her hand away. "We are speaking of my son! It is my duty to guide him properly, to see he pursues a path in accordance with his best interests."

Antonio shook his head. "Your son is a grown man. You no longer have the right to decide what is in his best interest. You are keeping him from two things he loves. You have not the right, Katarina."

She did not like his words. Even less did she care for the deep gentleness of his tone, or the look in his eyes. It was almost one

225

of—of pity! It was not to be borne. "You do not know whereof you speak, Antonio. A duke of the realm has certain responsibilities. He needs must take his place in the government, among the ton. Are you suggesting that my son *draw* for a *living?*"

He chuckled. "In a certain fashion, *cara mía*, it is what *I* do. Ah, I know, you will tell me I am not a *duche*. However, my cousin is. And I am a younger son of a noble family. But my papa did not try to stop me, though others did. But you cannot stop an artist, Katarina, or you kill him. Did you ever stop to wonder what it would mean to your son to design a building in London? To be able to leave that behind him, a legacy for generations?"

"He should be leaving a legacy of sons," she said stiffly.

"Ah yes, sons." He took a sip of coffee and stared down at his cup. "And for this you and the Lady Truesdale decide little Lucy will do well."

She looked at him sharply. She had never said any such thing. "I am an artist, *cara*, remember," he went on, meeting her gaze with dark eyes twinkling. "I see things. But you—" he sighed—"I am afraid there is much you do not see. He and little Lucy would bring each other misery, Katarina. Is that what you wish for your son?"

She did not like the tone of this discourse at all. No one had ever spoken to her in such a manner. But it was difficult to be truly angry with him when his voice was so soft and his eyes regarded her with such—such . . . was "tenderness" the word?

"Lucy is a very pretty behaved girl," Katherine said defensively. "Adam is thirty-one years old and has had ample time to find himself a suitable bride. It is his duty to his name and heritage that he produce an heir."

He sighed deeply and shook his head. He actually looked . . . disappointed. In her? Did he not understand what she was saying? He rose, and she found herself standing as well. "Where—where are you going?" she asked, despising the unaccustomed weakness in her own voice.

He shrugged. "I go to my chamber. I will sketch. I have some of my charcoals here."

She knew that he was walking away from her. Why did it

226

signify? But it did; after last night, it signified very much.

"Antonio," she said quickly, putting a hand to his sleeve to detain him, "you—you said I was keeping him from two things he loves. What—what is the other?"

He smiled then, and patted her hand. She had not realized until that moment how much she had come to—to love that smile that brought laugh lines to his dark eyes, and to enjoy the warmth of his hand on hers. "Can you not see, *cara mía?* It is very plain for *all* to see."

It was her turn to sigh. Slowly she walked to the window and looked out at the snow. It was coming down more lightly now, even sporadically, and there did not seem to be *that* much on the ground. Perhaps they would all leave this day.

"You are speaking of the doctor's daughter," she said at length in a tired voice.

"Of the *bella* Miss Rustin, yes. Do you ever see, really see, Katarina, the way they look at each other?"

She shook her head. "It is impossible, Antonio. Surely you can see that. The House of Damerest cannot align itself with—with a doctor's daughter, a midwife, for pitysake!"

"We are not speaking of houses and alliances, *cara mía.* We are speaking of a man and a woman, once again, eh?"

He took her chin between his thumb and forefinger and forced her to look at him. "I do not want to see you hurt, *bellíssima,* and you will be. For you will force him to choose, and he will choose her."

"No," she whispered. "He—he desires her, that is all. He does not wish to wed her. If he would but assuage his—his desire—"

"And do you think, Katarina," he said in the softest, most gentle voice she'd ever heard from him, "that desire is all I feel for you?"

"I—I do not know," she rasped.

"Tsk, tsk. I see there is much you did not learn last night." He put his hands to her shoulders. She looked around surreptitiously, lest someone appear in the doorway. "I think it is time for more lessons, *cara.* Come."

Her eyes widened. "What—now? But—but—'tis broad daylight!"

He chuckled, but his voice was husky. "My little innocente!

227

Do you think such things are not possible in the light of day? Besides, Katarina, there is little else to do just now. Unless you would care to join the game of whist Colonel Plunkett spoke of?" She shook her head slowly. "Then a stroll through the picture gallery with the good doctor and the little Mrs. Weeksgate?"

She shook her head. Grinning, he took her hand and started for the door. "Antonio!" she squeaked. "What will people say?"

He did not break stride, merely pulled her along. "They will say, *cara mía*, that I am sketching you, in preparation for the painting of your portrait." He paused and turned to gaze into her eyes. "And I think, Katarina, that finally you will get that smile right."

She smiled then—indeed she could not help it—and allowed him to convey her abovestairs. Not but what she did not feel a twinge of nerves. Last night had been wonderful . . . sinfully delicious in point of fact. It amazed her what those sensitive artist's hands could do, what her own body, the body she'd lived with nigh onto fifty years, was capable of. But in broad daylight? Katherine Damerest, Duchess of Marchmaine, was truly shocked.

Chapter 15

"And so you see," Lady Hart was saying as they stood in a long-abandoned salon in the south wing, "this entire section will need to be extended."

Diana watched Adam's face as he listened intently. He took in the peeling wallpaper, the mustiness, the ominous cracks in the ceiling, just as Diana did. But his eyes shone with the excitement of possibilities, just as it had during the rest of their tour.

"I should like a solarium here, for all my guests, but most especially for my niece, Alexandra." Lady Hart patted several of the myriad curls atop her head into place. "Dear Alix is an artist, you must know, and this room has an eastern aspect. I own it will be quite perfect! Alix studied with Signor D'Orsini when she was here. He told me she was enormously talented, but she has got a late start because her papa—my brother, you know—did not think it at all the thing for a lady to dirty her hands with oils." She finally paused for breath, her green eyes meeting Adam's for a moment before sweeping quite innocently about the room.

"It truly amazes me how a parent can be perfectly blind to a child's talents, and to what signifies the most to that child," she observed nonchalantly. Adam's mouth tightened.

"Well," she went on, her hand fluttering to her breast, "that is neither here nor there. Dear Alix has only just married the Viscount Weddington—they were matched by the Valentine Lottery. Goodness me, 'twas more than a month ago. Do you know the viscount, Marchmaine?"

229

"We have met, Lady Hart, but I believe he has been out of the country these many years."

She let forth a trill of laughter. "Yes, indeed, amassing a fortune, you may be sure. You will like him, Marchmaine. I shall have to bring all of you together at some time." Her gaze flitted over Adam and then Diana to include her in the "all of you," and Diana felt a pang. Oh, dear Lady Hart, I do believe I know what you are thinking, and you will be doomed to disappointment.

But Lady Hart went blithely on. "Well, and of course, Derek has swept Alix away to his estate in Herefordshire, but I am persuaded they will be back, as will my other two nieces. Why, and one is already in the family way, and so I should like nursery quarters in this wing, Marchmaine." She peered out the window where the snow could be seen falling in very light, sporadic flurries.

"I suppose I shall lose a good part of my rose garden, more's the pity. Unless you can perform some miracle of design, dear boy. Why do you and Diana not go outside to see what the structure of this wing looks like from the garden. I am persuaded the snow is about to stop."

Diana did not think it a very good idea for her to be alone with Adam in the snow. She remembered the last time, and its aftermath, when he had ministered to her frozen feet, far too well.

"An excellent idea, Lady Hart," Adam replied. "But perhaps you have a pair of warm boots for Diana. She has very . . . sensitive feet."

Diana hoped no one noticed the flush that suffused her face at the memory of the fact that her feet were not half so sensitive to cold as to Adam's hands.

Lady Hart promised the boots and said that if they were amenable, she would meet them in a half hour's time in the library, where there would be paper and pencil at the ready. Adam was most amenable, and in short order Diana found herself wrapped in her cloak, standing in Lady Hart's snow-covered rose garden.

Adam kept his hand at her elbow, and she did not feel half as cold as she ought to. The flurries brushing her face were not at all unpleasant; the closeness of Adam's head, tilted toward

230

hers, was not at all unpleasant either. He gazed up at the house, and then down at the garden, quite intently, then moved with her to stand farther back. The silence between them was companionable, and Diana enjoyed watching the myriad expressions cross his face as he pondered the lines of the house. He nodded, as if coming to some conclusion.

"'Tis quite a rambling old house, is it not?" she asked at length.

He smiled down at her. "Yes. Classical, originally. But it has been renovated several times over the years by persons of whimsy."

"Hence the few Gothic touches," she rejoined, thinking of a few turrets and flying buttresses visible from various vantage points in the extensive gardens.

His smile deepened. "Hence the Gothic touches," he echoed. "And the rambling northern wing. It all gives one a bit more freedom in planning future renovations, for one is not locked into a given style. Although, oddly enough, the house does have a sense of balance."

"It suits them quite well, does it not?" she asked softly.

"Quite well, indeed. Sir Horace could not have brought a more fitting bride to this house."

His tawny eyes regarded her now with the same intensity with which he'd regarded the house just moments ago. She had the feeling that he was assessing her in much the same way— for possibilities. Those possibilities made her shiver—neither from cold nor fear.

"Are you cold, Diana?" He pulled her closer, draping an arm about her shoulders.

Oh, Adam, you mustn't do that, she thought, but did not pull away. "No. I—I am right. The—the snow has almost stopped."

"Yes," he uttered, turning her to face him, putting his hands now to her upper arms. When, he wondered, did the air between them become so warm, so—so charged? He leaned closer, his breath grazing her face. "And your feet? Will you need me to . . . warm them, again?" Good God! Whatever had possessed him to say such a thing?

Oh, Adam, I will always need you to warm me, Diana cried inwardly, but you will not be there.

231

With great difficulty she steeled herself to pull back from him. "That—that will not be necessary," she lied. "Perhaps we had ought to go back now."

The expression on Adam's face was as bleak as she felt. He nodded and led her inside.

There was a cheerful fire burning in the library when they arrived, and Lady Hart, trailing yards of violet silk, floated in a moment later. Adam had to remind himself to concentrate on her, not on Diana, still clad in that achingly sensual satin gown she'd worn last night. And he would not look down at her feet, encased now in delicate matching slippers. He did not want to recall that walk in the snow at Rossmore, when she'd nearly given herself frostbite and he'd warmed her feet, and discovered she was impossibly, delightfully ticklish.

No, he would concentrate on Lady Hart, waving paper and pencils now as she came toward them. "Now then, dear boy, what *do* you think?"

He grinned. "Why, that you have a charming house with a history that I make no doubt is fascinating."

Her light laughter trilled in the air. "How right you are. But tell me, have I a chance of saving my rose garden?"

Adam's gaze shifted to Diana. "What do you say, my dear?"

"I?" she asked, incredulously.

"Yes, you. What does your aesthetic sense tell you?"

"I—well—I was wondering if perhaps a courtyard might not answer. The rose garden could be saved and—"

"Good girl!" he exclaimed, catching her hands in his. "You have seen the courtyard in the northern wing, have you not?"

She nodded, almost shyly, he thought. "I remember what you said about balance," she ventured, and he grinned at her, then turned to Lady Hart.

That lady's quizzical gleam recalled him to himself. He released Diana's hands and cleared his throat. "I would most assuredly advise a courtyard, Lady Hart," he said evenly, "and there are many possibilities to accommodate your other requirements."

Lady Hart placed the pencils and sketch paper on the desk behind them. "Marchmaine, if you would like, please feel free to make some preliminary sketches. But I do not mean to pressure you, dear boy, about taking this on. You must do exactly as you please." She pivoted and sashayed across half the width of the room toward the door.

"I will only say, dear boy," she said, pausing and whirling round, "that I do believe that each of us must follow our own lights in this life, and not the dictates of others. Why, if Signor D'Orsini had not done so, he might never have picked up a paint brush, nor would my niece Alix have done, nor would my dear Horace have married *me*."

Adam blinked at that; Diana's eyes widened. Lady Hart let forth a bubble of merriment. "Oh, my dears, you do not for a moment think *I* was Mother Hartcup's first choice? Oh, goodness me, no! She said I simply *wouldn't* do! And where would my dear heart be without me today? Well now, I've said quite enough, and probably spoken out of turn. I'll leave you now. See you at nuncheon, children."

And with that, the extraordinary Lady Hart pirouetted gracefully and danced out of the room.

Adam and Diana exchanged a bemused glance, and then they both burst out laughing.

"Quite an amazing woman, is she not?" Diana finally asked.

"Yes. A delightful original," he replied genially. "I expect I'd better get on to my drawing. Perhaps I *can* do some rough preliminary sketches for her today."

The laughter had vanished from Diana's face. She regarded him in all seriousness. "Yes. I—I shall leave you to your work now."

She turned to go, and before he knew what he was doing, his hand shot out to grasp her arm. "Don't go." She looked up at him, the question in her eyes. He did not try to hold back his next words. "I value your opinions, and your company. Stay with me, Diana. Perhaps you'd like to take a book and—read by the fire."

She smiled, that smile he knew, and loved, so well. "I should like that very much, Adam," she said quietly. And then she cocked her head to one side. "Do you mean to take Lady Hart's commission?"

He realized that he still held her arm, that it was bare—for the satin dress had only the tiniest of sleeves—and that his

233

hand fairly burned where it touched her. Very slowly, he released her. But he stayed where he was, mere inches from her, his eyes locking with hers.

Did she realize the significance of the question she asked? It was not just a matter of this commission; it was a matter of defying his mother; it was a matter of deciding, once and for all, whether to pursue his passion for designing buildings as a career. And it was far, far more. Did she realize that accepting this commission would keep him in Rossmore for an indefinite amount of time?

He gazed into the blue depths of her eyes and knew, of a certain, that she was well aware of all the ramifications of her question. It amazed him, shook him, that they could so often communicate without words, but there it was. He raised his hand to her cheek and felt her quiver from his touch.

"I do not know, Diana," he said at length. "In truth, I do not know."

She nodded in acknowledgment, and he knew he had ought to drop his hand. But he did not want to let her go. "What do *you* think, Diana?" he heard himself say. He meant the question only to refer to his work and wondered if she would understand.

She did. Perhaps without quite realizing it, she brought her hand up to cover his as it lay against her cheek. "Adam, you are very talented." She cocked her head, as if something had just occurred to her. "Tell me about the building the Regent wants you to design."

He smiled and kissed her hand, then let it go. " 'Tis a theater, Diana. He wants another royal theater. I can see it in my mind's eye," he said enthusiastically, waving his hands to emphasize his words. "It would have a magnificent staircase with intricate ironwork. There would be a domed entryway, which would juxtapose a bit of the Gothic with the classical pillars that would flank the portico. And it would be set in a park, with small domed pavilions here and there, for light afternoon dramatic fair."

Diana gazed up at his tawny eyes, gleaming with suppressed excitement. She thought she could feel the creative tension in him, and knew there was only one answer.

"Adam, I believe you must not waste your talent. Perhaps it

means more to you than even you realize. I am not an artist, but I—" she paused and sighed almost imperceptibly—"I know the anguish of having to deny oneself that for which one's very being cries out."

He heard the anguish in her voice and suddenly pulled her close. "And what have you denied yourself, Diana?" he whispered huskily.

Tears glistened in her eyes, and he thought he would not wait for an answer. He lowered his head.

A knock at the door had them springing apart. Adam darted behind the desk and cleared his throat. "Come in."

Rusty ushered Winifred Weeksgate across the threshold. "Forgive the interruption, Diana, Adam. Lady Hart said we'd find you here." His sharp eyes moved from Diana to Adam and back. Could he tell that neither of them was breathing quite steadily?

He took a blushing Mrs. Weeksgate by the arm and brought her to Diana, his genial face splitting in a smile. "There—there is something we would like to tell you, Diana."

Diana looked bewildered, but suddenly Adam knew exactly what was coming. "I'll—ah—come back in a little while," he said, moving back around the desk toward the group, and the door.

"Nonsense, Adam. Stay," Rusty insisted, and looked his daughter in the eye. Adam found himself watching her face carefully.

Rusty took Mrs. Weeksgate's hand. "Diana, will you wish us happy?" he asked quietly.

Diana's beautiful blue eyes widened a moment in surprise, and then welled up. But a huge smile suffused her face. She clasped her hands together at her breast. "Papa! You—and—Mrs. Weeksgate?"

Rusty nodded. Poor Mrs. Weeksgate looked apprehensive. "Oh, Papa! I'm so happy for you!" Diana squealed, and threw her arms around her father.

He enveloped her in a hug, and when they drew apart, she turned to Mrs. Weeksgate. "I do not know how this came about—indeed, I shall expect a full accounting from Papa—but I am all out of mind delighted, Mrs. Weeksgate. Papa likes to pretend otherwise, but I have always believed he is very much in need of a wife, and I am persuaded you two will suit perfectly!" She hugged Mrs. Weeksgate, and that lady looked at her with tears in her eyes.

"Thank you, dear. Please, won't you call me Millicent?" Diana nodded, and the little lady regarded her gravely. "Are you certain, dear, that you will not mind? I do not want to usurp your place. You have been mistress of the house for so long and—"

"Oh, fustian, Millicent. I do assure you there is quite enough work for both of us, especially since our housekeeper, Mrs. Barrett, is rather getting on in years. And if I do not mistake the matter, what with Papa otherwise occupied, I shall find myself with a good many more sick calls to make."

Millicent Weeksgate looked decidedly relieved, and Rusty's eyes twinkled at his daughter, and then his bride-to-be.

"Come, Adam," Diana said suddenly, spontaneously holding her hand out to him, "and wish my papa happy."

Adam, oddly enough, had not felt at all like an interloper in the past few moments. He had simply enjoyed watching everyone, especially Diana. Now he did not hesitate, but took her hand briefly and came forward.

He offered his most sincere and hearty felicitations, clapping Rusty on the shoulder and kissing his intended's hand.

And then a beaming, besotted Rusty was leading a blushing Millicent away. Just before he reached the door, Rusty called over his shoulder, "Lady Hart said to tell you that you will not be disturbed again, Adam. Diana, she said you needed to—ah—help him. But I am persuaded he will only need a few minutes of your . . . help." And with that, Rusty led his intended away, closing the door softly behind him.

Adam thought he understood Lady Hart's convoluted motivations very well, but why was Rusty leaving him alone with his daughter, even for a designated "few minutes"?

He did not ruminate about it overlong, however. He would make the most of the time they had.

Millicent put her hand to Rusty's arm and stopped them several paces from the library door. "Rusty, dear, do you think it wise to leave them alone, even for a few minutes? I mean to say, 'tis not at all the thing, is it?"

He chuckled and patted her hand. "No, my love, I don't suppose it is. But, then, I think 'tis a good idea nonetheless. For only a few minutes, of course."

"Oh, I see. Sits the wind in that quarter? I had wondered."

He smiled warmly at his bride-to-be. "I hope so, Millie dear. I truly hope so," he murmured, and together they strolled away.

Diana was regarding with a genuine smile the closed door through which her father had just passed. Adam turned her to him, his hands at her elbows.

"You amaze me, Diana," he said. "You meant every word you just said, did you not?"

"Of course, Adam. Did you not see Papa's face? I cannot remember when last I saw him so happy. I do not know Millicent well, but she is charming and sweet and quite obviously besotted with Papa. Do you not think they will suit, Adam?"

"Oh, I do indeed. I simply do not think there are many women in your position who would have reacted as you did. No hesitation, no jealousy, no concern for yourself. Simply joy for them."

His hands moved up her bare arms in a caress that drew her closer. Her breathing became unsteady again. The satin of her gown whispered against his green velvet coat. Suddenly it felt much too confining, but he dared not remove it. His eyes swept her length; he could not help himself. His hands ached to follow his eyes, to caress the curves beneath the plum-colored satin. His fingers itched to run through her hair, dislodging the pins and sending the raven curls cascading down her back. Instead he kept his hands on her arms, feeling that extraordinary heat rise between them. He sensed that he was making her nervous, but he could not bring himself to release her. Nor did she attempt to pull away.

"People—ah—" she stammered as his hands moved up to splay across her bare shoulders. "People do not realize, because Papa is so very good-natured, that he—that he is lonely, and has been these many years. He has never before shown more than a passing interest in any woman since Mama, and yet, he is a man who needs a woman."

And what of his daughter, he wanted to ask. Is she a woman who needs a man? He did not ask, but attempted to find the answer in the oldest way known to man.

He put his hand to the nape of her neck and drew her face close to his; his lips hovered a hairsbreadth from hers. "Diana," he whispered.

She put her hands up between them to push him away. "Adam, please, I—"

"Don't fight me, Diana," he rasped. "I only want to kiss you. I *need* to kiss you. It's been so long."

Diana knew that she was ten times a fool, but she was not proof against a plea that she knew was genuine. Nor was she proof against the tall, lean body, so close to hers, so taut with tension that he seemed about to explode. Nor could she deny that she, too, needed this.

Her hands relaxed against his chest; her eyes fluttered closed; her lips parted. He had spoken the truth a moment ago, Adam thought. He had gone beyond wanting to a need so deep it utterly frightened him. And then he shut off all thought and took what she so sweetly offered.

Her lips were soft and warm, as he remembered. He took them gently at first, and then more insistently, as she yielded and opened to him and allowed his tongue entry. And then he was plundering her, drinking thirstily of her sweetness, thrusting his tongue into the warm, moist recesses of her mouth.

His hands slid up and down her back, her sides, over bare skin and smooth satin. His hands burned; his blood pounded wildly. Dear God, if she did not stop him soon. . . .

Diana heard herself moan and could do naught but sway to him, let her hands creep round his neck and into his thick chestnut hair as she pressed closer and closer. She loved him, and this was all she would ever have of him. God help her, she wanted more, needed more. She did not know herself. Her body had become hot flowing liquid; she could not control it.

He had kissed her before, touched her, but never had she been this responsive. Yet there was something more, something he did not understand. There was a kind of desperation in the way she clung to him, in the way her tongue danced with his. It was as if she was trying to tell him something, but for once he did not understand.

His hand came up to caress her breast. Surely she would stop him now. But she shuddered and moaned again and arched her hip in a way that nearly sent him over the edge. Hellfire! She could have no idea what she was doing. But he knew, and he had got to be the one to stop.

Somehow, he wrenched his mouth from hers. He put his hands to her face and gently pulled them apart. His body shook; so did hers. He gasped for breath. She stared at him, completely dazed. Bloody hell! Whatever had he started?

As soon as the shaking stopped and her breathing became more steady, she stepped back from him. She shook her head, and wrapped her arms about herself, a picture of despair. "Adam, I—I do not know what—that is, I've never—I'm sor—"

"No!" he interrupted harshly. "No apologies. And no shame. You did nothing wrong. And I—I could not help myself."

Adam had no idea how he got through luncheon, or the leave-taking in the afternoon. For the snow had stopped, the sun had come out, and everyone said their farewells. Nor did he recall what he'd said to Edward and Georgie on his return. He remembered now, late in the night, only how wonderful, how right it had felt to hold Diana in his arms this morning, and how painful it had been to let her go.

She had once warned him that they were playing with fire, and she had been right. And now it raged out of control.

Chapter 16

The days passed slowly. Diana looked forward to the ball and dreaded it at the same time. She did not know how she would face Adam; she longed to see him again, to talk with him, to dance with him. It was as well Papa was walking about in a besotted cloud, else surely he would have sensed her despair, her distraction. . . .

They visited Rossmore on Saturday; but Georgie was up and about, and Diana knew this would be the last of these visits. She told herself it did not signify; Adam would likely be leaving after the ball. Unless, of course, he took the commission at Arden Chase. And how she wished it for him! She knew it was the best thing for him to do, even if it meant weeks, perhaps months of bittersweet torture for her. To have him so near, yet so far beyond her. . . .

She sat with Papa, Edward and Georgie in the morning room, she and Georgie on the yellow sofa. Talk centered on the ball. Papa said that as Georgie appeared so well-mended, and the babe would be a month old by then, she might attend the ball. But only, Papa added, if the weather was mild and she did not stay overlong. He reminded her that full recovery would take many weeks, and she must not tax her strength. To everyone's amazement, she did not immediately clap her hands in glee and launch into a discussion of ball gowns.

Instead she smiled and said, "Thank you, Rusty. And you, Diana, for everything. I own I am much relieved to be feeling more myself again. Although I am sensible of the fact that I do not have my full strength. And I should love to go to the ball.

But it will be up to Edward." She turned to her husband. "What do *you* think?"

Edward tried to keep his expression sober, tried to hide how very pleased he was at Georgie's words. "I think, my dear, that we shall decide on Wednesday morning. We shall see how the weather appears, and how you are feeling." And with that, Georgie appeared to be content.

Rusty and Edward drifted out of the room after a time, and Diana told Georgie she was in excellent looks, and added that Edward seemed quite happy.

A slight flush came to Georgie's cheeks. "Yes, I—it really isn't all that difficult to make him happy. I simply have to stop and think sometimes about what I am about to say. And he—well—he has become so attentive, Diana, as he was when we were courting. I—I can hardly credit it!"

"Well, I can," Diana replied, laughing at Georgie's pleased expression. But then Georgie's face sobered.

"The only problem is that—that I can't always hold my tongue, you see. And then if I say something to displease him—even a little thing such as a suggestion that his valet put more blacking on his boots—why, Edward becomes all het up! He rails at me quite as if he hadn't been holding my hand not five minutes past!"

Diana felt out of her depth. She spoke from instinct, not at all sure of what she was going to say. "None of us is perfect, Georgie. Not the gentlemen, nor the ladies. You must allow him those times, and yourself, and do not despair. I am persuaded those times will become fewer and fewer."

Georgie smiled at her. "What a wonderful wife *you* would make, Diana! You are still young, not at all on the shelf. You really must reconsider your commitment to the single state," she said, and then mercifully shifted the subject to her mother.

"Whatever happened at Arden Chase, Diana? Ever since that dinner party—well, it was almost a house party, was it not?—Mama has simply not been herself. Only once has she made reference to Mrs. Brownlow's shortcomings, and it *was* a rather insipid soup! And she actually had a kind word for Nanny Haycock yesterday! And she has suddenly become very dedicated to that portrait of hers. Why, she and Signor D'Orsini spend *hours* in his studio every day!"

Diana did not quite know what to say. She was not blind; she had noticed something different about the duchess and Signor D'Orsini the morning after the dinner party. They had not been gazing besottedly at each other as had Papa and Millicent, but still, it was plain that they were rather . . . close. She did not quite understand, for though Signor D'Orsini appeared to be a most romantical gentleman, the duchess seemed hardened to romance and gentlemen in general. And as to those hours spent in the studio, well, Diana could speculate. But surely it could not be that—oh no! Of course not! Not the proper, formidable Duchess of Marchmaine.

She cleared her throat, to clear the cobwebs from her head.

"I own you are in the right of it, Georgie. I could see even at Lady Hart's that something was different, but I vow I have no notion what it is," she answered honestly, if evasively. And then she added, "Perhaps you had ought to ask Adam."

"Ask Adam what?" a deep voice queried, and Adam sauntered into the morning room.

He came to the yellow chintz sofa, bent to give Georgie a kiss on the cheek, and took Diana's hand and held it for a moment. She felt his warmth and had to force herself to meet his tawny eyes. Were the circumstances of their last meeting etched as indelibly in his mind as in hers?

The piercing look he gave her, full of heat and memory and gentle understanding, told her all she needed to know, and also set her immediately at her ease with him. He stood before them, his hands tucked negligently into the pockets of his camel coat. He looked marvelous, Diana thought, his long, lean frame encased in riding boots, britches, and the superb-fitting coat. His chestnut hair was windblown and his cheeks ruddy from exercise. It was obvious he'd just come from riding, and she had the absurd urge to run her fingers through his hair, to feel its fullness and then smooth it into place.

She quickly lowered her eyes as Georgie answered him, repeating her question about her mother's odd behavior. "Ah, yes, Mother *has* been acting a bit . . . strangely," Adam replied bemusedly. "And what does Diana think?"

Diana's head snapped up. He was addressing Georgie, but his eyes were on *her*. The corners of his mouth twitched.

"Diana hasn't a clue," Georgie said, and Adam lifted a brow

242

in a subtle gesture of disbelief before turning to Georgie.

"I believe, Georgie, that Mother and Signor D'Orsini have become—er—friends, and that she has decided to be most cooperative in the matter of the portrait. I expect she is too preoccupied to concern herself overmuch with domestic affairs."

"I am persuaded you must be right, Adam," she responded, apparently satisfied.

"By the way, Georgie, I have just come from the nursery. It seems there is a very hungry young lad up there awaiting your company."

Georgie jumped up, and Adam escorted her to the door. But she turned at the threshold and looked pointedly at Adam and then Diana. Damned proprieties, Adam thought irritably, knowing exactly what was on Georgie's mind. He supposed she was right, but that did not mollify him. "I'll leave the door ajar," he murmured, and Georgie nodded and left.

Diana watched Adam come back and lower himself onto the sofa just two feet from her. He had left the door slightly ajar, for all she did not suppose anyone could see the sofa in passing at all events. He hitched his arm over the curved back of the sofa, just inches from her shoulder. Diana swallowed hard. Did he not realize he was too close? He mightn't be touching her, but she could still feel his heat. She remembered all too well the dangerous heat that had flared between them the last time they'd been alone. Did he not realize the danger, the open door notwithstanding?

But he appeared quite at his ease. He lifted his brow again, and there was a gleam in his eyes.

"Haven't a clue, have you?" he drawled, recalling her back to the conversation with Georgie.

Diana's lips curled and a faint blush rose to her cheeks, and Adam wondered why he hadn't let the subject rest. Why was he more willing to discuss it with Diana than with his sister, a married woman?

"Well," Diana began, her eyes dancing, "I own I *have* wondered just how—er—friendly they've become."

Adam let forth a roar of laughter. She was a delight! He leaned closer to her and murmured, "And I shan't enlighten you, as I suspect the answer is not fit for your ears."

243

She turned to him, opening her mouth to speak, and suddenly their lips were just inches apart. And then he realized his folly. What had he been thinking, to allow himself to be private with her, to sit so close, to quiz her on such a subject? Now he could hardly breath. Her lips were moist, soft, parted just as they had been that day at Lady Hart's. She was not breathing very steadily herself; her eyes told him she recalled that day all too well.

He cleared his throat and sat up straight. He did not look at her. "I—ah—I actually came to tell you something," he said soberly.

"Yes?"

He heard the apprehension in her voice and pivoted to face her, keeping a foot between them. But he could not resist taking her hand in his. "I wanted you to be the first to know that I—I've decided to accept Lady Hart's commission."

"Oh, Adam!" she exclaimed, squeezing his hand. "I'm so happy for you! I truly believe it is the right thing for you. And after that—"

"After that, I *am* considering the Regent's offer quite seriously."

"That's wonderful, Adam. It pained me to think you were bottling up all that talent. And perhaps now, with the duchess otherwise . . . occupied—"

"I am afraid my mother will never be that occupied," he countered, grinning, "but it no longer signifies." He took a deep breath and released her hand. "Diana, you—you do realize that if I am to do the plans for Arden Chase, I shall be here—"

A knock at the threshold interrupted him. He stood abruptly, which was a good thing, for Rusty came in looking for Diana. It was time for them to leave.

Adam helped her on with her cloak, wrapping it round her shoulders and fastening it at her throat. Her eyes were deep blue pools, fathomless. She had known exactly what he was going to say before—that he would be here for an indefinite amount of time. He wondered what she would have said in response.

They could not go on as they were; that much was clear. But how could he remain in Rossmore and not see her?

He stood at the window of the morning room and watched Rusty's carriage clatter away. He did not hear anyone come in.

"Care for a drink?" Edward asked.

"No, thank you. 'Tis too early in the day," he replied absently.

Edward handed him a snifter of brandy nonetheless. "You look as if you can use it."

Adam took the drink and went back to staring out the window. He heard Edward sink down onto the sofa.

"Georgie's been acting differently in the past few weeks, Adam," Edward began in a seeming non sequitur. "Matters are much improved between us."

"I've noticed. I am very happy for you." Adam sipped his drink.

"Yes, well, I am persuaded that much of it has to do with some things that Diana told Georgie. And I know that you encouraged Diana to talk to Georgie, and Georgie to listen." Edward rose, and from the corner of his eye Adam saw him stroll toward the door. "And so I've decided," Edward went on nonchalantly, "that in a round-about way I owe you one." What the devil was Edward talking about?

Edward sighed. "I came here to tell you that I think you're a prize idiot, and to ask you what the hell you're waiting for!"

"What?" Adam exploded, whirling round. But the door had just closed with a resounding snap. Adam downed his brandy in one gulp.

"Prize idiot" was he? What did Edward know? And what the bloody hell was he talking about at all events?

Hah! As if Adam didn't know! He stalked to the decanter and poured himself more brandy. Edward sure as hell was not speaking of which buildings Adam had ought to design. Strange that *that* decision, which had plagued him for years, had been the easier one, after all. Of a certain it signified less. But this, *this!*

Damnation! Until just moments ago he hadn't known, hadn't wanted to admit, that he had a decision to make at first stop. *What the hell are you waiting for?* He hadn't been waiting; he'd been denying the truth.

From the very beginning he'd reminded himself that he had no intention of marrying. His parents had been miserable, as, with very few exceptions, were all his married acquaintances. And every impeccably born, bred, and dressed debutante his mother had presented to him over the years had reminded him too much of her!

He'd had no intention of leg-shackling himself. And Diana, for reasons buried in her past, had been of like mind. And with an illicit liaison out of the question, they had made the ludicrous attempt to be friends.

Friends! Lord, what a failure they were as friends! He did not dream of friends, ache to touch them, feel the need to shelter them from harm.

He gulped the brandy, pacing the room, feeling tension in every cord of his body. He could not bear it whenever she left, when he did not know when next he would see her. He could not bear not having the right to protect her. He could not bear having to keep her at arm's length when he did see her.

And how did she feel? He laughed mirthlessly. How blind, how stupid could a man be? A woman such as Diana did not cling to a man in passion the way she did, did not run to him, instead of her father, in time of danger, unless. . . . And even if not for that, it was in her eyes every time she looked at him. Was she aware of it? Did she know that she—she—

Say the word, Adam, he told himself, and set the brandy down on a table. She loved him . . . And he loved her.

He loved her! He ran a hand through his hair. He had gone beyond wanting—wanting to touch her, kiss her, make love to her—to needing—needing her smile, her softness, her extraordinary combination of fire and serenity—to loving—loving to hold her, talk with her, be with her always. But most of all, he wanted to be there *for* her, to give her joy, warmth, protection. He needed to claim her for his own. He loved her.

He had never felt any of these things for another woman. So why the devil had it taken him so long to realize it, to admit it to himself? He began to pace again. Had he been afraid? Of what? His mother and her disapproval? Hardly. She deplored nearly everything he did, and he'd been flaunting his mistresses and his carousing before her for years. He knew that his mother disapproved of Diana, just as she opposed his architectural ambitions. Yet even now, when he had finally decided to defy her and take any commission he damn well pleased, still he had denied to himself the depth of his feelings for Diana. Lady Hart had said one must live life according to one's own lights, and he had thought of his art, not of his heart.

Why? Of what was he afraid? That she would reject him? And well she might; she had made her opposition to the nuptial state very plain numerous times. But he was confident that given their feelings, their love for each other, he could overcome her hesitation. Eventually.

Clearly he had another demon plaguing him. His own opposition to marriage came from not wishing to wed a woman like his mother, or Georgie, or their numerous female acquaintances. But Diana was nothing like any of them, and he'd known that from the beginning. Hell, Georgie was not like his mother any longer. Even *his mother* was not like his mother any longer!

But still he'd hesitated, until moments ago, when Edward had jarred him with his simple question. *What the hell are you waiting for?*

Something tickled at his brain—a conversation he'd had with Diana, one of their very first. They'd been speaking of marriage, of his parents' marriage in particular, and she'd said something that raised his hackles. It was about—about his father. He thought a moment, stopping his pacing to gaze out the window again, and then he recalled it all very clearly.

She'd said something to the effect that she wasn't certain if he was afraid that he'd marry a woman like his mother, or that he'd make the same mistakes his father had undoubtedly made. Whereupon he'd countered angrily that his father hadn't *made* any mistakes! Her response had been that marital difficulties could never be laid at one person's door alone.

He remembered then asking about her parents—had not her mother been the one responsible for their difficulties at first stop, and the one to change, to improve matters so dramatically? Yes, she'd said, but it was more complex than that. He tried to recall her exact words. "I believe Mama changed because Papa would not tolerate her waspish behavior, and because he responded so warmly to every overture she made."

And now he thought about Edward, unwilling to tolerate Georgie's waspish behavior, and his warm response to her attempts at change. Adam even thought of Signor D'Orsini, firmly but quietly putting his mother in her place. And perhaps, if Adam's suspicions were right, offering her a warmth she had never known before.

And what of his father?

He sat down now and stared into the fire and thought about that which he had never wanted to face before. His father *had* tolerated waspish behavior. He had not stood up to his mother; he had retreated into cold, sullen silences, erupting in anger now and again, but never really putting his foot down. And had he ever offered his mother a man's warmth? Adam suspected not.

His mother had been a Tartar, formidable and unpleasant, to be sure. But his father had been weak.

And Adam knew now what he had been most afraid of. He had been afraid that he would be weak, like his father. Afraid that he would prove a poor, ineffectual husband. He had tried to prove to himself, and his mother, that he was not weak, by defying her—refusing to marry, darting from one mistress to another. But he had not defied her in what was most important to him. He had not accepted the once-in-a-lifetime offer to design a royal theater in London. He *had* been weak, just as his father had been, just as he feared.

But no more! He was *not* his father. He would accept that commission, and go wherever his talent took him. And he would marry where he willed, without regard to his mother's notions of consequence. But most important of all, he would be a good husband, strong and loving.

And he had chosen for his wife a pearl among women, one whose inner luster radiated beyond her outer beauty. One who was soft and feminine, warm and responsive, yet possessed of a great inner strength.

And there, he realized, was the rub. She was quite adamantly opposed to marrying, and he did not know if his declaration of love would be enough to sway her. She had been badly hurt once; she had fears of her own. He was very tempted to fly to Three Oaks straightaway, to pull her into his arms and offer her his heart and his name. But something told him it would not be quite so simple.

Oh, Rusty would no doubt be delighted, and not very

surprised, Adam realized, recalling the times Rusty had left him alone with his daughter. And Diana might admit of more than a slight tendre for Adam. But as to her agreeing to marriage—ah, that might take a bit of doing.

He rose and went to retrieve his drink, then decided he did not need it after all. For he knew—he'd just realized—what he would do. He would wait until the Truesdale ball. There would be music and myriad glimmering lights and all those hot house flowers Lucy Truesdale had talked about. He would hold Diana close as they danced the first waltz, and then perhaps at the end he would waltz her to some alcove behind a set of potted palms. Or he would lead her to an empty salon when everyone else was eating supper.

He rose and strolled to the door, feeling calm for the first time since Edward had called him a prize idiot. One day soon, when his ring was safely on Diana's finger, he would thank his impertinent brother-in-law. For now he contented himself with the thought that he had made the right decision to wait until the ball. It was, after all, only four days away.

Never had four days loomed as such an interminably long time.

Diana chose her favorite of her three ball gowns to wear to Truesdale Hall on Wednesday night. The gown was an exquisite creation with its robe of silver net over a slip of midnight blue satin. The robe opened to the left and was looped all round with bouquets of silver lamé roses. The corsage was very small, and very tight, the sleeves tiny and the décolletage fashionably low. She had caught her black hair up in a sleek topknot, secured with tiny silver lamé roses, and she wore the sapphire pendant and earrings Papa had given her for her twenty-first birthday.

She did not delude herself as to why she had chosen to wear this gown. She knew very well that she had worn it for Adam. Just as she knew it was folly to do so. But she had gone beyond pretending to herself that she could keep from loving Adam, that she could protect herself from heartbreak.

It was far, far too late. She loved him, and she could not even fathom the depths of despair that awaited her when he finally left Rossmore. And her despair would be all the greater for the fact that he had decided to design the renovations for Arden Chase. He would be here indefinitely. They would not be able to avoid seeing each other. Nor, she suspected, would they have the strength to do so, for all it would be a kind of bittersweet torture to be together. And when he left. . . .

Dear God, she could not bear to think of that. Which was why she had decided to allow herself this one night of the Truesdale ball to enjoy herself, and Adam's company, fully. It was also why she had decided to attend the ball despite her aversion to the host. Tonight she wore a gown she thought Adam would especially like; tonight she would dance with Adam and let him hold her close. She would savor every minute and store up her memories. And on the morrow she would rein in her emotions and remind herself, and Adam, of the need to be restrained, and circumspect.

But not tonight. Just for tonight she would pretend that she was a woman like other women, entitled to love a man and, perhaps, be loved in return.

She took up her gloves and her silver net shawl and made her way belowstairs, where Papa awaited her.

Chapter 17

Adam straightened the folds of his starched white cravat and tugged at the sleeves of his flawless chocolate brown velvet coat. Where was Diana? Most of the guests had already arrived, and he was aching to see her.

He had just been asked by Lady Truesdale, in the reception line, to lead Lucy out for the first dance. He was not best pleased, for a first dance might hold a certain completely erroneous significance in the minds of some. Besides, he had wanted to ask Diana for the first set. That and the waltz and supper dance would have meant three dances, the number tantamount to a betrothal announcement. Which would have suited Adam quite well, indeed. But Diana was late, and Eleanor Truesdale had gotten to him first, and he hadn't been able to refuse.

And then finally, as the orchestra began to tune its instruments, he saw her. She shared her father's escort with Millicent Weeksgate, who looked sweet and glowing in pink chintz. Rusty, sporting a charcoal gray waistcoat and a cravat tied en cascade, looked enormously pleased with himself. And Diana . . . Diana looked breathtaking.

She wore a shimmering gown of silver net over a deep blue satin that made her eyes sparkle like the sapphires at her ears and throat. The net robe opened enticingly on the left side, and the satin beneath caressed her curves the way he longed to do.

Making a deliberate attempt to steady his breathing, he strode through the elegantly clad crowd to greet her as she emerged from the reception line.

"Diana," he uttered, taking her hand and smiling down at her, "you are beautiful, my dear." He brought her hand to his lips. "My only regret is that I've been commandeered to lead Lucy Truesdale out for the first set. I shall eagerly await our waltz."

"Thank you, Adam," she replied softly. "I, too, shall look forward to it. And I take leave to tell you that you look rather magnificent yourself tonight."

He grinned; had she ever complimented him before? He was still holding her hand and had done so far longer than necessary. He didn't give a tinker's damn. He did not want to release her, allow other men to kiss her hand, dance with her, whisper to her, as if she were theirs. She smiled up at him, that wide and lovely smile, and he thought she looked almost otherworldly in that shimmering gown. But he knew that she was very much of this world—very much a woman—and he felt a fierce bolt of possessiveness.

She's mine! he wanted to shout, so that all would know and take heed.

It was Rusty, clearing his throat, who recalled him to himself. Adam unabashedly relinquished her hand, and then turned to greet Rusty and Mrs. Weeksgate. He congratulated them on having the banns read this Sunday past, and was not at all surprised when Rusty led his betrothed out for the first set.

Percy, thank heaven, was partnering Mrs. Brixworth, and as Diana was dancing with Colonel Plunkett, Adam was able to relax as he executed the steps of the quadrille with Lucy Truesdale. This despite the fact that uttering two words to him seemed agony for the girl. At the end of the set, he handed her to her second partner, Captain Plunkett, the colonel's nephew. Adam could not say who was more relieved, Lucy or himself.

His relief was short-lived as he realized that Percy was making a beeline for Diana. Adam could not stop him—indeed, there was naught he could say without creating a scene—but he ground his teeth in frustration. Percy looked like a sly and hungry fox about to have his dinner. Adam did not like it one bit. He decided to sit this dance out and let his eyes wander the ballroom, although they were never far from Diana. The dance was a Roger de Coverly, and he could see the slight tensing of her mouth each time the steps brought her together with

Percy. Damnation!

The dance seemed to go on forever. To distract himself Adam noted the promised profusions of flowers, the potted palms creating intimate little corners, the myriad candles flickering in the chandeliers and wall sconces. His eyes scanned the room, looking for Diana again, and instead he saw . . . his mother!

She was dancing! With Signor D'Orsini. Adam could not recall the last time he'd ever seen his mother dance, if ever. She actually looked rather lovely, even stately in a russet and gold gown. He'd seen the gown before, but somehow it looked different on her now. It was, he realized, in the way she held herself, the way she moved, the way she smiled. Gone was the sternness, and in its place was a certain softness, even grace. Will wonders never cease, he mused, and decided that Signor D'Orsini, resplendent in black and gold, was himself one of the wonders of the world.

There were two more dances before the waltz. Adam partnered Lady Hart for one, then handed her to Sir Horace for the next. It was then that he noted Lady Truesdale and his mother in earnest conversation. Lady Truesdale had that same sly look as her son. The duchess looked uncomfortable. Adam felt a rather unpleasant gnawing in the pit of his stomach. Something was not quite right.

Finally, the first strains of the waltz could be heard. Diana, seated to the side, was some distance from him, chatting with Edward and Georgie. Georgie looked quite fetching in a rose-colored gown overlaid with white tulle, and thus far she had obediently sat out every dance. But now Edward rose, and took her by the hand to lead her out. Diana stood as well, her eyes quickly scanning the room. She smiled as soon as she saw Adam, and every other occupant of the room ceased to exist for him as he made his way toward her.

He took her into his arms as easily, as naturally, as if he'd been doing it all his life. He pulled her close, too close, and didn't give a damn who noticed. It was sheer joy to feel her warm body molding to his as he swept her round the room. It was torture as well, for his own body reacted instantly, the familiar fire rising in him. But he calmed himself with the thought that very soon he would be able to put the fire out.

He bent his head so that his lips grazed her ear. "Mmm. You smell delicious," he whispered. "You always do. Some mysterious and feminine scent that is pure Diana."

She looked up at him and smiled, but there was a hint of sadness in her eyes. It was only then that he realized that her body was just the slightest bit tense. "Oh, Adam, it feels so good to—that is, you—you dance very well."

"I would say, my dear, that we dance very well together. But you might relax a bit more, you know."

Instead, he felt her stiffen. Without missing a step, he followed her gaze. Percy was staring at her from across the room. Adam cursed inwardly. "What is it, my dear? Has he said something tonight to upset you?"

She nodded. "'Twas whilst we were dancing. He—he said I looked good enough to eat, and that he always finished what he started."

This time Adam cursed audibly. The blackguard! Adam should have run him through at dawn following his intrusion into Diana's room. And he should never have permitted Diana to come tonight, should not have come himself. But it was not his place—yet—to decide where Diana might go, and their absence would have occasioned comment, given grist to the gossip mills. No one else seemed to know of the debacle at Arden Chase, and it was best to keep it that way.

And so here they were, with Percy not scrupling to hide his still-undaunted dishonorable intentions.

"Diana," Adam said in a soft voice edged with steel, "he will not hurt you again." Adam pulled her closer. "Do you understand? I will not allow it!"

Her velvety blue eyes, gazing into his, were somber. This was his opening, his opportunity to declare himself. But he refused to do it on a crowded dance floor, where he could not kiss her and demonstrate exactly what his words of love meant. Instead he tightened the arm that held her waist. "I will protect you, Diana!" he whispered fiercely. "Trust me."

Something flickered in the depths of her eyes, some emotion that he could not fathom. But her lips curled into a smile again, and when he told her to relax, she did. And he savored every minute that she was in his arms.

Diana did not know how Adam could protect her, only knew

254

that she desperately wanted, needed him to. And knew that being in his arms like this was sheer heaven and that she would put her fears aside and enjoy every moment. His body was long and lean and taut with power; his breath fanned her face; his muscular thighs brushed against hers as he led them in the swirls and dips of the dance. She felt her face flush and her body begin to turn to hot, burning liquid. And she revelled in the sensations, for all they were only hers for this night.

The waltz ended much too soon. She danced the next few sets with Signor D'Orsini and then Edward and Captain Plunkett. She noted Adam standing up with Lucy again, and wondered how Lady Truesdale had maneuvered him into it. The poor man did not look as if he were enjoying himself.

At length Papa came to claim her for the second waltz. He asked if she was enjoying herself, and she answered quite truthfully in the affirmative. She did not see the point of worrying him with Percy's vile innuendoes. And she did not need to ask him the same question. His enjoyment was written all over his face, and Millicent's.

Adam danced the supper dance with her, and then led her into the supper room. They sat with Edward and Georgie. Georgie was glowing, but admittedly quite fagged. She did not cavil when Edward said they had ought to leave straightaway after supper. The four of them chatted easily, rather like old friends, or family. Or like . . . two couples, she thought wistfully.

Several feet from them sat Papa and Millicent with the Hartcups, the duchess and Signor D'Orsini. All of them—even the duchess—seemed to be in high spirits. But every once in a while Diana caught Her Grace casting a glance at her own table, and she did not look happy. Diana would have thought it was *her* presence with the little family gathering that would have peeved the duchess. But it was not pique Diana saw on her face; it was preoccupation, almost discomfort. Unfortunately she had not a private moment with Adam to ask him about it.

Adam wanted to lead Diana surreptitiously away the moment the last lobster pattie had been consumed. Indeed, he would not have minded skipping the supper altogether; but Georgie had hailed them right after the supper dance, and there had been no help for it. But now, Edward and Georgie were

255

saying their goodbyes, his mother's table seemed still to be eating their buttered oranges and walnut pudding, and the time was right.

"Diana," he whispered after Edward and Georgie had gone, "I should like to speak with you about—er—something of moment. Would you come for a stroll with me? I am persuaded that our absence will not be remarked just now."

She gazed quizzically at him, and he could see her considering the impropriety of being private with him versus the desire to do that very thing. "Very well, Adam," she said at length, and he grinned at her and took her hand.

They had just reached the threshold of the supper room when Adam espied Percy coming toward them. Diana saw him, too; Adam could feel her stiffen beside him. "Ah, Diana, there you are," Percy said smoothly. "The orchestra is just now beginning the waltz. I believe this is *my* dance, Marchmaine." He cocked his head insolently, a smug smile on his face.

Adam's jaw clenched. Diana looked up at him, her feelings written plainly on her face. She did not want to go with Percy. And worse, she was afraid. Dammit! He would do anything to erase that look from her beautiful face. But for now his hands were tied. Percy, bounder though he be, was their host, and there was no way short of creating a dreadful scene that Adam could prevent him from claiming his promised waltz. Nor could Diana at this point refuse, and she knew it. Even did she claim not to be feeling at all the thing, she would be obliged to sit the dance out with Percy hovering solicitously by her side.

Adam cursed to himself profusely. He should have done something, anything, to keep Diana away from here tonight. As it was, all he could do was smile bracingly at Diana and try to assure her without words that she would be all right. It was only one dance at a very public ball. Adam would not take his eyes off her.

Percy extended his arm, and she schooled her expression to one of calm before taking it. "I look forward to watching your excellent form on the dance floor," Adam said evenly, by way of warning Percy and reassuring Diana, lest their silent communication, for once, have failed. And for good measure, for his own sake as much as hers, he managed to give her hand a surreptitious squeeze before relinquishing her.

Diana hated every minute of her dance with Percy. She hated his hand at her waist, his face so close to hers, his breath grazing her cheeks. Where Adam's touched warmed, Percy's sent chills up her spine that she hoped he could not sense.

"You feel very good in my arms, Diana. I always knew you would," he whispered, and Diana thought she would be ill.

Every time she was turned toward the terrace doors, she caught a glimpse of Adam, standing there, a deep frown on his beloved face. She should not have let her fear show when Percy came for her. She had known there was naught Adam could do. But she had needed his smile of reassurance, that final squeeze of her hand.

It was only a dance, she reminded herself. Repulsed as she was by Percy's touch, even he could not harm her in the middle of his mother's ballroom.

It was only a dance, Adam reminded himself. The gnawing at the pit of his stomach, the sense of foreboding, was a very bad case of jealousy and possessiveness. The waltz would end, and he would take Diana aside, and tell her what was in his heart. And never again would he be in the frustrating position of having no right to publicly protect her.

The waltz was going on an interminably long time, he thought. Why was Percy leading her so close to the potted palms? She was like to knock one over with her gown! A footman approached with a tray of brandy and offered a snifter to Adam, which he gratefully took. He needed it. For a moment the distraction caused Adam to lose sight of Diana. When he saw her again little prickles of apprehension touched his neck. Percy was holding her in the sweep of the dance, but he was leading her in and around the palms, behind several large pillars, where for seconds at a time Adam could not see her. He did not like it one whit, and started forward with determination.

It was then that the second footman approached him. He was a tall fellow, and standing in front of Adam, he effectively blocked his view of the potted palms and Diana. Adam inched to the side but still could not see her. Impatiently he asked the man his business. It seemed there was a messenger from Damerest Hall awaiting him at the servants' entrance. Damerest! Why the devil would there be a messenger from

Damerest? He had left his eminently capable steward in charge.

"Tell the fellow I'll be with him shortly," he said dismissively, craning his neck to look for Diana, whom he still could not see. "And have him brought up to some anteroom near here. I've no wish to run the fellow to ground in the servants' wing."

"But, Your Grace, beggin' your pardon, I'm sure the chap said as how he was in all his travel dirt and could not come abovestairs, but I was to tell you it were a matter of great urgency."

Urgency? What the devil? Adam felt alarmed for the first time. But he still could not see Diana. He dismissed the footman, telling him he would come as soon as possible. And then he went in search of Diana. Damerest Hall could wait. She could not.

Diana had been decidedly uneasy when Percy had led her behind the potted palms and the pillars. Uncomfortable as she felt in his arms, she had at the least felt safe in full view of the crowded ballroom. The palms accorded a measure of privacy that she could not like, however. She had been about to tell him so when suddenly Lady Truesdale had come rushing up to them, wringing her hands in distress.

Percy had brought them to a sudden standstill behind a wide white pillar. He released Diana and asked his mother what was wrong.

"Oh, dear heavens, Percy! 'Tis Lucy!" she cried in an undertone. "She has disappeared. I—I can't find her anywhere, and I fear she's gone off with that Captain Plunkett. He is not anywhere to be found either. And you know what any *hint* of impropriety can do to the reputation of one so young as Lucy. Why, she hasn't had her London come-out yet!"

"Calm down, Mother," Percy soothed, peering through the row of palms to scan the ballroom.

Diana did the same, inching away from Percy and closer to his mother. When it became obvious that neither Lucy nor the captain were to be seen, Lady Truesdale beseeched Percy to help her look for them.

"Do you come as well, Diana," she added, surprising Diana. "Percy will ring a peal over the child, and I shall likely turn into a watering pot. You will be a comfort to her, I make no doubt."

Diana was aware that under ordinary circumstances Lady Truesdale felt her rather beneath her family's notice, but these were not ordinary circumstances. And while Diana was not foolhardy enough to go off somewhere alone with Percy, no matter *what* the urgency, Lady Truesdale's presence put another color on the matter. Besides, Lucy *would* be in great distress when found. She was a sweet girl, had always been kind to Diana, and Diana hated to think of her left to the tender mercies of her brother.

At all events, the choice was taken out of her hands, for Percy strode toward a nearby door, and Lady Truesdale took Diana by the arm and, sniffling into a handkerchief, propelled her forward. Diana had not the time for a glance toward Adam, to signal him and let him know she was all right.

And now, some minutes later, they were wending their way down yet another cold corridor, the first three salons they'd tried having been empty. Lady Truesdale suggested they try the conservatory, and shortly they pushed open the door to that large, glass-enclosed room. Diana had by this time no idea where in the house they were. Percy carried a candle, which he lifted to scan the room. The large and numerous plants made it difficult to see, and he called out Lucy's name.

There was no answer, but Lady Truesdale thought she heard a scuffling; and so they separated, and each began searching as best they might in the dim light.

But several minutes later no one had found them. Percy's candle flickered in the far corner of the large room, and so Diana assumed the footsteps behind her belonged to his mother. "Lady Truesdale," she began, turning round, "I do not—oh! Sir Percival! You startled me! Where is your mother?"

"Why, she had to go back to her guests," he said in a tone that suddenly made her skin crawl.

"But—but what of Lucy?"

He smiled mockingly and began walking toward her. "I believe Lucy tore a flounce on her gown, or thinks she did."

It took a moment for his words, and the implications, to register. And when they did her eyes widened. She wasted not a moment on speech, but turned and bolted for the door.

She heard his evil, condescending chuckle as he came after her. "Really, Diana. Do you think me a fool? The door is locked."

She yanked on it anyway and began to scream.

"No one can hear you, my dear. We are far from the festivities, and even the servants are well-occupied."

She felt him at her back and tried to sidle away, tried to keep the panic at bay. She had been insane to come here, no matter what his mother's plea. But she would find a way out of this. She would!

He grabbed her and whirled her round. "We have unfinished business, you and I," he said silkily, one hand holding her shoulder, and with the other running a finger down her cheek.

"We have *no* business, Percy!" she spat and shoved at him, but he restrained her easily, pinning her to the back of the door with his hands and his body.

She kicked and pummeled his chest, and he merely laughed and grasped both her hands, raising them above her head. She squirmed and kicked out at him.

"Little hellcat!" he grunted, sidestepping her knee. "Do save your strength for later, my dear."

He leaned closer. He was going to kiss her, and she did not know if she could bear it.

"This time I have taken pains to see we have privacy, Diana, and plenty of time," he whispered, his hard thighs pressing her against the door.

No! She would not let him do this! She was not a frightened twelve-year-old girl. Frantically, she looked around for the nearest weapon to hand. A potted plant would do, but first she had to reach it.

She lunged to the side at the same time that one of his hands released her and went to his pocket. Still he held her, and when his hand came up once more from the pocket, he held a handkerchief. And then she understood that he was not going to kiss her after all. Not yet.

Shocked at the depths to which he would sink, she fought

him. She kicked and bit him and clawed at him, but in the end it was to no avail. He secured the handkerchief most effectivly to gag her mouth.

"You may scratch me all you wish later, my sweet, when I bring you passion," he taunted, and then picked her up and dumped her quite unceremoniously over his shoulder.

Her screams came out as muffled cries, her flailing fists did not break his stride as he strode off toward the other side of the room, and her kicking ceased abruptly as he wound a length of rope about her ankles.

How dare he, she raged inwardly, more furious now than frightened. How dare he truss her up like a chicken and sling her over his back! Somehow, she would find a way to escape him. But this was not the time, and she ceased her struggles to conserve her strength. He opened a door, and she was aware of a blast of cold air just before he threw a blanket over her and carried her off into the dark night.

Adam was frantic; his fury was rising. She wasn't anywhere near those damned palms, nor could he see her in the ballroom. Percy was nowhere to be found either. It was too cold for a tryst in the gardens, and so Adam strode into the corridor to begin a search of the main floor salons. And he vowed that if that swine harmed so much as a hair on Diana's head, he would put a bullet through his heart. If the blackguard had one.

Katherine sat with Antonio on a love seat positioned such that she had a perfect view of the ballroom. She had enjoyed her waltz with him very much indeed. She'd had no idea that the scandalous dance could be quite so much fun. But her enjoyment of the ball was marred by a preoccupation that was growing worse by the minute.

She saw Adam scan the crowded ballroom and knew very well for whom he was looking. His expression was a mixture of anger and apprehension and . . . desperation as he moved hurriedly toward the doors. Katherine felt a pang in the region of her heart.

A moment later she saw Lucy Truesdale come into the

261

ballroom, followed soon thereafter by Eleanor, who had a self-satisfied grin on her face. And that was when Katherine knew everything was going according to plan. Lucy began looking about, presumably for Adam. Soon it would be time for Katherine's own part.

"Katarina," Antonio whispered in her ear, "perhaps now you tell me what is wrong. First you are happy, smiling, and now you frown and turn down your mouth."

The image of her son's face flashed across Katherine's mind. She looked at Antonio, thought of how he had changed her life in a few short weeks, and knew that she had made a terrible mistake. She had made several. Oh, dear God, she must stop this!

She grasped Antonio's arm. How could she tell him? He would never forgive her, never. And yet, what choice had she at this point? "Antonio, I—I have done something—allowed something dreadful to happen." She jumped up. "I must go find Adam straightaway."

Adam was just racing out of the library when he nearly collided with his mother and Signor D'Orsini.

"Oh, Adam! Thank God," she exclaimed, looking rather distraught. "I must speak with you."

"I'm sorry, Mother. You seem overset, but I really cannot take the time just now. Perhaps Signor D'Orsini—"

"But Adam, I—I know something about—about where she is. Well, not where exactly but—"

"Where *who* is?" he demanded, grabbing her hands, hardly able to breathe.

"Diana Rustin. It is she you are looking for, is it not?"

Adam stared at her in amazement. "Yes," he said tautly, with underlying menace in his voice. "What do you know of this?"

"Percy Truesdale has her. It was all arranged. I—could we go inside the library and I'll explain quickly."

He nodded as they entered the dimly lit room.

His mother sat, wringing her hands; Adam paced. D'Orsini stood by the window, his face a mask of anger and . . . disappointment as the duchess spoke in a choked voice.

"It was Eleanor's idea," she began, "and, God help me, I went along with it. Lucy and Captain Plunkett were to be got out of the ballroom by various ruses, and you were to be distracted by some messenger." Blast! The mysterious message from Damerest. "Then Diana was to be lured away by Eleanor and Percy, under the guise of searching for Lucy and Captain—"

"Yes, yes, I see how it came about, Mother. But *where is Diana* now? Where has Percy taken her?" he queried fiercely.

"I do not know, Adam," she wailed. "He was meant to take her to some far-off room in the house and—and keep her there long enough to . . . compromise her reputation. They would come back to the ball just before it ended, and meanwhile Eleanor and I were meant to—to start the tongues wagging."

Adam cursed bitterly. "Why, Mother?" he demanded savagely, towering over her, his body shaking with fury. "Why did you not put a stop to this villainy? Lady Truesdale would have listened to you. What did you hope to gain? Do you hate Diana that much?"

His mother turned beseeching eyes to D'Orsini, seeking support of some kind, but the Italian's face was twisted in shock.

"I—I thought it for the best, Adam," she mumbled. "Eleanor wanted to bring about a match between you and—and Lucy, and I agreed. And, we both thought that with Diana—"

"With Diana compromised I would turn to Lucy?" he finished in scathing tones. "Goddammit! How could you be so cruel, so criminally stupid as to think I would ever—Or that Percy would stop at merely ruining her *reputation?* Bloody hell! Never mind. I've got to find her!" He whirled around and strode toward the door.

"May I help you, Marchmaine?" D'Orsini called. They were the first words the man had spoken. Adam turned and looked from him to his mother, whose fist was in her mouth as she fought back tears. Adam had never seen his mother cry. "Thank you, D'Orsini," he said quietly, "but please, if you would, take care of Mother. And keep her away from Lady Truesdale!"

"I am sorry, Adam," his mother rasped. "I realize I made a mistake. But I was only thinking of you."

"No, Mother. You were thinking of yourself," he said with

cold fury. And then, just as he reached the door, he asked sardonically, "To what do I owe this change of heart?"

"I—I saw your face, when you were looking for her, and I—I understood what she meant to you."

"Good," Adam said coldly. "Then perhaps you will understand that no matter what happens tonight, she will be mine."

The duchess nodded slowly, and Adam strode from the room.

"Dear God, Antonio," Katherine whimpered, "what have I done?"

Antonio did not move. His face was set implacably. "You have done a very bad thing, Katarina. Very bad, indeed," he said pitilessly.

She reached a hand out to him for comfort, but he remained where he was, his face a mask of grim disappointment. And Katherine bowed her head and, for the first time in years, wept bitter, scalding tears of regret.

Chapter 18

Adam was riding hell bent for fury in the dark, cold night. Lady Truesdale had refused to leave the ballroom when he and Rusty asked to speak with her, claiming responsibility to her guests. And when Adam had demanded, sotto voce, that she tell him where Percy had taken Diana, she had looked at him as if he were quite addled. Percy had some matter to deal with belowstairs regarding the servants, and as for Diana—had she gone to the ladies' withdrawing room, perhaps? That was when Adam had ruthlessly informed her that he would blacken her precious Lucy's name from here to London town did she not accompany them straightaway. Lady Truesdale had paled and shown Adam and Rusty to an anteroom.

Adam had quelled her further protestations of innocence by describing what he would do to Percy if he dared to touch Diana.

"He—he has her in the conservatory," she stammered, beginning to look ill, "but—but you must know he means only to detain her, until—"

"You really do not know your son very well if you believe that, Lady Truesdale," Adam said scathingly, and bade her lead them to the conservatory.

The door to that room was locked, but she produced a key in short order. Adam was not surprised when the large room proved empty. Rusty suggested they search the house, but then Adam found a rear door open and knew Percy had taken Diana from the house. He cursed volubly; Lady Truesdale nearly swooned.

By then Lady Hart had found them. She took in the scene at a glance and said simply, "He has her, doesn't he?"

Eleanor Truesdale moaned. Lady Hart apparently had feared that Percy was planning some villainy. Now she ventured that there was an abandoned shepherd's hut just off the road between Arden Chase and Rossmore. And she recalled that Percy had a hunting box on the north end of the estate. There was more to Lady Hart, Adam decided, than one might assume to look at her with her Eighteenth Century haircomb and her endless purple gowns.

There were also, it seemed, two inns in the vicinity, the Horsefeathers and one other. It was decided that Rusty would search out the inns, Adam the hut and the hunting box. Lady Hart would inform Millicent of what was transpiring and would attempt to keep up appearances by accounting for the various absences from the ballroom. Adam very strongly admonished Lady Truesdale to do the same. "I shall say Miss Rustin tore a flounce on her hem," his hostess said weakly.

"Do that," Adam responded curtly, and then extracted directions to the hunting box from her before striding out with Rusty.

Neither he nor Rusty felt the slightest compunction borrowing Percy's horses. If Diana were . . . all right, they would bring her back here, to make a brief appearance. If . . . if not, they would take her home and send Millicent to stay with her whilst Rusty and Adam dealt with Truesdale.

And so now Adam rode as if the hounds in hell were after him. He had decided to seek out the shepherd's hut first. He thought he recalled seeing it on the way to Lady Hart's last week. Besides, Percy's own hunting box seemed too obvious.

Thank God, Adam thought, that the moon was bright, else it would have taken him twice as long to find the hut. As it was, however, the shepherd's hut was pitch dark, and very much abandoned. Cursing violently, he bounded onto the gray stallion he was riding and headed north for the hunting box. He made several wrong turns before he found it, and would have missed it had it not been for Lady Hart's last-minute, vague recollection that it was nearly surrounded by rows of tall spruce trees.

Adam approached slowly, quietly, although it looked as if

this structure, too, was empty. But a walk round the back revealed the muted glow of candlelight; there must have been a curtain on the window. He had retrieved his pistol from the hidden pocket of his carriage before setting out. It was tucked now into his coat pocket, ready to be used on a locked door . . . or on Percy Truesdale, if he was, indeed, here.

The rear door was locked, but the front, to Adam's surprise, was unbolted. That and the candle were a measure of Truesdale's arrogance, Adam thought. He really had assumed no one would follow him. Why? Because no one would have figured out that he had Diana? Or was it that he assumed Adam would not want Diana after. . . .

Bloody swine! Adam thought savagely as he took the stairs two at a time, trying to keep his tread silent. His heart was beating furiously with fear for Diana. How much time had Truesdale had with her already? If he had hurt her—and were they even here at first stop? Why wasn't there any noise?

At first Adam thought he was doomed to disappointment again. The house was eerily quiet; nonetheless, he pushed open each door along the dark upstairs corridor. Every room was empty. Then he heard a scuffling, then some muffled vocal noise, and finally a laugh. An evil, predatory laugh. The sounds were coming from the far end of the corridor, from behind a door he hadn't seen before. Adam bounded forward, his pistol at the ready. But he stopped in his tracks, and his breath caught in his throat as he heard Truesdale's voice from just beyond the door.

"Little fool," he said smugly. "If you would stop playing your little games and put that thing down, I could get close enough to take off that gag. And here you can scream your pleasure to your heart's content, my sweet. No one will hear you."

Adam felt a wave of blazing fury such as he had never known before, while paradoxically a wave of relief washed over him. She was here, and, apparently, he was in time. That did not reduce one iota his desire to do murder.

He stealthily turned the door handle. Blast! *This* one was locked! Percy had undoubtedly meant to lock Diana *in*; he was not concerned about keeping intruders *out*. It was a very solid, very heavy door. Adam did not think he had sufficient weight to break it down, and he could not shoot at the lock without knowing exactly where Diana was.

He did not have to wait more than seconds; indeed, did not know what he would have done had the sound not come when it did. For frustration gnawed at him even as his blood pounded in his temples. He heard Percy's heavy tread and then his odious voice again, this time farther away and edged with anger.

"That's enough, Diana! Now give me that damned thing!"

And then, from the far side of the room came a muffled cry—Diana's cry—and the sounds of struggle. In the split second after Diana's approximate location registered in his mind, Adam fired at the lock. It shattered straightaway, and he lunged into the room, pistol raised.

Truesdale spun about, shock followed by scorching fury on his face. Diana, holding aloft a fireplace poker, turned her head toward Adam but did not lower the poker. He saw the relief on her face despite the gag over her mouth. The sight of that gag made Adam shake with renewed rage.

"Back away from her, Truesdale," he shouted menacingly, advancing into the room. "Diana, come here."

Diana took one step, and Truesdale's arm snaked out and grabbed her by the hand that held the poker. The weapon clattered to the ground. "I could kill you for this, Marchmaine. Put that damned gun down. You've no more right to her than I do."

Adam felt his blood boil and barely kept himself from racing forward and wrenching Diana from his grasp. But Truesdale was perfectly capable of hurting her, and Adam wanted to avoid that if possible. "I am here as her father's emissary. And as to killing, that will take place at dawn. Have your seconds call mine."

"And again you will be her father's emissary?" Truesdale mocked. "Come now, Marchmaine. We both know 'tis not at all the thing to be duelling over mistresses."

Adam did not even think, had no idea how he got across the room, had no awareness of pocketing the gun. But he must have, for within two seconds of Truesdale's last odious remark, Adam's fist was connecting soundly with the blackguard's jaw. Truesdale staggered, releasing Diana and swinging at Adam, and catching him on the chin. Diana screamed from behind the gag, trying to untie it. Adam grabbed Truesdale by his coat, straightening him just enough so that he could land another blow to his left eye. This time Truesdale went down; Adam followed, pummeling him with his fists, ignoring the cur's vain attempts to fight back.

Diana's muffled cries became frantic. Adam felt her hands at his shoulders, trying to pull him away. Only then did he realize Truesdale was out cold. He put his finger beneath the man's jaw to check for his pulse. It was weak but steady. Satisfied, Adam rose, breathing heavily and wiping his hands as he turned to Diana.

"Are you all right?" he asked hoarsely.

She nodded, her beautiful hair tumbling in wild disarray about her face and down her back. Her magnificent blue and silver gown was askew but untorn. And she still had the damned gag over her mouth. But before he could untie it, she reached up with her hand to caress his bruised chin. "Oh, God, Diana!" he rasped, and dragged her into his arms.

He released her a moment later and turned her round. "Let me untie this blasted handkerchief," he said gruffly.

But the knot seemed excessively intricate and the light too dim. He led her to the table that held the candles, and still he fumbled with the knot. He finally undid one, only to find another, and another. "Good God! How many times did he knot this? No wonder you couldn't do it yourself."

When at last the hateful piece of silk fell to the floor, Diana spun about and buried herself in Adam's embrace. "Oh, Adam, Adam! Thank God! I did not even realize how frightened I was. I just concentrated on being furious."

She began to shake in his arms, and he rubbed her back up and down, holding her tightly. "And a good thing, too, my love. You were doing rather well at staving him off."

Just then Percy groaned, rolled to one side, then fell silent again. "Let's get the hell out of here," Adam said grimly, and grabbed her hand.

Two feet from the door he espied a length of rope, which Diana informed him Percy had used to tie her feet. Resisting the urge to coil it around the villain's neck, Adam contented himself with tying Percy's hands behind his back, very

269

securely. And then he led her quickly from the room and down the stairs, all the while sending up a silent prayer to God for returning her safely to him. He could hardly credit that she was here with him, that he could feel the warmth of her hand in his.

Not until they were outside the hunting box did he stop and take her by the shoulders. "Did he hurt you?" he asked meaningfully.

She attempted a smile. "Other than trussing me up like a chicken and tossing me over his shoulder, no, Adam. I—I am all right now."

As if to underscore her words, she stepped back from him and straightened her dress. Then she put her hands to her hair.

He smiled. His own Diana—calm, a bit ruffled perhaps but undaunted—was back. "Diana, we needs must get back. I have to get word to your father that I've found you—he's out searching as well—and then—ah—"

"What is it, Adam?" She was doing a remarkable job of pinning her hair into a semblance of order.

"I know you do not give great credence to proprieties, my dear, but if you are up to it, Rusty and I both feel that it would be best if you returned to the ball, at least for a brief time."

She smiled, a genuine Diana-smile this time. "Then, I shall do it for both of you." By God, he loved this woman!

He led her to where he'd tethered his mount. She glanced up toward the second floor of the hunting box. "Is he—is he all right?" she whispered.

"No; but he's alive, more's the pity. Let us get away from here before he wakes up."

He gave her a leg up onto the stallion and climbed up behind her. She turned her face up to him. "Adam, what—what you said before about—about dawn. You are not really going to—"

"I am," he cut in sharply, "and do not say another word on the matter."

She didn't.

The next few hours had passed in a blur for Diana. Seated now at her window, watching the birth of a cold gray dawn, she could recall returning to the ballroom on Adam's arm, talking fustian with whomever they encountered. She remembered

270

Lady Hart and Millicent trying not to make their relief at seeing her too obvious in the crowded ballroom. Papa's eyes had filled with tears when he returned and assured himself that she was unharmed. And Eleanor Truesdale had eyed the pair of them warily. The duchess was nowhere to be seen. Diana wondered if she was aware of any of this.

The ball wound to a close soon after her return. Millicent went home with the Hartcups, and Papa and Adam both conveyed Diana to Three Oaks. She turned to Adam at the base of the stairwell and, unable to help herself, had reached out a hand and whispered, "Be careful."

He had smiled and squeezed her hand and told her in gentle tones that she had naught to worry about. There had been neither the time nor the privacy for him to say more. He had waited belowstairs whilst Mrs. Barrett and Papa whisked her abovestairs and helped her into bed, and for their sakes Diana had pretended to be tired enough to sleep.

But, of course, sleep had eluded her completely. She knew well why Adam had waited for Papa. He meant to fight Percy, with Papa no doubt as his second. Papa would want to fight Percy himself, and Adam would refuse. Diana could almost hear their conversation in her head. She would not think too much now of the implications of Adam fighting a duel for her. Although it had not registered earlier, she was aware now that Adam had called her "my love" last night. She did not think he had used the phrase casually, and part of her felt joyous at the thought that he returned her regard. But her joy was tempered by her knowledge that nothing, really, had changed; she could not wed.

Yet none of that signified compared with the far greater concern that preyed now upon her mind. Adam could be seriously wounded—or worse—in this duel, this man's business that a female was powerless to stop. Percy was accounted a good shot when not in his cups; Diana had no idea how much he'd imbibed last night, nor what state he would be in after the thrashing Adam had given him. Of a certain, he would not be in top form. Diana took hope from that. As to Adam, was he, indeed, the crack shot he'd told Percy he was that dreadful night at Arden Chase?

And if he did kill Percy, would he be forced to flee the

country? Dear God, would she ever see him again? Oh, Lord, why was it taking so long? Was it not over yet? Why did not someone—Adam, Papa, a messenger—come banging on the door to tell her all was well?

What was to become of them all?

Adam *was* accounted a crack shot, a fact which he had not shared with Diana last night. There'd been no time for private discourse once they'd entered the ballroom. And besides, he had not wanted to elucidate just how he knew this about himself. For the sordid fact was that he had duelled twice before, and neither incident redounded to his credit, except, of course, as proof of his marksmanship—he'd gotten his man both times.

The first sorry incident had involved a married woman of loose virtue, a very irate husband, and a very young Duke of Marchmaine. Adam had winged the poor man in the shoulder, and had stayed clear of married "ladies" ever since. The second episode, five years later, had involved a disagreement over cards. Adam's opponent had been guilty of sleight of hand, and so Adam felt there was some poetic justice in the ball he'd shot into the scoundrel's arm. But he hadn't been proud of himself.

This morning, as he gazed down at the pale, still form of Sir Percy Truesdale, even now being ministered to by Dr. James Rustin, he *was* proud of himself. Proud that he had had the privilege of fighting for Diana's honor, proud that he'd had the forbearance not to kill the bastard, which he'd so longed to do.

But a man contemplating matrimony ought to have no black stain to mar his conscience nor to give his gentle lady a disgust of him. And so Adam had let the villain live. But he'd thought it poetic justice to shoot the fellow in the thigh, very high up and very close to a rather important part of his anatomy.

The stunned look on Percy's bruised face when he realized he'd been hit, his own shot gone astray, had been most gratifying. But not half so much as the howl of anguish he'd let forth upon looking down and seeing the dark red stain suffusing the general region so dear to every man. He'd started to shriek and, indeed, had fallen and lost consciousness before

Rusty could tell him his manhood, such as it was, was intact.

Now as Rusty staunched the flow of blood and tended the wound, he and Adam talked in low tones. Percy's second was readying the carriage for his trip home. He would have a long and painful recovery, and when he could walk again, Adam would see that he took another trip, a very extended one on the Continent.

Rusty urged Adam to go home. There was no sense in them both freezing out here on this desolate hilltop. Rusty would follow Percy's carriage home and remove the ball at Truesdale. He would send a message to Diana that all was well, and Adam was welcome to call later in the day if he wished.

He looked pointedly at Adam as he said this last, and Adam grinned.

"You know perfectly well I wish to visit, Rusty, and you know perfectly well why; and I do not mean to wait all day to do it!"

"'Tis just after daybreak, Adam. She'll be asleep."

"No, Rusty. She'll be awake. Waiting. I do not want her to hear from a messenger. I'll send a messenger to Rossmore instead, letting them know all is well. But I shall go to Three Oaks."

"Oh, very well," Rusty grumbled, wadding more clean linen against the gaping hole in Truesdale's thigh, "go now, then. But as to the other, you have not asked my permission, you know."

"No, I haven't. But I seem to recall your once saying, during a rather inane conversation which I initiated, that if my interest became personal, we would talk about Diana's need for protection."

"And?" Rusty tried to sound casual, his hands never faltering in their brisk, knowing movements. If he thought it incongruous to be tending the man who had meant his daughter so ill, it did not show in the care he gave that man. Such, Adam supposed, was the calling of a doctor.

"And," Adam answered at length, "my interest *is* personal. Very *very* personal."

Rusty finally raised his eyes; this time it was he who grinned. "About bloody time, Adam, is all I can say. But, Adam—" Suddenly Rusty's expression sobered. "I am not certain, that is, despite what she may feel, Diana is not—"

"Disposed to wed," Adam finished for him. "Yes, I know. I do not suppose you'll tell me why?"

Rusty shook his head. "'Tis for her to tell you, Adam. But I—good luck, Adam."

Rusty made it sound as though he would truly need it. For the first time, as he rode briskly over the bleak dales to Three Oaks, Adam pondered deeply just what he might be up against.

Diana had fallen into a light doze, her head against the front window of her bedchamber. The sound of hoofbeats woke her, and she opened her eyes and felt tears of relief well up. He was here! Adam was here, and quite safe and whole. "Oh, thank you, God," she cried aloud, and then wondered with sudden apprehension where Papa was. Without a thought for the impropriety of her dishabille, she belted her wrapper and dashed from her chamber.

It was Diana, and not one of the servants, who opened the door. She wore a blue velvet wrapper over an ivory satin night rail, and Adam had never seen a more welcome, beautiful sight, the dark circles beneath her eyes notwithstanding. She also looked delectable, her lovely form so clearly outlined beneath her wrapper, but Adam set that lascivious thought aside for later.

"Adam," she said huskily, stepping aside so that he could enter. "You're all right."

He smiled down at her, pushing the oak door shut behind him. "As you see, love. Did you doubt?"

She smiled ruefully, and somehow—he was not sure who moved first—she was in his arms. "No, but I also did not sleep. Oh, Adam, it seems every time I see you lately 'tis with more relief, and happiness, than the time before."

She snaked her arms about to clasp him round the waist, seemingly not at all discommoded by the rough feel of his greatcoat against her delicate nightclothes. Adam, however, was most discommoded by that warm, scantily clad body pressed so close to his. And by the luxurious black hair, confined at her back with nothing more than a thin ribbon.

It was Diana, however, who separated them, jerking her

head up and stepping back just a bit. "Adam! Where is Papa? I expected to hear the carriage by now—"

He chuckled. "Your esteemed papa is doing what he always does—tending the infirm," he replied, pulling of his hat, gloves, and greatcoat. Diana took the garments from him and set them aside.

"Just exactly what are you saying, Adam?"

He sighed. "That in deference to your sensibilities, and my conscience, and a great desire that I have just now to remain on English soil, I let the miserable cur live. Which is more, I assure you, than he deserves."

"I know that," she said quickly. "But I am glad you did not kill him."

Adam grinned. "Yes, well, for a while I daresay he'll wish I had."

She cocked her head at him. "Adam, what—ah—did you—"

"Another time, my dear." He took her hand and brought it to his lips, kissing her fingertips. Then he tucked her hand into the crook of his arm and began strolling toward the stairs. "I find I do not wish to speak of that wretched excuse for a man any further. Suffice it to say, for now, that it will be sometime before he can walk again."

She looked at him curiously, but with that marvelous talent she had for knowing when to be silent, said nothing more. She did, however, invite him to breakfast, which invitation he gratefully accepted, with the proviso that she change her clothes. He let his eyes sweep pointedly over her until she understood the need for this modification. She called to Mrs. Barrett, the housekeeper, before ascending the stairs, and asked that an extra place be laid for breakfast.

Mrs. Barrett looked at Adam with eyes wide, apparently a good deal more concerned with the impropriety of her mistress inviting a man to breakfast than Diana was. The woman's eyes went from Adam to Diana's retreating back and returned to Adam.

"You fought for her this morning, didn't you?" she asked bluntly. The old woman, who last night had murmured soothing, motherly things to Diana as she and Rusty led her up to bed, now eyed Adam piercingly.

This time Adam's eyes widened. No ordinary servant, this.

He eyed the plump, wrinkled gray-eyed woman warily. "Yes, I did," he said uncompromisingly.

"And Dr. Rustin?" she inquired.

"He is tending the wounded."

Mrs. Barrett's ancient face split into a smile for the first time. "Ah. Well, then, I expect you'll be very hungry."

Adam grinned in return. "I would at that, Mrs. Barrett," he replied, and watched her trundle away toward the rear of the house.

Diana returned in remarkably short order. She was attired in the same deep blue wool merino dress she'd worn the first time he'd seen her. Adam decided that was a good omen for his purpose here today. They made quick work of the delicious breakfast set before them, and then, telling her he wished a private word with her, he escorted Diana to the front parlor. They met Mrs. Barrett just emerging from that very room. She gazed pensively at the two of them, and Adam thought a bit of diplomacy was in order.

He allowed Diana to precede him into the parlor. He made to follow, but turned at the threshold to whisper to Mrs. Barrett, "Dr. Rustin is aware that I mean to speak with Miss Rustin this morning."

The housekeeper nodded, smiling faintly. She did not seem surprised. She did surprise *him*, however, by saying, "Good luck, Your Grace."

That was the second person who had wished him good luck this morning. Somehow, that did not auger well. Adam straightened his shoulders and stepped inside the room, closing the door behind him. It was time to put his fate to the touch.

Diana was seated on the ruby-colored damask sofa, and Adam went to sit close beside her. He looked at her a moment, at the beautiful oval face framed by ebony curls now pinned up demurely, at the expressive, deep blue eyes, and knew with complete certainty that this was right, and that he would make it right, despite any objections she might have.

He had not thought specifically about what he would say, and now the words simply began to flow naturally. He took both her hands in his.

"Diana, you must know—"

"Adam, did I thank you for what you did this morning?" she interrupted nervously. "It really was not necessary, but I do appreciate it. And as to last night, I—I simply do not know how long I could have—"

"Diana," he whispered, putting a finger to her lips to silence her. "I have never before known you to babble." Indeed, her unaccustomed chatter led him to the conclusion that she knew what he was going to say, to ask, and wanted to forestall him. He was having none of that.

"It will not do aught of good, at all events, for I mean to have my say," he went on gently, then stroked her soft cheek with his knuckles. "Do you know how very much I love you, Diana? Do you know that you occupy my thoughts all day, my dreams at night?"

She bit her lip, and her eyes welled up. "Adam, I—"

"Diana." He cupped her chin with his hand. "I want you to share my home, my name, my bed . . . my life." He brushed at a tear that was trickling toward her mouth. "Am I so wrong in believing that you—that you return my regard?"

She lowered her eyes and sniffled. "Am I so wrong, my dear?" he repeated. "Do I not feel your love when I hold you, when I kiss you? Do I not see it in your eyes? Look at me, Diana." He tilted her face up to his, a finger under her chin. "Am I wrong, Diana?" he uttered.

"No," she replied hoarsely. "You—you are not wrong."

He breathed an inward sigh of relief but knew he had only just passed the first hurdle. He took her gently by the shoulders, his mouth hovering just above hers. "I love you, Diana," he whispered, and took her lips in a kiss that held more tenderness than passion. Nonetheless he felt her shudder. "Say the words, Diana," he breathed into her mouth. When she stared at him mutely, two more tears rolling down her cheeks, he commanded a little less gently, "Say the words, Diana."

"I—I love you," she rasped, and tried to turn away.

He held her fast. "You love me, but your tears tell me you will not marry me."

She broke away from him then and darted up, going to stand

277

near the window. She kept her back to him, but he knew she was wringing her hands at her waist. "I—cannot wed you, Adam," she said in a voice growing thick with tears. "I told you from the very beginning that I—I am not a woman meant to wed."

He rose and went to her, clasping her shoulders and pulling her back against his chest. "And I have told you, you are wrong. It makes no sense. How can you love me, how can you respond the way you do in my arms, and still claim—"

"No, Adam!" She twisted away and moved forward to the window itself, wrapping her arms about herself. "Surely you must see that it is impossible. Why you—you are a duke of the realm. You cannot possibly marry a doctor's daughter. Your own mother would have the apoplexy. She thinks I'm no better than a—"

"I think it safe to say my mother doesn't know *what* she thinks anymore," he said from behind her. "And if truth be known, I don't give a tinker's damn." He moved several steps and breathed the next words into her ear. But he did not touch her. "'Tis *you* I cannot live without, Diana. The duchess has naught to say to the matter. And as to my rank, our differences are not so great. Why, the Duke of Milburne married the family governess not one year past! And, let me see, the Earl of Westmacott married his mistress of fifteen years, and—"

"Adam, that—that is not the only problem," she interrupted with a kind of desperation. She put her brow to the cold windowpane, trying to distance herself from the heat of his breath caressing her ear. She *had* to make him understand. Somehow she had to, without telling him the whole. And then she must send him on his way. For though his rank was not the only problem, it was a far greater one than he could possibly know. Robert, a mere baronet, had spoken of the purity of his bloodlines. How much more important must that be to the Duke of Marchmaine? And then there was the other matter that concerned not a duke and a doctor's daughter, but a man and a woman. A man had a right to expect his wife to be a maiden. It was as simple, and as complex, as that.

Idly she noted that the sky had darkened, rather than lightened, as the morning advanced. The bleakness suited her mood. She wondered if it would snow again. She sighed and forced herself to go on, "You do not understand. There are—there are things you do not know about me."

He put his hands to her shoulders again and turned her slowly to face him. "Then, I think 'tis time you told me those things. And then you will understand that it makes no difference to me. There is naught that can change what is between us."

She shook her head in despair. "I was betrothed once," she said softly, and then was amazed that she hadn't told him before.

Adam took a deep breath, letting her words sink in. "Was he the man you told me about, Diana?" She lifted a brow in question. "The one who hurt you, very badly. Seven years ago, was it?"

She nodded. "I was nineteen."

"What happened?" he inquired gently, brushing a stray curl back from her brow.

She made a pitiful attempt at a smile and shrugged. "Robert—Sir Robert Easton—breezed into my life at an assembly in York and—and swept me off my feet. I thought I loved him. He said he loved me."

"Do you still love him, Diana?" Adam asked, and held his breath.

"Oh, no, of course not, nor have I these many years passed." Adam expelled his breath. "I—I suppose I was infatuated with him, but I—I did not understand what it meant to love a man until—until I met you. And even my infatuation died quickly when he cried off."

"*He* cried off?"

"Oh, yes, although he put it about that I had done the jilting. A gentleman to the end, Robert was. But when he left, he had made it very clear that—that I was not fit to be a wife."

He grabbed her shoulders, feeling anger rise in him at this unknown man. "What did he do to you?" he asked ominously.

"No, no Adam. You—you misunderstand. He—he did not *do* anything. It was rather that he said things that—that I knew to be true. Things that I—" her voice dropped low, so that it was almost inaudible—"I had told myself did not signify. But they did. And they still do."

Adam frowned but did not release his hold on her. "Diana,

279

my dear, do you not trust me enough to tell me what the deuce you are talking about? Surely you must see that none of this makes sense to me. There is naught you could possibly—"

"Please, Adam. You must take my word on this. It is not something that I can ever tell you."

"Why, dammit?" He shook her lightly, beginning to feel desperate. "Are you protecting someone else?"

"No. 'Tis nothing like that." She tried to twist away. "Please, Adam, let me go. I was—I was so afraid it would come to this. I never wanted to fall in love with you, never wanted to hurt you." She was crying openly now, if silently. She brought her hand to his cheek. "I am so sorry," she rasped, and turned away.

"Why, dammit?" he demanded, jerking her back, forcing her to look him in the eye. "Why can you not tell me what turned Easton away?"

"Because—because it would give you a disgust of me," she ground out, and then wrenched herself from his grasp and ran from the room.

Adam cursed volubly into the quiet of the empty parlor. He stood stock-still for the next few minutes, considering his options, and then he strode from the room. He nearly collided with Rusty as soon as he reached the corridor.

"Adam!" Rusty exclaimed. "I just saw—oh, devil take it! I'm sorry." He patted Adam on the shoulder.

"Don't be, Rusty. I'll be back," Adam replied determinedly. "How goes the blighter?"

"He'll do, which is more than I can say for that mother of his. Shrieking and wailing enough to tear the rafters down."

"Serves her right," Adam said scathingly. "Damned viperous female planned the whole thing; I'm sure of it." Rusty nodded, and Adam went on, "She needs her come-uppance. I am thinking that the cut direct, administered by the Dowager Duchess of Marchmaine in a London drawing room, will serve admirably."

Rusty smiled grimly. "I agree, Adam. But if 'tis to be the *dowager* duchess, then I'd better have a word with my daughter, eh?"

"If you wish, Rusty. But, 'tis between the two of us. She—" he sighed—"she has got to learn to trust me, Rusty. But I do not mean to give up."

"I'm glad, my boy, very glad." Rusty smiled a genuine smile and saw Adam to the door.

Diana had run to her room oblivious to the whispering maids she passed en route. She had slammed the door and thrown herself on her bed to weep in a way she had promised herself she would never again weep for a man. She had known it would come to this. She had tried to stop it. But she had not known, could not have known, how it would cut her to the quick to refuse his offer.

For it had been not only her own desires, her own needs, that she had repudiated, but Adam's. She would never forget the intense, burning, even desperate look in his eyes as he asked why she could not trust him enough to tell him the truth. But even that look was better than the look of revulsion and disappointment the truth would engender. For a man was a man, and love, as the poet's claimed, did not conquer all.

She had calmed herself and was seated dry-eyed, if emotionally depleted, when Papa came into the room. She did not turn her head from her contemplation of the snow flurries that had begun to fall. "Hello, Papa," she said listlessly in response to his greeting. "How—how did you leave your patient?"

"He'll do. I'm not certain about you, however, or Adam. Diana, why did you turn him away?"

"Please, Papa. Do not ask me that. You know perfectly well—"

"You did not tell him the truth, did you?" he interjected gently. He drew a chair up and sat near her in the window embrasure.

She turned to him then. "Oh, Papa, of course not. I—"

"You did not even give him a chance, Diana. Do you not have a care for him?"

She lowered her eyes. "I love him more than my life, Papa," she whispered hoarsely.

She felt Papa's direct blue gaze on her as silence stretched between them. "Adam Damerest is not Robert Easton," he said at length.

281

"I know that, Papa. But he is a man nonetheless." She turned to stare out the window once more. "Forgive me, Papa, but I do not wish to discuss this further."

"Well I do, by God!" Papa exclaimed with unaccustomed ferocity. "I've let you go your own way since that debacle with Easton seven years ago. I told myself you were a woman fully grown, who had suffered enough and knew her own mind. And I think I was right. Truth to tell, no man worthy of you came along in all that time at all events. But this is different. Adam is different. I cannot keep silent."

"Papa, please!" She bolted up and began to pace the carpet in front of the window. Papa jumped up as well and confronted her head on.

"No, blast it all! I will have my say. That man is besotted with you, Diana. Any fool can see it. And 'tis plain as pikestaff the two of you cannot keep away from each other." Her eyes widened at that. "Did you think I would not notice that you stole every possible moment to be private with each other, that you flaunted all the proprieties right from that first day I saw you together at Rossmore, he with his hand on your cheek? Did you think I hadn't noticed, Diana?"

She felt herself flush and turned away from him, but he went relentlessly on. "And yet you would throw away any chance either of you has for happiness because of fear of something that may not even occur!"

She put her hands to her temples, her back still to him. "That's enough, Papa!" she cried, trying to choke back her tears.

"Are you so afraid, child?" he asked, his voice suddenly gentle.

"Yes!" she retorted on a sob. "I cannot go through, again, what I did with Robert. To see the look on his face when he—"

"Diana, do you want me to tell him?" he asked quietly.

She whirled round. "No! Dear God, no! Promise me, Papa, that you will not tell him. I couldn't bear it!" she sobbed.

He pulled her into his arms and held her. "All right, Diana. I promise. But I take leave to tell you, my dear child, that I think you are making the mistake of a lifetime."

282

The mistake of a lifetime, she reflected once he'd gone. Was it? Or would the mistake be to tell him, and instead of having his declaration of love to remember all her life, she would have only his look of disgust as he walked away? Papa was right about one thing. She was afraid. Afraid to put Adam's love to the test. She could not do it.

Chapter 19

Adam stormed into Rossmore Manor and was greeted by Edward and Georgie with heartfelt felicitations upon his safe return. Dear God, did everyone know about that blasted duel? The messenger he'd sent had merely been told to deliver the discreet news that he was well and would return sometime that morning. Nonetheless, he accepted their good wishes and pleaded the need for some sleep and a change of clothes.

Georgie asked if he mightn't want a late breakfast, which he declined. But it was Edward who noticed that he was not in the mood for felicitations. He looked pointedly at Adam and, when Georgie had gone ahead, asked if he wanted to talk about last night. The servants' grapevine had apparently run amuck all morning, mostly about the duel, and the duchess had offered only incoherent smatterings of information.

Adam succinctly repeated the events that transpired after Edward and Georgie had left the ball, and the results of this morning's meeting at dawn. And then Edward asked Adam where he'd been since early morning.

Adam regarded his brother-in-law thoughtfully for a moment. "I've been to Three Oaks," he said at length.

"And is Diana all right?"

Adam rubbed the back of his neck. "Yes, she—she will be all right."

Edward's gaze, as he stood there in the chilled entry lobby, was far too penetrating for Adam's comfort. "Adam, I know 'tis none of my business but—"

"You are right, Edward. 'Tis none—oh, hellfire! I am not

284

the prize idiot you seem to think me, Edward. But Diana is—is stubborn."

"Ahh." There was far too much comprehension in that monosyllable.

"But I haven't finished with her yet!" Adam growled, and strode off toward the stairs, ignoring Edward's maddening grin.

He was met at the first-floor landing by Mrs. Stebbins with the unwelcome news that the duchess awaited him in the morning room. He grimaced, not at all up to any sort of confrontation just now. And what else could an interview with his mother be? But he decided it was the better part of valor to get it over with, and sent word that he would be along after he'd changed his clothes.

He put himself into the efficient hands of his valet, and reflected that perhaps—perhaps—once he'd paid his duty call on his mother, he could snatch a few hours of sleep. And then he would plan his next move with Diana. He knew, of course, that he could force her hand. He could use that fiery passion that was between them to put her into a position where she would feel she *had* to marry him. But he did not want to do that. He wanted her to come to him in wedlock of her own free will. And he wanted her to trust him enough to reveal this apparently dark secret of hers.

What could it possibly be? Had she foolishly committed some youthful indiscretion, such as allowing a swain to lead her into a secluded garden arbor? Had they been found out, and her reputation torn to shreds, despite the innocence of the encounter? Was that enough to send her fiancé packing? Did that account for her disdain for the proprieties?

Or was it something far more dire? Had she unwittingly hurt someone, perhaps in the course of her work with Rusty? Had she caused a death?

And did she really think any such thing would make the slightest difference to him? When all this was over he was going to throttle her for having so little faith in him.

What had that bounder Easton said to her to make her believe she was unfit for marriage? Perhaps it was nothing that she had done, however unwittingly. Perhaps that blighter had wanted to cry off for reasons of his own, and told her some odious lie about herself, about her—her desirability as a woman. Was that what she had meant when she said the truth would give him a disgust of her? How *could* she be so foolish?

Blast it all! He would have the truth out of her by week's end, come what might!

The duchess was seated on the yellow chintz sofa in the morning room. To Adam's surprise, Signor D'Orsini sat in one of the adjacent blue wing chairs. Adam found his curiosity piqued; what sort of interview was this to be? He was further surprised, as he greeted them, to note that D'Orsini looked unaccustomedly grim, and that his mother's eyes were red-rimmed.

Red-rimmed? Had she been crying? He'd never thought to see the day!

"I am glad to see that you are well, Adam," she said quietly. "I have not slept a wink."

"As you see, Mother," he said guardedly, taking a seat in the Queen Anne chair to her left, opposite D'Orsini.

"And—and Miss Rustin?" she inquired.

Adam kept his face impassive. "Diana is well. I found her in time last night."

Was that relief he saw on his mother's face? She looked to D'Orsini, but the painter gave her no sign, no encouragement whatever. His mother twisted her hands in her lap. Adam volunteered no further information. She seemed about to say one thing, then appeared to switch to another.

"You—you do not have to flee the country?" she ventured.

"If that is a roundabout way of asking after Truesdale," he said caustically, "then the answer is that the rotter took a ball in his thigh. It will be a long and difficult recovery."

His mother nodded. There was no censure in her eyes. Just what did she want of him this morning? Surely information could have been got from other sources. He remained silent; he would not make this easy for her. A glance out the window told him it had begun to snow. The bleakness of the day suited him.

"Adam," she began again, and he forced his eyes to her. "Have you offered for her?"

Adam's eyes, and his voice, hardened. "Yes. And you might

286

as well know that I have been refused. But do not rejoice overmuch, for I shan't take 'no' for an answer."

She winced at his caustic words. Even D'Orsini frowned. It occurred to Adam that his mother was in genuine distress and that he was being deliberately cruel. It was unlike him, and yet he was still seething from last night.

"Adam," she went on, "I meant it last night when I said that I was sorry. Not only for my part in that wretched episode, but—but for many things."

Adam blinked. Was he hearing right? The duchess never apologized! And twice in less than four and twenty hours? Her eyes welled up. Tears? Again? He waited to hear what "things" she was sorry for before replying.

But instead of elaborating she surprised him further by turning pleading brown eyes to him. "Perhaps it would—would—help your suit with your Diana if you would tell her that I—I will welcome her into the family."

Adam stopped breathing for a moment. Had she really called her "his Diana?" Had she said she would welcome her to the family? He could not credit it!

"Why?" he asked baldly.

The duchess sniffled into a handkerchief. "Be—because she makes you happy. And I can see that you—you need her. I have never before understood what it meant to—to need someone."

And that was when Adam understood. Everything. He turned to D'Orsini and smiled. The painter smiled back. And then, for the first time since he was some sixteen years old, Adam went to his mother and enveloped her in a hug. She clung to him, weeping softly.

"Thank you, Mother," he rasped. "That will—that will mean a great deal to her. To both of us."

She nodded, and he kissed her brow and shook D'Orsini's hand as he departed, feeling a bit misty-eyed himself.

And Katherine let the tears fall copiously again, but this time they felt like a kind of blessed release. And this time she was not alone. For Antonio hauled her up and into his embrace.

"'Tis all right, *cara*. You need not cry anymore. Everything is very much all right."

287

She nodded, but the tears continued to flow, quite soaking his pristine blue coat and his white shirt. "Come abovestairs with me now, Katarina. I will take care of you."

She looked up at him, a question in her eyes. He wiped the tears from beneath her eyes. "I will always take care of you, *cara mía*," he said hoarsely.

And Katherine Damerest decided that when all was said and done, it was very nice to have someone to take care of her at long last. She reached up to press her lips gently to his, and then allowed Antonio D'Orsini to lead her up the stairs.

It had been snowing steadily since mid-morning. Papa had entreated Diana to come down to luncheon, and so she had done. But she had touched nary a bite, said nary a word. And though Papa went out of his way to discuss all but the most important topic, Diana knew he was very disappointed in her.

And so she was actually relieved when Papa received a summons from Midvale straightaway after luncheon. It seemed the newborn Caldwell twins had contracted some kind of croup, and Mrs. Caldwell was much alarmed. Diana sent him on his way in the carriage, admonishing him to be careful in the snow and to stay overnight if need be. He looked doubtfully at her.

"I shall be all right, Papa," she assured him, and did not add that what she most needed just now was solitude.

And she wondered, as she made her way to the privacy of her own chamber, if Papa realized the irony of it all. It had been snowing, and he had been called away to Midvale, on the day she'd met Adam. To be sure they would have met eventually at all events, but it was the intensity of those first days, snowbound together, that started their relationship on its inevitable path. And now, on the day their relationship ended, Papa was called away again, and the snow was falling.

Somehow Diana was not surprised when she, too, received a summons not an hour later. Farmer Clayton's wife Mavis was brought to bed with their first child. Diana piled two blankets, instead of her usual one, into the gig for protection against the brutal cold of what might turn into another blizzard. And then she set off for the Clayton farm. She would deliver the child in Papa's stead.

It was a day for ironies.

"Bloody hell!" Adam muttered as he sipped his brandy and paced the floor of the library. It was still snowing, harder than ever, and it looked as if the wind was picking up. It might very well be another blasted blizzard; they could be snowbound for days. And he would be miles away from Diana. No! He couldn't bear it. He would go out of his mind. If he was going to be shut in by this relentless weather once again, he would damned well make sure he was under the same roof as Diana.

He informed only Stebbins of his departure, but Edward, with that annoying perspicacity he seemed to have developed lately, waylaid him in the entry lobby. "Hell of a time for an afternoon call," his brother-in-law said genially.

"I agree, Edward. It is after the noon hour, is it not?" Adam countered.

Edward ignored the question. "Anyone fool enough to venture out right now would have to know he mightn't make it back home."

"Would he now?" Adam retorted. "You know, Edward, 'tis very cold here. Why do you not go abovestairs and—er—keep your wife warm or somesuch."

Edward grinned. "I believe I will, old chap. And I do—hope you'll find it . . . warm, wherever you're going."

Adam cuffed his brother-in-law on the shoulder. "Tell them not to wait dinner for me," he said, and then made his way out into the frigid Yorkshire storm.

Mrs. Barrett informed him that the doctor had gone to Midvale and that Miss Rustin had set off for the Clayton farm hours since.

Damnation, Adam thought. What a time for her to be riding off alone through the countryside! From Mrs. Barrett's directions he guessed the farm to be about halfway between here and Arden Chase. Not terribly far, but in this weather. . . .

And he wondered with a sense of foreboding how stable that gig of hers was. Why, there was no telling if she'd even made it to the farm! And if she had, how the devil would she get back? It would no doubt be dark by the time she was finished, the snow a thicker blanket on the ground. Would she be forced to spend the night in the farmer's cottage, or would she be fool enough to venture out?

A woman should not be out alone on a day like this. At least he, on horseback, could provide a more reliable mode of transport. He wondered, as the snow whipped about him, blinding him and soaking his greatcoat, if Diana would agree with him. Would she be pleased to see him, or would his presence overset her?

Diana's primary emotion at the moment was one of intense frustration. The Clayton farmhouse, which she'd been inside only once before, consisted of one large room partitioned by a makeshift curtain. One section housed the cooking hearth, table, chairs and settee. The inner "room" held a hand-hewn four-poster bed, linen chest, cupboard, and now, a cradle awaiting the newborn babe.

The babe, however, was refusing to be born. Mavis Clayton was a large, stoic woman who, knowing the excitable nature of her husband, had waited until the last possible moment to tell him that her time had come. By now her pains were coming frequently, but the child was taking its time about descending into the birth canal. Diana's assurances to the farmer that such was normal for a first child fell on deaf ears.

In point of fact, Diana thought she was like to go deaf if Clayton did not cease his wailing. She had finally banished him to the kitchen, forcing him to relinquish his death grip on Mavis's hand. She had closed the curtain between the two areas of the cottage, but she could not silence Clayton's desperate admonishments to Mavis not to die. Nor could he seem to honor Diana's request that he build up the fire. The air was becoming increasingly frigid inside the small cottage.

"'Tis all right, Mavis," she soothed when another pain had come and gone. "The babe is coming in his own sweet time."

Diana gazed out the window, rubbing her hands over her arms to warm herself. In a few minutes she would have to leave Mavis and see about the fire herself. She did not even know if there was kindling inside, but something would have to be done. The snow was still falling, and the sky was darkening. It was going to be a long night.

Adam could hear a wail go up inside the cottage as he approached. But somehow he did not think it sounded like a woman in childbed. Puzzled, he knocked at the door. There was no answer, and he was absolutely freezing. Damn! Even his horse was warm and fed by now, sharing the small barn with Diana's horses, gig, two plowhorses and a cow.

He tried banging the second time, and that was when he heard Diana's voice, above the roar of the wind. "Clayton, for pitysakes will you answer the door!"

It was her tone that alarmed him. Never had he heard such exasperation, such frustration from her. What the devil was going on?

Without waiting for Clayton, he pushed the door open and shouldered his way into the tiny cottage. He closed the door behind him, turning and stamping his feet to shake the snow from his boots and riding britches. He noted the scarred oak table in front of him, the mismatched chairs, the uneven blue curtain separating what must be the bedchamber. He heard whispers coming from behind the curtain, but from beside the hearth came what sounded like a sob. Adam shifted his gaze and saw the man he took to be Clayton.

He was standing with his back to the door, oblivious to Adam's arrival as he stabbed desultorily at the dying fire with a poker. "Don't let her die, Lord. Not my Mavis!" he cried.

Good God, Adam thought, and then heard Diana's voice. "That's it, Mavis. Grip my hand. Just a bit longer. Good! Very well now, relax."

He heard a rustling sound, and then the curtain was pulled aside. "Clayton, who—Adam!" Her blue eyes widened, and then very slowly, her beautiful, tired face broke out into a smile. "Oh, Adam, thank God!" she cried in relief, brushing two stray locks of hair from her face.

He felt his own wave of relief. She was happy to see him! She clutched at the curtain as if she could no longer stand on her own. She very likely had not slept at all last night and had been

291

here for hours.

"Diana," he said, taking a step forward, needing to touch her, knowing it was not the time. But then Mavis Clayton cried out.

"Adam, please, can you add kindling to the fire? 'Tis freezing in here," Diana whispered, just before disappearing behind the curtain.

He divested himself of his gloves and greatcoat and realized that it was, indeed, icy cold within the cottage. Damnation! Diana must be chilled to the bone. She wore only her blue wool merino dress with an apron over it. And that poor woman in the bed was probably wretchedly cold as well. There was a small pile of kindling next the hearth. It would do for now, but Adam knew if this went on long enough, he would have to go out for more. Clearly Farmer Clayton was useless at present.

He took the poker from the distraught man and worked intently for several minutes until a roaring blaze filled the chimney grate. Then he guided Clayton into a chair at the table, such that his back was toward the curtain. Adam could hear Diana's soothing voice coming from behind the curtain, and Mavis's restrained cries. He suspected the woman was trying not to alarm her husband. Hellfire! A woman ought to be able to cry out at a time like this. There was at present only one remedy for what ailed the farmer, and Adam began searching the cupboards.

He set a jug before Clayton and poured him a mug of ale. "Drink," he commanded, and the man, so dazed with fear he had no idea and no curiosity as to Adam's identity, obeyed.

Adam refilled Clayton's mug and then went to the curtain and called softly to Diana. "Can we not open this curtain and allow the fire to heat the entire room, Diana? You and Mrs. Clayton are like to freeze otherwise."

"Oh, yes," she answered after a moment. "That would be wonderful. But I do think that perhaps you had ought to— ah—ply Clayton with spirits first."

"'Tis already done, my dear," he said, and shoved the curtain aside.

Mavis lay under a mound of blankets. She gave a small, embarrassed smile, and opened her mouth to speak, but suddenly her face contorted in pain. Her hand clutched

Diana's tightly. Diana looked exhausted but undaunted, her body bent over the bed, as she wiped the woman's brow and murmured soothingly to her.

Mavis Clayton shifted her eyes to him as soon as the pain eased. "Your Grace," she said hoarsely. "I thank you for—"

"Save your strength, Mrs. Clayton," he responded kindly. "You just concentrate on birthing your child."

But to Diana he said, in hushed tones, "What else can I do?"

Diana gave him a smile that would have rendered him completely besotted had he not already been so, and began to tell him what to do.

And so began the seemingly endless hours of working together in a strange kind of intimacy as they helped Mavis Clayton birth her child. The pains grew harsher, and more frequent, Clayton became clean raddled and fell asleep, and Mavis finally allowed herself to scream. The child was not making it easy for any of them.

In the end it was Adam who, at Diana's instruction, gently pushed on Mavis's belly as Diana guided her child into the world.

"'Tis a boy, Mavis!" Diana cried at a few minutes before midnight. "You have a son, Mavis!"

The farmer's wife began to cry. Diana deftly cut and tied the cord that connected mother to baby and began to wash the child, wrapping him in the clean linen Adam had prepared an hour since. And then Diana placed the child in his mother's arms and finished tending to Mavis.

Moments later, Diana was covering mother and child with the blankets. Diana's eyes looked misty, and Adam felt none too steady himself. He had actually witnessed the birth of a child! He and Diana had done this together! He looked at her, her hair dishevelled, her apron splattered with blood, and felt an acute sense of longing. He wanted her, and he wanted her child. She met his gaze across the width of the bed, oblivious for the moment of the woman and child now warmly bundled under the blankets. She felt his longing, and returned it. He knew it as well as he knew his own name.

Suddenly, Diana felt the air between them vibrate with tension. She could feel the heat between them, even though they were not touching, had not, in fact, touched all night.

293

They had just delivered a baby together! For the first time the intimacy of the act, indeed of the entire night, truly hit her. She felt her pulse accelerate and her knees go weak. She could not tear her eyes from Adam's.

It was he who broke the spell. He cleared his throat and stepped back toward the kitchen area. While Diana cleaned up in the aftermath of the birth, Adam added to the fire from the pile of kindling he'd brought in from the woodshed hours ago.

He almost wished more kindling was needed; the cold air would do him good. His task completed, he woke Clayton and informed him, as he handed him a cup of black coffee, that he had a son. Clayton wiped his fuzzy eyes and drank half the cup before the news began to register.

"A son? I have a son?" he asked somewhat incoherently, turning bloodshot, bewildered eyes to Adam.

Adam nodded and gestured for him to finish the coffee. He downed it in two gulps and then swivelled to face the blue curtain, which Diana had once more drawn closed. "Mavis?" he whispered, his face twisted with fear.

Adam smiled. "Mavis is fine. Why do you not go and see?"

Clayton bolted from his chair so fast that he knocked it over, stumbling and nearly falling down himself. Adam poured him more coffee; it was clear he needed it. Clayton, meanwhile, had jerked the curtain aside and dashed most unsteadily to the bed, where Diana was helping Mavis to position the child for suckling.

"Mavis?" the man rasped, falling to his knees and clutching his wife's hand.

Adam swallowed a lump in his throat. What would it feel like. . . .

"We have a son, Clayton," she whispered, smiling tiredly.

"Are you—are you really all right?" Clayton entreated.

"I'm fine, Clay. Come and have a look at your son."

Clayton looked, an expression of awe on his face, but then he turned to Diana and asked about Mavis again. He looked pointedly down at Diana's bloodied apron. She assured him that it was all quite normal, that Mavis would need a good deal of rest but would be right as rain in a fortnight's time, and that his son had all the right number of fingers and toes.

Whereupon the farmer began to thank her profusely. Diana

cut him off gently, accepting his thanks but suggesting that he have another cup of coffee while she and Mavis helped his son with his first meal. And then Diana introduced Adam.

Farmer Clayton turned red in the face. "Your—Your Grace! I had no idea. Beggin' your pardon." He bowed awkwardly. "I reckon I been actin' mad as a March hare. Not offerin' you nowt to eat nor drink nor—oh, Lordy! 'Tis *you* who's been awaitin' on me! I—"

"Whoa! Clayton!" Adam interjected, lips twitching. "'Tis all right, truly. 'Tis not every day a man becomes a father for the first time. It has been my privilege to be here."

"Thank you, kindly, Your Grace." Clayton's crimson flush receded to a mere pink. "Will you accept a posset, and some bread and cheese, then? And you, too, Miss Rustin? I do not know what all would have become of us had you not come."

Adam caught Diana's eye, then answered for the both. "We should welcome a bit of refreshment, Clayton, but first you must allow Miss Rustin to finish with your wife and son. And I do think you had ought to finish that coffee."

Adam drew the curtain closed once more, and while Diana continued her work behind it, Adam plied the farmer with sufficient coffee to steady him. He wanted to be sure the man could care for his family when he and Diana left. Of that he was convinced by the time Clayton had stoked the fire, then set upon the table two warm possets and plates of bread, cheese, and currant jelly.

When Diana emerged from behind the curtain, Mavis and the child both having fallen asleep, she sat down at the table with the farmer and Adam. The posset of warm milk and ale was most welcome, as was the food; Adam had not realized how hungry he was. They rose to take their leave, Diana giving Clayton instructions about Mavis and the babe. And then Clayton turned rather red-faced and stammered an offer of pallets by the fire for the night.

"'Tain't what you be used to, Your Grace, but I reckon that storm be somethin' fierce. I can't be givin' you the bed, seein' as how Mavis—"

"Of course, you cannot, Mr. Clayton," Diana interrupted. "And thank you very much, but we shall be fine."

"Yes," Adam put in before she could go on, "we'll take my

stallion. He's quite sure-footed in the snow. Diana, I do think it best we leave the gig here."

Clayton agreed, and after a moment's hesitation, Diana acquiesced as well. Adam counted out several gold coins and set them on the table. Clayton frowned. "A gift for your son," Adam said, "and to cover the feed of Miss Rustin's horses. We'll retrieve them as soon as the snow lets up."

Clayton protested that he should be paying *them*, but Diana merely smiled and said he was welcome to take the matter up with her father, and that she would return as soon as the weather permitted to check on Mavis and the child.

Adam and Diana took their leave soon thereafter, bundling up as best they could, and retrieving Diana's two blankets from the gig. Adam secured the blankets with his own in his saddlebag. Neither of them spoke the obvious—that if the storm proved too harsh and they were forced to seek shelter before reaching Three Oaks, the blankets would be crucial.

Adam had thought for a moment to have her ride pillion, so that his body could shield her from the worst of the storm. But he decided that she was too exhausted. She might not be able to hold on to him, let alone sit upright. So instead he took her up before him in the saddle, instructing her to straddle it; there was no room for her to sit sidesaddle. It was brutally cold, the snow falling relentlessly, but at the least the wind had died down. With any luck the snow would slack off now as well.

His stalwart chestnut stallion, Plato, made his way slowly, steadily over the frozen terrain. Adam pulled Diana back against him, enveloping her in his greatcoat. He was pleased that she had the good sense not to resist.

"Better?" he murmured, already feeling warmer himself. She nodded. "Good," he went on. "Why don't you rest your head on my shoulder? You can turn your face away from the snow, and perhaps you can sleep."

"No, Adam, thank you. I do not want to burden you any more than I already have. I cannot thank you enough for—"

"Diana," he interrupted, a bit more curtly than he intended, "you are not, nor could ever be, a burden to me. Do you understand?" He tightened his arm about her waist for emphasis, until she nodded her acquiescence. "And furthermore," he continued, softening his tone as he breathed into

296

her ear, "I do not want your gratitude. I believe you know what I want of you."

Diana felt his warm breath at her ear, felt the security of his strong forearm holding her close to him, felt the hard, muscular width of his chest supporting her, and ached for what she could not have. He had come after her tonight out of concern, had stayed to help her through a difficult time, despite the cold and discomfort and the humblest of circumstances. He loved her, and she was afraid he would never understand why she was refusing him.

"Oh, Adam, I tried to explain—"

"Not now, my love. You will have ample time to do your explaining later. For now let us just concentrate on keeping each other warm, hmmm?" With that he tightened his hold on her and kissed the top of her head.

And Diana, despite the warning bells that went off in her head at the thought of "doing her explaining later," felt herself relaxing against him. She felt a contentment she had no right to feel, and the snow notwithstanding, sighed and gave herself up to it.

And thus they rode in companionable silence for some minutes, Adam quite hopeful that they would reach Three Oaks without undue difficulty. But then the wind picked up again, and the snow began to swirl fiercely about them. Now Diana did burrow her head in his shoulder. Adam slid his arm from her waist, needing both hands for the reins.

The snow fell now in a thick curtain; visibility became worse by the minute. Plato stumbled twice. Diana shivered and burrowed deeper beneath the folds of his coat and hers.

Adam felt his sense of direction deserting him. Everything before them was a sea of white. He could no longer see three feet in front of them and realized, when Plato stranded them in a snowdrift, that the stallion could no longer keep them to the roadway.

The sudden ferocity of the storm and its devastating effect astonished him. Adam had truly thought they would make it to Three Oaks within the hour. He had taken the blankets as a precaution against a very remote possibility. Now that possibility was becoming an imperative. And with nary a light nor house in sight, he felt the first twinges of alarm. He should have accepted Clayton's offer; he'd had no right to subject Diana to this.

"Diana, I'm sorry. I should have—"

"Adam, do not take responsibility for this. If anything, I'm the one who left home after the snow had started."

"You are not frightened, are you?" he asked, marvelling. His body was rigid with tension, but she lay back against him, relaxed and trusting.

"No, I am not frightened, Adam. I am with you, after all," she said simply.

Adam found her cheek and kissed her, feeling the tension and even fear fall away from him. Did she really think, after a statement like that, that he would ever, could ever, let her go?

One or two landmarks, a circle of bare oak trees whose branches seemed to reach out toward each other, a high hill with edges of black rock still visible, put them on the correct path again, but it was clear they would not make it to Three Oaks. He would always think afterward that it was Diana, and thoughts of taking her out of danger, that put the inspiration into his head. For he recalled the shepherd's hut he had vainly searched last night when Percy had abducted her. It was just off the road between Arden Chase and Three Oaks, and while those two houses were too far to hope to reach tonight, the hut, if he was not much mistaken, was not far west of them.

It was little more than a hovel and would make the Clayton farmhouse seem a palace, but such niceties were much beside the point. Despite Diana's brave words, she was freezing. Adam was not in much better state, and he did not know how long Plato could keep going.

The next quarter hour seemed the longest of his life. He guided Plato with gentle words and a firm hand, praying that his sense of direction was still in operation. The wind howled. The air was white and frigid. And somehow, no doubt with providential intervention, they found themselves coming to a halt before the delapidated, abandoned shepherd's hut. No Palladian mansion had ever looked so inviting.

In short order he had Diana, the stallion and himself inside. He found a partially used taper on an overturned barrel and lit it, watching Diana's face as she surveyed the cold, barren room. The floor and walls were earthen. The barrel, one straw pallet and a rickety wooden chair were all the furnishings the place could claim.

"How did you ever find this place, Adam? I own it will serve admirably," she said as she rubbed her arms against the cold. "Why, look, there's a fire pit, and I do believe there is a pile of kindling. How *did* you find this? I cannot imagine 'twas an accident."

"No," he replied, smiling, and told her about his search for her last night. And all the while he wondered how *he* had ever found such a remarkable woman.

"I know this land like I know the rooms in my house," she said when he finished, "and yet I did not recall this hut, nor would I have been able to find it in this blizzard. You are a remarkable man, Adam," she finished softly.

She stood about three feet from him. Her words and the look of admiration on her face made him feel like he'd had the wind knocked out of him and could not breathe. Suddenly he did not feel cold, not at all. Suddenly the full ramifications of this night hit him with the force of the storm. The air became charged; he knew by the subtle change in her eyes that she felt it as well. Christ! How would they get through this night?

Abruptly, he turned away and went to rub Plato down. Diana went to the straw pallet and began to examine it, Adam supposed, for any unsavory creatures. He covered Plato with one of the blankets, and having no food with him, he pulled a flask of brandy from his saddlebag and went to Diana. She was standing near the fire pit in the center of the room.

"Drink this," he said, "and then I'll build a fire."

She stared at him wordlessly and took the flask. Their gloved hands touched, then jerked apart. She drank, her eyes on his, then closed them as the brandy went down. She opened them again and handed him the flask. He put his mouth over the opening, the same place her lips had been. He drank deeply, then gave it back to her.

"Take some more," he said hoarsely.

She did not wipe the aperture, nor press her closed lips to it, but opened her mouth to envelop the opening fully with her moist lips before she tilted her head back and drank. Adam swallowed hard.

How *the hell* would he get through this night?

299

Chapter 20

Adam set the flask aside, unable to tear his eyes from her. "I—I shall see about the fire now."

She nodded, her eyes deep and luminous in the candlelight. Did she know, as well as he, that the fire had already been lit, that it was burning at a low flame, but that the next touch might well ignite it into a blaze?

She watched him in silence as he built the fire and then handed him the taper to light it. When it was done he stepped back and shrugged out of his greatcoat, setting it on the chair. The only task left was for them to bed down for the night. He removed his hat and gloves and turned back to her.

"Shall I help you with your cloak, or do you want to wait for the fire to warm the room?" he asked into the silence.

"No, I—I shall take it off now." Her hands went to the catch at her throat, and he moved quickly round the fire to stand behind her. He drew the hood down and then lifted the cloak from her shoulders, his hands brushing her lightly. Quickly he stepped back and went to lay her cloak on the chair over his own coat. Then, as if drawn by a magnet, he returned to her.

"Take off your gloves," he said quietly. When she complied he set them aside, then enveloped her small, cold hands in his. "Are you getting warmer?" he asked.

"Oh, yes. The room is small and the—the fire is strong." That, he thought, was an understatement. "And your—your hands," she went on, and he wished she hadn't, "are so warm, and so large. They make me feel—"

"Diana, I—I do not think this conversation is such a good idea."

"Oh," she said, and pulled her hands back. There was a world of understanding in that one word.

His eyes scanned her face, taking in the black curls softly brushed from her smooth brow, the deep, velvety blue eyes, the lips—dear God, but he wanted to kiss her! Reluctantly, he stepped back and rubbed the nape of his neck. He glanced over to one corner of the room.

"We had best go to sleep," he said, knowing full well he would not sleep a wink. "Is that straw pallet usable?"

"Yes, I think so." Her voice was soft, raspy, as if their circumstances had just fully dawned on her. She took a step back.

"Very well. You take the pallet," he said.

"But you—"

"I'll do fine with a blanket on the ground, Diana," he fairly growled, and whirled round to retrieve the blankets. Damnation! Could she not leave well enough alone?

When he turned back, blankets in hand, she was standing where he'd left her. Her face was pale; she rubbed her hands up and down over her arms. He did not want to think that the look on her face was one of hurt, and so he asked, "Are you cold?"

"No."

"Your feet. They're very sensitive," he said, belatedly recalling a certain day in the Rossmore library. "Are they—"

"My feet are fine, Adam. I was not really walking in the snow, you must know. I—ah—" She walked toward him. "I'll help you with those blankets."

"No!" Hellfire! Did she not know what this was doing to him?

She stopped in her path. "I'm sorry, Adam." She turned abruptly away from him. She could not bear that look of hunger on his face. Hunger she had engendered, but could not assuage. Nor did she know what she was going to do with her own hunger.

He was so strong, his panther's body tall and lean and powerful. His handsome face was taut now with the effort of a man trying to keep his emotions in check. She had done this to him! Dear God, how were they to get through the night? She

301

stifled the sob that rose to her throat.

Suddenly she felt his hands on her shoulders. "Diana. It is I who should apologize," he said hoarsely. "Forgive me for snapping at you." Slowly, he turned her round. He kept his hands at her shoulders as he gazed at her out of those piercing tawny eyes. "'Tis only that I love you, so very much. And this—" his hand swept the room—"this is so hard."

She swallowed, not certain if she could speak. "I know," she finally managed. "It—it is hard for me as well."

She saw the carefully banked fires flare in his eyes. His fingers tightened on her shoulders.

"Why?" he rasped. "Why will you not wed me?"

She tried to pull away, but he would not let her. Had she been icy cold only minutes ago? Now her body was warm, far too warm. "I—I do love you, Adam. You must believe me."

He smiled, a gentle smile full of understanding. "I *do* know, love. That is why I cannot comprehend—"

"Oh, Adam," she interrupted, lowering her eyes, "there are so many reasons why we cannot—cannot wed." She twisted her hands at her waist, needing to make him understand, and if she was unable to do that, needing to divert him. "You—you may make light of the difference in our stations, but I do assure you no one else would. Least of all your mother."

"Ah, my mother." He raised her chin with his forefinger. "There are a few things you needs must know about my mother. I am afraid Percy did not plan his dastardly deed alone." Diana listened with ever-widening eyes as Adam explained just how her abduction was planned and executed. Lady Truesdale's very active role did not surprise her, but the duchess's more passive one made her sick at heart.

She swallowed with difficulty. "You must see, Adam. That is what I have been trying to—"

"No, love, 'tis *you* who does not see. 'Twas my mother who came to tell me of the scheme. And though she did not know your whereabouts, she told me enough to—"

"B-but I do not understand. Why did she have a change of heart?"

He grinned and kissed her brow. "I believe, my dear, 'tis because she herself has had a change of heart. I believe that for the first time in her life, my mother has *given* her heart."

Diana smiled back at him. "Signor D'Orsini."

"None other. You were right, you must know, Diana, when you alluded—oh, so long ago—to mistakes my father made. He was a good man, but—" he sighed and forced himself to go on—"but he was weak, and I do not think he was a very good husband."

She put a comforting hand on his arm. "I believe," Adam continued, "that our Italian friend has—has given my mother that which my father never could. I asked her the same question about a change of heart, you must know, albeit far less politely than you just did." He covered her hand with his.

"What did she say?"

"She said that she'd seen the look on my face when I was looking for you, and understood how much you meant to me."

"Oh, Adam," she uttered tremulously.

"And furthermore, love, she sent you a message this very morning. Her exact words were, 'Perhaps it would help your suit with your Diana if you would tell her that I shall welcome her into the family.'"

Diana blinked. He went on without giving her a chance to speak. "I think it safe to assume that such a welcome will extend to a proper introduction to the ton. I do assure you that when the dowager duchess sponsors the new Duchess of Marchmaine in Town, none will raise any questions about stations. And we can always, if it makes you feel better, trot out your great grandfather, the earl.

"Now then, love," he went on, kissing her chiselled nose, "that we have got all of that straightened away, perhaps you will tell me the real reason for your refusal. We both know it has naught to do with families and stations."

At that she tried to pull out of his grasp. He simply moved his hands to her elbows. "Answer the question, Diana."

Diana suddenly felt as if she could not breathe. He was too close, the hut overwarm. She must get away! She jerked out of his grasp and backed up.

"Be careful of the fire!" he shouted, and grabbed her.

Her heart was pounding. She had been only a step away. . . . Whatever was wrong with her? He led her some feet from the fire pit and then dropped his hands.

"I am waiting for my answer, Diana. For the truth," he said

303

with quiet urgency, his hands clenched at his sides.

Her eyes welled up. She *would not* cry, she told herself. "Adam," she said raggedly, "I—I tried to explain before, as much as I am able. There are—are things I cannot speak of. And I could not bear it if the look in your eyes turned to—to—one of revulsion, as surely it must if—"

"For Godssakes, Diana," he exploded, grabbing her upper arms, "do you not know that there is nothing—absolutely *nothing* you could say that would change the way I feel, or my intention to wed you? Why do you not understand that? Why do you not trust me, dammit?"

He did not wait for her reply. He was furious and desperate and so full of need that he could not think straight. He pulled her close and ground his mouth onto hers. But all his anger dissipated at the touch of her soft lips. He gentled the kiss, and that was when he realized her hands were pushing at his chest, as she struggled to free herself.

"Don't fight me, Diana," he commanded hoarsely. "I won't hurt you, love. Just let me kiss you. Only that. In the morning we shall talk."

This kiss was different, and Diana knew it straightaway. It was a kiss of infinite tenderness, a kiss that only hinted at the carefully banked fires beneath it. He held her face in his hands, almost reverently, and she felt as if he were reaching into her very soul.

She answered his kiss with all the longing she felt, wondering if he could hear the pounding of her heart. But when her hands came up to clasp him behind his neck, he broke away from her, ever so gently, but resolutely. He brought her hands down from his neck and held them in his.

Sweet heaven! Adam thought. He hadn't even touched her—not really. And yet, her hands were quivering and his blood was pulsing wildly. It was as if the fire between them blazed ever higher every time they were together. How could she respond to him the way she did, and then insist they could not wed? But he had said they would talk in the morning, and he would keep to his word. Prudently, he released her hands.

"I think," he said unsteadily, "that we had ought to go to sleep."

She nodded and swallowed hard. "G-good night, Adam," she

uttered and turned toward the blankets.

He watched as she spread a blanket over the straw pallet. She lay down on one half of the blanket and pulled the other half over herself. Adam picked up her cloak and covered her with that as well.

"You'll be cold later when the fire dies down," he murmured.

"Thank you, Adam," she whispered, and closed her eyes.

Adam wondered if she would sleep any better than he.

Diana drew the blanket up to her chin. How long had it been since she had listened to the sounds of Adam preparing his own bed? Thirty minutes? An hour? She did not know, only knew that the night was interminable and that she could not sleep. The fire was dying down, and the hut was becoming decidedly frigid. This despite the fact that the wind was no longer howling and the snowfall was abating somewhat.

Now it was the storm inside Diana that raged. Her body was restless with longings that Adam's kiss had engendered. And she was tormented by the look she'd seen on his face as they'd parted for the night. She'd seen a mirror of her own need, but she'd also seen the confusion, the pain caused by her refusal of his offer.

She loved him so much! She had not meant to hurt him. She had not meant any of this to happen. She stifled a sob, and in a rare bout of self-pity cursed the Fates that had decreed that she could not live as other women. She could not love, and wed, and bear children. She recalled all the times, as she was growing up, when Papa had told her that one day she would wed a man who loved her. And then she would discover the magic that takes place between a man and a woman in the marriage bed.

She would never have that marriage bed. But—suddenly her body tensed as an idea took hold—she was a woman, in love with a man. And he loved her. She could not be his wife. She would not be his mistress. But they were here, together, in the dark of night. Her reputation, tarnished as it was, would be further blackened by this night's escapade, even if they stayed on opposite sides of the dying fire!

305

Who would know whether or not they had lit their own, very personal fire, secluded here as they took shelter from the snow? She had to deny herself a lifetime of love. Could she not have this one night, to store the memories against all the cold and lonely nights ahead? And could she not give this one night to Adam, as a gift of her love?

Of course, when it was over he would know why she could not wed him. He would be shocked, disappointed, and perhaps, he *would* look at her with revulsion. But perhaps—was it not possible that he might instead merely thank her for this night of love, agree that they could not wed, and go off on his way? That, too, would hurt, but it would not be like Robert's rejection. Either way, she would be prepared. And she would have the memory of this night. Nothing that happened after could take that away. For just this one night, she would know what it meant to be loved, truly loved, by a man.

Quickly, silently, before she thought better of it, she crept out from her blanket and around the fire to Adam. She had no idea what to say, or do. It didn't signify, she told herself. She loved him. Surely she could make him understand what she wanted. Surely, he would not refuse!

"Adam," she whispered, kneeling beside where he lay wrapped in his blanket and greatcoat. He whirled round, yanking the covers with him.

"Diana!" he exclaimed, propping himself up on his elbows. She thought he had not been sleeping any more than she. "Is anything wrong?"

She swallowed. "It—it cannot be very comfortable for you on the cold, earthen floor. Come and share the pallet with me."

Good God! Adam thought, sitting bolt upright. Had she lost her mind? "Diana, I—I am fine. I cannot share the pallet with you."

"'Tis very cold, Adam. I cannot sleep like this."

Bloody hell! Adam gritted his teeth. She simply could not be that naive.

"I'll rebuild the fire," he ground out, and neatly skirted her as he rose in his shirtsleeves and stockinged feet to do so.

When he had got a healthy blaze going in the pit, he turned to see Diana reclining on that damned pallet. She was propped on one elbow, half covered by the blanket, a corner of which was turned down. Her eyes met his, and then, amazingly, she patted the blanket.

"Come, Adam," she said softly.

"What?" he fairly shouted.

This time she smiled faintly and extended her hand. "Come here," she repeated. "You'll be much warmer."

He gulped. She obviously had no idea of the picture she presented, lying on that blasted pallet in such manner. She still wore her dress, of course, but several locks of her hair had come loose and tumbled about her shoulders. He felt his breathing alter.

"Ah, Diana," he finally managed, "I cannot sleep there . . . with you. You—you do not understand what you are asking."

Her smile changed. If he did not know her better he would think it flirtatious. "I am not a child, Adam."

He fought to control his breathing. She could not mean what he thought she meant! He hunkered down so that he was at eye level with her.

"Diana," he said, careful not to touch her, "there is no way that I could share this—this bed with you and—and not—ah—"

He stumbled to a halt, rendered quite speechless by the look on her face. For he read the truth in those velvety blue eyes, twinkling up at him, and in the mysterious smile on her face. It was the saucy Miss Rustin he beheld before him, but she was quite serious. A bubble of incredulous delight welled up inside of him, and his heart began to pound. But still he restrained himself.

He knelt beside her, still not touching her. "You are not making sense, Diana. You will not wed me, but you—"

"Adam," she breathed, reaching up with one hand to caress his face, "don't fight me. Not now."

He caught her hand and kissed the palm. "Why?" he whispered huskily.

"Because . . . 'tis all I'll ever have," she rasped.

And that was when he took her in his arms. And with that small part of him still capable of rational thought, he told himself they were merely anticipating the wedding night a bit, whatever Diana might say. He hadn't wanted to force her hand in this manner. But perhaps, after all, it was the best way to bind her to him. And bind her he would, with a special license and the nearest parson, as soon as the snow let up.

For now, he was not a saint; he would not fight her.

For one frantic moment Diana had thought he might refuse her, but now he lay full length against her, his hands caressing her softly, slowly, even as his tongue lovingly stroked her lips. His touch, even through the fabric of her clothes, was causing warm ripples of sensation to course over her. Suddenly she did not want his gentleness, and she could no longer bear the barrier of their clothing. She opened her mouth to him, her tongue meeting his, and fumbled with the buttons on his shirt.

Oh, God, Adam groaned inwardly. He had wanted to be gentle with her, not to frighten her, even though his blood was pounding, his body so rigid with need he thought he would explode. But then her hands went to his shirt, and he was lost. He ran his hands through her dark hair, sending it cascading down in long luxurious waves.

He kissed her deeply, his lips crushing hers, and somehow, in seconds, divested them both of their clothing. And with shaking hands he stroked the smooth, silky skin of her back, her sides, her hips. Her arms snaked around his nape. He could hardly believe that she was here with him at last, his Diana. He caressed her breasts, kissed her throat. She moaned and arched to him. Never had he known a more responsive woman. His hands became frantic, his mouth voracious; he could not help himself. He could not get enough of her, and she began to respond in kind, her hands massaging his hips, his thighs.

"Dear God," he murmured, and rolled her beneath him.

Diana felt his full weight upon her and revelled in the sensation. His hands were everywhere, kneading, caressing, turning her body to liquid heat. Papa had been right. This was nothing like what happened so long ago in the woods behind Three Oaks. For she felt Adam's love with his every touch, every kiss. And she wanted, needed more. She felt an emptiness only he could fill. And if in so doing, he would know her secret, it would have been worth it. He sought out her most hidden places, making her moan and gasp in delight, making her thrash wildly beneath him.

Adam knew she was ready, and he could not wait a moment longer. He took her face in his hands, afraid he would hurt her.

308

But she was beyond words; indeed, so was he, and so he kissed her deeply and brought them together in one swift, hard thrust. And then he moved slowly, waiting for the cry of pain that never came, just as there had been no barrier when he—

Suddenly he went still, as full realization hit him with the force of a Yorkshire blizzard. Suddenly he understood so much. Not all of it, but enough. Damn her for not trusting him! She lay utterly still beneath him, her face averted, eyes tightly closed. A tear trickled down her cheek, and a wave of tenderness swept over him, mingling with the desire he had only temporarily banked.

"Diana," he whispered raggedly, "look at me."

In answer she turned her head, her eyes still closed, and sought his mouth with hers. She clutched him tightly to her, and he felt her desperation, also knew this was not the time for conversation. Later, they would have a reckoning. He kissed her moist eyes.

"I love you, Diana," he rasped, even as his hands began touching her again, all over.

She reacted instantly, arching her body into his, and he was nearly undone. He began moving within her, slowly and gently until the fires were unleashed once more. He kissed her, stroked her, and she began writhing beneath him. He answered her urgency, taking her higher and higher in a throbbing rhythm that she matched, until together they reached the shattering, pulsing crescendo.

She cried his name as her body shook wildly, and she clutched at him for dear life. He cried his love for her as he took his own release, and then held her tightly as they descended slowly, pantingly, dazedly, from the peak.

It was several moments before he could catch his breath. "Diana, I—"

"No!" she whispered urgently, putting a hand to his lips. "You—you said we would talk tomorrow."

Very well, he thought. He was beyond coherent discourse now at all events. Tomorrow he would teach her that the past was past and that *she* was his future. And then he would throttle her for doubting him. For now, a delicious languor was suffusing him, and he gave in to it, turning onto his side and pulling her against him, her back to his chest. He draped his

309

hand possessively over her waist and kissed the nape of her neck. She snuggled back against him, purring her contentment. Never had he felt so replete.

Diana felt the warm, solid length of him behind her and felt a sweet languor overtake her. Come what might on the morrow, she would always have the memory, the joy of this night.

It was just as she drifted off to sleep that she heard him murmur, "I love you," into her ear. She could not have heard aright. She must be dreaming. Surely he could not mean that. Not now, not anymore. No matter, she thought sleepily. He *would* have loved her, had things been different. She had no regrets.

Chapter 21

Adam's first thought as he slowly came awake, his eyes still closed, was that the sun was shining. His second was that his foot was touching the floor and the bed seemed inordinately low to the ground. And then, suddenly, he remembered. Everything. Eyes still closed and fuzzy with sleep, he groped for Diana and felt only a tangle of blankets. He opened one eye, then the other, then jerked his head up, scanning the hut.

She was gone, blast her! He bolted from the pallet, shrugging into his clothes. He yanked his boots on, noting that her clothes were gone, as was *his* stallion. Muttering an expletive, he dashed for the door. There was Plato, just outside, basking in the bright sun of what must be mid-morning. Of Diana there was no sign, and all that greeted his call was silence.

And then he noticed the small footprints, leading far and away from the hut. Good God! Had she been that eager to get away from him that she would risk a trek over freshly fallen snow? She'd had the good sense to let Plato outside. Why had she simply not mounted him and gone off? Her boots notwithstanding, surely she must know Adam would fare better on foot than she. But, of course, Diana would have done no such thing. At the moment she probably wanted nothing at all to do with him.

Well, he would not give her that luxury. He donned his coat, hat and gloves and saddled the stallion quickly. He gathered up the blankets and his empty brandy flask and set off over the densely packed snow. Her footprints told him she'd gone back to the Clayton farm to retrieve the gig, which was just as well.

311

It was undoubtedly closer than Three Oaks. After a moment's reflection he decided not to go that way, however. Instinct told him Diana had probably been up at dawn. She would be long gone from the Claytons by now. No doubt she was holed up in her bedchamber at Three Oaks, having given strict instructions that she was not to be disturbed *by anyone.*

Hah! They would just see about that! Plato was in the mood for a gallop, and Adam obliged. He rode at a steady pace, and went straight round to the stable at the back of Three Oaks. He threw the reins to a startled groom, noted with grim satisfaction the presence of the gig, and strode back round to the front of the house.

He pounded on the door and rushed right past Mrs. Barrett as she opened it. "Where is she?" he demanded, appalled at his own lack of manners but needing desperately to see her. Enough was enough, after all.

"Why, Your Grace," replied the elderly woman, quite flustered as he handed over his greatcoat, hat and gloves. "If you mean Miss Rustin, I—I'm afraid she's given orders not—"

"Adam, good morning!" came Rusty's genial voice.

Adam looked up to see him emerge from what he thought was the breakfast parlor. Millicent Weeksgate was at his side. Rusty gestured him up to the main floor, and Adam took the stairs two at a time.

"Good morning, Rusty, Mrs. Weeksgate," he said perfunctorily. "I'd like to see Diana."

Rusty's lips twitched. "Yes, I can see that, Adam, but she's resting now. Had quite a night of it over at the Clayton farm. Mavis—"

"Rusty, might we speak privately?" Adam interrupted ruthlessly. "Forgive me, Mrs. Weeksgate, but—"

"'Tis all right," Rusty interjected, pulling the lady's arm through his, "Millie will be family soon enough. Say what's on your mind, my boy."

Adam took a deep breath, telling himself he mightn't be acting the gentleman, but he was most certainly acting like a man. A man who wanted, needed, a certain woman. "Rusty, Diana did not spend the night at the Clayton farmhouse," he said soberly.

Rusty looked confused. "But the baby—I thought—"

"Yes. She delivered the child. I was there. I helped her. I had come here, and when I heard where she'd gone I became worried, because of the snow. We left the Clayton farm around midnight, intent on returning here."

"But you could not get through because of the snow," Rusty ventured.

Adam nodded. "We spent the night in that abandoned shepherd's hut between—"

"Yes, yes, I know the one." Rusty frowned. "This puts rather another complexion on things," he said. His betrothed turned pink.

"I need to see her, Rusty. 'Tis time we settled things between us. You know that she refused me yesterday, and last night she would not speak of it. I—"

"I understand all that, Adam, but truth be told she *is* exhausted. She's been through a great deal these few days past. Perhaps if you gave her more time . . ."

"There *is* no more time, Rusty!" Adam said emphatically and stalked to the staircase leading to the upper floor.

"Adam! You can't go up there!" Rusty shouted, following him.

"Watch me, Rusty!" Adam growled, and began ascending the steps. "She's not exhausted, I assure you," he called over his shoulder. "She slept very well last night. *Very* well, indeed!"

"Adam, what the hell are you implying? Dammit, you cannot just go marching into her bedchamber!" Rusty dashed up and caught him by the arm.

Adam whirled round. "Oh, can I not? I am going up to shake some sense into your daughter. And then I am going off to find a special license this very day!"

"Now, Adam," Rusty said placatingly. "Perhaps you're being a bit hasty. Really, old chap, 'tisn't at all the thing to storm her bedchamber."

Adam sighed. There really was no wrapping it up in clean linen. He lowered his voice, for Mrs. Weeksgate was not that far behind them. "You're rather closing the gate after the pony's bolted, Rusty," Adam said bluntly. Rusty blinked in confusion. Oh, blast, Adam thought, and whispered in exasperation, "Did she tell you, when she barricaded herself in her room, that she might *even now* be carrying your grandchild?"

"Good God! Diana!" Rusty roared, and raced up the stairs ahead of Adam. Moments later it was Rusty who whirled round. "Adam! Then you—you know. I mean—"

"She hasn't told me a thing, Rusty. But . . . there are some matters a man can figure out for himself."

Rusty's blue eyes were narrowed, penetrating. "And you still—"

"Bloody hell, Rusty! Did you also think I'd walk away?"

Rusty grinned. "No, Adam, I never did think that. Not at all."

Adam grinned back, and the two men strode off, leaving a crimson-faced Millicent Weeksgate behind.

He was not surprised to find Diana's chamber empty and with a muffled curse raced past Rusty and belowstairs. He bolted out the door, heedless of the cold, and strode round to the back of the house. He espied her behind the stables making rapid tracks on foot, toward the woods. He was going to throttle her!

As he drew closer he saw that she wore only a woolen shawl over her dress, and a pair of flimsy leather slippers. Dammit, she was going to hurt her feet again, especially after that trek this morning.

"That's far enough, Diana," he called when he was but two yards behind her.

She broke into a run. He went after her and caught her in short order, grabbing her by the waist. She twisted and stumbled and fell down into the snow, taking him with her. He rolled deftly until she was on her back, stretched out beneath him.

He grinned down at her. He really could not help himself. "Well, well, my love. Is this not where we left off last night, in just this position? And were you not saying that we would talk in the morning?" Suddenly his expression sobered, and he grasped her shoulders tightly. "Well, my dear, 'tis morning. Now, let us talk!"

"Please, Adam, I—there is truly naught to talk about. What happened last night was—was wonderful. I shall never forget it. But—"

314

"Was it, Diana?" he murmured. "Was it wonderful?" He brushed his lips across hers, feeling the heat of her body against his, despite the snow beneath and on all sides of them. He wanted this little discussion over and done, so he could kiss her in earnest and feel the fire build between them, right here in the cradle of the pure, white snow.

"Yes," she breathed, "but—but it is over and we must go our separate ways. Truly, I understand—"

"What fustian do you speak, Diana?" he demanded, shaking her gently. "You understand nothing! Did you really think I would spurn you because of a youthful indiscretion with a man to whom you were betrothed? Blast it all, Diana, you—"

"No, Adam!" she cried. "*You* do not understand. It—it . . . was not Robert. It was—it was something else entirely."

Perhaps it was the faraway look in her eyes, or the odd tone of her voice, but for the first time Adam felt the chill of the snow. He felt cold prickles on the nape of his neck. This would not be a brief discussion, after all. Wordlessly, he hoisted himself to his feet, then reached down to pull her up as well.

He took her bare hands in his. "Diana, you do not have to tell me anything you do not wish to. But, I think, for your own sake, it is best if you—"

"I—I was twelve years old," she said flatly, and tugged her hands away. She turned her back and took two steps from him. He let her go. She wrapped her hands about herself and continued in the same dull, blunt tone. "It happened in these woods, a good way back from here. Far enough so that no one could hear me scream."

Oh, God, he thought, no! "Diana, please," he pleaded, stepping forward to put his hands on her shoulders, "you do not—"

"No!" She jerked away, keeping her back to him. "Let me finish. There—there was a man. A large man. A vagrant of some sort. I thought he was cold, that he wanted my cloak. But he—he wanted something else. I fought him, but he—he—"

She caught her breath on a sob, and he pulled her into his arms. "Shh. 'Tis all right, Diana. You do not have to say another word." He stroked her back, fully expecting her to cry her pain out. But instead she sniffed back her tears and raised her head.

The blue eyes that regarded him held a hardness he'd never seen in them, and the voice a bitterness he'd never heard as she said, "Perhaps you thought you could accept the notion of Robert and . . . and me, though I have my doubts. But this is something else entirely, isn't it? I know very well that you cannot mar the purity of your ducal bloodline with—"

"Mar the—" Adam spluttered, beginning to feel a red-hot rage building within him. "Is *that* what Easton said?" he asked with ominous calm. She nodded, her eyes a mask of anguish. "Goddammit, Diana!" he exploded, storming three feet away from her lest he shake her till her teeth rattled. "How *dare* you compare me to Easton, assume that because he was an unmitigated cad that I would be the same! I *love* you, dammit! You say you love me. Could you not have trusted me?"

She looked utterly confused. "B-but Robert made me see that no man could accept—"

"Bloody hell!" he ranted, grabbing her by the upper arms. "I had ought to throttle you, you little idiot. I *love* you! I am completely besotted with you! I daresay you are the only one for miles around who doesn't see that!"

The anguish receded in the velvety blue eyes, to be replaced by a faint glimmer of hope. "You—you mean—"

"What I mean, my dearest idiot, is that what pains me about what happened to you as a child is that you were made to suffer so heinously. It has naught to do with how I feel about you, except to make me treasure you and want to protect you all the more."

Her eyes welled up, but not before he saw the dawning wonder and joy in them. "Oh, Adam," she whispered. "I love you." Whereupon she collapsed onto his chest, sobbing profusely. But her tears were cleansing ones, tears of happiness. He held her tightly, blinking back the moisture in his own eyes.

She was his, at last.

When the tears subsided into hiccoughs, he kissed her eyes and rested his forehead against hers. "I think we'd best be going back, my love. We neither of us have coat nor gloves. And your feet! You are wearing naught but flimsy slippers! 'Tis a wonder you have not caught chilblains already!"

"Fustian, Adam!" she said fuzzily. "My feet are fine. I—"

"But I'm not taking any chances, love." Adam grinned down at her before unceremoniously swinging her up into his arms and starting for the house.

"Adam! Put me down! I can walk!" she protested.

He kept walking. "I am persuaded those feet will need special attention after all this time in the snow. I remember that you have *very* sensitive feet!"

"No! Adam, you wouldn't dare!"

"Oh?" He chuckled roguishly and proceeded into the house and up the stairs, cradling Diana in his arms. They passed a startled Mrs. Barrett and only paused at the top of the stairs where they were met by a grinning Rusty, and his wide-eyed fiancée. Diana by this time was clinging to him, her head buried in his shoulder. Darling that she was, she always knew when to keep silent.

"Is there a fire in the front parlor?" Adam demanded of Rusty.

The good doctor blinked. "Ah, why, yes. May I ask—"

"Good. If you'll excuse us," Adam cut in ruthlessly, and strode away with his precious cargo.

He carried her into the toasty warm parlor and resolutely kicked the door shut behind him.

Rusty smiled at that closed door, pulling Millicent close to his side.

"Rusty dear," she asked uncertainly, "does this mean they are betrothed?"

"I would say so, Millie, yes indeed."

"Even so, dear, do you think it proper to leave them alone togeth—"

"No, Adam!" came his daughter's voice from behind the door. Millie stiffened, but Rusty patted her hand reassuringly. "No, I won't let you do it, Adam!" Diana exclaimed, but he heard the love, and the laughter in her voice.

"Rusty," Millicent asked again, "do you think it wise to leave them—"

"Oh, I do, Millie. Yes, indeed, I do," he replied knowingly.

"No!" Diana's word was punctuated with a giggle. And then another. "No, not there! Oh, I cannot bear it!"

His daughter began to giggle uncontrollably, and he heard a deeply satisfied masculine chuckle. Rusty looked down to

317

see Millie blushing.

"Oh, my goodness me, Rusty! Should you not intervene?"

"I should say not! I haven't heard my girl laugh like that in years, Millie."

"But what—what are they *doing?*"

Rusty grinned wolfishly. "I do not know, my dear, but why don't you come along with me to my sitting room, and we'll endeavor to find out!"

Epilogue

Adam peered out the window of the master bedroom of Damerest Hall and muttered an expletive. Why the devil was there always a blizzard when babies decided to be born?

"Because, my love, babies have their own inimitable schedule," Diana replied softly. He hadn't realized he'd spoken aloud. Diana's face was serene now that the latest pain had subsided. But *he* was anything but serene. "Besides, Adam, this babe was started in a blizzard, was it not?"

He went to sit beside her and took her hand, kissing her fingers gently.

"Indeed, love." He smiled rakishly at the memory of that night in the shepherd's hut. "But it would have been politic of him, or her, to await the arrival of his doctor—grandfather. As it is, the babe is early, Rusty and Millicent are probably holed up in some ramshackle inn miles from here, Mother and D'Orsini have not returned from their wedding trip, and even the Damerest physician will never make it through in this weather! What a damnable coil!"

"Adam," she said, regarding him soberly, "I know that the housekeeper is quite shocked by your presence here, and if you'd rather not remain . . ."

"Madam wife," he replied gravely, "I find I do not care a rush for proprieties, any more than you do! That is not the point and well you know it!"

She grinned saucily at him. "Ah yes, the point. Well, I did tell you once, a very long time ago, that husbands are fairly useless at a time like this. And so I do understand if—"

319

"The devil you say, Diana! Not another word!" he growled with lips twitching. "I delivered Farmer Clayton's babe—I can damned well deliver my own!"

Which was exactly what he did. And quite well at that. For Arabella Katherine Damerest, named for her grandmothers, made her noisy way into the world some seven hours later. She would be called Bella, which anyone who'd been around Signor D'Orsini long enough knew meant "beautiful." And so she was, like the love between her parents.

And though she would one day have two brothers and a sister, only of Bella could Adam and Diana say that she was born the same way she was conceived. That is, with only her mother and father present, with the snow whirling on the outside and the fire of love burning within.